"Ross's lush, evocative writing is the perfect counterpoint for her spell-binding tale of a wickedly refined, elegantly attired rake who is redeemed by one woman's love. Ross, whose combination of lyricism and sensuality is on par with Jo Beverley's, skillfully builds the simmering sexual chemistry between Alden and Juliet into an exquisitely sensual romance and luscious love story."   —*Booklist*

"A gripping novel starring two wonderfully tainted romantic skeptics as lead protagonists."   —*Midwest Book Review*

"Brilliant [and] scorching . . . With its fascinating characters, intriguing plot, and engrossing, rewarding romance, it is a story not to be missed . . . A beautifully woven tale of an unexpected love that succeeds against all odds. This will be ranked as one of the year's best."
                                                         —*The Romance Reader*

"Rich, delicious . . . Books like this are treasures . . . Put it at the top of your summer reading list."   —*The Oakland Press*

"An extraordinary story . . . A superb example of Ms. Ross's outstanding storytelling talents and exceptional writing abilities. Intense emotions and passionate, strong characters are the complement to a complex love story, replete with such dastardly villains as Shakespeare might have crafted."   —*Historical Romance Reviews*

continued . . .

My Dark Prince

The
Wicked Lover

Julia Ross

B
BERKLEY BOOKS, NEW YORK

This is an original publication of The Berkley Publishing Group.

A Berkley Book
Published by The Berkley Publishing Group
A division of Penguin Group (USA) Inc.
375 Hudson Street
New York, New York 10014

First Edition: February 2004

Library of Congress Cataloging-in-Publication Data

Ross, Julia.
    The wicked lover / Julia Ross.—1st ed.
        p. cm.
    ISBN 0-425-19406-X
    1. Undercover operations—Fiction. 2. London (England)—Fiction. 3. Women
spies—Fiction. 4. Treason—Fiction. I. Title.

PS3618.O846W53 2004
813'.6—dc22

2003063666

The
Wicked Lover

CHAPTER ONE

~V~

$\mathcal{H}$E HAD A REGRETTABLE WEAKNESS FOR BEAUTY: IN HORSES, in clothes, in art, in women. He was known for it. That he was also generally considered dangerous amused him, though not because that assessment was false. He was just about to discover his mistress burning his clothes in the street in front of his townhouse. Yet Robert Dovenby's first reaction was simply that it was a damned unfortunate moment to be riding a young, half-trained stallion in Mayfair.

Abdiel reared.

With a slightly corrosive smile, Dove brought his mount firmly back to the ground.

A bloodred flame of muscle and spirit, with fine-boned glossy black legs and the fierce eye of an angel, the bay sidled and fretted, the bit clinking.

A light mist curled about the chimneys. Moisture lay on stone and wrought iron like fresh paint. Yet a crowd had gathered on foot, abandoning carriages and sedan chairs to the encroaching winter dusk, while a fitful column of smoke rose from their midst.

Dove glanced up. His bedroom window stood open, a scrap of lace caught forlornly on the sill.

With their canes and quizzing glasses, silks and lace, the flower of London society was obviously waiting for him, Robert Sinclair Dovenby, to return home.

He wove a cocoon of persuasion with legs, back, and reins. Abdiel minced forward.

Like a field of daisies honoring the sun, every powdered head turned in anticipation as the stallion cleaved through the crowd. At their center Lady Margaret, Countess of Grenham, was feeding a bonfire with a fortune in clothes.

His clothes.

Shock and disbelief tore his first wry impulse to mirth into shreds.

Clever and splendid, daughter and granddaughter of dukes, Meg was the toast and arbiter of fashionable London. Her favor had brought him indulgence, granted him opportunities, opened doors, and given him some of the loveliest days and nights of his life.

He owed her everything.

Now she was publicly shattering his social survival, his credit, his future—and their relationship. He had no idea why.

Yet the audience waited. The air shimmered with their eagerness: to witness a duel of wits—if not of blood—with every expectation, in their ravenous world, to see the loser eaten alive.

Whatever his distress, whatever his feelings about Meg, Dove could not afford to lose. Neither, of course, could he afford to win.

Her hem brushed through drifts of exquisite embroidery, discreet silks, translucently fine linens, scattered haphazardly over the cobbles. She selected a coat of dark-gray cut velvet and tossed it into her fire. The velvet smoldered, belching ruinously expensive smoke, before the flames caught and the coat blazed.

The glorious, unassailable Lady Grenham, destroying a triviality.

Hooves rang an uneven staccato on the flagstones.

By pure force of will Dove rode his agitated bay up to the bonfire. The fire crackled. The horse's fractured breathing reverberated. All human sound died away.

Meg glanced up, her face lovely, intelligent, bright with anger.

"So what do you make of my bonfire, sir? A pretty enough blaze, don't you think?"

Dove bowed from the saddle and spoke, as he must if he was going to survive this, not only for her. "Indeed, Lady Grenham. A perfect funeral pyre to our friendship, so well represented by these few gaudy trappings. Let them burn!"

It was a monstrous untruth, or had been, but she laughed and began to throw his boots, then his shoes, into her fire. Buckles melted in a blaze of multicolored flame.

"Do you dare to hold me at no value, sir?"

"Ma'am, you are a diamond among pearls: more brilliant, more valuable, more magnificent—and with a sharper cutting edge, of course."

The crowd laughed behind flamboyant handkerchiefs. Meg gathered an armful of fabric.

"Yet you would allow your cheap strumpet—"

"I' faith, ma'am, to which strumpet do you refer? London breeds strumpets faster than your bonfire consumes shirts."

Billowing silk hit the fire. "But do they all burn as furiously—"

"As you did for me? Hard to say, ma'am."

The audience's amusement exploded. Abdiel careened sideways. Color flooded Meg's skin, like paper catching fire.

"Lud, sir, you deserve to get thrown!" There was—appallingly—heartbreak as well as anger in her voice. "Damn you for a faithless, brazen-faced bastard!"

"Allow me to claim brazen and bastard, ma'am, though I defy any horse—even this one—to unseat me."

Daring fate, he slipped the reins into one hand and unbuttoned his coat. The bay skidded as Dove tossed the contents of his pockets—pistol, snuffbox, his pair-cased silver watch by Joseph Antram of London—to his groom, who now stood, mouth agape, in the crowd.

Bending Abdiel in a tight circle, Dove managed to shrug out of the coat sleeves. A feat of some difficulty, but he was just lucky enough to do it.

"Pray, burn this jacket, also, ma'am. I never cared for the cut." He flung her his full-skirted coat, then winked as he swept off his tricorn. "And this hat has gone quite out of style!"

The onlookers cheered as Meg caught the hat.

Her eyes now held a hint of trapped laughter, as if she already saw the absurdity in what she had done and in his outrageous response to it. "You will spend a cold winter, sir!"

"Without you, or without my coat, ma'am? It's a damned paltry comparison." On the knife edge of chaos he stripped off his waistcoat and held up the ivory satin, examining the silver-thread roses with deliberate gravity. "Though this? Alas, I always rather liked it. But let it burn, by all means!"

"You cannot afford this!" Meg cried suddenly.

"You think not, ma'am? But it makes such rich fodder for the scandal sheets—"

The waistcoat sailed into the flames. The spectators shouted with glee as Abdiel rose on his haunches. Dove would have to take both hands from the reins to pull off his shirt, and everyone knew it.

Meg's eyes blazed with horrified mirth as the snorting horse dropped back to the cobbles. "You're mad, sir! Insane! That stallion will kill you!"

"What will you wager on it, ma'am? One last exquisite night?"

"My nights aren't up for wager, sir, though your death will be, if you don't dismount this instant."

"But I never abandon any creature, once mounted, ma'am, unless by my own choice."

Hilarity detonated like cannon fire. The stallion's muscles convulsed. Foam flew back from the bit as four iron-shod hooves clanged desperately on the pavement. Dove held the bay on the brink, reassurance firm in hands and legs: *Easy, my brave fellow! It's all right, Abdiel. Trust me!*

The stallion calmed, just enough. A tiny relaxation shimmered through reins and seat. Dove signaled his groom. The boy ran up and seized the bit, allowing Dove to vault to the ground. Dragging the groom, the stallion skidded away—beauty in every line of arched neck, flared nostrils, startled eye.

"Anyone would think you adored that hell-begotten bay," Meg said.

Her voice held a certain regret, along with a determination that Dove couldn't quite fathom. No doubt his own conveyed the same. Neither of them could undo this now.

"Since you found him for me yourself, ma'am—whether in hell or out of it—perhaps I do. So you concede the game? I still live."

"What a pity!" Meg waited until the crowd's silence was more palpable than the ash filtering down over her feathered hat. "The scandal sheets cannot give you the triumph, sir, for the trump is still mine. Far more heat is being generated by my bonfire than could ever be found in your glacial bed."

Faces swiveled, waiting for Dove to deliver the deathblow.

Yet he bowed. "I' faith, in affairs of the heart, ma'am, the lady is always right. If I could not love you as you deserved, it is my loss. As it is my failing that I was not rid of such an unsightly wardrobe a long time ago. My homage is yours, Lady Grenham, along with my undying gratitude." He took her fingers and kissed them. "Even for Abdiel, though he came deuced close to making a bloody fool out of me."

Meg laughed. Leaving the crowd in bewilderment, Dove strode into his townhouse.

Two losses: a wardrobe and—far more important—the favors of a lady he truly cared for. One more loss would make three. Didn't they say trouble always came in threes?

Dove knew with certainty that this disaster had only just begun.

* * *

THE HALLWAY YAWNED EMPTY AND SILENT, AN ABSURD VAC-uum of servants.

There was no one in the drawing room, the dining room, or his study. In their basement sanctuary the kitchen staff worked on undisturbed, ignorant of any embarrassment abovestairs. Dove found his two footmen locked into the butler's pantry. Not bothering to question them, he left them there in a mortified huddle and went straight to his bedroom.

He stopped at the door and took a deep breath.

Had he been in love with Meg? A times, certainly. It was a damnable weakness, he supposed, that he had never wanted cold-hearted sex, certainly one he preferred the beau monde not discover. His reputation had given him his entrée into the fashionable world. He had nothing else—no title, no fortune, no noble breeding—to recommend him. Only that the incomparable Lady Grenham had been his patron and his acknowledged lover. Until today.

Yet you would allow your cheap strumpet—

He had a damned good idea what he would find in his bedroom. If it was the right lady, she might get exactly what she'd come for.

Dove lifted the latch and opened the door.

He stopped dead.

A girl sat on a chair near the window. She did not look like a strumpet. Beneath a French straw hat, her angular face was flushed, apprehensive, vaguely pretty only because she was young. Yet she seemed more annoyed than frightened. As he entered she struggled against what appeared to be her own hat ribbons, which had been used to efficiently truss her to the chair.

The girl's eyes narrowed, assessing him, before her glance slid away to the bed.

A young man stood spread-eagled at the foot of Dove's four-poster, arms stretched uncomfortably. Each wrist had been securely tied to the bedposts with the cords from the hangings.

Long-limbed, neatly made, the young man stared defiantly at Dove. His wig boasted white curls and a queue. The shoulders bunched on an ill-fitting blue coat. The bed canopy cast his angry, fine-boned face into shadow, the skin chalk-white, startling in contrast to vehement lapis lazuli eyes, ringed with fatigue as if bruised.

Potential explanations splintered into myriad possibilities—none of them without danger, several of them rich with delight. Closing the door behind him, Dove leaned back against the panels and folded his arms. His premonition of peril seemed absurd, yet the scent of it lingered, along with the faint smell of smoke.

"I enjoy uninvited female company," he said, "as the lion enjoys the gazelle. The presence of a manservant, trussed like a hare for jugging, seems sadly superfluous."

The girl's freckled nose turned pink.

"My mistress is not at fault, sir." The young man's voice was light, cultured, hard to pin down. "She's already afraid. If you would be pleased to untie her?"

"Why? She does not look afraid."

"We did not intend—" the young man began.

"Whether it was intentional or not," Dove interrupted, "the gazelle is at a distinct disadvantage, if she voluntarily enters the lion's den."

The French hat dipped over the girl's powdered hair. Green ribbons trailed across fingers marked here and there with pinpricks. Neither a strumpet nor a lady. He nevertheless gave her a small bow.

"We have not been introduced, ma'am. Robert Sinclair Dovenby, your servant. The world sometimes calls me the Dove."

"And your friends?" The manservant jerked angrily against his bonds. "What do they call you? Sinclair—or just Sin? An appropriate enough name for a man of your reputation."

Dove smiled at him. He was also young, but not too young: a hint of wary experience marked the high cheekbones and stubborn chin, and lurked in the pout of the full bottom lip. An odd grace traced the long legs and slender arms, half hidden by the coarse blue jacket. Interesting! He wondered fleetingly how well—or if—this intruder could handle a sword.

"Your mistress was brought here by tales of my notoriety?"

The young man's bravado was almost tangible.

"She was brought here on a whim, sir. It means nothing."

"*Brought* here? May I ask your mistress's name and business, sir? I admit I'm agog with curiosity. Though I'm sure her company promises infinite delights, I did have other plans for this evening."

The young man looked away at the ceiling. "Of course. You are busy. My mistress's name is Mademoiselle Berthe Dubois. We arrived recently—and with some difficulty—from France. She only came to search—to fetch something."

Search? The word numbed like a shower of ice water.

"She came to *fetch* something? From a complete stranger? Pray, what did Miss Dubois hope to find in my bedroom? Her own stray wits, perhaps?"

The stubborn chin set in defiance. "Only an item of your clothing. Anything would have sufficed. It was quite random—a wager."

"Ah!" Dove walked around the room, closing empty drawers. "A wager."

"A chance thing," the young man said. "We met a party of ladies—"

Dove stopped by the girl's chair and smiled down at her. "How very, very naughty of you, Berthe Dubois. A chance meeting, where my undoubted infamy was discussed? You wagered that you could walk into my bedroom, take an article of my clothing, bring it back to the other ladies, and win—one hundred guineas, perhaps?"

"Two hundred," the young man said.

Dove laughed. "Then how tragic that I have no clothing left, except what remains on my person. Though I'm charmed by the brilliance of her revenge, Lady Grenham has burned my entire wardrobe. Unless I disrobe further, your mistress cannot win her bet."

"You would not undress in front of a lady," Berthe Dubois said in French. It was not the accent of Versailles.

"Not unless invited." Dove took a knife from his boot and sliced one green ribbon. The girl pulled a hand free and with a small sound rubbed her wrist over her mouth. "Yet I am disappointed," he added in her own tongue, "that your manservant did not put up a better defense and so allowed another lady to bind you to a chair."

"I am unarmed." The young man also spoke French, slipping easily from one language to the other. "Lady Grenham had a pistol. When she found us here, she became rather discomposed."

"I can imagine. Rifling through a man's shirts is such an unfortunately intimate task to perform in front of his mistress. So you introduced yourselves?"

"She introduced herself, Lady Margaret, Countess of Grenham." The young man broke off and took a deep breath, then began again in English. "I didn't think it politic to determine whether her pistol was loaded—"

"I assure you that it was. So with the help of her firearm, Lady Grenham forced Miss Dubois to help truss you to my bedposts. Then, also at pistol point, she tied your mistress to that convenient chair?"

"What could we do, when faced with a gun?" Berthe said, still in French. "Then she tore into your dressers—"

"Which you and your manservant had already conveniently opened."

"—and threw everything from the window like a madwoman. We couldn't stop her," the French girl added helpfully.

Not sure if he could trust himself to keep his mirth hidden, Dove walked to the window, tossing the knife in one hand.

"But why the devil couldn't my servants stop either of you? Are my footmen helpless clay in the hands of a woman? Is my house open to every stray female who presents herself at the door, whether trailing her manservant or not?"

"It's not your servants' fault," the young man said. "I used a ruse to lock the footmen into the pantry."

"Then I shall have to get an entire new staff, it seems." Dove looked down at the smoldering ashes in the street. Meg had left. The crowd was drifting away. "And, thanks to you, a new lover."

"No harm was meant, sir," the young man said with steely politeness. "You'll be pleased to release us, I'm sure. You *are* a gentleman?"

"But what if I'm not a very nice gentleman?" Dove closed the window, shutting out the oncoming night. "Perhaps I am very nasty indeed to young ladies who force their way into my bedroom?"

Their eyes watched him as he strolled about the room. He caressed random objects: his washstand, his brushes, the candlesticks, a stack of leather-bound books abandoned on a table: Defoe, Milton, Molière, Henry Fielding.

"After all, no one consulted me, did they?" He picked up a volume and smoothed his thumb down the spine. Nothing seemed to have been touched except his clothespresses. "By the requirements of your wager, without my agreement I was cast as the angel of benevolence, unwittingly donating clothing to strangers." Dove set down the book: *Tom Jones*—another rogue who hadn't known his true parents. "Whatever your motives, you have just cost me my wardrobe, as well as a delightfully experienced mistress. They will both be very expensive to replace."

"No doubt you can win sufficient at the tables," the young man said.

"Of the sins of a rake, I prefer wine and women, which is unfortunate for Mademoiselle Dubois. What if my pleasure is a little too inventive for her tastes? Do you really think that she can match the naughty habits of an experienced lady like Meg Grenham?" Dove picked up a silver-and-ivory box from a side table and took a pinch of snuff, the gesture as deliberately insulting as he could make it. "Though *you* are safe, of course, being a man."

A blush ran like a flame across the youth's peerless bones. "Are you foxed, sir?"

"To ride that half-broken stallion in town, I must have been. However, the sight of Lady Grenham's bonfire and the resulting calculation of the loss to my purse sobered me instantly. I am now in complete possession of my wits. Fortunately for Mademoiselle Dubois, I rather wish to be alone with them. I shall call a sedan chair to take your mistress wherever she would like to go."

"You'll let us leave?"

Dove closed the snuffbox with a snap, sliced the remaining ribbon with his knife and helped the French girl stand. "I shall let *you* leave, ma'am. Your man, I think, must stay and answer a few questions."

"I won't leave without him," Berthe Dubois said stoutly.

"Because you are *his* faithful servant, are you not?" Dove asked gently. "His cook, perhaps?"

The Frenchwoman's resolve faltered. Her gaze slid again to the bed.

"Oh, devil take it," the young man said. "Yes, she's my servant. Go back to our lodgings, Berthe."

"*Mais—*"

"Monsieur Dovenby is owed his explanation, that's all. After which, as he has said, he prefers to be alone. I shall be quite safe."

"You have your orders from your master, Miss Dubois," Dove said. "Besides, you have no other choice. If you don't go willingly, I shall be forced to lay hands on your person, which I believe you would hold in some distaste."

He laid the cut ribbons into her pinpricked hands. Without

thinking, she folded them carefully. Not a cook, then, a maid. A lady's maid.

Dove rang the bell. One of his footmen, sheepish still, appeared immediately. With a few quick instructions, Dove saw the French girl escorted from the room.

Poor Berthe Dubois! She was brave and stalwart enough, though not quite as stalwart as her companion, still tied spread-eagled at the foot of his bed. The Frenchwoman would certainly be carried anywhere she wished to go, but the ride would take the best part of the evening. Dove did not want his interview with Meg's remaining captive to be disturbed by anything.

He studied the long neck and high cheekbones, the pale face marked by those extraordinary blue eyes. The curved line of hip and waist, revealed where the jacket had fallen open. Was she an actress, hired by a rival as part of a deliberate plan to rob him of Meg and his security in society? Or was she here to discover his far more dangerous secrets? Either way he thought he might enjoy finding out.

She met his gaze, then glanced down. Small white teeth scraped over her ripe bottom lip. Erotic images fired like grapeshot.

For as Robert Dovenby had recognized on his second glance, the individual tied to his bedposts was not only young and beautiful, but a woman.

CHAPTER TWO

❧

THE CORDS WERE BEGINNING TO BITE. HER SHOULDERS ACHED. Otherwise her plan was going better than she'd dare hope. She was alone with Robert Sinclair Dovenby and she had his attention.

His eyes seemed surprisingly intense, his face brutally masculine in contrast to the elegant shimmer of silver at forehead and temples. There was something unholy about a man in a formal powdered wig stripped to breeches and shirtsleeves, as if for a sword fight. Apprehension and excitement shivered down her spine.

"I'm to stand here like a trussed goat?" Sylvie asked.

"My imagery, sir, concerned a gazelle." His smile pleated deep lines in each cheek. "I am not fond of goats."

He moved Berthe's chair next to the fireplace and sat, then leaned back, arms crossed behind his head, balancing the chair on its back legs with his booted feet propped on the fender.

"But you would keep me tied up like this?"

"Why not? You surely don't suggest that I free you to do me further injury?"

"It wasn't my intention to harm you."

"Yet you have done so. I think you owe me some recompense, don't you?"

Sylvie clenched her fists against their bonds, though she was neither angry nor afraid. In spite of her awkward stance, a secret mirth danced in her bones. The knots were not very secure.

"Very well. Perhaps. But I don't have any money."

"Then I must take out your obligation in flesh and blood. However, darkness would be so much more discreet for a discussion between gentlemen. You and I shall have dinner, sir. A little pheasant and rare beef, perhaps, with red wine?"

"I cannot possibly stay to dinner," she answered.

"Why not? You're too pale. Red wine and red meat will do you good. In the meantime, I must bathe and write some letters. I am lamentably flecked with ash. You will not mind waiting?"

"Are you serious? You will keep me tied up like this, so that we may dine together?"

"Would you prefer to work off your debt by carrying my coal and hot water?" The chair legs thumped on the floor as, in one fluid motion, he stood. "Though when I compare that with the value of what I have lost today through your agency, sir, I fear you would be laboring for me for several lifetimes."

He strolled across the room. His reflection moved with him in a freestanding mirror. Images of flexible shoulders, trim waist, narrow hips shimmered in the dying daylight, crafting ghosts. He moved superbly, mind and body attuned, as if trained for war. A man for other men to fear. A man for women to covet. A man who through her interference had just lost his mistress and, in spite of his cool manner, was angrier than he knew.

He untied his cravat and tossed it aside, then unbuckled and laid the gilt scabbard containing his smallsword on a side table.

"A pretty toy," he said, staring down at it. "A gift, you may have guessed, from Lady Grenham. Regrettably I shall now feel obliged to return it."

Yes, very angry. He walked back to the mirror and slid the silver wig from his head. Dark hair hugged a neat male skull, then sprang under one pass of lean fingers to tumble over his forehead. Without his wig he seemed primitive, like a pirate, with no gloss of civilized restraint.

He rang a bell. Another footman appeared. The two men talked, too softly for her to hear. She caught only a few words, *bath* being one of them. Lud, he really was going to bathe! Sylvie swallowed a smile. Of course, he thought she was a boy.

She watched him stride across the room to a table with a writing case, once again wringing his fingers through his hair. The dark strands caressed his high collar, leaped thickly over his ears. He seemed pleasantly aware of his state of undress, that nothing lay between his skin and the still smoky air but that single layer of linen. The skin of his throat gleamed against the open neck of his shirt.

An answering awareness flickered, unbidden, in her belly. How much simpler to have moved directly, as she had practiced so often, into those masculine arms—

"What's your name?" he asked.

"George." It was close enough to the truth. "George White."

"You're experienced with women, George?"

"Not as you undoubtedly are, sir, though I am skilled enough, I believe, in the rituals of courtship."

He turned to look at her, brows raised. "Faith, for such a stripling you're very sure of your boast!"

"I have sometimes been required to perform certain services in that capacity for my employers—"

"Then since you're such an expert, you may advise me in what I should write to Meg."

She tried to appear contrite. "If you would allow me, sir, I could write your letter for you. My penmanship is excellent."

He laughed and hooked a chair with one booted foot, then sharpened a quill with a few quick scrapes of his penknife. "So is mine," he said.

She watched his supple back and dark head as his pen danced rapidly over the paper. No corrections or hesitation, apparently. He blotted the damp ink and stood, turning to face her.

"Allow me to read aloud my letter to my ex-mistress," he said. "You may let me have your opinion."

Sylvie stared at him, at the clever mouth and firm jaw, trying to ignore the ache that burned in her shoulder blades—and the inconvenient new ache that lay so much deeper.

"My pleasure, of course."

" 'My dear, incomparable Meg,' " he read. " 'I believe we have just made history—or rich food for gossip, at least—though it will no doubt amuse you to learn that my man has found some unburned shirts and stockings just returned from the laundry—' "

"So your losses aren't as great as you wish me to believe," Sylvie interrupted.

"They are great enough. Allow me to read on: 'I am also given to understand that you left me four coats and five waistcoats—accidentally, since they had been taken downstairs to be brushed—but one is your favorite opal silk. Several pairs of shoes and boots have also survived by the stratagem of being cleaned. Very wicked footwear to so cozen a lady!' " He stopped and lowered the paper. "What do you think so far?"

"Very sweet," Sylvie said. "She will admire your cool dismissal of her stratagem and no doubt be piqued that she did not destroy everything."

"No." Humor radiated from the corners of his mouth. "She'll be pleased. Meg is more generous than you are, George. Of course, this next part is what counts—"

"Where you swear to take revenge?"

"Where I tell her the truth." He began reading again. " 'Perhaps you will dismiss these next words as the coquetry of a rogue, but I do care for you, my dear Meg, very much. I am sorry it is over. I hope we

can meet next as friends who will find laughter in our shared catas-
trophe. In faith, I admit—though it earn me your ridicule—that
what you did was magnificent. You have my admiration, my regrets,
and my deepest apologies. I shall, of course, return the smallsword
and other gifts that you were pleased to bestow on your unworthy
lover. My groom will deliver Abdiel to your stables at first light. I
am, Your Ladyship's most humble, obedient servant,' et cetera, et
cetera—" He looked up. "Lud, George, you are faint?"

It had begun almost at the first sentence of this second para-
graph, a dreadful vertigo, as if all clarity drained from her head,
leaving her dizzy.

I am sorry it is over. . . . I do care for you, my dear Meg, very much—

"You're still in love with her?" Her voice sounded husky.

"In love?" Hot wax dropped like rose petals as he sealed the letter.
"What a romantic soul lurks in that skinny chest of yours, George!
I thought you claimed to be experienced with women."

Blood rushed hotly to her face. "I only wondered—in an attempt
to gauge how far you will desire to punish me."

"I have no desire to punish you," he said. "Only to settle the debt
you owe me." He strode up to her and with two strokes of his knife
cut her bonds. "If you intend to honor that obligation, you will be
pleased to sit, sir, in that chair by the fire."

For a fleeting moment she stared into his eyes. Changeable hazel
depths, dark and bright, almost hidden beneath thick black lashes,
his gaze was both compelling and secretive. It was as if he deliberately offered her a challenge: *This is your chance to leave, if you wish.*
Sylvie immediately looked away. Her heart hammered as she walked
to the fireplace, dropped into the chair he had indicated, and kicked
her feet out in front of her.

His smallsword lay on its table. He had deliberately disarmed
himself. Yet he had the confidence to free her, even though she might
be an enemy.

"As for Meg," he said. "I wish I could have loved her as she deserved, but if you had any understanding of London society, you would know there's no going back on what happened out there in the street."

"So pride is what counts?"

In a single neat movement he wrenched his shirt over his head. Light gleamed over his naked back, the deft muscles of his stomach and chest. Her mouth went dry.

"For a man, George, you're overly concerned with emotion. Meg is brilliant both in and out of bed. I am bloody annoyed to have lost her, as well as what her patronage means to me in London society." A knock sounded at the door. At his response the latch lifted. "You cannot match any of those attributes. Pride has nothing to do with it."

Footmen entered carrying a slipper bath and pails of hot water. Dove sat to allow one of the men to tug off his boots. Another servant began to strop a razor. Water hissed into the tub. Towels were arranged, soap set out in a gilt-edged dish. His boots were tugged off and carried away, along with his heartbreaking letter to Lady Grenham.

Sylvie sat ignored, while reflections chased and danced in the mirror.

I shall, of course, return the smallsword and other gifts that you were pleased to bestow on your unworthy lover. My groom will deliver Abdiel to your stables at first light. From her seat near the window, Berthe had described, moment by moment, this man's mad insistence on riding his young stallion right up to the bonfire and his defiant, brilliant participation in the burning of his clothes.

"*C'est magnifique!*" the maid had said at last, meaning both horse and man.

He stood up and—as casually as a bather at the beach—Robert

Sinclair Dovenby stripped off stockings, breeches, and smallclothes.

Her breath caught, raggedly.

Reflected in the mirror and in the polished surface of metal, he strode to the tub. Shadows flitted across unambiguous muscle, followed the long line of calf and ridged thigh, waist and back, his genitals prominently nested in crisp curls of black hair. Light danced up the hard forearms, stomach, the tender curl of bone at his throat and across the arch of his ribs. Flames caressed hard, pale buttocks as he stepped into the water. The deadly male animal so recently and wittily hidden beneath all that silk and lace.

A yearning for all that sheer power and beauty seized her by the throat.

Water sloshed as he leaned back, lifting his chin. The servant began to shave his jaw, while his master's hands rested, relaxed, on the metal rim. Bronzed skin, male sinew and bone, and lean, swordsman's fingers.

All caught in a moment of stunning vulnerability.

Sylvie forced herself to breathe normally, though the irony almost choked her. He thought she was a boy. He thought she wouldn't notice. Faith, she noticed! The mad craving sank bittersweet roots straight down to her bones.

He lay for a long time in the hot water, saying nothing, long after his menservants had left, long after the daylight had faded away outside. Sylvie watched his closed lids, the shuttered face, as her pulse throbbed, dull and heavy in her veins.

She regretted, quite bitterly, the necessity to let him think her a man.

But if she became his lover, their liaison might be confined to the bedroom. It would probably be short-lived. Not enough time, not enough access, to penetrate his life, his secrets, to learn what he kept hidden from the world. To do that she must become an indispensable and unchallenged part of his household: a young man who owed him a debt and had no other way to pay it, except through his labor.

She had accepted the mission and the terms. How could she have foreseen that her blood would ring with this hot, unbidden awareness?

A single manservant stepped back into the room. Though the man's slippered feet were silent, Robert Dovenby held out one hand. Water ran, slicking the dark hair on his forearm. A tiny silver runnel spiraled from his elbow to the carpet.

"A reply?"

"Yes, sir," the servant said, placing the sealed paper into his master's fingers. "From Lady Grenham."

No emotion showed on the lean face as he read. At last, he dipped the paper into his bathwater until the ink ran and blurred, before balling it up and tossing it into the fireplace. The sphere hissed, then began to char. Dove snapped his fingers and his servant handed him a towel. Streaming water, he stood and wrapped himself in the folds of white linen.

"Are you hungry, George?"

"I have at last regained the feeling in my arms," Sylvie said. "But I am indeed wretchedly overwhelmed with famine."

"But before we eat, perhaps you would also like to bathe?" asked the breathtaking man she had come to London to destroy.

S HE STOOD AND TUGGED HER CHEAP CUFFS INTO PLACE. HER eyes shone, like delft, like gentians, beneath dark honey lashes. Yet like this, severe, upright, with those clean bones and strong hands, no one would ever guess that she wasn't a boy. The male jacket conspired to hide that betraying curve of hip and thigh. Her soft throat had disappeared behind the man's collar and cravat. She even held her chin like any stripling, proudly, with a hint of disdain.

A challenging woman!

"I hardly think it necessary, sir," she said. "I'm not overly fond of plunging into other men's hot water."

Dove laughed. He felt splendidly aroused, though he had enough self-control not to let himself show it.

"Yet you have, of course, already done so. Meanwhile my men have placed hot water of the physical kind in another room. Since you're to remain there until our meal is served, you might as well wash away that unpleasant scowl."

"I do not wish—" she began.

"Your wishes, George, if you haven't realized it by now, are of no consequence. I must attend to a little business. You will wait. Whether you take advantage of that time to repair your attitude and appearance is up to you."

He took her by both arms and propelled her to the door. Another door opened as his footmen leaped to obey his glance. Without ceremony, he thrust her into a nearby room and turned the key in the lock. He stood for a moment, wondering if she would hammer at the door or shout. She did neither. The sound of her boots faded away. The heels clicked once. Then silence.

Dove walked thoughtfully back into his bedroom. He had behaved as provocatively in front of a woman as he knew how, giving her every chance to flee or object. "George" hadn't even looked away. Though the betraying color had washed and retreated over her face like a sunrise, she hadn't given herself away by any deliberate gesture. Which suggested, among other things, a delightful level of familiarity with the bodies of naked men.

It did not say, of course, why the devil she was dressed as a youth, nor what she was really doing in his house.

What would it take to really shock her?

His manservant had laid out clean linen, rescued from the laundry. Dove pulled on shirt and smallclothes, chose stockings, shoes, cravat. The opal silk coat and breeches—with the muted colors and subtle sheen of the bird he was named for—had been Meg's favorite.

He glanced at himself in the mirror as he slipped on his wig, hiding his dark hair beneath the necessary gloss of fashion. Odd how its glimmering elegance seemed to change his face, as if he were two people. As he was, of course. Fully dressed he walked to the fireplace and stared at the ball of damp paper lying half burned at the edge of the grate.

Meg could never take him back after such a public display. They had both known it.

Her ink had melted away in hot water, but he remembered every word:

My regrets equal yours, sir. You were—you will always be—the most exquisite lover I shall ever know. But I rather burned my boats as well as your wardrobe. I am sorry for it. Alas, for my wretched temper! Pray, keep the sword and the horse. How can you continue to be London's most glorious chevalier without them? As for your little strumpet, I think she has trounced both of us. Enjoy her.

He could imagine her rueful smile as she added the last sentences:

Young Hartsham is coming to call on me tonight. He has neither your wit, nor your skills, but he is heir to an earldom. Yet you must know that some of the gifts I plan to bestow on him will come, indirectly, from you. You are generous, my dear sir, to consider me still a friend, as I am honored to so call you—Meg Gregory.

So that door had closed, with a gentle enough warning.

Not for the first time, Dove wondered why Meg had chosen plain Robert Sinclair Dovenby when they'd first met—long before they had spun their inescapable web of mutual debt and obligation. Her favors until then had always been shared only with the most dashing and powerful sons of the peerage.

Lord Hartsham was young and keen and a man who would matter to Britain one day. Meg had found a worthy enough object for her patronage, though it would be a very one-sided exchange, all the endowment going from the beautiful widow to her new lover—

He shrugged, burying the unwelcome burn of emotion. Distaste? Hurt? He wasn't sure. At least Meg had agreed to the social truce he had worked for so hard when he had discovered her burning his clothes in the street. Surely that was all that mattered in the end?

And the rest, as Meg knew, would remain—as it had remained for so long—lost in silence.

It did not take much time to examine the house. Bedroom, study, library. The inlaid boxes, lacquered Japanese cabinets, elegant desks and tables. All the places that George and Berthe Dubois might have searched. Nothing appeared to have been disturbed. Was George too clever to have left any traces, or was her intrusion truly innocent? Not that she would have found anything damaging. Dove did not keep such papers at home.

*N*IGHT FOG AND COLD ENVELOPED HIM AS HE WALKED OUT to the mews. Abdiel filled his stall, munching hay. At his master's step the bay lifted his head and nickered. With soft endearments to his brave and foolhardy friend, Dove stroked the fine neck, groomed now to glossy contentment.

A rapid and delicate training had taken place at the bonfire, though Dove would not have chosen to do it quite like that. Yet Abdiel would face sulfur and brimstone for his rider now and not falter. Leaving the horse to his meal, in the sweet, grassy warmth of the stable, Dove waited.

Abdiel shifted, his hooves striking dully in the straw bedding, the sounds muffled by the thick walls, the bulk of stored hay. Only a slight change in the air currents betrayed that someone had come in.

"Mr. Brink," Dove said quietly. "I'm glad to see that you have not lost your edge, sir."

"I trust not," the newcomer said. "Since that's what you pay me for."

Tanner Brink peered up from a face like a walnut, his dark skin betraying his Egyptian blood. Secretive and clever, he winked one black eye. Gypsies were not generally loyal outside their own kind. Neither, probably, was Tanner Brink his real name. Yet it was a relationship of very long standing.

"I shadowed the little French girl, as you asked," the Gypsy said. "She gave the sedan chair fellows directions to a damned poor inn, where she arrived last night with the young man." He spat once into the straw. "Your men proceeded to carry her off in the opposite direction."

"So you had time to visit her lodgings before the young lady arrived home. What did you discover?"

"It's not a place I'd want to leave my brother or sister."

"Your brother or sister would not be happy in any place that had walls," Dove said. "I'll see that the girl is moved. What else?"

"They came from France with a nice purse, they told the landlady, but were robbed of their money by the boatmen who brought them. So they took some kind of bold wager with some ladies they met at an inn, in hopes of mending their fortunes."

"There's no disturbance at the workshop?"

Tanner Brink pulled off his moleskin cap and scratched at a flea. "All quiet as a mouse, sir, unless you go downstairs—"

"Thank you, Mr. Brink. I would like to trace this odd couple's movements before they arrived in London, the young man and his French servant. The smugglers—probably—who brought them to

England. Inns where they stayed on their journey. Anything you can discover."

Tanner's ivory teeth gapped as he gave a broad grin and disappeared.

D OVE WALKED BACK INTO HIS HOUSE AND GAVE FURTHER directions to one of his footmen. He could not leave the French girl alone in the place Tanner Brink had described. She was barely more than a child, and Dove had a strong feeling that none of this was her fault. So Berthe Dubois would have to be taken somewhere safer, while whatever possessions she and George had with them were recovered from their landlady. Those possessions would be discreetly examined, of course, before being delivered back to their owners.

In the dining room the next step of the game waited for its two players. Set with twinned glasses and finger bowls, white napkins and pretty ranks of cutlery, the table gleamed in the candlelight. Perhaps George wanted nothing more than to steal his silver, but if so, she had chosen a damned odd way to go about it.

His heels clicked as Dove climbed the stairs, then strode to the room holding his intriguing prisoner. The key turned with well-oiled ease. Knowing that this stripling was in truth a woman was strangely erotic, ripe with the hidden potential of secret meetings in dark places, offering all the sensual promise of the forbidden.

George was sitting on a chair by the empty grate, apparently staring at nothing, though the hot water and towels had been used. Her hands, certainly, had been washed. Such valiant hands for a woman, with strong knuckles and practical nails, though also supple and long-fingered and with soft, plump pads at the fingertips.

Unbidden, the vision invaded: those hands dressed in rings; her arms and wrists revealed by a gown, instead of being hidden by a man's cuffs; those cushioned fingertips laid lovingly on his bare chest. Was she as lovely beneath the boy's clothes as he imagined? Was she, as her skin and eyes suggested, palely blond beneath the wig?

How would that gilt hair feel falling free, damp with passion, over his naked skin?

Dove wanted, quite forcefully, to find out. His pulse hammered— with desire, with annoyance at his own lack of control. Making sure that none of those thoughts showed in his eyes, he leaned casually in the doorway and crossed his arms.

"You mentioned penmanship, George," he said. "What other skills do you have?"

"What do you mean?"

"You have grown up in too soft a household, sir. If you're angry, try 'What the *devil* do you mean?'" He was delighted to see color flood her face. Not embarrassment. Annoyance. "Who taught you to talk? A nun?"

"A nursemaid." As if her fair skin had not already betrayed her, she stood up and strode boldly toward him. "Who taught you?"

"The inside of a basket. It was woven tightly enough to force my infant mewling early into blasphemous channels. I'm a foundling, George. Did you know that?"

"How the *devil* could I have known?"

He thought that, at least, was the truth. She hadn't known.

"You should have found out before choosing me for your target, sir. It means that I have no particular personal wealth and no expectations of inheritance. It means that your careless destruction of my relationship with Lady Grenham will have unfortunate financial consequences. It means that I intend to take out the value of my lost wardrobe, damaged opportunities, and good credit in hard labor. Your labor."

Her lip curled. "And the value of your lost mistress?"

"Is beyond your ability to repay. My taste does not run to boys. Neither is your servant, Berthe Dubois, to my liking."

Real anger flared for a moment across the perfect cheekbones. "Lud, sir! Berthe Dubois is young enough to be your daughter."

"Alas, I was not *quite* that precocious as a lad. She must be at least fifteen. And yourself? You are—what—seventeen?"

"I'm nineteen." That was, probably, not the truth either. He would guess her to be around twenty-three or four. He knew with certainty that she wasn't a virgin.

"And your tastes, George? Do you like little girls like Berthe, or do other boys enthrall you?"

"Neither," she said flatly.

"You like older ladies?" With a practiced flick of the wrist, he took a pinch of snuff. "Then we're both doomed to be frustrated to-night."

"You cannot go for one night without a woman in your bed?" Her question held depths of contempt.

"I prefer not to. An inclination I share with most men, except you apparently." He held out the box, an amiable confection of enamel and gold. "Try my blend, George. You'll like it."

"I don't take snuff."

"Whatever happened to the ardor of youth? No sex. No snuff. Don't you indulge in any of the vices, sir?"

"Only thievery. And that is limited to cravats, which is all I would have needed to secure two hundred guineas tonight."

"I refuse to disrobe again because of you, George," Dove said. "Especially before dinner. As for your wager, you may have my cravat when I go to bed tonight. Shall we dine?"

He stepped aside to allow her to walk out of the room, but she stood as if rooted, staring at him. Her eyes blazed like daylight. "You would let me win the wager to put me even further in your debt? How do you expect me to pay you back?"

"That depends," he said. "On what you can do besides read and write. You *can* read, I take it?"

She picked up a small book, left lying on a table beside her. Dove recognized *The Book of Common Prayer*. It belonged to the last occupant of this room.

" 'For the enemy hath persecuted my soul,' " she read, opening the volume at random. " 'He hath smitten my life down to the ground; he hath laid me in the darkness, as the men that have been long dead. Therefore is my spirit vexed within me and my heart within me is desolate. Yet do I remember the time past; I muse upon all thy works.' " Her blue eyes met his in open challenge. " 'Yea, I exercise myself in the works of thy hands. I stretch forth my hands unto thee; my soul gaspeth unto thee as a thirsty land.' "

"If you're addressing that last entreaty to me," Dove said dryly, "it is charmingly close to blasphemy."

She closed the covers with a snap and set the book down. "I have all the usual skills," she said, "though I don't consider either excessive piety or blasphemy among them. I can count, calculate, read, write, understand a legal document, craft a letter or an invoice. I know how to address a bishop or an earl. I can recount the adventures of Hercules or name the gods of Olympus, in Latin if need be. In short, sir, I have the normal education of any gentleman."

"Except decent manners. Shall we dine before our roast beef congeals in its juices?"

Dove spun about and led the way to the dining room. She walked stiffly behind him. He wondered for a moment whether she would hesitate as if she wore skirts, but she marched directly to the table and sat. The footman obviously did not question her gender as he slid her chair into place.

The wine soared. The roast steamed in succulent splendor. The fish, the bread, the vegetables, the sauces, each perfect in its way. Nutty cheeses, ripe fruits. A pretty sugar-spun trifle of coffee ice.

The seductive meal he had expected to share with Meg. A question briefly presented itself at the thought. He filed it away to ask later.

Meanwhile, his interesting companion was obviously familiar with the rankings of glasses, the multiplicity of cutlery, the silent nod to an attentive footman to serve or remove. She must in the recent past have been hostess of her own table. In which case, what was she really doing here, dressed like this?

Dove leaned back, toying with the spiral stem of his wineglass. Candlelight sparkled in drops, like red blood, on the rim.

"You're still annoyed with me?" she asked.

"Certainly."

"The last meal for two shared here was with Lady Grenham?"

"As this one was designed to be. Yes."

She lifted her glass, matching his gesture. "After which you retired upstairs?"

He took a single sip. His mouth filled with rich darkness. Grapes, time, and magic. "To that bed to which you had the misfortune to be trussed? Yes."

Her gaze met his as she took a swallow of her wine, then set down her glass. "You will find another mistress."

Desire flared again, like the light in the red wine. Dove smiled, savoring the warmth running through his blood. Desire. And anger at her cavalier reminder of what she had cost him.

"I certainly don't intend to live without one."

She tore a corner from her bread roll. "Another bone to pick with me."

"We'll get to the bones later, George, after we have devoured the flesh. Firstly, I would like to know how you found yourself in such an awkward position that you must break into a stranger's dressers in search of his cravats."

White teeth bit neatly into bread. "I came to seek my fortune in

London, but was robbed on the journey. With the peace not yet concluded, it wasn't that easy to cross from France."

"So you traveled with smugglers or vagabonds who fleeced you. Now you wax indignant, though you're fortunate to still have your life. Pray go on."

She colored a little. "I don't have any immediate family. I've had to live by my wits, sir, as it would seem that you have."

"Lud," Dove said. "Another foundling!"

"Not at all! My parents were English, but had the misfortune to pick the wrong side in that unhappy business with the Jacobites."

"Yet they named you George? How very original of them!"

"My grandfather was also named George. In honor of the saint, not the Hanoverian kings."

"And your father? He was a dragon slayer, too?"

She laughed. "Or he would hardly have supported Charles Edward Stuart? Either way, my father was too proud to return, cap in hand, to the country he'd fled in such panic. So though I was born in England, I grew up in Italy."

"How did your family survive?"

"My parents ran a business in antiquities. Rather poorly, as it turned out. There wasn't much left when they were carried off in a fever." She watched as he refilled her wineglass. "In fact, there were creditors. I thought it wise to salvage what I could and try my luck in my lost homeland. Though I see now that my choice of conveyance might have been foolhardy, I didn't plan to lose my savings."

It might be true. The story would explain both her perfect English and her unusual education, even why she might have traveled in breeches—though not why she should disguise her gender now.

"I am sorry for your loss," he said in Italian, just to make sure.

The blue eyes gazed frankly into his as she replied without hesitation in the same language. "I try to pay my debts, Mr. Dovenby.

I satisfied my father's creditors. If it can be done with honor, I shall pay you back what you believe I have cost you."

He sipped wine, meeting her gaze, and spoke again in English. "What you *have* cost me, I fail to see how you can possibly pay back."

She glanced down to cut an apple into neat slices. He watched her hands moving beneath her shirt cuffs, the feminine fingertips caressing the red rind, separating the white flesh and the intricate star of seeds at the center. If he didn't still feel a certain loyalty to Meg—and if he didn't need to uncover this young woman's game—he would be tempted to let George know right now that he saw through her disguise and that he liked what he saw. Though he had never before made love to any woman for revenge.

"Ah, yes," she said. "Your mistress. You will miss her tonight."

He smiled, genuinely amused, though it did not soften his anger. It was hardly something one man would say to another. "With considerable urgency."

"Then you don't think celibacy good for the soul?"

"I consider celibacy an unnatural abomination."

"Because you enjoy fornication?" A smile lifted the corners of her mouth as she began to quote. " 'Marriage was ordained for a remedy against sin and to avoid fornication, that such persons as have not the gift of continency might marry and keep themselves undefiled.' You should marry, Mr. Dovenby."

His laugh broke free this time, forcing him to set down his glass. "Faith! You cite the marriage service? Don't tell me you're *married,* George?"

She ran one finger around the rim of her wineglass and matched his grin. "No."

"Thank God for that! A wife and gaggle of infants would unduly complicate matters between us. As I'm sure you've noticed, this is a bachelor establishment, sir, of regrettably loose morals."

"I rather thought everything in it had been chosen primarily for beauty," she said. "You are partial to loveliness?"

"You are perceptive, sir." He poured her more wine. "But everything in this house—especially what is beautiful—is designed only to fulfill a man's basest needs."

Awareness flared in her eyes, but she answered him with defiance. "Except *The Book of Common Prayer?*"

"Remind me never to leave you locked in a room with a prayer book again."

She leaned back, saluting him with the glass. "I would prefer not to be locked in at all."

"That depends on your behavior."

"Oh," she said. "I thought my future right now depended entirely on yours. Certainly it would appear to depend on your whim. Why do you warn me that you share all the usual weaknesses of our sex? That's been painfully obvious, sir, from the start."

"*Weaknesses?*"

"You cannot survive without a woman in your bed. Such a craving for sex only makes men vulnerable. It's a weakness that allows the female the upper hand in every dealing she has with a man."

He signaled the footmen to remove the cloth and bring the brandy. "And in fear of that, you cling to celibacy, George?"

She shrugged. "If you like."

He wasn't surprised that she would pretend a vague piety, a convenient excuse not to womanize in order to maintain her disguise. Yet this went deeper than that. Did she truly believe that men were more sexually vulnerable than women? The idea was strangely compelling—and a definite invitation to indulge a little wickedness.

The footman left the room, leaving them gazing at each other across the polished mahogany.

"You believe that women are never desperate for sex?"

"Not as men are," she replied. "Men crave it. Women only give it. A man becomes a fool over his desires in a way that a woman never does."

"If so," he said, "perhaps it only means that the woman in question has never met the right man."

The candles had begun to burn low, guttering occasionally, offering a new dance of softer light and greater intimacy. With Meg, this part of the evening had always been sweetly, urgently, a readying for bed. In some part of his heart, that festered like a sore.

"And you're always the right man?"

"Always," he said merely to goad her. "Aren't you?"

A betraying flush washed over her cheeks. "I can't afford to make a wager with you, sir. But you're wrong. If you believe otherwise, your lovers have been lying to you."

"But every young man should devote himself to learning how to please a woman in bed."

"You would encourage me to investigate sin?" The pulse beat hard beneath the turn of her jaw. "How should I begin a seduction, sir? With a conversation over dinner, perhaps?"

"Why not? Your every attention must let her know how very lovely she is to you, how much you desire her. It's called flirtation. If she desires you, she will breathe a little faster. Her cheeks will flush with color. Once she invites you with her eyes—"

"I assume touch comes next?" she asked. "Where?"

"Wherever the woman desires." He stroked the stem of his glass as he gazed into her eyes. He was beginning to enjoy himself. "A woman's body is a shrine of sweet places, begging for a man's worship. Her wine-soaked lips. Her tongue. Any of her soft, scented, hidden spots: the little depression at the base of her throat, the swell of her breasts, her instep, the hollow behind her knee, the tender curve of her thigh—"

Her pupils dilated into jet. She turned her head and naked skin flashed white: the spot where the supple column of her neck met the pink lobe of her ear.

If he set his fingertips there, his mouth—

That one glimpse of tender female flesh, just that, was giving him an erection.

Her hand trembled a little as she reached for the decanter, her breathing unsteady. "But if you seek to teach me a rake's technique, sir, tell me this: how long do you linger over such places?"

"As long as it takes for her to offer me even sweeter places: her waist, her belly—"

She looked back at him, her cheeks stained with carmine. "Why wait for her to offer? Why not just take what you want?"

Hard and imperious, his erection throbbed. He knew that his eyes were as dilated as hers, his skin just as hectically burning. His imagination fired as if with a madness.

"What I want is her tongue desperate to entangle with mine, her nipples inexorably rising to meet my palm. I want to hear her whimpers when one peak can't bear any more, though the other breast begs for the same attention. I want her to beg for my tongue to explore—"

The brandy flask rattled onto the table. "Yet you still maintain your vaunted control?"

"Control? Yes. But over myself, not her. Even when she offers my hands and my mouth the sweetest place of all: between her legs."

She bit her ripe bottom lip. "You are never at her mercy?"

"Of course. But she is equally at mine: when shattering need meets shattering need, when the flame of sensation consumes us both in the same crucible. Yet however intense my ardor, I wait for hers, because the sex is always sweetest when the lady's desires drive the pace."

"It's a manipulation," she said, clenching her fingers on her glass. "Where you make yourself her slave. She will never become as desperate as you."

"Yes, she will. If a man has never caused a woman to want him as much as he wants her, it means only that he's a damned selfish lover."

She pushed up and leaned forward, resting both fists on the polished mahogany. In the guttering candlelight her eyes were shadowed with indigo. The lace at her throat quaked like apple petals in a spring breeze.

"Yet Lady Grenham disposed of your vaunted skills in the bedroom quickly enough, didn't she?"

"Meg had no choice." Though his blood raged in his veins, he set down his empty brandy glass, then slid it across the polished surface to chink gently against hers. "Thanks to you and your plain little maid."

"So how long does it take you to make a lady beg for more, sir? One night? Several? Since I cannot fulfill your base needs myself, would you like me to scour the streets to procure you a harlot for tonight?"

He looked her up and down, deliberately cataloguing her slender bones and fair skin, the blue eyes, the lovely fingers beneath her lace cuffs. "How about a tall, strapping woman, dark-eyed enough to drown in, but shy as a mouse? I abhor bold women."

"Long legs or short? Lush lashes? Large breasts?"

He almost choked. "You're kind to offer, sir, but I prefer to procure my own lovers."

"Then what service may I perform for you, sir, to redeem my debt? You are not, I assume, simply going to let me walk out of here?"

Dove waited until his pulse slowed and his erection died away. "Why not? That's exactly what I'm going to do, since it's time to retire."

"And my fate?"

He stood up, walked to the fireplace, and stripped off his cravat, watching her reflection in the mirror over the mantel. A poignant regret pierced his mixed mirth and anger. He missed Meg. He was facing a cold, empty bed tonight. Those two things were certain. Nothing about this young woman was, least of all her real motives.

"What the hell can you offer me, sir, that I cannot more easily and more cheaply obtain elsewhere?" The strip of linen draped from his fingers as he turned to face her. "Here, take this."

Her face drained. "You'll let me win my wager?"

"Why not? This would seem to be a night for taking liberties. To balance some of yours, I have transferred your lodgings. Mademoiselle Dubois is already ensconced at your new abode. The two hundred guineas riding on your possession of my cravat will help you pay the reckoning."

She scrambled around the table. "What have you done? Where have you taken her?"

He smiled down into the indignant blue eyes and wondered what she would do if he kissed her and let his resentment and hurt burn hotly into her mouth.

"Lud, sir! I have only moved her to a more suitable address than the disgusting place you had chosen. A sedan chair will take you there."

He folded the cravat, picked up one of her hands, and placed the white fabric into her cupped palm.

"And my debt?" she asked.

"Is still owed."

He strode to the doorway, where he stopped for a moment, letting his eyes run over her perfect bones and brave profile, filing away every detail.

"Meanwhile, sir," he said, "you know where the front door is. By all means, use it."

Dove bowed and left the room, only to lean back against the wall in the corridor to allow himself a moment of silent hilarity. There was no clink of silverware sliding into her pockets. He did not hear the sound of crystal wineglasses or gilt candlesticks being disturbed, though she had observed and judged everything in the house. Instead her footsteps tapped lightly back and forth as if she paced, deep in thought.

Just as he had already surmised: not simply a thief, unless it counted that she had stolen a certain peace of mind.

He strode away down the hallway to his study, sat down at his desk, and pulled out paper and ink. It wasn't necessary to make notes to cover all the little trains of investigation he had already set in motion, with various servants, with Tanner Brink. He held every detail of his web of inquiry perfectly competently in his mind.

Just one query needed to be put into writing, the thought that had occurred to him so forcefully at dinner.

He snapped open the silver lid of the inkwell.

My dear Meg: Thank you for your gifts, my dear, though they are but poor recompense for the loss of your company. I grow verdigris on my soul over Hartsham. Be kind to the boy. There is just one small question that in addition to the lack of your shining presence will keep me from sleep tonight. I shall be forever in your debt, if your kindness allows you to send your answer by return.

He stopped to dip the quill back into the ink, before coming to the crux of the matter.

Can you tell me, my dear, why you arrived here so very early, when our appointment for dinner was not until nine? You find me, as always, Your Ladyship's humble, obedient and most bereft of servants, Robert Dovenby.

A footman took the note, with instructions to wait for a reply. Dove walked to the window and looked down into the street. It was entirely dark now. Around the far corner, lit brightly by the flare of a passing coach lantern, the sedan chair was disappearing, carrying its interesting burden. He closed his eyes and allowed himself to recall each slender finger. The turn of her neck. The soft skin and fierce gaze. The woman's scent just discernable beneath the powder. The flare of passionate interest in her eyes that she hadn't quite been able to hide.

He wanted her. In spite of his feelings for Meg, he felt that desire with considerable intensity.

He did not consider it a weakness.

He was too practiced, too experienced, and too cynical for that.

Whatever his ardor, he was not blinded to the facility with which she had slipped from one language to another—English, Italian, French—or the ease with which she had negotiated the complexities of a dining table. Nothing he had said or done, however outrageous, had genuinely shocked her. George had studied not only the ways of high society, but the ways of men, which meant that she was either a widow or a courtesan—or both.

She had meant to interest him and she had succeeded, though perhaps in more ways than she had quite intended. There was only one way she could outwit him now and that was to disappear without trace. Since he was certain that the ransacking of his bedroom had not been in the least random, he did not imagine for a moment that would happen. If it did, he was doubly damned.

He would have misjudged the game and lost track of a potential enemy.

Even worse, he would have lost from his life a woman who was undoubtedly experienced but—provocatively—had never yet learned what it meant to crave the touch of a lover.

Chapter Three

SYLVIE SAT BACK IN THE CHAIR AS TWO SERVANTS JOLTED HER along the cobbles. A third led the way as link boy, his smoking torch cleaving the damp night. Her blood still pulsed, hot and urgent. She took a deep breath of frosty air and tried to ignore it.

Round one—to whom? She felt as if she had been scorched in a furnace, yet she believed she had given nothing away. If she had been overly keen to leave, he would have wondered why she had really been in his house to begin with, yet if she'd let herself seem too reluctant, he would have become even more suspicious.

Irritating man!

She had learned precisely nothing so far, except that he was clever, charming, and damnably overconfident—and had a face and body for women to worship. *A woman's body is a shrine of sweet places. . . .*

His cravat lay folded in her hands. Without thinking, she lifted the strip of linen to her face. The scent of fresh laundry. Tantalizing undertones that spoke of shaving soap and witch hazel. A whisper of the potent aroma of clean male skin. A shiver scurried down her spine. Unlike her, he was a man. A real one. And dangerous.

It was damnable that she should feel this unwelcome fascination. So he was attractive—so he knew how to please a lover! What of it? She had known other lovers. No man had ever enthralled her yet.

She glanced out at the jostle of London, dark and shadow alternating with the flare of lantern or torch and the dim sheen of oil streetlamps. Crowds mobbed the pavements. Carriages rumbled by. He would no doubt be having her followed.

With a defiant grin she leaned from the window and gave a new address to the porters. The men's shoes clunked on the paving as they turned into a fashionable modern square. The link boy extinguished his torch in the open mouth of a cast-iron dragon, set there for the purpose, then banged on the knocker. The door opened. Sylvie climbed out and walked up the steps.

Moments later she was being shown into a drawing room. Several ladies and gentlemen turned their powdered heads to examine her as she entered. Robert Dovenby may have absurdly claimed it was bedtime, but most of fashionable London had only just begun to enjoy itself. Any excuse for flirtation and gambling would do. At Number Eighteen she had interrupted a card party.

"Faith!" exclaimed one of the ladies, clapping her hands. "It's our pretty fellow from the Royal Oak on the Dover Road. Remember, everyone? I told you about him." She rose and came to greet Sylvie with both arms outstretched. "You haven't *already* won our wager, sir?"

Sylvie bowed over her soft hands, vaguely kissing the air above several valuable rings. "But of course, Lady Charlotte. An article of Mr. Robert Dovenby's personal linen is yours."

With a flourish she draped his cravat over the lady's open palm. The room erupted in laughter and applause.

"Now," cried one of the ladies, "if you could only capture the man for us as easily, sir!"

"Wine!" Lady Charlotte called. "Bring wine for Mr. George White, then he may tell us the whole tale. Will a duel result, do you suppose?"

"Alas, ma'am," Sylvie whispered in her ear as a footman approached with a glass. "I have already taken too much of Mr. Dovenby's wine. I am not used—"

She shrugged and made a face. It was almost true. Her breath would certainly carry the aroma of Dove's excellent brandy and her head felt light, almost as if something soared in her heart.

"My poor boy! You are unwell? You would like to be private?" The lady turned to the company. "Our pretty fellow is overcome by so much elegant company, my dears."

Taking Sylvie by the arm, she led her from the room.

"My poor young sir," Lady Charlotte said. "You are tired. You would like to lie down? My chamber is yours."

With you in it? Sophie suppressed a giggle at the thought.

"Alas, ma'am," she said bluntly. "I think I'm going to be sick."

The lady's face crumpled. "My dear boy! In here." She opened the door to a small study with a chaise longue. "I will send a maid with a basin."

"You will not forget our wager, Lady Charlotte?"

"But, no! I will write you a draft immediately for your one hundred guineas."

"Two hundred," Sylvie said, sagging dramatically onto the chaise longue and continuing in French. "Oh, ma'am, I thought to be charmed by an evening in your amiable company. I am wretched with chagrin."

She groaned, clapping one hand over her mouth.

"Yes, two hundred!" Lady Charlotte backed rapidly from the room.

The door slammed. Sylvie curled herself into a ball, stuffing a fist in her mouth to stifle helpless laughter. There was—perfection!—a key in the lock. When the maid arrived, she would find herself locked out. If she knocked, she would hear only a wail begging her to leave the basin and go away. Then Mr. George White, sadly overcome by an excess of spirits, would appear to have fallen soundly asleep on the chaise longue and would remain that way for the rest of the night.

It took only five minutes to complete that phase of the plan. The maid left, clunking the basin onto the floor outside the locked door after rattling at the handle. Sylvie retrieved the basin, locked the door again, opened the window, and stepped over the sill. It had begun to drizzle, sealing the night with damp and silence, like a blanket. Since she had left her hat with the footman in the hallway, Sylvie held the basin over her head to protect her wig from the rain.

THE DUKE OF YVESHIRE FROWNED OVER THE PAPERS PILED ON his desk. His dressing gown snaked with gold thread. The designs glittered in the candlelight and the glow of the dying coals in the grate. A linen nightcap covered his skull and shadowed the lean line of cheek and long jaw. He wrung one hand harshly over his face and sighed. He seemed pinched and unhappy, as if carrying too great a burden.

Sylvie watched him quietly for a few moments more before she tapped on the windowpane.

Yveshire looked up, reaching for a small brass bell with one hand. His eyes burned, too dark in his white face. Sylvie slipped off her wig and gestured for silence.

Leaving the bell undisturbed, the duke strode to the window and lifted the sash.

"Lud, ma'am," he said. "You make a damned attractive boy. Welcome to England."

"Thank you, Your Grace. May I come in?"

"You have news? Already?"

"Not quite. I can't bring you much right now but night air and dampness, I'm afraid, but I thought you'd like to know that I have successfully made contact. He doesn't suspect a thing and he's about to take me into his household. I could tell you more comfortably, perhaps, by the fire?"

Tall, elegant, Yveshire stepped back and allowed her to scramble into the room. His skin gleamed like ivory, then flushed with borrowed warmth as he sat down beside the fireplace.

Sylvie set down the basin, pulled down the sash, and closed the shutters behind her.

"It was not wise to come here," the duke said. "You might have been followed."

"I *am* being followed," she replied. "But only as far as Number Eighteen, three doors down in the next street."

He raised both brows.

"They're having a party. I met one of the houseguests, Lady Charlotte Rampole, a few days ago at the Royal Oak on the Dover Road. I learned she'd soon be a close neighbor of yours, and I'd already set up an excuse to visit her. Dovenby's porters took me there."

"*Dovenby's* porters!"

"No need for concern. The men didn't want to wait in the rain. So when I suggested it, they left. The additional hound Mr. Dovenby set on my scent for that very eventuality is still watching the house. The discreet inquiries he will make among the servants will confirm that I retired from the drawing room with Lady Charlotte. She had designs, I think, on my virgin manhood, but I was sadly taken ill and had to beg for that basin."

Yveshire laughed.

Sylvie hung her wig on the back of a chair and walked up to the fireplace. "So young George White is locked, drunk as a lord, in a study with a convenient chaise longue. Meanwhile, this palace of yours was easy to find. Dovenby won't discover that I left the house."

"But if he does—"

"He won't. I'm a professional, Your Grace. As you are." She took the poker and jiggled the coals so they erupted into flame, then held her palms out to the warmth. "It suits you to be a duke, even in your night attire."

The dressing gown cast gilt ripples over his shoulders as he shrugged. "My father's death was not unexpected, though there were circumstances that regretfully hastened it. I am certainly enjoying the title. It would be absurd to pretend otherwise."

"Because you've always liked the associated bowing and scraping?"

His lean face split in a wary grin. "Being a duke's eldest son always brought certain advantages."

"No doubt, Your Grace," Sylvie said with mock gravity. "May I sit?"

He waved her to the chair opposite his. "If you want brandy, serve yourself. For obvious reasons, I cannot summon any servants to wait on you."

"I've already taken more wine and brandy tonight than I quite have stomach for. This male obsession with drinking may prove to be a nuisance."

She sat down to thrust both booted feet onto the fender, then realized she was imitating the stance Dovenby had used in his bedroom. She shrugged, grinning, and left her boots where they were.

"The joke?" the duke asked.

"Only that in spite of that—or perhaps because of it—it is really rather liberating being a man!"

The duke sat back and steepled his fingers together. "It seemed the wisest choice for this particular assignment, though I'm damned if I can quite reconcile those breeches with the way I last saw you: in silver tissue and diamonds, mesmerizing lords and princes in a ballroom in Vienna."

"The diamonds were fake, and that was also acting of a kind, Your Grace. You, of all men, should know that."

"Should I?"

Sylvie switched back to something safer. "I agreed that this disguise was less dangerous on the journey, yet I have wondered why you insisted so vehemently on my continuing it for the whole mission. Can you tell me?"

He met her gaze without flinching. "I could not, in good conscience, let you become this man's mistress."

"Your Grace—" She had to stop to take a deep breath, but she still could not keep the bite from her voice. "You give me my assignments. You pay me very well for the information I send you. You do *not* control when, or with whom, I share my bed."

"Perhaps not. That does not stop me from wanting to keep you out of the bed of a monster."

She stared at him, while shock sank to her gut like a stone. "A *monster?*"

"Lud, ma'am!" He laughed. "You are no naive miss. He is charming. Attractive. Handsome. Witty. Brave. Intelligent. His manner is impeccable. Of course. But you know very well that charisma is one of the Devil's most useful attributes."

Sylvie tugged at her cuffs to cover her odd moment of panic. "I'm using this disguise only because you need me to enter so absolutely into Robert Dovenby's confidence," she said. "And because he was known to be absolutely faithful to Lady Grenham, and so might not be vulnerable enough to my usual methods. However, I suppose if my male attire keeps me from a Black Mass and congress with Beelzebub, that's all to the good."

"I do not jest, ma'am."

"I didn't think for a minute that you did. Do you know he rides a stallion called Abdiel?"

Yveshire looked blank. "What?"

"Like Abdiel in *Paradise Lost,* the angel who resisted Satan's revolt. 'Faithful found among the faithless, faithful only he.' I suppose it's rather appropriate."

The duke stood, gold rippling from his shoulders as he smashed his fist onto the mantel. "*I do not jest, ma'am!*"

Sylvie took another deep breath. She felt as if the air were being squeezed slowly from her lungs. "You will learn, soon enough, how

I entered his house, though the version you will hear will bear little resemblance to what really happened. Suffice it to say that I successfully liberated Mr. Dovenby of his powerful mistress and of a fortune in clothing. He was very annoyed."

"It's not enough. He must be completely destroyed."

Sylvie stared up at him. She had never before seen the duke this close to losing control.

"Why? What has he done?"

Yveshire strode away across the room, his slippered feet silent on the carpet. "Of all the tasks that you did for me in Europe—" He stopped, leaning both fists on his desk to stare down at the scattering of papers. "This is different. I need more than one or two pieces of information. I must know everything. How he lives. Where his money comes from. His habits. His weaknesses—"

"I have accepted that he is the devil incarnate, but you didn't tell me that this mission was also personally motivated. Though I suppose I should have guessed, considering the size of the payment you promised."

"I did not tell you when I wrote to you, but I am telling you now: Robert Dovenby is a criminal. He deserves death. But yes, this assignment also intimately involves myself."

"I will have to know exactly how, or I cannot help you," Sylvie insisted.

He strode back to stand over her. His anger and bitterness sparked as clearly as his gold thread. "Dovenby is responsible for the death of my brother."

"I am sorry, Your Grace," she said. "I didn't know."

The tendons of his hands stood out starkly as the duke grasped the arms of his chair and sat down. "Dovenby ruined him, then saw that he was murdered in cold blood. My younger brother."

She supported her head on both hands, remembering her unwelcome craving at the sight of that lean body, the firing of her senses as they jousted over dinner. Had she lusted so ferociously after a heartless assassin?

"I am sorry," she said again. "What was your brother's name?"

"Edward. Edward Frederick George. We weren't close. There were five years between us. But he shared my blood and my name. He was my father's favorite."

"Can you tell me how he died?"

"He was beaten to death. That's when I discovered what Dovenby had done. My father suffered a stroke at the news. It was his deathbed wish that I avenge him."

"So this is why you need to know everything about Dovenby—?"

"I consider his destruction a sacred duty."

Sylvie pushed to her feet and walked to the side table where a bottle reflected the candlelight. Her hand felt unsteady as she poured the pungent brandy into a glass. She walked back to thrust it into the duke's fingers. He took the glass and swallowed half the contents in one gulp. A red spot flared brightly on each cheekbone.

"Don't be afraid that my personal feelings will in any way compromise our mission, Sylvie. Robert Dovenby is far more than a personal enemy."

"But he knows you suspect him?"

"Absolutely, which is why your association with me must remain secret."

"You say he is criminal. How?"

"That's what I want you to discover. I know only that he is an evil man and a canker on society. Thanks to Meg Grenham, he has moved freely among the *ton,* yet I believe he leads a double life. Before my brother died, there were rumors—"

"I'm not a child. You can tell me."

He looked uncomfortable. "Edward always defended him—said the idea was an absurd calumny—yet the rumors persisted: of unspeakable vice, of girls who disappeared—"

"I understand. Nothing was ever proved?"

"I have hired men to follow him. I know only that Dovenby freely visits parts of London that no gentleman should dare go."

"What kind of places?"

"Every time I set a tail on him, he loses it. My men are waylaid, misled, sometimes even set upon—though in ways that seem random. He is clever. He will not be easy to unmask."

Her blood seemed to run ever colder, like a winter stream in the oncoming night. "Yet you think I can do it?"

"If I thought anyone else could do it, I would not have suggested you take on the task." He drained the rest of his glass. "I don't expect you to put yourself in danger. I trust you in that."

In danger! She studied the duke's face, the fear for her—in spite of his words—that he was trying to conceal. Lud, she knew him so thoroughly!

"You think Dovenby will simply tell me his secrets?"

"I think you are just as clever as he is. I think you alone can penetrate his mind."

"Without sharing his bed?" she asked dryly. "I can do all of this while masquerading as a man?"

"Why not?" The duke tipped back his head to drain the rest of his drink. "And I truly believe you can do it without risk. I would never forgive myself if any harm came to you from this, Sylvie!"

"Yes, Your Grace, I know that."

He smiled. "Yet perhaps you understand now why men indulge in a little too much brandy now and again?"

"I have always understood," Sylvie said, taking his empty wineglass. "You must recall, Your Grace, that I understand men very well."

Yveshire's eyes lit like coals. "We *will* see him brought to the gallows."

In spite of herself, Sylvie shivered. She walked away, set down the glass, and picked up her powdered wig.

"He keeps nothing incriminating at his house. I have already searched. However, I promise I will discover everything you need to know when he hires me as his secretary."

The duke leaped to his feet. "He has already offered that?"

"No," she said, setting the wig over her carefully pinned hair, "but he will."

T HE FOOTMAN BROUGHT BACK A REPLY FROM MEG WITHIN the hour. Dove read it standing beside his empty bed.

You are importunate, sir, to call me away from my pretty new project. Hartsham is pouting. Enclosed is the answer to your question. Your ever devoted and regretful, Meg Grenham.

Folded in her lavender-scented sheet was another. He smoothed out the creases. This note was unsigned.

Your Ladyship would be advised to visit a certain well-renowned bird this afternoon. At his invitation, another little bird is about to take up residence in a nest Your Ladyship has been used to call her own.

He allowed himself a wry smile. As he had suspected, Meg had been deliberately summoned to discover the trespassers in his bed-room. Not only that, she had been alerted to expect to find a young woman there, one who planned to supplant her. That she had dis-covered a rather plain French girl and her manservant would only have added to Meg's rage and pain. As Dove felt to be replaced by a pup like Hartsham?

He read the note again, then walked to the fireplace, burning brightly now to ward off the night chill. He dropped the paper into the coals and watched it turn into ash. Rain was tracing freely down the windowpanes. Nevertheless, five minutes later he slipped out of the back door of his townhouse, a dark cloak flung over his silk.

Rain gurgled in gutters and dripped from the eaves. The hilt of his smallsword nestled comfortably against his hip, Dove strode toward the new address his porters had given him on their return. George had not allowed herself to be taken to the lodgings he had secured for her, the safer place where young Berthe Dubois now waited alone. She had instead given his men an address in a fashionable new square.

He located his spy waiting patiently under the scaffolding of a half-built house at the end of the row. The man looked up as Dove approached. Water stained his collar and dripped from his chin.

"A miserable night," Dove said.

"Yes, sir," the man replied. "The young man stopped there, sir." He nodded toward Number Eighteen. "The footman says they're having a party. The young man arrived to fulfil his wager with Lady Charlotte Rampole, who's a guest there. They met, so the footman says, at an inn on the Dover Road. They left the room together, but the young man claimed to be ill. He's lying in a downstairs study with the door locked. He appears to have gone to sleep."

"And the windows?"

"A maid brought him a basin. The ladies were talking about him, about how handsome he was. The maid was upset that he locked the door against her. She said that when she went out later to the necessary, the shutters obscured most of the room where he was sleeping. She couldn't see him lying on the couch, but a candle still burned and the window was closed and latched."

Dove grinned. "A conveniently nosy housemaid."

"Yes, sir. The maid also swears she heard the young man snoring. He cannot have left the house."

Dove pulled his tricorn more closely over his forehead. Water shone and dripped as rain sheeted along the street. The maid could have heard nothing in this downpour.

His boots splashed as he walked around to the backs of the houses. A slim beam of light glimmered from one window. He stood quietly in a dark corner by the mews and waited.

It was late. It was cold. It was bloody uncomfortable. The rain gave way to sleet, frosting the puddles. At last the candle in the room where George supposedly lay went out, plunging the back of the house into yet deeper darkness. Perhaps she was innocently and snuggly asleep on that chaise longue, the richer now by two hundred guineas. Perhaps she really was snoring. Perhaps everything she had told him had been the simple truth. Perhaps all along she had wanted nothing from him but his cravat.

Yet it was easy enough to close and open such a window from the outside by slipping a knife into the slot between the sashes to knock back the latch, especially if the screw had first been loosened a little.

The shutters, though almost closed, had not been locked into place with their iron bar.

And Meg had been deliberately summoned.

He was prepared to wait all night, if necessary.

At last light footsteps rapped toward the stables. Dove drew farther back into the shadows as she walked up to the house. He grinned when he saw that she was using an upturned basin to keep her wig dry. She glanced around once at the dark buildings, then pulled a paper knife from her jacket pocket. He could imagine the slight click as the latch gave way. Without looking back again, she lifted the sash and stepped in through the window.

Moments later the shutters closed. This time, no doubt, the bar was dropped to secure them. Her entry into the house had been fast and disturbingly professional.

So she had already outwitted him. There was no way to know where she had been, and obviously he could not reveal his presence here, lurking in dark corners like a spirit of the night.

Dove strode back into the square, where he gave the spy his coin and dismissed him. Next time he would set two men to follow her. Either that or go himself. Unless, of course—in spite of this midnight adventure, however unlikely it might seem—there was nothing sinister at all in her intrusion into his life.

Yet an empty bed lay waiting at his townhouse. His dressers and maybe his house had been searched. Whatever happened now, he and this interesting young woman had just begun a most provocative game.

He would—since he held all the cards—win.

But when he eventually chose to unmask her—when he found out if she was indeed blond; when she welcomed him to explore her soft woman's skin; when she offered him the sweet flare of her waist and hip and thigh; when she sighed his name and told him hers—then he would uncover without mercy the heat of female passion that she carried hidden in her heart.

Though if his suspicions were correct, it would be the first time he would ever have made love to an enemy.

LIGHT AND THE RATTLE OF VOICES STILL FLARED FROM THE front windows of Number Eighteen. Dove walked up the steps and hammered at the knocker. A footman opened the door to stare up at the unexpected visitor, rain streaming from the corners of his hat, the glint of a sword visible beneath his wet cloak.

"Good evening," Dove said, placing his engraved card—*Robert Sinclair Dovenby*—into the man's gloved hand. "You will be pleased to take this directly to Lady Charlotte Rampole."

COLD WOKE HER. COLD AND A FAINT SOUND. THE AIR IN THE study was arctic. Her fingers fumbled as she groped for her tinderbox, until welcome light flickered from the candle on the small table next to the couch. Shadows chased into bitter, dark corners. Her boots were still damp and there was no fuel in the grate.

Sylvie adjusted her wig and shrugged into her crumpled jacket before she unlocked the door. The sconces shone brightly along the hallway. The hands of the clock stood rigidly at attention: six o'clock. It wouldn't be daylight for hours, though the servants had already dragged themselves from their attic beds to renew lights and begin tending fires. They would start in the kitchen and bedrooms, of course, not in this chill room with its icy chaise longue.

She walked back to hold her hands over her newly lit candle and shiver.

You know very well that charisma is one of the Devil's most useful attributes.

The words had seemed merely melodramatic last night in Yveshire House, but now in the cold reality of a winter morning, they resounded like a death knell.

I consider his destruction a sacred duty.

In a vain attempt to warm herself, Sylvie began to pace. She had worked for Yveshire for years, long before his father died and he became duke. France and England were at war. She had sent him information about French plans, about indiscreet or foolish Englishmen; reported on the gossip at the courts of Europe and the threads of discontent in the German states. It had been an interesting and lucrative enough way of earning her living, though it had all been done for a country she barely remembered.

Her reflection frowned back from the mirror over the mantel. She had never before participated in the annihilation of a personal enemy. Was she—for the first time—truly out of her depth?

"So you glower even at yourself," a voice said from the doorway. "Really, sir, I sometimes wonder why I bother with you."

Sylvie spun about, the breath frozen in her lungs, though her pulse leaped in recognition, as if scalded.

Dressed in his opal silk coat and neat silver wig, a fresh cravat tied elegantly at his throat, Robert Dovenby stood in the open doorway. Formidable. Challenging. Smiling. He held a candlestick in one hand. Light flared over his cheekbone and jaw. For a moment, she yearned to explore those fascinating shapes with her fingertips, though, unlike her, he did not appear to have spent a cold or uncomfortable night.

He met Sylvie's gaze, then his smile deepened as he glanced down at his companion.

Lady Charlotte, her hair tumbled becomingly around her flushed face, stood at his elbow. A dressing gown draped from her shoulders. The lining of apricot fur framed her white face and lovingly embraced her ankles and wrists. It was a seemingly casual déshabille that might have taken hours to perfect, yet her eyes were sleepy, soft with contentment, as if she had just risen from a warm bed.

Dove's fingertips touched lightly on the back of her hand. She gazed up at him, adulation shining at the corners of her mouth, clear in the soft turn of her neck.

Something fragile seemed to crack in Sylvie's heart.

"You are kind, Lady Charlotte," he said. "I must apologize once again that my young friend disturbed you so thoughtlessly last night."

"Not at all, Mr. Dovenby." Lady Charlotte seemed painfully vulnerable. "The boy meant no harm."

"Ma'am, I cannot regret that he brought me to this house and thus into your entrancing company."

"But you won't stay for breakfast, sir?"

"After we shared such a feast last night?" Dove bent to kiss her knuckles. "How could I still be hungry? Return to bed, my lady. It is cold. I shall deal with our young reprobate."

Lady Charlotte blushed like a girl. "Until next time," she said. Her slippers padded away down the hall.

Dove leaned one shoulder casually against the jamb. "A beautiful woman," he said.

Sylvie stared at him. She felt faint, almost as if she had been beaten. "She's in love with you?"

"Hardly! She's lived abroad for the last several years. We just met again for the first time last night." He set his candlestick on a table. Flame shone over his hand for a moment, his long fingers redly translucent.

"You followed me here *last night*?"

"I arrived in time for supper: a perfectly civilized hour, though perhaps a slightly intimate one. Lady Charlotte deserved some small recompense for the scurrilous way you have used her, don't you think?" He flicked open a silver box to take a pinch of snuff. "You were sadly indisposed, I gather, and so missed the meal. A shame, sir. The cold grouse was excellent."

It was still hard to breathe. "You spent the night with her?"

His eyes were both amused and cold, as if he addressed an importunate servant. "Where and how I spend my nights, George, is none of your business."

She walked back to the chaise longue and sat down. Candle flames danced and streamed. Perhaps the flickering shadows would hide the absurd unsteadiness in her knees. Why should she care? She didn't care! And she was slipping dangerously out of character. What boy would ask such questions?

"It damned well is my business, sir," she said, leaning back and kicking out her booted feet. "Lady Charlotte offered me a wager and lost it. She promised me a draft for two hundred guineas. All of which now seems to have been conveniently forgotten."

"The lady's debt is void. You knew at the Royal Oak that your wager was dishonest."

"I knew no such thing!"

Dominating the cold spaces, he strode into the room. "No, but that's what I told Lady Charlotte. Did you think I would collude with you in cheating this lady? You did not successfully steal my cravat. I gave it to you. I'm amazed that you did not admit as much to Her Ladyship. However, she now thinks the entire wager was just a small jest, for which she has forgiven you."

"You gave up *my* claim on *my* wager over some tenuous, absurd point of honor? You deliberately leave me penniless?"

"I could have you thrown into prison for debt, sir. Instead, as I informed Lady Charlotte, you will today take up a position as my secretary. It will be without salary, but with room and board, until you have redeemed what you owe me."

Her breath stopped entirely, as if she had just been plunged under water, as if she must thrash to regain the surface. He had just proposed exactly what she had worked for! Air rushed back into her lungs as she regained control.

"Why would you offer me any such thing?"

He gazed up at a painting on the wall, a black horse rolling its eyes at a diminutive groom. "You're an educated young man of considerable wit and inventiveness. I need a secretary. You need a position. You also owe me a considerable sum of money. It's an ideal solution."

"But you think I'm dishonest!"

"I think you were desperate. If you try to cheat me, I shall beat you."

With room and board . . . He had fallen right into her trap, so why feel as if he had outwitted her? "And Berthe Dubois?"

"I need shirts. She may also join my household and earn her keep with her needle. She can sew?"

"Yes."

He turned to smile at her. "So that's settled. Shall we go?"

"Wait," she said, standing and facing him. "Don't you already have a secretary?"

"I did. He served me in several capacities, but now—thanks to you—I can no longer afford his salary. I've sent him to Lord Hartsham, who could use the polish."

"Lord Hartsham?"

His gaze pierced like a sword thrust. "Lady Grenham's new lover. Appropriate enough, don't you think?"

Something rattled. A maid stood in the doorway with kindling and coal, giving Sylvie a moment to recover.

"Ah," she said. "A fire!"

The maid curtsied and glanced up at Dove.

"By all means," he said. "Though we shan't stay to enjoy it. Come, George, it's time to go."

She rubbed her frigid hands together, though the blood pulsed hotly in her heart. "But surely we can warm ourselves first?"

Devastating creases marked both cheeks. "Why? I am perfectly warm."

In one stride he had seized Sylvie's wrist. The maid scrambled aside, clattering her coal scuttle, as he hauled his new secretary through the doorway and along the hall. A footman handed him a capacious cloak, gave Sylvie her hat, then flung open the front door. Light streamed out into the street.

Framed against the darkness, frost flakes flurried and swirled in a white haze.

Dove released Sylvie's wrist as the door closed behind them. Stinging ice fell without hurry to burn onto her cheeks.

"You have a carriage?" she asked.

"I don't keep a carriage. We shall walk."

"But it's snowing!"

"I noticed," he said.

"I don't have a cloak."

"You're my servant, George." His voice mocked. "Surely you don't suggest that I give my cloak to you?"

He spun about and strode away. The houses and railings were

blurred under a fresh blanket of white. Streetlamps flared yellow over frosty steps. Doorways yawned into pitch shadow. No one seemed to be about. Sylvie thrust her hands deep into her pockets, hunched her shoulders, and hurried after him.

The pavement underfoot became slushy. The streets stank faintly of horse piss. Snowflakes melted as they coated her wet jacket and dripped from her wig. She did not know London. The dark hat and cloak of the man leading the way ahead was her only compass. Sylvie cursed silently under her breath as she tried to match his long strides.

The ballrooms of Vienna had not quite prepared her for this!

They walked for some time in silence before he plunged down an alley where a new scent assaulted her, as if they were suddenly enveloped in a mantle of warm spice.

She almost bumped into him when Dove stopped.

"Are you hungry, George?" he asked. "Cold?"

He hammered at a door recessed beneath an overhang. Snow flurried, forming small drifts. Her feet were blocks of ice. The door thudded open. Heat and light flooded into the street. The scent of spice burgeoned into the heavenly aroma of warm dough, hot ovens, and yeast. A face grinned out at them, the man's black skin and hair dusted like a sugared plum.

"Good morning, Mr. Finch," Dove said. "My young friend here needs a pie."

The African laughed and made a sweeping gesture with one arm. Flour rose in a white cloud from his apron. "Then I'd say, sir, that you've come to the right place."

Her feet stumbled as she stepped inside. The door slammed behind her. Dove walked away with Mr. Finch to exchange a few words, their two heads frosted: one with an elegant wig, the other with flour.

Apprentices scurried back and forth, carrying fuel, kneading dough, rolling out pastry, chopping apples, suet, mutton, and onions. Fires glowed red. Beneath ranks of oil lamps, stands of flour-dusted wooden trays held pastries ready to be baked. Near the brick ovens, slatted racks groaned beneath a wealth of hot loaves and pies, their crusts crisp and brown. The scents mingled into one glorious, mouthwatering perfume.

Sylvie stood dripping in the roaring interior of the bakery and stared at her new employer: tall, lean, and terrifying.

Her mouth filled with hunger.

CHAPTER FOUR

"**S**IT DOWN," DOVE SAID, WALKING BACK TO HANG HIS WET CLOAK on a hook by the door. "There, on that barrel near the fire."

She sat where he indicated, propping her feet close to the blaze. Steam rose from her boots. Mr. Finch handed her a hot pie, scooped onto a small wooden paddle. The crust sparkled with sugar. With icy fingers she clumsily broke off a piece, forced to wait while the pie cooled a little. At last her teeth sank into warm raisins and apples. Spices and honey exploded on her tongue.

"Mince pie." Dove smiled down at her. "My friend Matthew Finch is famous for them."

"Deservedly," Sylvie said. For no reason at all, she felt like weeping or laughing. "I never tasted anything closer to ambrosia in my life."

"My pie-sellers will be here soon," Mr. Finch said. "We bake all night. The boys sell all day."

The African grinned, teeth as bright as his apron, then walked away to oversee a new batch of bread.

Sylvie licked a stray currant from the corner of her mouth, then sucked without shame at her sticky fingers. Simple gratitude bubbled in her heart. For just this one moment—in this hot, innocent, floury place—she felt free. As free as if there were no Duke of Yveshire setting her such unnerving tasks. As free as if this strange man were not standing over her, his shadowed gaze following her every move. As free as if she were a child—but that had been so long ago!

"Matthew Finch?" she asked. "How do you know such a splendid person?"

"He's a baker," Dove said.

"Nonsense! He's a magician. This mince pie is heavenly. You're not hungry?"

"Yesterday you and I ate supper at nine. Later, while you snored in that study and went without food, I shared another supper with Lady Charlotte. I'm not hungry."

She mopped up crumbs. "Don't tell me you stopped here just for me?"

"Why not?" he said. "Do you think me a monster, George?"

The pastry almost stuck in her throat. It was the word Yveshire had used. "A *monster*? Why would I think that?"

"Something lurks in your eyes this morning that was not there last night. As if you were afraid of me."

"Not afraid. Dismayed, perhaps."

He leaned back against the wall and crossed his arms. "You believe that I sleep with women too carelessly?"

She avoided his eyes by taking another bite of pie. "Lady Charlotte may have welcomed you. I'm sure she *did* welcome you, but now she is besotted."

Apprentices glanced at them as he laughed. She looked up, trying to keep her pulse steady. Faith, he was devastating!

"Lud, George! What a sensitive—if inconsistent—heart hides beneath that damp coat! Yesterday you told me that women are less vulnerable than men. I thought you believed it. Now you tell me that a shared supper and a few games of cards is enough to send a lady into a decline." His eyes smiled wickedly into hers. "Surely you don't really believe that Lady Charlotte Rampole was so undone by a single night in my company?"

"A supper and a few games of cards? Was that what made her look at you this morning as if you were Sir Lancelot?"

"Is that what she was doing?" He brushed his hand over the empty wooden paddle and sucked a little stray sugar and powdered almond from his fingertips. Sensuous. Leisured. Her pulse hammered. "You're an odd fish, George. You have so much concern for Lady Charlotte's tender emotions, yet you would have robbed her without compunction of two hundred guineas."

"Better to deplete her purse over a *perfectly* honorable wager," Sylvie insisted, "than to misuse her in bed and break her heart."

"Misuse her?"

He took the paddle and set it on a shelf. Sudden, unwelcome, the vision flooded in—of that strong hand on Lady Charlotte's white skin. The sensitive fingertips and sugar-kissed lips touching the lady's bent neck. *When shattering need meets shattering need, when the flame of sensation consumes us both in the same crucible.* Lud, yes, it did bother her—which only disturbed Sylvie more.

"What else would you call it?" she asked.

"Allow me to set your mind at rest. I chose not to let you cheat her of her money, but Her Ladyship does not possess much heart."

"How do you know? You slept with her, but you don't give a fig for her feelings?"

"Whether or not I choose to bed a lady is—as I was forced to remind you before—none of your damned business. Frankly I'm amazed that you cannot better contain your curiosity." He turned back to her, hazel eyes lit only with amusement. "Are you jealous, George? Do you regret spending the night in the cold study rather than in the lady's warm bed?"

"Of course not!"

"Your loss, sir. Lady Charlotte would have devoured a pretty boy like you without a backward glance. In spite of your romantic fancies, you would undoubtedly have found the experience instructive. Don't tell me you're a virgin, George?"

She looked directly into his eyes as she stood up. She felt like a fool. Her lips flamed, almost too aware to form words. She ran her tongue over them, tasting sweetness and tension.

"That," she said, "is none of *your* business."

"So are you satisfied?" Mirth still lay vividly at the corners of his mouth. "Are you warm? Are you adequately fed?"

She nodded. His lips and tongue would taste of sugar and almonds and man. Warm, satisfying—and far too dangerous.

"Then let us go home, sir," he said. "I don't want food, but after playing such hazardous games all night with Lady Charlotte, I do want coffee."

THE PRAYER BOOK WAS MISSING FROM THE ROOM NEAR HIS bedroom, where she had been imprisoned only the day before. This time the room was warmed by a fire, a tub of hot water, and Berthe.

"Well," the French girl said. "This is a pretty mess, I must say."

"We have a roof over our heads." Sylvie tossed aside her wig to pull the pins from her hair. "We have a fire. You have honorable work for which you will be paid. I'm grateful that you played your part so well yesterday, but I would be just as grateful if you would now help me to take off my boots."

Berthe knelt to tug off Sylvie's wet boots, then busied herself gathering towels as her mistress peeled off the damp layers of men's clothing. At last she was able to untie the binding she had used to flatten her breasts.

"Lud," Sylvie said. "How fortunate that I'm not too well endowed!"

"You've enough." Berthe laughed as she turned away to poke at the fire.

Sylvie sank gratefully into the hot water. She had achieved the first part of her plan. She was to live in this house as his personal secretary. She would win his confidence and trust. Then one by one she would uncover his mysteries, so that she could give the Duke of Yveshire everything he needed to destroy Robert Dovenby.

He is charming. Attractive. Handsome. Witty. Brave. Intelligent. His manner is impeccable. Of course. But you know very well that charisma is one of the Devil's most useful attributes.

In spite of the hot bath, she shivered. What if Yveshire was wrong? Then this would be the most dishonorable task she had ever attempted.

Sylvie sank deeper, letting the water close over her face. The duke had never been wrong before. In every mission he had set her, she had found evidence that justified everything she had done. No doubt the same would happen this time. Yet it was a life of trickery and deception. Why had that never bothered her before?

She was not a romantic. Her marriage and its aftermath had cured her of that. If she had learned anything about men and women, it was that cold-hearted manipulation was the way of the world.

To stay in character as George White, she had pretended a prudery that was alien to her. How could she object if Dove had shared an intimate supper with a virtual stranger and—though he had not directly admitted it—had probably shared the greater intimacies of that stranger's bed? In her previous life as Sylvie Georgiana, Countess of Montevrain, she had done no less herself. There had been times when the fate of nations had turned on her success.

Yet Robert Dovenby had stopped at Matthew Finch's bakery to give her a mince pie and let her warm her cold feet, because he was aware that she was hungry and cold.

Sylvie pushed her wet, floating hair back from her forehead as she surfaced, her face streaming water. Her eyes stung, almost as if that liquid were tears.

$\mathcal{D}$OVE PICKED UP HIS CUP AND INHALED THE AROMA OF HOT coffee.

Berthe Dubois was helping her bathe. Obviously the French girl knew that the supposed George White was female, but presumably no one else was aware of her secret—except whoever had hired her. He was almost certain that someone was paying her to spy on him.

If so, her deception had been well and thoroughly planned. Her bags had contained only men's clothing, all of which was of considerably better quality than yesterday's blue jacket. She had even packed razors and a shaving kit, the brushes slightly worn. An uncannily thorough and professional preparation, which could only mean that she had expected someone—him?—to examine her belongings.

He set down the cup and walked to the window to open the shutters. It was almost light. The snow had stopped. London lay smothered under an icy fog.

With surprisingly keen anticipation, he glanced at the clock. As it chimed the hour there was a rap on the door.

Just like the rest of the carefully chosen clothes in her baggage, her coat and matching waistcoat were neither extravagant nor humble. The suit was green, with darker piping around the facings and pockets. With her freshly powdered wig, clean shirt, and neat black shoes, she looked like a gentleman—as she must have seemed when she met Lady Charlotte at the Royal Oak and made her wager.

He sat down, leaned back, and surveyed her.

She had nice legs.

Silence stretched for a moment.

Her stockings curved over her shin and sleek woman's calf.

Very, very nice legs.

"I am ready to begin work," she said. "Sir."

Arousal stirred hotly, pleasurably, in his groin.

He suppressed his smile and kept his voice noncommittal. "Then let me explain your duties, George. Your position here will be both intimate and personal. You will work for me, but you will also sometimes accompany me on social occasions. I may wish you to observe and make notes for me afterward."

"Observe what, Mr. Dovenby?"

"Whatever I request, plus anything your inquisitive mind thinks may be relevant. You'll understand better later on."

"Yes, sir."

"You will also attend to my personal needs, whatever they may be, day or night, which is why I have installed you in a bedroom near to my mine."

Her chin jerked as she impaled him with the full force of her blue gaze. "Personal needs?"

"Tie my cravats. Shave me—"

"*Shave* you?"

He took a single pinch of snuff. "Faith! Does that disturb you? Do you think you might cut my throat?"

"I thought I was to be your secretary," she said. "Not your valet."

"The man you are replacing was both."

Her mouth set in a stubborn grimace. "Very well. It doesn't really matter, Mr. Dovenby. I don't intend to be here very long."

He placed a sheet of paper on the desk in front of her. "An inventory," he said, "of my lost wardrobe, together with the cost of replacing it."

Her eyes widened as she read. "Oh," she said. "Yes, I see. Only the very best quality. You've even included the value of the cravat you gave to Lady Charlotte."

"Of course."

She laughed, surprising him with the wry gaiety of it. "I will go to my grave, ancient and wizened, with a gray beard to my knees, and still not have redeemed all of this."

"That's the idea," he said.

"Unless I work *particularly* hard?"

"There's just one more thing before you start your labors of Hercules. An accounting, if you please, of your immediate past: where you lived, what you did, and why that French girl is with you."

He watched carefully, but she gave nothing away. She simply shrugged.

"I was taken ill at an inn near St. Omer. Berthe was a maid there. She helped me. I was grateful. So when she said she wished to flee an abusive lover and find a position in England, I agreed she could travel with me."

"And before that?"

No hesitation was visible. She would, of course, have a story prepared. It all sounded plausible enough. A young man cast loose on the world, taking whatever work offered itself: clerk, secretary. The tale was even enlivened with convincing little details—witty, astutely observed. Yet her story couldn't be true, because she was not a young man. She was a woman that he wanted to take to his bed.

"But England and France were at war," she finished. "My situation had became too uncomfortable. So here I am."

Dove rested one hand on a stack of receipts. "Then you'd better start now. I need all of these copied in a fair hand into this ledger."

She opened the cover, her fingers delicate and supple on the leather binding. "May I ask, sir, the nature of your business?"

"I run many concerns, George. You'll learn as much as you need."

"Or as much as you see fit?" She grinned.

His impulse was simply to kiss her—as he had wanted to kiss her, rich in sugar and spice, in the bakery—but instead he gestured her toward the chair. "Perhaps those figures will tell you the nature of my nefarious dealings. They should certainly tell you whether or not I am making a profit."

She sat down and sharpened a quill before beginning to neatly transcribe the figures. It was bold handwriting for a woman, strong and rapid. He imagined he was going to get to know it quite well. Of course, she would learn precisely nothing from the ledgers, or from anything else in his study. Though he was certain she would search.

The interesting question was why? Or rather, for whom?

Meanwhile, she had just unwittingly answered one question of his own. *At his invitation, another bird is about to take up residence in a nest Your Ladyship has been used to call her own.* As her handwriting was busy demonstrating, the supposed Mr. George White—the wretch—had herself written the message summoning Meg. It was convincing evidence that she had planned almost everything that had happened since then.

Leaving her bent over the ledgers, he walked out into the street. Abdiel stood saddled by the mounting block, his groom holding the bridle. Dove patted the sleek neck before he rode his proud bay into the clammy, fog-enshrouded streets of London.

SYLVIE STROLLED INTO THE STABLE YARD. THE LAMP BESIDE the kitchen door soaked the woolly air with an egg-yolk stain. Her nostrils curled at the smoky damp, underlain with the scent of horse. Beyond the yard it was pitch dark.

Hands thrust deep in her pockets, she walked over to the stables, where another lamp shone dully through the fog. Abdiel was gone once again.

She almost laughed. Damn him! She had absolutely nothing to report to Yveshire. For two days Dove had kept her hard at work, making copies of receipts and innocuous correspondence. To her mixed relief and regret, he hadn't demanded that she shave him or tie his cravat, for he was almost never at home. Yet a hot wave surged in her blood at the thought of touching his face.

Her casual questions to the other servants had revealed nothing. He left and arrived at odd hours. No one seemed to know what he did with his time.

"You're the new secretary, Mr. White," the housemaid had said. "If you don't know where the master went today, how should I?"

It was too dangerous to press them further. If she wanted to learn anything, she would have to follow him. So she had attacked the despised ledgers, working fast to get ahead of his expectations and hiding the results. Yet she was still helpless. She couldn't follow him. She didn't have a horse.

Abdiel's stall rested quietly, breathing dark secrets and grassy smells. The groom had already mucked out, tossed in new bedding, and forked down fresh hay, ready for the stallion's return. The other stalls lay empty. Nothing moved, not even a mouse.

Sylvie turned to go back to the house.

A stranger blocked the doorway.

"You are looking for someone, sir?" She tried to sound belligerent, boyish, though her heart drummed.

The man pulled off a moleskin cap. White teeth fractured a face like a nut. "Happen you're doing the looking, young man?"

She thought rapidly, checking that she had given away nothing by her offhand inspection of the stable.

"I work here," she said. "What do you want?"

The man scratched at his chin, still grinning. "No harm meant, young sir. Just collecting a little charity from your cook. I'll be off."

He turned his back and disappeared.

Sylvie stared at the empty doorway for a moment, then walked over to take a better look. The man in the moleskin cap had vanished into the fog, his footsteps silent, like those of a hunter. Yet his voice hissed again, as if he were still standing beside her.

"Though if you were smart, young fellow, you'd be looking for me!"

The whisper echoed for a moment in her ears, while her pulse thundered. Then the fog settled back onto the cobbles like a broody hen sheltering chicks.

Cook smiled absently when asked. Yes, she had given a few scraps to the Gypsy. She often did.

THE NEXT DAY DOVE STROLLED INTO THE STUDY PERUSING A letter. It was getting dark outside. The lamplighter had already passed down the street. Dove had obviously just come in, but he had shed his hat and wig and changed clothes. Sylvie looked up from her work, ludicrously giddy at the sight of him. Her heartbeat surged, every nerve fired with sensual recognition.

He propped one lean thigh on the corner of the desk, the skirts of his jacket spread behind him. The rich fabric shone. Modestly frilled cuffs draped the backs of his hands.

"I have worked you too hard, George," he said. "Would you like a little innocent diversion?"

"I'm not sure, sir," she replied, laying down her quill, "that any of your diversions are innocent."

He smiled. "You're probably right, especially about this one. Lady Grenham has invited us to an evening of rustic pleasure."

"Lady *Grenham*?"

"Why not?"

"You said 'us.' She invites *me*?"

Dark hair tumbled over his forehead as he picked up her day's work to leaf through it. She was disturbingly conscious of his scent: that potent mix of clean linen, maleness, and witch hazel. Her skin wanted to absorb it. Her lungs greedily breathed it in.

"You're a gentleman. You have a cosmopolitan enough education. Are you afraid you'll disgrace me, if allowed into polite company?"

"I am afraid, sir, that in the circumstances the company may not be very polite."

"Nonsense. Meg has impeccable manners."

"No doubt. So when and where does she choose to display them?" He tossed the ledger back onto the table.

"Tonight. We go masked to Grenham Hall to cavort in Meg's famous pleasure gardens beside the Thames."

"Gardens? But it's winter!"

"Meg hosts the Muscovy ambassador and holds a little Christmas season frolic in the Russian style. There will be lanterns and bonfires and sleigh races in the snow. If the weather holds cold enough. Otherwise, sleigh races in the slush."

The pulse of awareness throbbed in her blood, but she grinned. "A plowing contest?"

"In which case, George, I hope you know how to plow." He dropped the letter into her hands.

She read it rapidly. "But this was planned months ago. Surely you were already invited?"

"The only new addition to the guest list is you, which seems appropriate, since you're responsible for the regrettable rearrangement of what will happen in Lady Grenham's private apartments once the party is over. But never fear, you and I will be cheered by hot mulled wine and roasted chestnuts. Do you have a warm enough coat?"

She stood and walked to the fireplace to hold her hands to the blaze. If he had searched her bags as she suspected, he knew perfectly well what clothes she had with her.

"You amaze me, Mr. Dovenby. I don't recall your being so concerned for my comfort when we left Number Eighteen."

"You needed a small lesson."

She turned to look at him. Dark head bent, he was studying some letters she had written for him concerning mundane payments for candles and paper. If only he were not her quarry. If only she were someone different, someone less complicated—

"A lesson? What kind of lesson?"

He glanced up, humor clear in his hazel eyes. "That the offer of a lady's warm bed should never be turned down. Such a memory may be all that sustains a man cast out into the cold. Meg will send her carriage for us. Be ready at seven."

THEIR BREATH MISTED AS DOVE AND SYLVIE STEPPED DOWN from Meg's carriage. The floor had been lined with warm bricks. They had covered their laps with thick robes, tucked their hands into huge fur muffs. She watched with regret as the empty carriage lurched away over the ruts in a crunch of iron-shod wheels.

The previous day's fog had gone. The cold had deepened. The facade of a great house gleamed beneath a full moon. Meg's country home: Grenham Hall.

Windows blazed with light. Thousands of lanterns lit the waterfall of outside terraces. Musicians manfully sawed away under canopies of lamps. The light and the music streamed out across the shrouded gardens and outlying fields, frost diamonds sparkling on the snow, arpeggios tinkling in the icy air.

"Lud," Sylvie said. "It's a fairyland. But won't the ladies get cold feet?"

"Due to the labors of untold numbers of men this morning, the flagstones are dry and covered with carpets. The lower terrace is also the roof of the orangery, which is already heated. The ladies won't even get cold shoulders."

"How could they," she asked, "when the masquerade requires them all to be covered, like us, from head to toe?"

They both wore half-masks, his black, hers white, beneath the hoods of capacious dark-crimson dominoes. It was a complete enough disguise unless you knew a person well—or knew his mouth well. That recognition disrupted her breathing for a moment. Faith, but he had a lovely mouth!

She looked back at the house, the country seat of Lady Grenham, his lover until she had intervened between them. "So whose was the devious mind behind all this?"

"Devious? It's only a party, not some Machiavellian intrigue."

"But masked," Sylvie said, "which would seem to allow intrigue enough."

"The purpose of a masquerade isn't intrigue. It's sin. Which is not always the same thing."

They walked up onto a carpeted terrace, already mobbed with people. Towering over the crowd, cast-iron nymphs and satyrs gazed at the distant moon. Echoing the stars, myriad small holes glowed among their iron drapes, in their upturned hands, amidst their strands of metal hair. The air was warm, as if an invisible sun shone among the cloaks and costumes.

"This is more than just waste heat from the orangery," she said. "It's like summer. Lady Grenham can even change the seasons?"

"A gift from Olympus." His voice sounded amused. "Try touching a nymph."

Sylvie put her hand on a statue. The metal was warm. She glanced up at the moon-drenched sky. A thin column of smoke rose from the head of each statue to waver away into the still night.

"Charcoal braziers?" she said. "Very clever!"

"Along with seats built over pipes diverting heat from the orangery, and the charmingly medieval whole beef roasting over its spit down there. No one will get cold."

He leaned on the stone parapet to look down across terrace after terrace, all thronged with milling guests.

Sylvie stood beside him, setting both hands next to his. His lean fingers, the deadly strength of tendon and bone, contrasted painfully with her own hands, mostly hidden beneath her long shirt cuffs. An inch closer and she could touch him. Warmth flooded her blood. She smiled a little grimly. No woman standing beside such a man would ever feel cold.

"Most of the aristocracy of England are here, hiding their wicked thoughts behind the safety of their masks," Dove said. "Those expensive cloaks trimmed in fur mark the Russian Ambassador and his friends. Will they be impressed by our tame English frost palace, do you think?"

On the lawn at the bottom of the terraces a miniature castle had been built from blocks of ice. Light glittered in its frozen turrets. An outdoor kitchen, just far enough away not to threaten the walls with its fires, was obviously providing a wealth of food and drink. Away to one side lay the dark yew hedges of a maze, the path leading to its entrance strung with paper lanterns.

"There are dining tables and chairs inside the ice palace?" she asked.

"Along with a warren of fur-lined alcoves, just private enough to be sinful, just public enough to be naughty."

Sylvie laughed. "I suppose when a masked lady disappears into a bed of fur with a masked man, who, though incognito, most definitely isn't her husband—"

"And the walls of that nest are semi-transparent—"

"—it is generally considered both sinful *and* naughty. I think someone most definitely possesses a Machiavellian mind, sir!"

He turned to smile down at her. "If so, the maze is his only failure. Though intimate enough, it must be impossible to heat. I doubt if the Aphrodite at the center will witness much sin tonight."

A little lightheaded, Sylvie turned, leaned back against the parapet, and folded her arms.

"But Lord Hartsham is our host and responsible for all this? What would he have done had it been snowing?"

"It isn't snowing," he replied. "It wouldn't dare."

"But if it had, we all could have retreated into little fur-lined nests in the ice castle?"

"If it had," he said dryly, "everyone could have retreated into the house. Come, George, we need wine."

In a swirl of crimson, he ran lightly down the steps to the next terrace. Sylvie followed. A footman pressed mulled wine into her hand. Gratefully she breathed in honey and spices, and wrapped her cold palms around the warm glass.

The air was balmy, the crowd streamed past, laughing and joyful, but now Dove had moved away from her, her blood felt like ice. He was here because of Meg, and she had separated them.

Dove swept her a short bow as he retreated. "You have wine, food, music, and ladies in abundance, sir. Enjoy yourself, for now I shall abandon you. Make merry!"

"You go to find a woman?"

He stopped to look back at her, his expression lost behind the black mask. "We are certainly being invited. Look at all those ivory-and-silk fans, dancing their language of desire and flirtation!"

She gulped down hot wine, not tasting it. "I despise it," she said.

"Lud, sir! You admit to ignoble envy?"

The drink burned a path of heat past her heart. "Envy?"

"Of the power of the ladies. As men we are dumb." He smiled. "We don't carry fans."

He walked away to be swallowed by the crowd. Sylvie retreated to a dark corner. Was she envious? She felt lost, caught between two worlds—the only guest here who couldn't flirt and play—while Dove would find himself a partner: for a flirtation, for a dance, for a retreat to a fur-covered bench. For the night?

Clutching her domino, she ran down the steps toward the maze. She strode along the lantern-lit path and stepped in through an arched doorway of yew to be immediately lost in the dark passages.

She glanced up once at the sky and was forced to laugh at herself. Lud, no, she wasn't envious! She was sick with jealousy.

EG SMILED AND HELD UP HER HAND TO BE KISSED. DOVE touched his lips to her knuckles, then her cheek.

"You are happy, ma'am?"

"With my party? You clever man, it will be the talk of London for years. And you? Are you happy, Dove?"

"How can I be happy when I have lost you?"

"Ah, my dear, don't be gallant!"

Still holding her hand he sat down next to her. "Meg, sweetheart! What is it?"

"Do you think I gave you up lightly?" Her smile was bright, brave. "Do you think a boy like Hartsham could ever be more than mildly amusing to me?"

"He's younger than I by ten years," Dove said. "I imagine his ardor is inexhaustible."

She laughed. "Boringly so!"

"You will teach him. You taught me."

"No. You are unique." Meg brought his hand to her mouth and kissed his palm once, hard, before letting go. "That's why I had to give you up. Don't interrupt! It's not only because I could never publicly ignore what I did in front of your townhouse. It's also because, in spite of what you think—and in spite of everything we share and shall always share—you do not love me enough."

He stared at her fingers. "I assume I would waste my breath to argue that?"

"I'm not fool enough to marry, Dove, or make promises I can't keep."

"Because only as a widow are your freedom and your fortune your own." It was a statement, not a question.

She took her hand back. "I intend it to stay that way. So better to end it now. As friends."

"Yet there was once a man wholly worthy of your heart, wasn't there, Meg?"

"Perhaps, long ago. After what happened with my daughter, it was impossible."

Dove ran the lace edging at her elbow through his fingers. "And I thought you had abandoned me because a plain French girl had invaded my house?"

"Lud, sir! That silly child! No, I had to end it because of George White."

Her lace almost tore in his hands. *"George?"*

"You forget: I tied her to your bedposts. Otherwise, I'd never have found out."

"Yet you said nothing? How very naughty of you!"

"Her secret is safe with me. But be careful, Dove." She stood up and gave him a wry smile. "I don't know what her game is, but I'm deuced sure she does not know how to love."

Dove watched her as she walked away—beautiful, glorious Meg. She was lovely. She was clever. He did not believe that she had ever really loved him, except because of what she thought she owed him. He didn't know if he had ever really quite loved her, other than as a friend and in gratitude. Yet he still liked her and he strongly missed sharing her bed. With a small surge of rage, he stood up to go in search of his mysterious new secretary.

* * *

*I*T WAS DARK IN THE MAZE. DARK AND COLD. SNOW HAD BEEN shoveled from the pathways. Braziers had been set at each dead end. Yet the thick yew hedges, higher than a man's head, trapped the winter air and prevented the heat from the fires from penetrating more than a few feet. In the summer the maze must be an idyllic place for couples. Now it was deserted.

Wrapped snugly in her domino, Sylvie sat at the center on a wrought-iron bench and listened to the footsteps striding along the frosty paths, retreating and advancing with every turn of the labyrinth. Her heart kept the same rhythm, as if it knew that her destiny was stalking toward her. At last a masked figure walked into the small space where she was sitting. He leaned crookedly against the statue of Aphrodite—the prize at the heart of the maze—before tipping back his head to smile at the moon.

There were many crimson dominoes here tonight. In the hooded cloak and with his face covered with the black half-mask, he should have been impossible to recognize. Sylvie only knew it was Dove by his height, his scent, and by the shape of his mouth.

That beautiful mouth!

Everything else was lost in darkness, as she was, safely ensconced in the shadows. She waited, not even sure if he had seen her, her breath feathering softly into the night, her mouth alive with sensitivity.

He turned, then recoiled as if startled when he saw her, though he recovered with admirable ease to give her an unsteady bow. He had been drinking? Then he might be vulnerable, careless—perhaps she could use this? If so, she *must* use it! Yet she sat quietly, leaving it to fate.

"Ah, ma'am," he said. "What is a man to do when his mistress abandons him?"

Lud, he thought she was a woman? Sylvie kept her silence, thinking fast.

The moonlight might glimmer a little on her white mask, as it shone tonight on a hundred other white masks, but the hood of her domino hid her wig. The long folds covered her masculine coat and breeches. He had no way of knowing that—foxed—he was making a fool of himself with his secretary. *He thought she was a woman!*

She pulled farther back into the shadows and spoke softly, seductively, while her heart hammered at the risk.

"I don't know, sir," she said. "Find himself another mistress?"

"Heartless advice, ma'am," he replied. "You would have me kiss a stranger?"

The quiet was absolute, as if they both held their breath, a cocoon of silence among the dark hedges. She had only to open the domino and step into the moonlight to let him know. Yet a moment like this might never come again.

Sylvie stood, keeping the fabric wrapped tightly over her betraying clothes and man's wig. She was a wraith, lost in cold darkness. With her back to the moon, the hood must completely shadow her face.

"Isn't kissing strangers the purpose," she asked, keeping her voice breathy, insubstantial, "of a masquerade?"

He reached out one hand. His fingertips brushed her jaw. "You are kind, ma'am."

"You've been drinking, sir?"

"Regrettably." His tone was rueful. "And I'm cold to the bone. Would you warm me?"

"What if I, too, am a frozen creature?"

The moonlight that cast her so deeply into shadow lit his masked face. Entrancing creases bracketed his mouth as he smiled. He still clasped Aphrodite's stone robes, as if he might fall without the support, but with the other hand he tipped up her chin. "Nevertheless, you would kiss me?"

Her pulse beat like a trapped bird. Did something in her yearn for a moment of warmth, a moment to be female again? Did she want to slip back into those familiar pathways? Could she leave him craving a woman who would no longer exist in the morning? She was rooted with horror at the stakes, yet an overwhelming desire also burned: to hazard it, to find out what she could from his body.

"You should return to the party," she said.

"No." He touched loving lips to the corner of hers. "I should kiss you."

Warm, supple—the electric contact of his mouth to her skin! She stood stunned as her soul began to quake.

"Why not choose another of the myriad incognito ladies at this masquerade?"

"I'm choosing you." His breath burned, his voice murmured. His fingers left her chin to stroke softly over her palm. "Unless you say no, I think I *must* kiss you."

The drums in her heart pounded a crescendo. She felt almost faint at the thought of the risk: if he guessed, if he uncovered her disguise! She could not allow him to touch her body, to discover the boy's clothes, but—

"Your mouth trembles, ma'am. I am a helpless witness to the beauty of your upper lip, the charm of the pouting curve beneath it. I think you will taste of honey."

"No," she said. "Of mulled wine."

Sylvie grasped his free fingers in hers, closed her eyes, and let it happen. His lips touched. Ineffable sweetness flooded her tongue.

His mouth was bliss.

Bliss!

She felt the shock of it—at the brilliance, at the exquisite sensitivity—before sensation invaded, blazing through her blood. Forgetting restraint, letting desire meet desire, she kissed back.

He tasted of wine and wickedness, forged by skill into genius. Sensation shivered, pooling heat in the groin. Palm pressed against naked palm. Mouth pressed to open mouth. Tongue touched tongue.

Hunger roared. She was enveloped in the glorious heat of his body. Her fingers clung to the hard length of his. Their palms pressed together, rubbing, twisting. His tongue played with hers, suckling, plunging. His lips teased, demanded, insisted, sparking a tumult of longing.

Crushed against his strength, Sylvie kissed back, wanting more.

She wanted him to touch her. She wanted those lovely masculine hands to explore her softness, her weakness. She wanted his palms and fingers and mouth to worship in her soft, scented, hidden spots. She wanted his tongue between her legs—

A wave of flame scorched from his lips.

With his free hand he still gripped the statue. With hers, she gloried in the muscled strength of his back and waist. Her blood caught fire. Her legs quaked as his erection swelled against her belly. She slipped her hand between their bodies and closed it over that glorious hardness. The pulse of his arousal thrust against her palm.

The locked fingers of her other hand slipped from his—

Before it was too late, she forced herself to pull away, leaving him clinging only to the statue. Her blood raced hot and sweet. Her mouth swam with honey. Her lips blazed. Her groin ached with passion and the void of sudden loss—

To fold down onto the iron bench to carry him there with her! Down onto the cold stones to be bathed in his fire! Down, down until this insatiable longing was burned away and fulfilled! Lud, what the devil was happening to her? She wanted, wanted, wanted—

The bewildering ferocity of it hurt.

Clutching the folds of her domino she reeled to the exit to stare out at the dark pathway. Vienna. Rome. Paris. She had calculated every move, offered herself only when necessary and always with cynicism, with discretion. She had taken pride in her delicate, measured control.

Until now!

"Don't leave," he said. "Devil take it, ma'am. Don't ever leave!"

"You're drunk, sir," she said. "You bestow your gifts at random."

Damn him! Damn him!

All that luminous intensity would have been offered to any chance-met stranger—would have been given just as freely to any lady in a white mask? She shivered.

He was feral. He was inspired.

She had met her match.

In the worst possible circumstances—when she had solemnly undertaken to destroy him, when she was living in his household as a spy, when it was too late to begin again—*she had met her match!*

"Faith, ma'am!" He sank to his haunches at the base of the statue and stared up at the sky. "Will you marry me?"

"Marry Aphrodite," Sylvie said, choked. "She is no colder than I."

She stumbled away through the maze, leaving him there, his kisses deserted, his lovely, indiscriminate skills abandoned to lie empty in his hands.

Blind alley after blind alley trapped her, before she burst at last onto the path to the terraces. In the space in front of the ice castle, guests moved and swayed to new music. Reflecting the frosty stars, the ladies' evening gowns shone with diamonds and pearls. Powdered hair curled onto naked necks and shoulders.

Dominoes and masks discarded, the guests were dancing.

Sylvie tore away her own cloak and mask to march out into the crowd. A young man again, a ruthless, invincible tool for the duke, she walked straight into Lady Grenham, the lady to whom Robert Sinclair Dovenby had once given his heart.

CHAPTER FIVE

*M*EG HAD BEEN WALKING WITH A GENTLEMAN, DARKLY handsome and ferociously young. He glowered once at Sylvie, then kissed Meg's fingers and disappeared. Meg smiled over her fan with a genuine, if rueful, pleasure.

"We meet again, Mr. White," Meg said. "In slightly happier circumstances this time."

Sylvie swept her a bow. "Your servant, my lady."

"I am forgiven?"

"There is nothing to forgive, ma'am," Sylvie replied gallantly. "The fault was all mine."

Meg slipped her hand into the crook of Sylvie's elbow. She was about Sylvie's height, but she could never pass for a boy.

"No, it was mine, which is why I sent Lord Hartsham away. I would be private for a moment. Walk with me, sir. Tell me, how do you find your new employer?"

Sylvie almost tripped. Her mouth still burned from his kisses. He had very likely spent a night in Lady Charlotte's eager bed. But Meg Grenham still cared.

"I hardly know, ma'am."

Meg's fan fluttered closed. "Do you think he still loves me?"

"I am only his secretary, Lady Grenham."

"He does not." Meg's skirts rustled at each step. "He likes to think that he does, but I was never his grand passion."

Sylvie stared at the exquisite complexion, the smooth skin of Meg's throat. He had loved this woman, kissed her, run his hands over her yielding waist, taken her to ecstasy in his bed.

"Ma'am, I can hardly believe—"

"You doubt me because you're a man. A woman would know better, sir. There is only one true grand passion in a lifetime. Perhaps he could have been mine. I was never his."

Sylvie tried to hide her dismay. "Ma'am, I'm quite sure he still wants you."

The fan fell open again in a lace-and-silk waterfall. "Ah, yes. But nothing is more pitiable than a woman pining for a man who doesn't return the same depth of feeling. Pray, sir, do not waste your youth."

Meg released Sylvie's arm to sink gracefully onto a bench. Moonlit grounds spread away from the terrace. Shadows from the balusters marked the snow like elongated chessmen.

"I am ten years older than he is, Mr. White. I have a fifteen-year-old daughter and a nine-year-old son. Sophie is with my sister in Brussels. Augustus is staying with his tutor at Oxford for the month. I cannot offer any future to Mr. Dovenby."

"But you are lovely," Sylvie said. "Beautiful."

Meg opened and closed her fan gently as she gazed away into the dark. "When I look in the mirror I can almost see the face of the old lady I will one day become. It lies like a shadow beneath the face of the young lady I once was. If I were truly his grand passion, it wouldn't matter. I am not. Meanwhile, the man who would have offered me his whole heart, I let pass many years ago. If I wanted love, I have left it too late." She sighed. "Besides, love demands surrender. I could never risk it."

"So you maintained control?"

Meg laughed. "Over *Dove*? Are you serious, sir? No woman will ever control him. I have simply retreated with dignity—before he let me go, gently, kindly, and with unbearable courtesy."

"Fight for him," Sylvie said. "Lud, ma'am. If you want him, fight for him. He's yours for the taking."

"You say that because you are young, sir. The young think sexual passion is something to die over. They think it is something that lasts. It is not. Love is the only thing that lasts. Have you ever loved, Mr. White?"

"No, my lady. Never."

"Then you have no idea what I'm talking about. We ladies don't have much time. Men have their entire lives. It's not fair, but that's how it is—"

A loud cheer and several shouts drowned out her voice. The music stopped. The chattering died away. The new silence was splintered with snorting and the mad ringing of bells. Meg stood to lean over the parapet next to Sylvie.

"Ah!" she cried. "The sleighs!"

Branding black holes in the snow a cavalcade pranced around the end of the terrace. Six Russian sleighs, each drawn by a team of three matched horses, harnessed abreast. Great hoops carried a multitude of tiny bells, ringing wildly. Two grooms rode beside each team, holding the sleigh horses by their heads as they shied and plunged. Steam rose from nostrils and glossy backs. Ice sprayed like broken diamonds from thirty stamping hooves.

"Lud," Sylvie said. "Are those teams even broken to harness?"

"Oh, I think so, Mr. White," Dove whispered in her ear. She spun about to stare up at him. Free of mask and domino, neat and unruffled in silver wig and silk coat, he grinned like a wolf. "But perhaps only yesterday? And not, alas, to a troika."

*   *   *

ITH A HAND ON HER ELBOW, DOVE DREW HIS SECRETARY to one side, away from the crush. Her eyes blazed like cornflowers under a summer sun, but her lips signaled something close to derision, prickly, unapproachable. Faith, and he had just kissed that ripe mouth! More—she had kissed him back with fervor, caressed him brazenly, openly, trembling with desire.

He had barely controlled his response. His palm was scraped, bruised, where he had gripped the cold statue, fighting the impulse to touch her. Yet she had abandoned him there unfulfilled, aching, and maintained her disguise, while Aphrodite laughed and the moon looked on with indifference.

Releasing her arm, he leaned back against the parapet. She turned to stand beside him, striking a similar pose to his, one buckled foot crossed over the other.

She certainly did not lack courage.

He wrung one hand over his mouth as if to annihilate the memory still lingering there, though it still burned in his blood. The longing was urgent, feral. He wanted to tear away her wig and man's jacket and take her into an alcove in the ice castle, thick with warm furs. He wanted to know if she could fulfil what that one searing kiss had promised. He wanted her unmasked.

But not yet! Not until he knew why she had taken such an appalling risk in the maze. Not until he knew who she really was.

The crowd began to shout. "The race! The race!"

A group of men in furs walked up to Meg. A footman blew a trumpet. Faces turned. Laughing and chattering, the guests formed a circle around their hostess. The Russian ambassador thrust a copper vase into her hands. Meg reached in to pull out a slip of paper, then another.

"What are they doing?" George asked.

Dove laughed, almost dizzy with the sensual force of his thoughts. A line of fires was springing to life like distant candles across the far fields. A rider carrying a torch moved like a wraith through the moonlight.

"It's a race," he said. "To be run over several miles out there in the night, the route marked only by those bonfires. Lady Grenham is drawing the names of the gentlemen foolish enough to enter."

"And with such a bright moon, everyone else can savor the mayhem from here. Besides risking a broken neck, what's the prize?"

"The winner may take home his team."

"Then how unfortunate that the horses seem to be objecting!"

"They don't like the snow. They don't like the shouting. And they don't like the fires."

"And I imagine," she said as the sky overhead burst into streamers of noise and flame, "that they really hate the fireworks."

Maddened by the pyrotechnic bang and whiz, the sleigh horses fought. One groom was jerked to the ground as a team entangled itself in its harness. The riderless mount galloped away. Within seconds the sleigh was a turmoil of flashing hooves, splinters and crushed bells. The other groom cut the traces to rescue the horses and lead them from the field.

"Five names only, ma'am," Dove called to Meg. "Not six."

Meg laughed. "Then I have them, sir."

The remaining teams steamed and fretted like the horses of the Apocalypse.

S YLVIE REFUSED TO LOOK AT HIM, AT THE SHINING WIG AND clean jaw. Wine must still swim through his blood. He was stunningly relaxed, careless, as if only he knew the answer to some grand joke.

She had a terrible suspicion that the joke might involve her.

This man, casually—because he was foxed—had kissed her and shaken her to her soul. Her nerves rang as if she had never been kissed before. Her blood yearned for him as if she had never known a man's body.

Yveshire had been right to insist on her disguise. With this one man, she dare risk nothing else.

Meg clapped her hands. In a shimmer of powder and lace, the guests gathered again. One by one Meg read from the slips of paper she had drawn. Applause thundered as each name was announced.

"Mr. George Finbank Lewisham." Loud cheers as that gentleman, barely able to stand, downed another glass of wine and roared with the rest. "Lord Hartsham—"

The clamor rocketed. Meg's new lover laughed and bowed to his audience.

"A foolhardy young man," Dove said dryly.

"Lord Bone." Green brocade flashed as that baron saluted the company with his glass. "Mr. Charles Mayhew." A group of cronies hammered on the back of a red-faced youth in blue velvet. Mayhew blinked and grinned.

"More foolhardy young men," Sylvie said.

Dove leaned close. "You don't count yourself in that class, Mr. White?"

"I'm a secretary, sir, not a wastrel in search of idiotic thrills."

"Your loss," Dove replied.

Meg held up the final slip of paper, her face alight with mirth as she turned to face Dove. "And Mr. Robert Sinclair Dovenby."

"Lud, sir," Sylvie said on a breath, while cheers ricocheted about the terrace. "*You* volunteered?"

"I want the gray geldings."

"Then you drank for courage?"

He turned to look down at her, his hazel eyes dark. "What else would you suggest a man drink for?"

"Is your neck worth so little? Those horses are unmanageable!"

"You're so concerned for my welfare, Mr. White?"

"Hardly," she replied with boyish bravado. "If you're killed, I'm out of work. I'm concerned for my job."

"Unfortunate," Dove said. "For your job depends upon your accompanying me now in one of those sleighs."

Her heart lurched—then she almost laughed with the dazed recognition that she was thoroughly trapped. She was not afraid of horses. She knew how to drive. But she was to trust her life to a flimsy contraption of ribbon and bells? To one of those hysterical teams? All to be raced at breakneck speed through the dark by men full of drink? It was a challenge that no genuine young man would turn down, and one that any woman would think either ridiculous or terrifying.

"If you don't come, sir, you're unemployed." Just as he had done in the maze, he tipped back his head to gaze up at the moon-drenched sky. His throat gleamed, smooth and hard. "Then I shall be forced to see you jailed for debt."

"You bastard," Sylvie blurted. "As you well know, I cannot pay it."

His shining wig framed his face as he stared down at her. "I am a foundling. I may or may not be a bastard. Either way, Mr. White, you will not so lose your manners again."

An uncomfortable wash of heat had already colored her cheeks. Was she going mad? Such a clumsy outburst was completely unlike her. Yet she was furious. Genuinely, icily furious to be forced into this. And perhaps she was more scared than she knew. She glanced back at the wild-eyed horses.

"You have my apology, Mr. Dovenby," she said stiffly. "I will not so forget myself again."

"You're afraid?"

"No," she said. "Of course not."

"Then come, sir! I intend to win."

He grasped her sleeve and ran down the steps, dragging her with him. The other drivers had also chosen partners. With raucous yells, they ran out to the sleighs. Only two of them looked less than three sheets to the wind: Lord Hartsham and his companion, a man who seemed to be his valet. No doubt only one individual involved in this idiotic race was totally stone-cold sober: Sylvie herself.

Snow crunched beneath her boots. Her pulse pounded in her ears, a drumbeat beneath the snorts of the horses and the ringing bells. The cacophony of the crowd reached a crescendo. A damnable disadvantage not to have one's senses blurred by drink!

"Faith!" she said. "They're laying wagers on the winner?"

"Nothing so enlightened," Dove said. "They simply wager on whether ten men and fifteen horses will live to see the end of the race. Life or death, Mr. White, the only bet worth making!"

"Then they should wager on death," she replied. "For I'm damned if I see how we can live through this."

The men were climbing into their seats and taking their reins. The sleighs seemed hideously lightweight, the runners fragile against the snow. The bells rang. Dove leaped up behind a trembling team of matched grays and hauled Sylvie up beside him. She thumped onto the narrow seat. Her thigh was crushed against his. His heat enveloped her. And he was as drunk as the rest.

"Don't worry," he said with a grin. "I'll drive."

The outriders still controlled their team's heads. Dove grasped the reins in one gloved hand, his whip upright in the other. The geldings plunged, rebelling anew as they felt the pressure on their bits, yet the grooms spun away. The sleigh lurched as the grays skidded forward, throwing Sylvie back in her seat.

"If we win, I'll give you a horse," Dove said.

"You mean that?" she asked through gritted teeth.

"Of course."

Her fingers clenched involuntarily on painted scrollwork. *A horse!* "Then let's win!"

"We'll be going fast. Use your weight to help balance the sleigh around the turns. You can do it?"

"I can do it. Did you think I would shirk now?"

His smile embraced the moon. "Not for a moment!"

Dove brought their team to a ragged halt. The grays tossed their manes, a froth of moving foam against the trampled snow. The sleigh shivered as if it, too, were alive.

Somehow the other drivers had also gathered their wits and their teams. The sleighs formed a rough line. Another burst of fireworks lit up the sky. One sleigh immediately ran sideways, tipped its occupants into the snow, and splintered. The horses careened off, dragging a tangle of bells and hoops back toward the stables.

George Finbank Lewisham was out of the race.

"Four," Dove said.

Whips cracked. The remaining sleighs again formed their ragged line.

A gunshot exploded over their heads.

Cheers and shouts followed them as twelve maddened horses bolted away into the night, the gray geldings chasing the others.

Sylvie clung to the scrollwork and knew she was petrified. The facade of Meg's house soared against the moonlit sky behind her, streaming light and human voices into the frosty air. Then all sound was lost in the hissing of the runners and the riotous ringing of sleigh bells. She had lived with risk all her life. But never anything like this!

She was jammed against Dove into the frail, narrow structure. Her blood raced, her heart pounding harder than the hoofbeats. Handling reins and whip, his powerful arm and thigh flexed against hers. Intimate. Reckless. Exciting. And more nerve-racking than anything she'd ever done.

"Don't relax," he said. "We don't have four teams. We have a herd of runaways. We'll lose someone at the first bend. I don't want it to be us."

Relax? She was wound up like a watch spring, but she glanced sharply at his face. The light from the first bonfire streamed over his features, then was lost behind them, but that glimpse was enough. He was far too confident and capable with the ribbons. Any semblance of carelessness or bravado had disappeared to be replaced by a calm, implacable will.

The shock sank in, carrying numerous, potentially uncomfortable implications. The *bastard*! So she was safer in the sleigh than she had thought, but he had deceived her—for how long? In the maze? No, surely he had truly been foxed then? It was impossible that he had recognized her and kissed her anyway?

"You can guarantee that we won't tip over?" Her words whipped away.

"No," he said, brilliantly sober. "Of course not. Hush, sir, I must talk to the horses."

Cold air rushed in an icy torrent over her face. The mysterious night opened, cleaved by speed and excitement. Her blood pulsed thick and dark as the black shapes of trees and the blaze of the bonfires flashed by.

The grays were galloping fast, flinging ice shards from studded shoes. Dove murmured a stream of endearments to them, as if he whispered to a lover.

"It's all right, my brave beauties! Steady, now. Steady, now. Easy. Come to me. Come to me. Steady. Steady. Easy. That's lovely!"

First one ear, then another, flicked back, as if the horses took comfort from the sound of his voice. Their panicked, uneven plunge began to smooth into a strong, even pace, still swift, but no longer as uncontrolled.

He was sober. He was brilliant. Damn him!

Little by little the geldings surrendered to their driver. Dove handled the reins softly, easily, with an enviable skill. His use of the whip was delicate, precise: a communication, not a punishment. The bells began to carol in unison, a rhythm of ringing chords forming a strangely ordered music. The other teams were still running in a frenzy, but the grays were now solidly in control. It had taken him— what?—ten minutes?

Up ahead the bonfires marked the first sharp curve around a stand of trees. The three leading sleighs flashed in and out of streamers of light, a temporary gilding. Their tracks tangled like an unraveled rope across the snow. Sylvie glanced back. Dove's tracks cut arrow-straight, right up the center.

With each stride the grays gained on Charles Mayhew. Hartsham ran ahead of him, just behind Lord Bone, who had kept the lead from the beginning. Mayhew's sleigh lurched wildly, bouncing over their ruts.

"Come, now!" Dove whispered. "Come, my brave boys!"

White manes streamed as the gray geldings responded.

Mayhew frantically flailed his whip. In a sizzle of crushed snow, Dove and Sylvie swept past, leaving him behind. Ahead, Lord Bone's chestnuts skidded into the turn, but Hartsham sliced into the curve inside them, runners cutting deep. For a moment the two teams ran neck and neck. But the chestnuts swung ever wider and Hartsham's sleigh pulled out in front.

Meg's new lover had taken the lead.

Dove's arm flexed as he eased reins. His sleigh hissed into the bend in Hartsham's tracks.

Sylvie leaned hard as she felt the runners shake and lift. In a shower of ice they passed Lord Bone. The trees swept past and they were running on. Only Hartsham remained ahead of them.

"Well done!" Dove said. "You'll do."

An odd pride flooded through her at his laconic praise. She could do this!

"Thank you," she said. "Perhaps we aren't about to be killed, after all?"

"We were never about to be killed."

Cursing broke out somewhere behind them. Sylvie looked back.

"Three," Dove added. "Charles Mayhew lacked a certain decorum as a whipster."

Mayhew's sleigh had flipped over coming out of the bend. The occupants struggled from the wreckage and ran to their horses' heads. Mayhew's companion waved his hat and shouted to cheer on the other three teams.

Ice showered, stinging her cheeks. From sheer exhilaration Sylvie laughed aloud.

"That's better," Dove said. "Now, let's have fun!"

She met his gaze, bright with mirth. Warmth engulfed her, a mad delirium. "We're catching up with Hartsham!"

"We'll overtake him at the next bend."

"But in the meantime you're deliberately letting him keep the lead, so our team saves its strength by running in his tracks?"

"Exactly. Though Bone is doing even better: the track is doubly packed for him."

She glanced back again. As he passed a bonfire Lord Bone's green jacket flashed once like a beetle's wing, then was gulped by the night. Running in their tracks, he was rapidly catching up with them.

"Now," Dove said. He spoke once to the team. The grays responded with a renewed burst of speed and Bone dropped back.

Sylvie clung, ready to balance the upcoming turns.

All feeling had coalesced into one exhilarated chant. Her pulse drummed a counterpoint to the rhythm of the bells and the thundering hooves. The sleigh flew. It soared. Her wild breath beat in her ears, amazing her. Ecstasy! No wonder men played such mad games!

She laughed aloud again, and heard Dove's answering mirth shout to the sky. They moved in unison now, she and this strange man, alert to the rhythm of the sleigh and the surprises of the night, creating a single harmony with each mutual flex of muscle and bone.

The grays surged, ever faster. Ahead of them Hartsham's sleigh was running fast. The bonfires marked a turn to the left, then hard right over a small bridge. A dark snake swallowing the snow, the water moved sluggishly beneath the stone arch, slipping past its lacy fringe of ice. Hartsham leaned forward and cracked his whip, but the grays drew level with his sleigh. Snow showered from the runners. The moon laughed overhead. Dove cut to the inside as both teams ricocheted around the first curve.

Sylvie was sharply, gloriously awake, as if defiance had worked dark magic in her bones. No trace of fear remained. She glanced at Hartsham's determined face as they ran neck and neck, six horses careening toward the black stream. The stone arch was narrow. Only one sleigh could cross it at a time: whoever got there first.

Eyes bright with hilarity, Dove spoke again to their team, his voice clear and calm beneath the song of the bells. "Now, my sweet birds!"

Slicing open the night, the grays pulled away, leaving Hartsham behind. They swept toward the final turn. The bridge was theirs! She was going to win a horse! She would be able to follow Dove when he disappeared into the mysterious streets of London. One of these lovely—

The bays surged up beside them again, running flat, ears pinned. As Dove's team spun smoothly into the last bend, Hartsham sawed at his reins.

Foam-filled mouths open on their bits, the maddened bays refused the turn, bolted headlong past the stone arches, and—sleigh bucketing like a cork on a wave—ran straight into the stream. Hartsham's horses skidded, breaking ice, crashing knee-deep in black water. The sleigh tipped, snapping wooden hoops, crushing bells. Lord Hartsham and his valet disappeared beneath a silent arch of runners.

"Two," Dove said as his grays thundered safely over the stone arch. *"Damnation!"*

The bonfires ahead led a clear path to victory. Three magnificent geldings to fill up Dove's stable, and one of them a gift to his secretary. Yet he guided his team into a wide circle, turning back. Beetle-green flashed as Lord Bone swept over the bridge and past the last bonfire. His sleigh hissed away into the night.

"Sorry, George," Dove said. "We just lost, after all."

He brought the grays to a halt. Before he could notice her face, Sylvie jumped down and ran to the horses' heads. Shameful tears stung her eyes. They had lost. Dove had abandoned the race. No horses. No winning. No more shared ecstasy under the extraordinary moon!

Whiskered nostrils blew warm innocence over her hands as Dove slipped down the bank toward the wreckage in the stream. The three bays stood, breathing hard, hanging their heads, making no attempt to move. Lord Hartsham dragged himself out of the water. Meg's new lover leaned one hand on the stone wall of the bridge and stared down at the remains of his sleigh.

"Devil take it," he said. "Is that you, Dovenby? Your bloody valet's knocked himself out."

Dove was already in the water, pulling the servant from the wreckage. Carrying the man as easily as if he were a child, he strode back to his own sleigh. Sylvie caught a glimpse of the valet's white wig and whiter face as Dove set the unconscious man on the seat.

Hartsham, dripping, brought up the rear, then stood awkwardly as Dove felt for the servant's pulse.

The young man shivered. "Lud, sir, is he sound?"

"He'll recover," Dove said. "It'll take more than a thump on the head to kill this one. But he's wet through and cold. Get him back to Grenham Hall, Hartsham. And yourself."

Lord Hartsham kicked at the snow with his shoe. "What about you, Dovenby? And your secretary?"

Dove's smile was soft in the night. "This sleigh will only carry two, my lord, and the grays are already tired. You are wet and in danger from the frost. We are not. We'll bring your team safely home."

Hartsham stared at him for a moment. He shivered again.

"I insist," Dove said. "Take my sleigh. Meg won't thank either of us, if you die out here of exposure." He grinned. "After all, Lord Bone's already won the damned race."

Hartsham nodded and climbed into the seat next to the slumped form of the valet. Sylvie stepped away from the grays' heads. The sleigh turned and sped off toward Grenham Hall.

She and Dove stood alone.

Silent dark stretched around them. White fields rippled away to the moon-bright horizon. The quiet was absolute, except for a slight chink of harness—as if to magnify the thump of her heart—from the bays standing in the stream.

His face ghosted in the moonlight, clever, lovely as a god. The shine of silver. The impenetrable dark of his eyes. The lovely, sensitive curve of his lips. His beauty pierced her. What if she just pulled off her wig, abandoned her mission and her promise to Yveshire, and let Dove kiss her again? She longed to know what he was thinking, if he too remembered that moment with a stranger in the maze—

Time stretched, as if a thin silk ribbon still offered a frail moment of connection, then snapped.

Dove spun away, waded back into the black water and pulled out a knife. His back flexed in the moonlight, limber and powerful. He shredded the harness, leaving the three bays with only their bridles and a shortened length of rein.

Sylvie splashed in to help hold the horses' heads. Ice water burned her calves, shocking her into harsh remembrance. *I am a boy! I do not wait to be enfolded, to be comforted, to be cherished as if I were fragile—*

"You do ride?" Dove asked.

"Yes."

"Good."

The horses followed them up onto the bank. Dove checked them for injuries, running his fingers over bone and tendon as Sylvie rubbed at the black noses. Her heart echoed as if with a great loss. She was cold. Grief assailed her, lonely and cavernous. Because she hadn't won a horse? Oh, God! *Simply because that glorious, heart-pounding race was over?*

She would have done the same to rescue Hartsham and his valet, of course, but that didn't lessen her wild regret. For the loss of the race. For the loss of that brilliant moment of shared lunacy—

"They'll be glad enough just to walk home." Dove's calm voice broke harshly into her thoughts. "Excitement over. Let me give you a leg up."

She bent her knee and allowed him to hoist her onto a bay back. She could, of course, ride. But never bareback, never astride, never with a trembling half ton of horseflesh steaming beneath her.

I do not wait to be enfolded, to be comforted, to be cherished as if I were fragile—and even when I was a woman, that was never truly what the world offered! She buried her ludicrous grief and grinned a little rue-fully to herself. Ah, well! Her life had surely bestowed other com-pensations—and now it offered a bareback ride in the moonlight!

Dove vaulted onto one of the other bays, leading the third horse beside him.

"Let's go back to drown our sorrows in dry Spanish sack," he said. "I've had enough warm, sweet wine for one night."

"Shall I say something first about how noble you are, sir?" She made her voice tease, offer impudence, like a boy's—though his had seemed taut, edgy.

He was surprised into laughter. "Lud, no!"

"We could have won. Lord Hartsham could have rescued the valet by himself."

"They were wet. The man was unconscious." Perhaps she had imagined the tension.

"Lord Bone didn't appear to have any such scruples."

"He didn't need to. We were already taking care of it. Which reminds me: my feet are bloody freezing. Shall we go?"

He turned his mount's head and started back toward Grenham Hall.

"I'm not sure I quite understand," she said, riding beside him. "I would have thought you and Hartsham would be enemies."

He glanced at her face. "Why the devil would you think that?"

"It's what anyone would expect."

"I rarely behave, George, as others expect."

"If my lover left me for another man, I wouldn't think of that man as a friend."

"I don't think of him as anything," Dove said. "I merely put the evening to good use."

"Good use?" she asked. "What good use?"

Moonlight cast deep shadows across the planes of his face as he smiled again. "You haven't guessed?"

"Oh, yes," she said. "I'm supposing to be observing for you, aren't I?"

"And did you?"

"As Lady Grenham's acknowledged escort, Lord Hartsham is our host. Yet the braziers in the statues, the ice palace, our mad race—I think it was all beyond His Lordship's imagination and capabilities. None of this was Hartsham's idea, was it?"

"That's a moderately shrewd observation, George. What else?"

"You created this party and you've been quietly running everything without taking the credit. Why?"

"To please Meg."

"Yet you risked her new lover's life in your insane race."

"No more than mine, or yours for that matter. Hartsham was a willing participant, and though he misjudged this time, he's a deuced good whip. He could—as you so astutely pointed out earlier—have saved himself."

"So what did you mean by *good use*?"

"I offered him a little training."

"Training?"

"An opportunity to stretch himself."

She glanced away at the sweep of snow-covered fields, only too aware of the attraction of that wry edge to his voice. "Why?"

"Because Meg is my friend."

"She deserves better," she said.

"Of course. But I have nothing else to give her. What else did you observe?"

The bay's back was warm beneath her thighs. She stroked one hand down the black mane and took a deep breath, before she plunged into even more perilous waters.

"I saw you going into the maze after a woman. You appeared to be foxed."

His led horse swung its rump. The three horses jostled together for a moment.

"A convenient deception, George. Ladies like a man to be a little foxed. The lady forgives the man his trespasses more easily because he can't help himself, and thus it is easier to forgive herself any small indiscretion."

Small indiscretion! Her heart had begun to pound, tolling into the quiet like a tocsin. "Did this lady?"

"I have no idea. It was dark. I wouldn't even know her again. Just a woman to kiss at a party."

She swallowed, knowing her voice would be rough. "So you kissed her. Did you like it?"

He set his horses into a trot and tossed his reply over his shoulder. "I hardly remember."

"You don't *remember*?"

"Surely you have kissed women yourself and forgotten it, George?"

She reined in her mount, letting Dove ride away into the black night. He had not been foxed. He had pretended to be drunk in order to trick a stranger into kissing him. Just for the diversion of the moment. A hoax. Yet the joke in the end was on him. He had exchanged those embraces with his secretary, and he had no idea of it.

"I have kissed often enough, sir," she said to the dark. "It has meant as much to me in the past as it obviously means now to you. I'm damned if I see why the hell I should care this time. I don't care. Yet it seems like such a waste!"

Pressing her horse into a canter, she caught up with him. They rode in silence back to the terraces. The noise of the party streamed out to meet them.

Lord Bone had been hoisted shoulder high and was being carried up the steps to thunderous applause. White flashed at the edge of dark eyes as his tired chestnuts clattered up the steps behind him. The three horses had been unhitched from their sleigh and were being led behind their new master by a trio of eager young men.

Meanwhile, a small crowd had gathered around what had been Dove's sleigh, where the grays stood quietly, breathing easily, held in the hands of a single groom. Hartsham climbed down. He began to explain something, waving his arms toward the open fields. Meg held out her hands to him and led him away. The valet was lifted down by several footmen. The man had apparently recovered consciousness, for he tried to sit up, though he was carried off on a makeshift stretcher. Dove's faithful team was led back to the stable.

Pain lanced Sylvie's heart as the white tails ghosted away.

They halted their bays at the base of the lower terrace. Dove abandoned his horses to a groom and was instantly swallowed up by an adoring throng. Obviously Hartsham had told everyone what had happened at the bridge. The story went from mouth to mouth, gaining in the telling.

Sylvie slipped to the ground and watched for a moment, stroking her hand over her mount's warm neck. Dove was a pet, a darling. Whatever fiction had been offered, everyone knew that his had been the wild mastermind behind the evenings festivities. They had known it for weeks. He had arranged everything, as if he directed a play. Even she had been simply a lowly player!

Wry admiration shocked through her blood as she saw the extent of it.

A groom took her horse. The crowd was following Dove up the steps.

"Sylvie!"

She spun about and stared into the shadows. In elegant wig and brocade coat, the Duke of Yveshire beckoned with one hand. They were momentarily alone, lost in the shade at the base of the terraces.

"Your Grace?" she replied softly, looking about. "Is this wise?"

His face glimmered, white and intense. *"Wise?* What the *devil* possessed you to risk your neck in that race?"

"I could hardly refuse."

"Lud, ma'am! He was drunk. You could have made any of a thousand excuses."

"One would have sufficed, but there was no risk. Do you really think the notorious Dove would imperil himself?"

"He was three sheets to the wind!"

"You think so?" Her mirth cascaded into hidden laughter, gathering strength. "Mr. Robert Sinclair Dovenby makes fools of us all. Don't you see? I created a social disaster for him when Lady Grenham burned his clothes. Now he's just fought a brilliant campaign to reinstate himself in the bosom of London society. It was carried out with a ruthless efficiency and is being crowned with sickening success. He's the hero of the moment. Any of a dozen ladies will soon offer him a bed for the night—"

"Sylvie." The duke caught her arm. His whisper cracked, betraying genuine concern. "His tastes are depraved—anything else is just a veneer. I did warn you!"

She pulled away, glad to breathe in her mysterious hilarity—the best defense, surely, against heartbreak?

"So you did, Your Grace," she said. "But he's not foxed. Faith! He never was."

CHAPTER SIX

*D*OVE ALLOWED THE CROWD TO SWEEP HIM UP THE STEPS. The evening's entertainment was moving into its final stage. The dancing had stopped. Pairs drifted, arm in arm. Violins wept and cajoled. With the aid of Tanner Brink, Dove had hired a band of Gypsies—all brothers or cousins, no doubt—to play wistful love songs.

The outlandish musicians were his final triumph: imaginative, unique, touching jaded hearts to unaccustomed depths. Powdered heads nestled on brocade shoulders. Heeled shoes tapped slowly, fading into silence. Love lay heavy in the air. Couples sauntered into the ice palace, or disappeared into the warm spaces of Grenham Hall.

With a joke and a wink, Dove escaped his admiring captors and left them to find their cups or their ladies. Tomorrow the beau monde would offer him credit, welcome him once again into London's innermost circles of power and influence. Success. Yet it hardly seemed to matter.

He walked away from the warm terraces and into Meg's knot garden. A drape of icicles had long robbed the hours from the sundial. The ghostly pattern of the interlinked beds—where in the summer thyme and rosemary offered their sweet solace—lay banked under snow.

He had unraveled Meg's mysteries and made love to her here for the first time as bees buzzed lazily among the herbs: the enchantment of a seduction where both parties clearly understood every nuance of the game. She had not expected him to be faithful, though it had been clear what the cost would be, if he betrayed her. Yet he had never particularly wanted to stray—and then circumstances had bound them more tightly than love ever could have done. In the end it had become more easy than passionate, while their shared secret had trapped them together.

Complaisant, clever Meg! He had thought he still longed for her bed. Why was anything more than friendship now so thoroughly in the past?

"Don't tell me you're alone?" a woman's voice asked.

Dove turned. Meg glimmered at the edge of her garden, an ice queen in her wide skirts, in her diamonds and lace, watching him.

He bowed. "As you see, ma'am."

"As I am," she said.

"But Lord Hartsham—?"

"I have sent him home."

"After all my efforts on his behalf? Why? I think he's most promising."

Her smile grew broader, lighting her face. "Oh, so do I. But I still sent him home. He was damp."

"You could have warmed him until he became dry."

"So I could, Dove. But I would rather warm you."

The snow serpents swirled at his feet, concealing the sleeping borders of bergamot and tansy. He stared at the dumb, timeless icicles, speechless.

"I made a mistake," Meg said. "I would rectify it. I am asking you to spend the night with me."

His hands hung empty at his sides. He had no idea what to say. "Meg—"

She stepped forward, graceful, lovely. "It's not fair for me to ask, I know. How can you refuse? You have just shown the beau monde what a force you are to be reckoned with, even independent of my favor. Yet I made that possible. I have just allowed you to use my home as a canvas for your triumph. If you spurn me now, how petty and mean that would seem! Is that what you're thinking?"

"Something like that. I am too deeply in your debt."

"The debt is more than equally mine, but I would not have you stay on those terms, Dove. I would have you stay with me tonight, without gratitude, without obligation, only because you wished it."

"Which still offers me no escape, Meg. What could I say that you could be certain would be honest?"

"I trust our friendship. You have every escape."

"Then you offer me my heart's desire," he said. "You offer me what I have longed for. Knowing I must refuse."

She walked away along the tiny snow-covered paths, her shoes leaving dainty tracks, like a deer's. "Refuse? Why, Dove?"

He waited until the turn of the knotted beds brought her back to face him. "Because we cannot go back."

"You are right, of course. I know we cannot go back. Perhaps I did not really expect you to accept. And perhaps, knowing that, I did not quite truly mean it. But that does not stop desire. Or memory."

"I am right. Though your loveliness takes away my breath. Though my desire roots me to the spot. Though I will never forget."

"And that knowledge has to be enough? Very well. Then it's enough."

"There is no one else, Meg," he said, as if that would answer everything.

"No, of course not. Though there will be."

His disorientation was bitter. "After you, how can there be?"

Why not begin again with Meg? She was infinitely alluring. He could take her to bed and burn away the night. She would wake warm and satisfied in his arms once again. Yet the thought was only profoundly disturbing, as if some deeper confusion annihilated his desire.

"Fustian!" Her mouth was rueful, though mirth lingered. "Whether you know it or not, you already want your mysterious new secretary. What else could have possessed you to force her into that mad sleigh ride?"

"A moment's misjudgment, obviously!"

"Ah! Did you think you would teach her a lesson? Don't tell me you thought she would shriek or faint!"

"If I did, she defied fear and mocked speed. Lud! She'd defy the damned moon in its orbit. Why the devil would I want *that* in a lover?"

"When the world catches fire," Meg said gently, "the candle, though warm, is no longer enough. Don't say anything more, Dove. Just kiss me and have done."

She stepped forward. Her familiar lips opened under his. Her kiss was sweet, poignant. Scented with honey and memory, her body fit warmly against his. If he did not take her to bed, he would spend the night alone. With the prescience of the damned, he knew he was doomed—for the first time in his adult life—to spend many more nights alone.

Meg was right: *Whether you know it or not—you already want your mysterious new secretary.*

A stone Aphrodite had witnessed his world spinning from his control, chortled as she saw the soul suckled from his mouth by a woman he neither understood nor trusted, yet craved as the moth craves the flame. It was a new and damned unwelcome sensation.

He broke the kiss—skilled, gentle, regretful—and pressed his lips once to her knuckles as he bowed and stepped away. "I like you too well, Meg. I trust we are destined to always be friends?"

She laughed, her voice breaking. "Yes," she said. "Damn you!"

Her skirts swayed as she walked back into her marvelous house. Though inevitable—though it was his own wish and he was certain now that it was hers also—it still felt like an irreparable loss.

Not even curses, every damn blasphemy he knew spoken harshly under his breath, could put this night back into its planned orbit. Damn George! Damn all of her—

The crash of breaking icicles shattered his thoughts. Dove spun about. Irony had stormed, rollicking, into the frozen garden. His secretary stood white-faced beside the sundial. His blood responded instantly, surging with passionate self-derision: the first woman he had kissed on this publicly triumphant—but personally disastrous—evening had just watched him kiss the second?

"Did I just observe the wrong incident?" George asked. "I only—"

"—wished to witness the practice of gallantry? Learn something of courtship?"

"From an expert?" Her voice mocked. "Lady Grenham might have preferred a little less noble self-denial."

"You may assume that I now feel about as noble as the heel of my shoe. Did you *plan* to witness this?"

"I thought *you* were in charge of planning everything here tonight, Mr. Dovenby. Especially such an affecting scene with your mistress."

"How much did you overhear?"

"Nothing. Like the best of lovers, you spoke only in whispers. But her wishes were obvious, and you were panting for her like a satyr. Why the devil didn't you take her to bed?"

If she were truly a man, he would have knocked her down. Instead he let his voice excoriate.

"You have an extraordinary facility, Mr. White, for appalling errors of judgment. You are my secretary, sir, not my friend. You are not in a position to venture half-baked opinions on the state of my soul, my manners, or my dealings with the fair sex—"

"Your tone could certainly peel the bark from a withy. I thought the offer of a lady's warm bed should never be denied?" Her chin had tipped in defiance, though tears glimmered in her eyes and her face had colored as if a shadow passed over the moon. "You said you wanted me to observe everything. That wasn't supposed to include your behaving like a monster?"

He stalked up to her. She backed a step, half-tripping over the hidden herb beds.

"You have no idea what you just witnessed and it is none of your bloody business. You forget: though I may have been destined to kiss women in mazes tonight, I go home by myself to a hideously virtuous bed—"

"As I go home to mine."

"Then I wish to hell you would hold your tongue until we get there."

More icicles crashed from the sundial as she turned away. "I apologize, sir, if I spoke out of turn. Your Gypsy music must have disordered my judgment."

"Really? I thought that our sleigh ride had done that."

"No." A fine tremor ran down her spine. "That was merely amusing."

"*Amusing!* Is that what it was?"

"Why, yes," she said, kicking angrily at the snow. "What would you have called it?"

The growing irony caught him out. His rage disappeared as he laughed.

"Damned stupid," he replied.

SHE MANAGED TO WALK AWAY WITHOUT LOOKING BACK, striding between ghostly statues, in and out of arched yews. Winter blurred as she fought back tears. Oh, Lud! *Tears!* No one—*no one*—had ever spoken to her like that. Worse. She had never seen any man kiss a woman like that before. Perhaps she had never even thought it possible.

Sylvie stopped at the edge of the top terrace, mostly empty now that the couples had drifted away to less public places. A few unattached men had taken solace in drink. They sprawled in untidy groups on the benches or against the warm braziers. Should she join them and drown her sorrows? *In dry Spanish sack?*

It was the tenderness. That was it. That heartbreaking tenderness. What kind of man could behave so tenderly to a woman he said he had loved and then refuse her?

She had known animal attraction. She had known condescension, patronage, weakness, supplication, malice. She had known strength. She had known fervor. Never had any man offered her tenderness. Faith! She had always received exactly what she had given, a fair enough exchange. It was madness to think she could ever offer or deserve anything else.

Yveshire had shown her gentleness, even kindness, but never— until that mad kiss in the maze—had she ever thought that passion, intensity, and a tender, aching sensitivity could all melt into one glorious mix—

"A song, sir?" The sibilant sounds caressed. "A ditty for your trouble? Or your fortune told?"

A Gypsy grinned at her, his violin tucked beneath his chin. Before she could reply he drew the bow. The strings resonated in a low, mournful chord. It was the man she had last met wearing a moleskin cap in Dove's stable.

"No music," she said. "I am hardly in the mood for the food of love."

"Then cross my palm with silver and I'll tell your fortune, good sir." The brown face split in a grin. "Which will it be? Your future? Shall I foretell riches? Shall I foretell true love? The hour of your death? The birth of your first child? Or should I tell you your real past?"

Her blood seemed to congeal. "My past? What the devil do you mean?"

He played a few bars, callused fingertips haunting the strings. "Past or future, young sir. It's all the same to me. I know the truth either way."

She leaned down to tear away a shoe buckle, hiding her sudden panic from the penetrating brown eyes. "Here," she said. "My future. I already know my past."

The buckle disappeared into the Gypsy's pocket. He propped the violin on a stone bench and took her right hand. One long finger traced the lines in her palm.

"I see a long life. I see riches. I see little sorrows and great joys. I see one great love, almost lost, then regained—"

She laughed. "This is what you tell everyone. What does my palm tell you about what I need?"

The shrewd gaze pinned her. "I see three gray horses lost. I see another horse in your future."

"Good," Sylvie said. "I hope it'll arrive soon."

"Soon as you like," the Gypsy replied. "My brothers and I, we trade horses."

She pulled her hand from his grasp. "I suppose this base fortune is all I can expect for a paste shoe buckle. I can't afford to buy a horse, sir, nor a real fortune-telling, so you're wasting your time with me."

He tapped one finger to the side of his nose and winked. "No time is wasted. My granny foretold how much I would have when I was still in my cradle."

The Gypsy tucked the violin back under his chin and walked away. A dance tune skipped lightly after him over the terrace. As if summoned by the music, a lady in green silk wobbled unsteadily up the steps from the ice castle. She turned, dipping and swaying, only to spin directly into Sylvie.

"Oh!" she exclaimed, peering up from slack-lidded eyes. "Mr. George White!"

"Lady Charlotte, your servant, ma'am."

Sylvie tried to back away, yet the other woman grabbed her by both arms. Her face floated palely in the moonlight, her pupils huge.

"You escaped from me once, Mr. White. I'll not let you go this time. You're my prisoner, sir." Lady Charlotte giggled. "The price of your freedom is a kiss!"

"My lady, I am charmed! Yet I value—"

"Just one!" The woman's hands clung ferociously. "I am desolate tonight. You cannot be cruel, sir. You're just a boy. One kiss!"

Sylvie turned her face away, swallowing both mirth and alarm. Lud! The devil had planned this night for kisses? Yet wicked men could laugh their way freely to their graves before she'd willingly kiss another woman, so unless she could break free, Lady Charlotte would unmask her.

"Faith, ma'am," a man's voice said at her elbow. "Why demand embraces from a lad, when mine are here at your command?"

Lady Charlotte's hands slipped from Sylvie's sleeves as she turned to smile tipsily at the newcomer. "Mr. Dovenby!"

Dove caught her as she folded forward. His eyes met Sylvie's for a split second. There was nothing in his expression but merriment.

Silk crushed as Lady Charlotte seized him around the waist. "Then I demand your kiss instead, Mr. Dovenby."

Her hands slid, until he caught them in both of his. "Why demand, my lady, what can be freely given?"

Lady Charlotte smiled up at him. Her eyes closed as he began to kiss her.

She ought to leave. She ought to turn around and walk away. With stubborn determination Sylvie crossed her arms and made herself watch. As if deliberately baiting her, Dove deepened the kiss, bending Lady Charlotte back over one arm, while his long fingers strayed at the base of her ear.

Heat rose to Sylvie's face as if someone had lit a bonfire under her heart. Even to a drunken, demanding woman who obviously meant nothing to him, he was tender, careful, passionate.

Unable to bear it, she bit her lip and looked down, trying to negate that hot flare of sensual awareness. Yet her mouth burned and her throat craved his touch, even as just one more among many. Damn the man!

Dove winked at Sylvie as he let the other woman sink onto the bench. Limp, malleable, Lady Charlotte leaned her head back onto the cold stone. She smiled dreamily and sighed. Within seconds she had subsided into slumber. Dove pulled off his jacket and draped it around the sleeping woman's naked shoulders.

"Three," Sylvie said, forcing herself to seem casual. "At least three ladies in mazes."

"Three is all you know about, George. Who's to say I've not been putting ladies to sleep with my kisses all evening?"

Taking her entirely by surprise, unexpected giggles built like water behind a dam. She gasped for a breath, then another, before she began to roar with laughter.

"With an entirely . . . unnecessary . . . thoroughness, no doubt!"

Dove folded his arms across the lean lines of his embroidered waistcoat. His shirtsleeves glimmered. "What the devil do you know about kissing women, George?"

She grabbed her aching sides. "Not enough, obviously! Is that what you did after your card game at Number Eighteen? Sent her to sleep?"

"Did you really think there was enough time between the diamonds and the clubs for fornication?"

Why did it all seem so funny? Sylvie collapsed onto the bench next to Lady Charlotte, who was now snoring beneath Dove's warm jacket, and tried to stifle her hilarity.

"Why not? Faith! How much time does it take?"

"To do it pleasingly takes long, slow patience, George, a time that wants to stretch to infinity. If there's one thing I *never* hurry, it's making love to a woman."

His profile shone clear and bright under the moon. Her pulse still ran wild, a deep disturbance eddying beneath her mirth. What would it be like to be ravished by a man who touched a woman *pleasingly,* with *long, slow patience*?

"You're offering more lessons, sir?"

"Lud, no! I was rescuing you. You were *not* uncomfortable at the idea of being used as a toy by Lady Charlotte Rampole? I misunderstood? Did I interrupt your first planned descent into debauchery with an older woman?"

"No." She had to look down before he discovered the desire pooled darkly in her eyes. "No. I am grateful, sir. Thank you."

"The pleasure," he said wickedly, "was all mine. As were the kisses. Come, George! Time for innocent boys to retreat to their virginal beds."

THE COACH, REPLENISHED WITH FRESH HOT BRICKS, CARRIED them back to London. In the dull glow from the carriage lamps, Dove studied the lines of her face. George had folded into the corner of the seat opposite his, wrapped herself snugly in a rug, and fallen asleep. Relaxed, soft, her upper lip curled just enough to reveal a glimpse of white teeth.

Aware of every sensuous nuance, he wet his dry lips with his tongue. Would she wake if he leaned forward to press his hungry mouth onto hers? Would she moan and sigh and admit aloud that she wanted him just as much as he wanted her?

Damnation! He had kissed three women tonight, but he only craved one of them.

So he was not in love with Meg, after all. He liked her. He respected and admired her. They shared something precious and important. Yet however much he thought he had come close to it, he was not in love with her. How long had Meg, in her woman's wisdom, known that?

Lady Charlotte with her wine-soaked embraces held no interest for him at all. He hoped by morning she would have forgotten the entire episode.

But what would George have done, if he had not come along to interrupt? Would she have pretended illness a second time? Or would she have risked being unmasked? Or would she simply have kissed another woman without a qualm? He swallowed a smile at the eroticism of that image.

His gaze traveled over the long lashes, the trim curl of nostril, the silken skin at her jaw.

He wanted to touch his mouth to her pulse, to suckle her heartbeat into his blood. He wanted his hands to shape the soft woman's curves beneath the boy's jacket; caress a breast that would just fit his palm; find her moist, silken heat to encompass his arousal. His pulse throbbed, bringing an intense response from his loins. *Long, slow, patient.* An infinity of time to build them both to a frenzy. An infinity of time to find his release again and again, and watch her face each time she found hers.

He closed his eyes before he followed the impulse to throw caution to the winds. Before he leaned forward to drink more kisses from her mouth. Before he could find out what she would do, if she awoke to find him kissing his secretary.

Yet even behind his closed lids, her image burned, her mouth was just as lovely. In his reverie her lips moved, shaping what he wanted to hear.

"*Yes.*"

His blood surged, hot beneath his clothes, while he tried to think of something else.

S YLVIE BEGAN THE NOTE RAPIDLY, IN THE CODE SHE HAD used for years.

Your Grace, I wish to inform you— She struck through the words. *My dear Yveshire, I cannot complete this mission—* The paper crushed beneath her fist. *Your Grace, I have found nothing—*

Tearing the paper into shreds, she leaped up and began to pace. Berthe was somewhere belowstairs, stitching shirts, gossiping with the other household staff. Dove had gone out. She was alone in her room in his townhouse. Alone to think about that catastrophic evening.

Everything about him took her breath away. The inventive gaiety of Meg's party. The lunatic sleigh race. That kiss in the maze. How the devil could she understand that? He kissed strangers indiscriminately, but he had embraced his last mistress with a gentleness and courtesy that must have broken Meg's heart. Even Lady Charlotte Rampole had been treated with kindness.

Nothing about him made sense. Meanwhile, she had achieved nothing for the duke. Their last two conversations seemed to have receded into absurdity. She did not understand Robert Dovenby, but how could she believe him evil?

Sylvie gathered up the shreds of her letters and burned them in the grate.

She walked downstairs to the empty study. Dove's desk had almost disappeared beneath more piles of tedious work.

Unable to bear it, she marched on through the house and out into the yard. A cold drizzle mingled with a miasma of coal smoke to form a greasy fog around the lamps. Kicking idly at the cobbles, she wandered over to the stables. If he had not stopped to help Hartsham out of the stream, if they had instead won the race, she'd have a horse of her own.

Something snorted. Sylvie stopped, heart hammering, and peered over her shoulder into the yellow fog.

The quiet was subtly broken. Breathing. An odd clink. Something bulky loomed, grotesquely misshapen, in the shadow of the stable.

"Who's there?" she asked. "What do you want?"

"My name, young sir," a familiar, hissing voice said softly, "is Tanner Brink. We last met over a palm and a ditty."

Iron shoes clopped on the cobbles. Mounted on a dun pony, the Gypsy rode forward into the light of the lamps. He was leading another pony, a piebald—the coat a maze of black-and-white shapes—by the bridle.

"I brought you a horse," Tanner Brink said. "You wanted to ride?"

"Oh," she said. Then she laughed. "Did your palm-reading also tell you where I wish to go?"

The Gypsy's gaze remained as calm as a forest pool. "Your lines of life strain after Robert Sinclair Dovenby's, young sir. Your palm speaks of fascination. Your thumb itches to trace his. I've known him since he was a lad, when we met on a moor. I know where he went."

Her pulse leaped erratically, pounding a nervous, exhilarated rhythm. She nodded at the piebald. "He hires you to bring me a pony?"

The Gypsy shrugged. "He hires me to play music. Where I go after that is my own affair."

"And mine if I follow?"

"None of us can escape our fate."

"Very well," Sylvie said. "Let's ride!"

She swung onto the piebald's saddle. For an entire week Dove had been disappearing without trace into London. She had found no way of following him, until now. Excitement surged. A fast, agitated beat.

Her pony butted its nose against the dun's tail and stayed there, while Tanner Brink led the way at a bone-jarring trot into a maze of blurred streets and alleys. The jostling crowds of the winter evening loomed and slipped away like shoals of fish in a murky pond, until the streets grew darker, with fewer lamps or link boys. The dun rump swayed and bounced. The moleskin hat appeared and disappeared as the fog swirled.

It had become quiet, the streets almost empty. The two riders had been moving as if wrapped in their own cocoon of yellow silk, when the moist haze suddenly lifted. A windowless wall loomed up on her left. The dun clattered around a corner: a crossroads, where four deserted streets disappeared into impenetrable fog-shrouded darkness.

"Here," the Gypsy said over his shoulder. "Wednesdays."

And vanished.

Sylvie pulled up her piebald pony. The blanket of smoky air wrapped damply. "Mr. Brink? *Mr. Brink!*"

Her mount whinnied, almost shaking her from the saddle, as the fog eased damp kisses on her ears.

She tried to urge her pony forward. The piebald dropped its head and appeared to fall asleep. Sylvie kicked in vain. The pony's breath rumbled. Without warning its knees folded. Sylvie sprang off just before the piebald rolled onto its back. Four steel-blue shoes thrashed as it writhed on the cobbles.

"Not a good idea," a man's voice said. "Guaranteed to wreck the saddle."

The mist thinned, opening like a turned sheet to reveal four glossy black legs and a horse's nose. Abdiel's nostrils dilated as indignant breath snorted.

Oh, God! *Dove!*

His face calm, moisture beaded like a halo around the rim of his tricorn, her quarry sat on his stallion's back, staring down at her.

"Lud!" she said, feeling the color rush to her face. The piebald grunted, still rolling. Sylvie tugged in vain at the reins. "What are you doing here, sir?"

The bay stepped daintily to one side, like a lady at a ball. Fog slid from the rider's tall boots and lean thighs, swirled away from the long tails of his coat, slipped from his smallsword.

"I might ask you the same question and with better cause, sir. I see that Mr. Brink has lent you a pony. How unfortunate that you can't control it better than that!"

"I have *never* allowed any mount to lie down with me before!"

The pony lurched to its feet. With a sudden shake of its head, it jerked the leather from her hands and cantered off down the street.

"I would venture that you've never ridden a Gypsy pony before," Dove said, gazing after the retreating rump. "They're all bewitched, every last scraggy, skin-and-bone animal."

"You paid him to do this?" The sound of sharp hoofbeats retreated like loose stones poured from a jar. "You paid Mr. Brink to dump me here?"

"I never bring anyone here. I imagine this is Tanner's idea of a joke."

Just beyond Abdiel's rump, an arched gateway loomed like a cavern. In the courtyard beyond, a pair of flambeaux cast flickering light over walls streaked with streamers of moss. The rest of the building lay in darkness. Sylvie hunted for some identifying mark, something that would enable her to recognize the place again. A stone carving sat in a niche above the gateway, a draped figure carrying something—a lamb, perhaps? There was also a motto, but the writing was impossible to read.

"Where the devil is this?"

Amused annoyance lurked at the corners of Dove's mouth. "This is where I go on Wednesdays, which is none of your business. Would you try to insist otherwise?"

"I can hardly insist on anything, sir," she replied. "I'm merely your employee."

"Then you're just out on an excursion? At night? In the fog?"

Abdiel stepped sideways, blocking her view. White glimmered at the edge of a liquid, dark eye as the horse watched her.

"I would seem to have become the butt of some peculiar Romany prank," she said.

"Then you did *not* intend to follow me as I practice my nighttime activities?"

"I was following Tanner Brink, Mr. Dovenby. Or rather my piebald was following his dun."

Dove's mouth quirked. "Then my activities do *not* interest you, Mr. White? You aren't here to discover whether I practice devil worship? Indulge in orgies? Pursue shameful depravities?"

She glanced directly into his eyes. Mirth still lay enticingly on the curve of his lips, as if he quelled the impulse to laugh.

"And *do* you, sir?"

"This place involves shame and sin, certainly," he said, "or the results of it, but there is nothing here to concern you. Shall we go home?"

"I no longer have a pony."

"We can ride double."

"On Abdiel?" she asked. "I don't think he would like it."

She wasn't afraid of the horse, but she felt very reluctant to face the erotic charge of straddling the gleaming bay rump behind Dove.

"Hardly my mount's decision, sir. If I ask him to carry us both, he will do so."

The stallion shook its black mane. Dove held out one hand, palm up, inviting her to put her fingers onto his.

Sylvie backed up. "I can walk."

Abdiel sidled after her, step for step, iron shoes ringing on the cobbles, head bent obediently to the bit.

"You can, but you may not. I require you to return with me now, sir, which is, we might say, another condition of your employment."

"Abdiel will buck," she said.

Dove grinned. "If he does, you may hold on to me."

The horse sidepassed again, until Sylvie found herself pinned between Dove's boot and a mounting block built next to the gate. The light from the flambeaux traced up and down its stone steps. The same light flared over Dove's face, the wicked mirth lurking deep in his eyes, the clean, beckoning lines of his outstretched fingers.

"Come, sir. Abdiel is becoming impatient. Mount behind me."

She was trapped. At the pure absurdity of it, she laughed. Without further protest, she climbed the steps and began to ease herself onto the broad bay rump.

Abdiel switched his tail.

"He doesn't like it," Sylvie said.

"I never thought for a moment that he would like it. I said only that he would do it."

Sylvie settled herself, then grabbed Dove's coat as the stallion skittered away. Hooves clattered. She slipped sideways and yelped as she banged her foot on the mounting block.

"Faith, Mr. White! Put your arms about my waist, sir. I won't bite!"

There was no choice. Sylvie slipped both arms around Dove's waist as the bay rump dropped in equine indignation.

"He's going to buck!"

"No, sir. He's going to take us home."

Muscles surged, man and horse moving together. One lean hand clamped down over both of hers, pulling her firmly against Dove's back. Abdiel plunged. The saddle rubbed against her crotch. The tops of her thighs pressed into Dove's. His coattails flew back to envelope her legs.

"Hold on, sir," Dove said.

The horse leaped forward and they rocketed away up the street. Sylvie clung to Dove's lean waist, the friction of coat and waistcoat, and the hard, moving muscles beneath. Awareness clamored. Of his strength. Of his clean scent. Of the lovely, curved indentation of his spine. Of the subtle dance of his shoulder blade beneath her turned cheek.

Damnation! Damnation! Damnation!

She was a boy. His employee. He thought of nothing but controlling his fractious mount. Only she knew that she held a man's body against her bound breasts.

Her vision filled with an image of him, lovely, strong, sliding naked into his bath. Yet her longing mouth was doomed to remain empty, lips clamped together in frustration. Her hands clutched only at each other. Her legs held only the meaningless rump of the horse—while her yearning arms were filled with the limber flex of his muscles, and her blood scalded in recognition.

DOVE RODE LIKE A DEMON. GEORGE CLUNG TIGHTLY BEHIND him, her arms about his waist. Abdiel skidded around corners; minced over cobbles; pranced, mane flowing, up the long avenue of trees in the Mall. Dove's fingers caressed the reins, speaking reassurance and appreciation, as his horse nervously carried its double burden back toward the stable.

He was burningly conscious of her fingers, her thumbs, the firm grim of her palms over his belly. He listened like a drowning man to her shuddering breath, echoing in his ears like the quick, trembling awareness of a lover. He stared straight ahead and tried to quell the mad images. Of George naked. Of George open and willing. Of George welcoming him into her bed and her body.

Lust clamored. Yet laughter fought suddenly for release. Why the *hell* had he forced her to ride behind him like this? He had achieved precisely nothing. He had only created an idiotic torment for himself. Yet he would do it all again just to feel her arms about his body—

"Fire," she breathed in his ear. "What's that bonfire for, there across the park?"

He focused on the distant flames. "Not for the further destruction of my personal effects, I trust."

Beyond the open sweep of St. James's Park, the moon cast an opalescent glow over Buckingham House. Tendrils of smoke from the chimneys blurred into the thinning fog. A white sheen draped the cornices.

Snatches of music danced over the frozen rectangular pool, known as the Canal, that split the park through its center.

On the other side of the ice, a couple of makeshift tents had been erected beneath a stand of trees. Ponies stood tied, heads drooping. Equine breath melted into the frail shreds of mist. Some men were jigging a dance near the entrance of the tents. More were standing around a downed tree trunk, bending over their violins. Flame fingers from their bonfires streamed out over the snow.

"Well, someone fiddles while the fire burns," George said.

Flashing in and out of the flickering light, like water beetles scuttling at random across a pond, a dozen figures—all men and boys—swooped back and forth across the frozen surface of the Canal. One youth fell suddenly, sprawling onto his back. Another crashed as he tried to avoid his downed companion. A stray dog raced out across the ice, then skidded past them into a snow bank. The dog scrambled unharmed to its feet, shook a white spray from its coat, then stood barking.

Dove spun Abdiel straight toward the mayhem.

"We're not going home?" George asked.

"No, sir, we're going to visit some damned interfering Gypsies."

"Oh," she said, pressing her cheek into his shoulder. "Not Nero?"

He laughed and brought Abdiel to a halt at the edge of the trees. "No. Tanner Brink. This is London, not Rome. Get down."

She unclasped her grip and lifted her head. The soft pressure of her breasts against his spine disappeared. Her thighs relaxed and fell away. He forced a breath, then another, keenly aware of the sudden bereavement, before he grasped her hand and swung her down onto the snow.

She looked about for a moment, then she stared up at him, eyes dilated in the dim light.

"Well," she said, "Abdiel didn't buck, after all!"

"Unlike you, sir, I know how to control my horse."

"As well as you know how to control yourself?"

She flushed scarlet, as if she instantly regretted the question, and walked away.

Dove dropped to the ground. He ran his palm down Abdiel's neck, then rubbed his fingers over the soft muzzle. The horse blew gently into his palm. George walked up to a bonfire and flung her arms wide to welcome the heat. She seemed as fragile and brave as hoarfrost.

"We'll have more cold later," Tanner Brink said.

"Ah, Mr. Brink! Since I know you'll never explain yourself, any more than you did when you first appeared to a boy lost on Lonscale Fell, you can go to hell, sir."

"You were a likely enough lad. You'd have rescued yourself whether I'd turned up or not." The Gypsy laughed and leaned his shoulders against the trunk of a tree. "We're only playing the merry fiddle to line our pockets with silver." He set his violin under his chin and drew one long, quavering note. "You want to know why I took your secretary to St. John's?"

"You had a pony that needed the exercise? You had an unforeseen attack of the megrims? In spite of those boyhood obligations, I don't pay you to amuse yourself by interfering in my private life, Mr. Brink."

Tanner grinned. "No, we're old friends, you and I. You pay me for information. Why question my ways of obtaining it?"

"There are times that I question my sanity in employing you at all, sir, but go on."

The Gypsy glanced across at the fires. Music chased around the slight figure of the young man who stood there, warming slender hands at the blaze. A group of youths sped past on skates, shouting at each other.

"A nice way for the lads to spend a chilly night," Tanner said. "No skirts in evidence."

"Though whores may haunt its fringes, ladies don't generally come out at night to join London's rabble on the ice."

Tanner Brink rubbed at his nose. "So we have a puzzle."

Dove waited. George was watching the skaters, hands clasped behind her back, the line of her shoulders defiant against the snow. Some younger boys skidded about on the far side of the Canal, shoes sliding without protest. The sound of their yells and laughter echoed faintly through the icy mist. Abdiel shifted, jingling the bit.

"Mr. George White is a woman," Tanner said.

Dove reached for his purse with one hand. His mouth had gone dry. To his intense annoyance, his pulse hammered so hard that he fumbled for a moment. "How did you find out?"

The Gypsy shrugged. "Does it matter? I know everything about her. She is lost."

"Lost?"

"My family is everywhere. France. England. Italy. It makes no difference to us. We can find out anything you want to know. She's not dangerous. She is lost. So there is a puzzle."

Abdiel snorted as gold clinked into the brown palm. "I thought the Romany liked puzzles."

"You think *we* are a devious people, sir? The puzzle is not why this woman pretends to be a man. The puzzle is why a man who so likes women hasn't already unmasked her—"

"Which is a riddle for me to solve, I think, Mr. Brink."

The Gypsy pocketed his payment, laughed, and played a few familiar bars. *Alas, my love, you do me wrong to cast me off discourteously*—

"She is lost," Tanner Brink said again. "You think we Romany should not like a puzzle? The labyrinth is our birthplace." He snatched a coin—apparently—from the air, then palmed it again. "You want her complete history? Here's her complete history—"

It was a simple enough tale, confirming everything George had already told him: a flight from France, a boat ride with smugglers where she had been robbed, a chance meeting with Lady Charlotte at an inn—with the single exception that the history belonged to a woman, not a man.

A childhood in Italy, followed, when she was orphaned, by a hasty marriage to an undistinguished lawyer who had left her widowed and in penury. With considerable courage she had then pursued whatever employment she could get. She had been a governess, not a secretary. A lady's traveling companion, not a messenger. She had even revived her parents' business in antiquities, which had, perhaps, given her an unusual self-reliance. An austere enough past, lived without much privilege on the edge of gentility. Nothing to arouse suspicion. Nothing to say that she hadn't indeed ended up at his house at random—assuming that Tanner Brink was telling the truth.

"Who is she working for now, Mr. Brink?" Dove asked.

A flicker of hesitation passed over the tanned face, but perhaps it was just a trick of the light. The wiry shoulders were eloquent with dismissal.

"No one, except you," the Gypsy said. "We have just the one riddle, and that an easy one: with this war winding down, it was safer for her to travel as a boy."

"So why have your pony dump her in the street by St. John's?"

"Just a small joke." Tanner winked. "Why not? She is lost either way."

Lost. She was a woman who had trapped herself in this masquerade and was no doubt afraid of what Dove might do if he unmasked her. He smiled to himself. Faith! She had no reason at all to be *afraid* of what he wanted from her. Curious, perhaps. But not afraid.

And the rest of her odd behavior? Who knew? But there was no evidence at all that she was pursuing any personal vendetta against him or that she was in any way dangerous. No evidence. Just this dark, niggling suspicion, and instincts that had never let him down before.

"Take care of Abdiel for me, Mr. Brink," Dove said. "That young lady is about to experience more of the joys of being male."

CHAPTER SEVEN

꧁

SNOW CRUNCHED. SYLVIE LOOKED UP. DOVE WAS WALKING toward her, swinging a tangle of iron, wood, and leather in one hand. Light from the bonfire flared across the planes of his face, shadowing the bracketing creases around his mouth. Her heart turned like a stooping hawk.

"Sit," he said, indicating the downed tree behind her. He seemed filled with gaiety.

She thrust both hands into her pockets, as if her arms didn't know the feel of his body, as if her legs didn't remember the fire of embracing his thighs.

"What's this? Another exaction of payment for my dreary debts?"

He began to undo buckles. Metal clanked in his hands. "Lud, no! These are purely for recreation. I've just paid Tanner Brink a minor fortune to rent them. Pray sit, sir, or you cannot strap them on."

Defiantly she set one foot on the tree trunk. "They look rather like instruments of torture to me."

He glanced up, his eyes brilliant, his smile ruinous. "You *can* skate?"

Once, in Vienna, she had been helped by an admirer to complete a few sedate rounds of a frozen lake, the man's arm at her waist, his enraptured mouth by her ear. They had done the same thing again the next night, before he told her everything she needed to know.

"No, not really." She laughed and sat down. "Not at all!"

"What the devil kind of childhood did you have, sir? All boys skate—even if it's just to strap on two bits of wood."

"Not me. We didn't have much ice where I grew up in Italy."

"A lame excuse. Any young man in my employ must be able to adequately propel himself across a frozen pond when required."

He dropped to one knee and grasped her left shoe. Too late to pull away, Sylvie stared at his bent head. He held her foot on his thigh, his fingers wrapped about her ankle. She bit her lip to stifle her rush of sensual awareness.

But I am not a young man. I am a woman. I know desire and how to be desired. Faith, sir, I am desolate right now with desire for you—

"Why are you doing this, sir? If you insist that I venture onto the ice, I can surely strap them on myself."

"But you don't know—having grown up in a hothouse—how to do it properly. You'd make a pig's breakfast of the entire business and break a leg."

One palm slid up the back of her calf—a matter-of-fact, impersonal grip—as he lifted her foot to fit the sole of the skate. He touched her as coolly as a doctor might touch a patient, but her face flamed and her flesh flooded with sensual delight. *Ah, don't stop!* The fleeting brush of his fingertips left a trail like a burn.

"You think I might break only one leg?"

He was busy with straps and buckles. "Lud, sir! A secretary with two broken legs would be entirely useless to me."

"Perhaps I'll just break a wrist." She clutched desperately at the rough bark beneath her palms. "Or two wrists?"

"Do that and I'll give you a beating. With a nice little switch. Bent over the desk in my study."

Her blush scorched, though she knew he was mocking. "I'm not an English schoolboy."

His mouth quirked. "Of course not. If you were, you'd know how to skate."

With deft movements, he closed buckles and straps and inserted a small peg into the heel of her shoe. One skate was fitted. He dropped that foot unceremoniously into the snow.

He met her gaze, his mouth lovely, his smile jubilant. "Your other foot, sir."

Sylvie held out her right foot, gulping back her shuddering breath, her flame of sensitivity. He rapidly set her second skate, then sat down beside her.

Pleasingly—the words echoed sweetly, as if whispered by ice crystals—with *long, slow patience.*

She rubbed at her calves, trying to negate the memory of his touch, while he strapped on his own skates, his hands limber, his fingers skilled.

He stood up. "Now," he said. "Onto the ice!"

The burn had gathered in the pit of her stomach and pooled in her groin. His presence filled her vision. If she reached out she could touch his hand, explore the sensuous invitation of his lean fingers. *Long, slow patience.* Blind for a moment, as if suddenly struck to the heart with the cold, she shook her head.

Dove stepped alone onto the frozen Canal. Instantly he was gone, sliding away across the ice, each strong leg pushing off in turn. The stray dog raced after him.

Sylvie watched them. Yearning beat at her heart. If she had not agreed to this disguise, if she had simply entrapped him as she had entrapped men in Paris, in Vienna—

Yet for the first time she couldn't bear to seduce a man dishonestly, though she had no idea how she could ever learn to do anything else.

He leaned down to scoop snow from the bank. As the dog skidded and yapped at his heels, he formed a snowball and threw it. The dog raced away. Dove spun in a small circle and came swooping back. The dog had disappeared into the mist at the far end of the Canal.

"What, sir?" he asked. "You haven't even tried to stand yet?"

"I'm thinking about that promised beating, sir," she said. "I'm not sure I dare risk it. What if I break both legs *and* both wrists?"

"Then I'll feed your useless carcass to that mangy dog. Come!" He held out one arm. "Hang on to my sleeve."

Four older men passed, skating arm-in-arm in two pairs like members of a church procession. On the far side of the Canal the boys clung to one another's coattails as they swung, screaming with joy, in a ragged line.

"There's no one close enough to witness your humiliation," Dove said. "And if you don't try, I'll beat you anyway."

She grasped his arm and stood up. Leaning on his strength, she managed to walk out onto the ice. "What if I fall *without* breaking any bones?"

"Five strokes of the switch on the backside for each tumble, Mr. White," Dove said. "Bent over my desk like a schoolboy with the tails of your coat tossed over your ears and your breeches—"

Her feet slipped. She grabbed frantically at his coat, but he had already slipped one hand behind her back to support her.

"Faith, if you can walk, you can skate," he said. "Like this: first one foot, then the other."

Sylvie tried to match his movements, stride for stride. Tendrils of fog snatched at her lungs. The ice hissed, each scratch eliciting its small protest. The lean muscles of his forearm flexed at her waist, firing her with awareness. Yet Dove skated steadily, holding her securely by his side until she found her balance. The half-remembered rhythm from her venture in Vienna began to seep back. *One . . . two. One . . . two.*

"You will not," she said, breathless, "get the pleasure of whipping me, after all. I can't possibly topple over while you prop me up like this, can I?"

He glanced down at her. "We'll see. Ready for a small turn? To the right, perhaps?"

She scrambled desperately as he steered her around a little curve. Her skates skidded, her legs flailed, but he supported her until she found her footing again.

"You *almost* had the chance then," she said.

"What chance?"

"To exercise your switch on my backside."

His lips moved close to her ear. "Alas, I've never whipped a servant in my life. Why start now? Let us skate on, sir, like two docile ponies in harness. You won't fall."

The expanse of gray ice stretched before them, marked with white tracks like a child's first scribbles. Trees loomed in silent clusters. Snow glimmered through the luminous mist, as if dusted with tiny diamonds. Once, mad with excitement in a sleigh drawn by wild horses, she had thought her heart might soar to the heavens. This was the opposite kind of enchantment—mellow, slow-moving, drifting through the frost-bound night as serenely as a ship sailing a painted ocean—yet equally enthralling.

She allowed her back to fit into the curve of Dove's arm, her palm to encompass his other wrist. Her blood surged warmly in her veins. Far fiddle music streamed through the mist, enlivened by snatches of shouts and laughter. Crisp ice hissed beneath her feet. The night seemed flooded with confidence, as if the faint sheen of moonlight had intoxicated the air.

"It's like a favored glimpse of the mystic land of the Faerie," she said.

"Where we poor mortals are bewitched?" Cold air had fired the skin over his cheeks, as if he smiled at a flame. His eyes seemed fathomless. Her pulse thundered.

"I'm under a spell, obviously," she said, "or I should have fallen long ago."

"No, you're a natural," Dove said.

She felt absurdly pleased. "Only because you're making it easy. It's nothing to do with me."

"Nonsense," he replied. "It has everything to do with you. See!"

Yearning filled her mouth as his arm slipped away from her waist, but without breaking rhythm he slid his hand down her sleeve to grasp her hand, palm to palm.

"As for me," he continued, "my motives are entirely selfish—I never had so much fun in my life!"

Bright with merriment, he steered her into another small curve. Sylvie stayed with him, his hand warm beneath hers, her fingers bound securely within his. She stretched out her free arm like a bird's wing, the fingertips trailing ice fog. She was almost skating by herself! Yet she skimmed along next to a fire, knowing with every stride the loveliness of its ardor and the stark contrast with the frosty air beyond.

I never had so much fun in my life! It was true for her, too! He was infinitely entertaining to be with: witty, exciting. A burst of pure happiness enveloped her. Her joy felt as pure a child's.

"Balance is all it takes, like dancing," he said.

"Not only balance, harmony—"

Barking exploded. The stray dog bolted out of the fog. In a blur of snow and fur and wagging tail, it bounded straight at them. Dove tried to spin her aside, but the dog had already launched itself. Sylvie floundered. As the full force of hurtling canine collided with her legs, his fingers ripped from her hand.

For an instant she tipped too far back. Then she fell forward, arms flailing, into the snow bank at the edge of the Canal.

She caught one glimpse of Dove's face, bright with hilarity, as the dog knocked his skates in turn from the ice. He spun once, flinging his arms wide, before falling straight back to land beside Sylvie. As if terrified by its own capacity for mayhem, the dog raced away, still barking.

"You fell tails over ears," he said. "I'm going to have to beat you, after all."

She pushed up on one elbow. "But you fell, too!"

Dove lay back in the snow and grinned, relaxed, merry, gazing up at her like a man waking from sleep in a disordered bed. "That doesn't count."

"Why not?"

"Because I make all the rules, sir. What were you about to say?"

"About to say?" she asked. "When?"

"When the dog knocked us down, you were about to say something. Something about harmony?"

"Was I? Lud, I've forgotten!"

Regret flashed over his features, before he laughed again and wrung both hands over his face.

Sylvie stared at him. A lump blocked her throat. She had taken so many lovers. Why did sex always make men and women so guarded and manipulative? Why was it so inevitable that they always woke in the morning to find they had slept, after all, with a stranger? He would never offer this carefree, open camaraderie to a lover, a relationship inevitably bound by restraint.

Yet if she had been dressed as a woman, she would already have known the scent and feel and brilliance of his body. She craved it as a shipwrecked sailor craves the shore. Alas, only a harmless, awkward boy could steal these precious glimpses of the brilliance of his soul!

She scrambled to her feet and began to brush snow from her arms and legs.

Dove lay back and watched as ice crystals scattered from her clothes to sting his hot skin. Reticence had dropped over her like a cloud bank. The words he had been about to say died unspoken on his lips.

I know, madam. I know your absurd, charming secret. Don't you understand that I am already seducing you to the very best of my ability? Why don't you tell me that you're a woman and welcome it?

But the moment was gone.

"No bones broken," she said, her voice filled with masculine bravado. "Arms, legs, all here."

She staggered unsteadily a few steps, then abruptly sat down again.

Dove rolled away, scooped up an armful of snow, and dumped it over her head.

"Excellent," he said. "Then you can skate on all fours. I'll race you home."

Her laughter and curses flew after him as he sped away across the ice, back to the tents and the bonfires, and away from the danger of a female secretary who was trying to masquerade as a boy.

Tanner Brink had gone. A Gypsy lad held Abdiel by the bridle. Dove stripped off his skates, pressed a coin into the boy's palm, and swung onto his horse. Within minutes he had ridden back around the Canal. George was walking toward him through the snow, her skates dangling from one hand.

In spite of the masculine clothes, she was lovely. Her mouth created a floodtide of ardor. Her eyes and face glowed.

She stopped and grinned up at him. "I'm steadier without the giddy presence of metal blades on my feet," she said, "though my stockings are uncommonly wet."

"Then let's get home and dry them. Leave the skates. I've already paid a boy to come and fetch them."

He reached down one hand. She hesitated for only a moment, then she dropped the tangle of straps and metal and set her palm onto his. He swung her up behind him.

As Abdiel sedately walked home carrying his double burden the moon broke at last through the mist, casting its silvery sheen over the frozen park, while desire raced hot and sweet in Dove's veins.

*   *   *

*H*E DEPOSITED HER UNCEREMONIOUSLY ENOUGH ONTO THE slushy cobbles in the stableyard. She looked sleepy and tousled, her wig and hat a little awry, her mouth blurred as if he had just kissed her.

His nerves sang. His blood chorused in delirious arpeggios.

Devil take it, but he wanted to kiss her!

She grinned like a boy and made a silly joke, before she turned to march away into the house.

Abdiel pawed nervously. It was not too late to rouse his groom, but Dove led his horse into its stall. He whistled softly as he stripped the stallion of saddle and bridle, and began the rubbing down. In spite of her wry insolence, her eyes had spoken clearly of her woman's longing and the rapid quickening of her heartbeat.

A quickening that matched his, beat for beat.

Tanner Brink had uncovered the harmless secrets of her past. She was innocent. Other than hiding her sex, George was innocent—or else she was the smartest adversary he had ever faced, smart enough to either fool or persuade the Gypsy. Either way she offered a fascinating challenge.

And she wanted him, just as much as he wanted her.

*D*OVE LEFT ABDIEL COMFORTABLY NOSING AT HAY AND walked thoughtfully up the stairs. What had he ever expected of women? Admiration, pursuit, flirtation, but always the safe retreat of Meg's bed, like Abdiel relaxing at last in the familiar stall—?

He stopped outside his bedroom door for a moment, his fingers on the latch. She would be asleep by now in that little room just down the hall. The temptation was simply to walk down the corridor and knock at her door. Would she welcome him?

If she did, what would that mean?

Dove had no intention—yet—of finding out. His bedroom latch lifted under his hand.

He stopped dead. The flame of a single candle stroked over a bare shoulder, an apprehensive smile, a tousle of loose female hair.

A woman lay waiting for him in his bed, naked.

His groin tightened. His blood roared. He was instantly erect. Yet anger flared faster and his voice lashed like a whip.

"What the devil possessed you to do this?"

THE DUKE OF YVESHIRE GAZED INTO THE FIRE, HIS FINGERS steepled together. His dressing gown glimmered. Sylvie had spent several minutes shivering on the balcony outside his bedroom, rapping at the glass with a pebble. Though she had roused the duke from sleep, he was immaculate now they had moved to his study, his gown draped in exact folds, his nightcap precisely framing his long face.

"I can't tell you how very relieved I am to have found you alone, Your Grace," she said.

"Then your relief is purer than mine," he replied dryly. "Every man prefers to share his bed."

She laughed and added more coal to the grate, stirring up the flames. It no longer felt strange that she should perform these menial tasks, as if she really were a boy and a servant.

"Hmm," she said, spreading her fingers. "How very capable they seem now! Who would think they had once been bedecked with rings—even paste ones?"

"Not Dovenby, I trust." Yveshire leaned back in his chair. "You are taking too great a risk to come here like this. His spies—"

Sylvie glanced at the clock on the mantel. "In the wee hours? Lud! They don't even know that I left. Besides, after a fickle moment of moonlight, another ice fog has descended on London like a smothering dowager."

"And your employer?"

"Is long abed by now—alone, as you were. It seems that London's most fascinating bachelors sleep alone more often than anyone thinks. He took me skating in St. James's Park. I never enjoyed anything as much in my life. Perhaps—for just a moment—he felt the same, as if we were both as free as children. We disported ourselves on the frozen Canal, along with several other restless young males and an overexcited dog. While he put away his horse, I came out over the roof."

"The *roof*?"

With open bravado Sylvie leaned her shoulder against the edge of the mantel. She felt as desperate as if she had just woken to find herself, completely without bearings, in another century, but it was only an hour since she and Dove had ridden home from the park on Abdiel.

"Why not? It was fun. Until I began this masquerade of yours, I had no idea how much I'd missed by being raised female. Do you know that boys get to run and scream and slide about on the ice like idiots? Of course you do. You were one of them once."

"As a duke's eldest son, I did not enjoy quite the same freedom as the street urchins—"

"But I sewed samplers, Your Grace. *Samplers!*"

He laughed. "You learned more than that."

She grinned at him. "Yes, but not how to skate, nor climb over a roof."

"This isn't a game, Sylvie." The duke wrung one hand over his mouth. "I am getting your messages, as we agreed. You should not come here in person, over the roof or otherwise. It's too dangerous."

"Yes. Well, it doesn't matter. I came here to tell you that this mission is over."

His glance impaled her. "What? You think he suspects you?"

"No! If he sends agents to Europe, he'll learn only the blameless and ordinary past of one George White, a very run-of-the-mill young man. Even if he were to discover that I'm female, his spies wouldn't discover anything. I laid that trail very carefully, too. A complete false history, involving various imaginary positions as governess or companion."

"Then why?"

She pushed away from the fireplace and began to pace. "You knew me years ago in Vienna. You knew me before that in France, when I was still married to the Comte de Montevrain—"

"You were the loveliest creature I'd ever seen," the duke said.

"So you were there to help pick up the pieces after Montevrain died. I'm grateful. I'm grateful that you gave me a way to earn my own living without my marrying again."

The clock ticked into a momentary hush.

"I couldn't marry you—"

Sylvie smiled. "A man destined to be a duke wed a ramshackle, penniless widow from nowhere? No, of course not. I can't imagine you seriously considered it for one moment."

"I considered it," he said. "When I first saw you."

"Only because you'd just broken your heart over someone here in England. Lud, a husband controls his wife's body, her person, her money, her children. Instead you gave me back my life to call my own. I wouldn't have had it any other way."

"Then why give up on this mission now?"

"Because in the years since then I've only rarely been able to offer any simple acts of thoughtfulness or generosity, and I've never had the chance to pursue a real friendship, nor a real passion. Yet I was so caught up in the game, I wasn't even much aware of it. Until now."

"It is not given to many of us to know much of either, Sylvie, though perhaps you and I have shared a small part of each. What makes you think that you want more now?"

"I don't know. All I know is that you've sent me in pursuit of a man who does understand these things—"

His knuckles turned white. The chair crashed back as Yveshire sprang to his feet.

"*Dovenby?*"

She plunged on, letting the words tumble, before she lost her nerve. "I don't believe Robert Dovenby killed your brother. Even if he did—accidentally perhaps—I don't believe he deliberately ruined him. Dove has secrets, yes. Who doesn't? He's certainly everything else that you told me. Except this: now that I've been with him, I cannot believe he is evil."

The duke's robe shimmered as he turned to face the mantel, his shoulders rigid. Time ticked for several seconds into an explosive silence.

"He has cozened you!" he hissed at last.

"You are wrong, Your Grace."

Gold flashed as Yveshire seized the clock from the mantel and smashed it to the floor. Glass cracked, spilling gilt hours and minutes across the hearth. He spun to face her.

"I am not wrong! God help us! Did you really think that the devil would look *more* wicked on closer acquaintance?"

A small cut glimmered on the side of his fist. Not trusting herself to speak, Sylvie held out a handkerchief. The duke took it and bound up his grazed hand.

"On the contrary, ma'am, that is the danger of this adventure: that the devil will seem so seductive that you will fall in love and swear him an archangel. I warned you. Faith! I warned you!"

Sylvie stubbornly faced him, shaken to the core by his vehemence. "I'm not in love. But if even every kindness is still evidence of his venality—?"

"If I weren't certain, I would not break clocks." The duke strode to his desk. A drawer unlocked with a click. "Lud! I have proof enough, if you want it, Sylvie." He pulled out sheaf after sheaf of papers. He flung them into a pile, then walked back to stare down at the ruins of the clock. "You know his handwriting?"

"Yes, of course."

"Then read those papers." The duke's chin tipped up as if he were in pain. "Read them, ma'am! Then tell me again that I am wrong!"

She sat at the desk and began to read, forcing herself to take in the unwelcome words, the treacherous sentences. The papers scorched in her hands. More than two years' worth of evidence: invoices, accounts, copies of ships' manifests. Letters to Yveshire's brother, Lord Edward Vane, promising untold wealth. A complicated plan for a new business venture involving the Russian fur trade.

Page after damning page.

All in Dove's unmistakable handwriting.

The strong black ink that had written heartbreaking messages to Meg. That had filled careful columns in ledgers. That spoke of his power and his charm. All contradicted by these documents that showed his promises to be only a network of false investments, guaranteeing ruin. Every step carefully, maliciously, inventively plotted— until Lord Edward had seen an empire of wealth dissolve without trace.

There was no error, no mistake. Dove had used all of his brilliance to ruin Yveshire's younger brother and then escape without blame. She felt faint, almost as if poisonous vapors had seeped into the room.

"Why?" The word cracked in her throat. "Why did he do this?"

"Jealousy, envy, a woman's disputed favors, who knows? Dovenby is a man from nowhere. My brother was a light in society. Edward once told me that Dovenby was the most charming man he'd ever met—"

"Charming?" She shivered. "He's devastating!"

The duke picked up the clock face. "Lud," he said. "What histrionics! I'm damned if I know why I had to destroy my favorite timepiece. You have my apologies, ma'am."

"Accepted, Your Grace." She even made herself smile. "Though I think we could both use a drink?"

To her amazement, Yveshire strode to the side table and poured out two brandies. He pressed one into her hand, then swallowed the contents of the other glass in one gulp.

"I did not want to have to show you all that. I wanted you to accept my word. That was foolish."

"No. After all the years we've worked together, it was foolish of me to question it."

The duke began to pace, his long strides devouring the carpet. "Robert Dovenby arrived in London like a comet, trailing brilliance. Edward saw such great potential there. He talked as if the man outshone the stars."

The brandy burned down into her ice-cold blood. Why did this have to hurt so damn much?

"Your brother used his position to aid a stranger, just because he thought he was talented?"

"Talented? As you have witnessed for yourself, Dovenby has the spark of genius. Edward couldn't bear to see such gifts go to waste. So my brother introduced him to the right people, offered him business opportunities. Without that patronage, Dovenby would be working somewhere today as a clerk. Instead, thanks to my brother, he was taken up in society. He caught Meg Grenham's eye right away and became the acknowledged lover of the most glorious and powerful hostess in London. After that, his fortune was made."

Sylvie rubbed one hand over her eyes. The duke's story even made some kind of hideous sense. "But *why* did Dove want to harm the man who'd befriended him?"

"Why was Iago driven to destroy Othello? Is it unusual for a street cur to turn on the hand that feeds it?" The duke stopped at the bookcase and extracted a sheet of paper that had been tucked inside one of the volumes. "Yet no street cur ever had Dovenby's devilish intellect, nor the patience to create another man's destruction, piece by iniquitous piece, even if it takes years."

"Exactly how did Lord Edward die? Can you tell me?"

Yveshire dropped the paper into her hands. "This is an invitation, ma'am, for my brother to go at dawn to the place where he would meet his death. Premeditated. Callous. Calculating. Dovenby was too much the coward to face my brother in a duel. Edward was one of the best swordsmen in London."

The note seemed almost merry, innocent, words flowing across the paper in that lovely black handwriting. An offer to a friend. *Everything is ready, my lord. The gold—* There was no need to finish it. The intensity of the pain it produced left her breathless.

"But something must have brought things to a head—"

"Perhaps Edward could prove that those vile rumors were true and Dovenby discovered that. I don't know, but my brother was shot down like a dog, and all of his wealth fell into the hands of his murderer: your employer, Robert Sinclair Dovenby."

"Why can't you prosecute him? You have all this proof. Faith, you're a duke!"

"Because, in spite of what you hold in your hands, that wealth has disappeared. I cannot demonstrate that Dovenby has it. He could argue that he was an innocent partner, also ruined by the failure of those ventures. And, though he arranged Edward's death, Dovenby was too clever to be there when he died."

Sylvie dropped her head into both hands. She felt sick. Shaken as if she burned with an ague.

"For you to use your title to manipulate the outcome of a trial is unthinkable, of course. I do see that. As it is for you to challenge him to a duel yourself. Why give him the satisfaction of settling something this enormous in one brief exchange of honor?"

"*Honor?* A clean death in a frosty meadow before dawn? I made my dying father a solemn vow that I would see Dovenby humiliated, as my brother was humiliated, before he dies. But I also need to fathom what makes such a man tick. Can you understand that?"

She made herself face it, forced herself to stand and walk to the fireplace, where Yveshire stood now with his hands spread to each side, as if stretched on the rack.

"I have kissed him," she said.

His head jerked up. "*What?*"

"I have kissed him. At Lady Grenham's masquerade. He mistook me in the dark for a woman and I kissed him. Were it not for my disguise, I would willingly have gone to his bed."

The duke set one hand on her shoulder. His palm lay lightly, not straying, demanding nothing, yet his voice rasped, whispering into the desperate night. "Then this mission ends now. You know I will pay you anyway. You know I'd have given you a home here in England—without strings, if you'd wanted it—without your working at all."

"But now I can't end it," she replied. "I'm already caught in his web."

His fingers tightened almost imperceptibly. "If you crave simple bodily comfort, ma'am, it's far closer than that."

"I am honored, Your Grace, though you must know my answer."

He stared at her for a moment, then smiled. "But should we be surprised, if we are tempted?"

She pulled his hand to her mouth and kissed the palm once, before she moved away.

"I'm only human and female. Of course I'm tempted. Alas, I feel hideously frail, as if all my skin had dissolved into a thin web of gossamer, but something else is happening here. You gave me a mission.

I accepted it. If, like a fool, I'd begun—in spite of all of my training and experience—to trust him, I was just mistaken, that's all. Now that you've shown me the true stakes, I will bring you your evidence—"

"Not if the personal cost to you is too great, Sylvie!"

She shrugged into her coat and glanced out at the dark beyond the windowpanes. It was snowing again, as if to mock her already clammy skin.

"There's no personal cost that matters. My living, and occasionally my life, have been dependent on my ability to judge men. I've never been this wrong before. My messages have already told you everything I know so far: He runs several businesses, one apparently at a deep loss, some at considerable profit. Large sums come in and are paid out, but nothing tells me the exact nature of what he does. He buys paper, soap, food. He pays employees. He goes somewhere every Wednesday and spends the entire evening there."

"Where?"

"A place with a carving over the gate. Though it was too dark to be certain, it seemed to be a man with a staff, carrying a lamb. The emblems of St. John, I think. Otherwise, he simply disappears or reappears at random."

The duke stalked to the side table to refill his brandy glass, then paced back to the fireplace.

"You will not sleep with him!"

The flakes outside fell softly, tiny crystals of ice. A terrible grief had invaded her bones.

"I don't know. That decision isn't yours, and I assure you it wouldn't affect my judgment either way. But if you wanted to protect me from that, you miscalculated—"

"How?"

She indicated her clothes, the wig hiding her hair, as her mysterious grief welled into anger. "All this! I don't know how to guard myself from him dressed like this. I don't know what I am, who I am. I should have made him my lover to start with, and proved to myself right away that he's just another man."

The duke's glass slipped from his fingers to spill its sweetness among the broken springs and wheels of the clock. His face blanched.

"*I forbid it, ma'am!*"

She whirled about to face him. "Damnation, Your Grace! What do you think sex is? A lady smiles and wagers and offers promises behind her fan, and a man thinks that he's winning her heart? Lud, men are so romantic! In most of the world, females cannot afford to have hearts."

"*I forbid it!*"

"Yes, *this* time! After paying me for all those other times? How do you think I've gathered your information for you in the past? Outside of a man's bed, how can I uncover his vulnerabilities, or witness his dreams? All that most women ever know is that they'll be paid for their favors, with marriage or with money, in the end it's all the same."

He looked stunned. "I didn't think—"

"How could you? It's not only sex without love that matters, Your Grace, it's whether a woman has any say in the matter. In a marriage, her body is her husband's to use, whether she wills it or not. If she falls into harlotry, she has no control at all. Haven't you seen them? The little girls waiting in the shadows, under bridges, in doorways, accosting strangers, offering themselves for sixpence. Girls who grew up with other hopes, other dreams. Girls from respectable, loving homes. Girls like Berthe."

"The Frenchwoman who brings your coded messages to my footman?"

"There are thousands like her, sliding inexorably into prostitution. By teaching Berthe to be a lady's maid, I wanted to give her a second chance, but only men have the freedom to moon over true love. Only men write sonnets full of sighs. Women are stuck with the practical choices."

"If it's any consolation, your information was always vital."

"And that work enabled me to carve a different path, where the choice whether or not to share a man's bed was mine alone. There were times when loneliness or desperation or compassion played a part, but it was always for a cause greater than myself, and I always had dominion over my own destiny." She gestured toward the treacherous papers on his desk. "Your evidence has presented me with a hideous discontinuity, as if everything I ever believed has been turned upside-down. I must find out the truth."

"We already know the truth."

"You believe that you do, but my judgment is my own and I must satisfy it."

Yveshire wrung one hand over his white face. Flames reflected in his eyes like two tiny candles.

"And when you find nothing but further proof of his depravity and guilt?"

She stared at the bitter frost creeping over the window.

"Then I will see him destroyed," she said. "I will see him shaking on the scaffold, pleading for one more moment in the sun before the hood is drawn over his handsome face. I will stand with you and watch Robert Dovenby hang."

"WHAT THE DEVIL POSSESSED YOU TO DO THIS?" The words seemed to echo about his bedroom, bouncing from the candlelit walls, resounding over the naked shoulders, the wild tangle of female hair in his bed.

The girl flushed scarlet.

"My master thought you might be lonely," she said in French.

Dove was at the bedside in two strides, all desire long evaporated. "Your *master*? Mr. George White is a pimp in his spare moments? I refuse to believe it!"

Berthe began to cry. "You don't think I'm pretty enough, sir?"

He grasped his dressing gown and wrapped it about the girl's shoulders. *Damnation!*

"You're as pretty as a marigold, Miss Dubois. Any man would be honored by your favors. I am—I was taken aback, that is all. You've done this before?"

"There's usually an extra coin in it, sir." Sobs welled like hiccups. "Or a bit of lace."

He strode away. "Then you must learn to strike a better bargain, ma'am. You should trade your favors for nothing less than a good man's heart."

She began to weep in earnest, the tears racing freely. "I never knew a good man, sir!"

Dove found a handkerchief and pressed it into her hands, then poured her a glass of brandy. "Is that why you came to England, to find one?"

Berthe gulped at the amber liquor. "Oh, no, sir! I had to leave St. Omer. Jacques used to beat me. He would fly into these jealous rages. I was afraid of him. I thought he would kill me."

"You did right." He stared from the window as revulsion warred with pity. She feared men, no doubt disliked sex. He had seen it in her face when he had first found her in this room with George. Yet she would have sold herself for a bit of lace? "Tell me about yourself, Berthe. Were you born in St. Omer?"

In disjointed bits and pieces it all came out. She had not been born there, but she had been a maid at a great inn, where Jacques had been the proprietor's son. With no family left in her home village, she hadn't known where to turn for help—who helps a maid-servant, when a man wants his way with her and won't take no for an answer?—then a young Englishman had fallen ill there. She had nursed him. In gratitude for her help, Mr. White had offered her passage to England. Every detail, every nuance was exactly as George had told him and as Tanner Brink had confirmed.

Except that Berthe, too, knew that her master was truly a woman. Otherwise Dove believed the essence of her story, though he was almost certain that she was lying about the exact nature of her relationship with Jacques.

Yet it would seem that George, for all her bravado, was a woman of considerable compassion—as well as courage—if she had burdened herself with this French girl only in order to remove her from the reach of a violent panderer.

ICE SCRAPED HER HANDS AS SYLVIE CREPT BACK INTO DOVE'S house. It was a difficult enough journey from the duke's splendid residence, passing down deserted alleys, climbing to the rooftops up the scaffolding of a half-built house, using cornices and chimneys, tiles and gutters, and eventually slipping inside Dove's attic window. Yet her palms and fingers had grown no colder than her heart.

She had been an abject fool. She knew Yveshire to be honorable to the core. She liked him. She had once, briefly, been a little in love with him. Perhaps a part of that feeling had never died. He was not lying. And he had shown her proof. Robert Dovenby had brought about in cold blood the ruin and death of an innocent man. And yet—

And yet, if that was true, it made all of his charm and his blandishments just that much worse.

Closed doors hid sleeping servants. The house breathed silence. She was almost to her room when she heard voices, soft, sibilant. Pressing herself into a dark corner at the base of the attic stairs, she peered into the corridor.

Berthe was standing in the open doorway of Dove's room. She

looked tousled and a little annoyed, yet with a deep contentment, as if she were a cat who'd stepped accidentally into liquid, but discovered it was cream. Dove said something, grinned at her, then thrust her bodily into the hallway. The door closed behind him. Berthe walked off and started downstairs.

Sylvie reeled away and leaned her head back against the wall. She felt as if she'd been struck. *I will see him destroyed. I will see him shaking on the scaffold, pleading for one more moment in the sun before the hood is drawn over his handsome face.*

Even Berthe!

In a few strides Sylvie caught up with the French girl and grabbed her arm.

"Where are you going?"

"Just to the kitchens for some water," Berthe said.

Sylvie indicated Dove's door with a jerk of her head. "What was that about?"

Berthe flushed scarlet, then cocked a brow. "What do you think?" The girl held out a pair of lace cuffs, worth a fortune to any servant. "Our pretty new master has just given me a present. I didn't tell him anything, if that's what you think. I only told him the story you concocted, the one you left all those false clues for."

Sylvie waved her away and walked back to her own room. A bitter pain pressed beneath her ribs like unwept tears, like another gaping wound in what was left of the night. It took only a few minutes to tear off her coat, cravat, waistcoat, and shoes, leaving herself in shirt and breeches, as if she had just risen from bed and dressed hurriedly.

Her white face ghosted in the mirror—the empty face of a phantom—before she stepped back into the corridor and marched up to Dove's door.

She hammered hard at the panels. The door immediately swung open.

Had he expected Berthe to return?

His eyes lost in shadows, Dove smiled down at her. He had already shed his coat and cravat. A long robe, open at the neck, dropped from shoulders to slippers. His dark hair was disordered, curling over his ears and forehead. He was stunningly, heartbreakingly handsome.

"You bastard!" she said, letting her voice drip venom. "You bloody, unconscionable bastard!"

"You wished to speak to me, George?" He did not seem surprised. "Would you like to come in, or would you rather stand there in the hallway and curse until you rouse the whole household?"

He stepped back, elegant, contained, infuriating, and gestured for her to enter. Sylvie stalked past him. A single candle burned beside his bed. The covers were rumpled, the pillow dented.

Dove closed the door and turned to face her. "So what the devil brought this on?"

"You bloody liar! You said you had no interest in her. Then just now—"

"Berthe? She told you? How extremely indiscreet of her!"

"I heard a noise and came to investigate. I saw her leave this room. Are you really that dissolute?"

He walked to the grate and stirred the fire with a poker. He seemed unconcerned. "Maybe. However, your alarm for Berthe is misplaced. Unlike you, George, she's not an innocent virgin."

Fury boiled. If this was true, she wanted to strike him. "What difference does that make! She's a child and afraid of sex."

"Pray come over here and sit down. If I'm to be berated by my own secretary, I would rather enjoy a modicum of comfort during the process."

"Sit down?"

He dropped into a chair beside the fire and propped his slippered feet on the fender. Shadows chased over his shoulders and the long line of draped legs. He leaned his head back, as if to offer his throat. Lovely. Treacherous as Beelzebub.

"Unless you sit, George, I will not discuss it."

Sylvie walked across the carpet to sit opposite him. "There's nothing to discuss. I want you to leave her alone."

"Then perhaps you could ask her to leave *me* alone? What the devil do you suppose happened? I returned here to find Berthe lying naked in my bed. She offered me her dewy favors in exchange for a strip of lace—"

"And you *obliged*?"

"She had the lace. I did *not* enjoy the favors. A damned uneven bargain." Light flickered across the bridge of his nose, his upper lip and firm chin. "The encounter was neither of my choosing, nor at my instigation. Perhaps it would interest you to know that she told me you had sent her."

Sylvie stared at him, barely comprehending. "That *I* had sent her?"

She was freezing. In spite of the fire and the cozy confines of the room, she was freezing. Why would Berthe do such a thing?

"The young woman you rescued in France is a sadly opportunistic little hussy, George." His voice seemed to drift from some great distance. "After what her life has offered her, I'm not surprised. However, no harm is done."

No harm. Sylvie leaned her head forward onto both palms. This night had already been feral with harm.

"Then I have made a fool of myself," she said, shivering. She felt faint. "You have my apologies, sir."

"When I said that girls like Berthe don't interest me, I told you the truth. But now it's your turn to tell me: Why would you have cared so damned much?"

Her head snapped up. "Cared?"

"Lud, George! Are you ill?" He dropped to one knee beside her chair and laid a palm on her forehead. "Damnation! You're as white as the wall. Drop your face to your knees. Now!"

She tried to lift her lids to look at him, but the room spun like a ship tossed at sea. Nausea swept up her throat to be lost in the gathering darkness. Somewhere very far away, a chair fell, clattering.

CHAPTER EIGHT

ERTHE RAN DOWN THE STAIRS AND WRENCHED OPEN THE bolts on the back door. The lace lay folded in her pocket. She shivered a little at the icy air, then walked across to the stable. Mr. Dovenby's stallion breathed hay-scented warmth into the cold darkness. The girl hesitated as the bay nickered softly.

"Not overly fond of horses?" Tanner Brink asked in passable French.

"No, sir."

The Gypsy leaned close and smiled at her. "You'd be better off to trust horses more and men less."

Berthe bridled. "What makes you think I trust men? I never thought I could trust Mr. Dovenby. I was right. I hate him."

"Do you, now? Why is that?"

She shrugged. "Nothing. I talked to him."

Tanner laughed. "Is that all you did? What did you tell him?"

"Only what was already arranged, same as you," Berthe replied. "Though he already believed you. He has no idea of her real past."

"Good girl." The Gypsy reached into his pocket and pulled out some coins. "And what happened?"

"He gave me some lace."

"But you didn't earn it, did you? Is that what's the matter?"

"He said I deserved a good man, not a rogue like him."

"So you do, lass." Tanner Brink pressed the coins into her palm. "For your trouble," he said.

Berthe bit gingerly at the metal discs, then nodded, satisfied, before she crept back unnoticed into the house.

Sʏʟᴠɪᴇ ᴡᴏᴋᴇ ᴛᴏ ᴍᴏᴠɪɴɢ ꜱʜᴀᴅᴏᴡꜱ. Lɪɢʜᴛ ᴄʜᴀꜱᴇᴅ ꜱᴏꜰᴛ patterns over the inside of a bed canopy. She felt empty, as insubstantial as mist. Her eyes focused slowly. Just firelight. Someone had put out the candle.

Her wig was gone. Her hairpins and the cloth that had bound her hair, gone. She was in a bed. Dove's bed. Her head neatly filled the dent that Berthe had left, and her hair had been combed out to spread across the pillows. She let the shock sink in unremarked for a moment. So she was discovered!

"Blond," his voice said: that beautiful, seductive, incubus voice. "I guessed as much, but not that it would be so lovely, like spun silk and gossamer. You fainted."

Sylvie closed her eyes and ran her fingers down her naked throat.

She was discovered and she had accepted a mission. Nothing must be allowed to distract her from that.

"When you carried me to the bed, you found out," she said. "Yet my modesty is preserved. You have covered me with the counterpane, but I'm still wearing my shirt and breeches. I am grateful for small mercies."

"If I hadn't caught you, you'd have fallen into the fire. Our prior exchange was melodramatic enough, I thought, without immolation."

Her hair dragged across the pillow as Sylvie turned her head. Dove was standing beside the fireplace. His robe fell from his shoulders in soft gray folds, like a bird's wing, his hair a startling shadow in contrast. A small brass burner sat beside the grate. A blackened kettle balanced above the flame.

"Will you dismiss me?" she asked.

"I don't know. I'm not sure we should discuss it while you are lying like liquid temptation in my bed. Would you like tea?"

"Tea would be excellent," she said. "Thank you."

She watched his deft movements. It was as if she were two people, a woman who lay intimately in a man's darkened bed—as she had lain in so many darkened beds—and a ferocious soul who had sworn to her closest friend this one man's destruction.

How could she have been so wrong this time? The disorientation was brutal, but she had other resources, other strengths, to draw on: pride, professionalism, intelligence, the cold desire for justice. Whatever this man was, whatever he had done, whatever he appeared to be, she would outwit him.

You will not sleep with him!

But that was before Dove had discovered she was female! If he wanted to dismiss her now, she would have no other choice. It was close to four in the morning. She was already in his bed. A smile, a gesture, an unspoken invitation, and she would become his lover.

A hot shiver, like a small shock, passed down her spine. However much she tried to call on detachment, desire made its own ignoble demands.

Dove poured a dish of tea and held it out. Sylvie gathered her hair in one hand to push it out of the way and sat up. She managed to walk quite steadily in her stockinged feet to the fire, where she chose one of the chairs as if nothing were wrong. She even smiled up at him, before accepting the teacup from his beautiful fingers.

"I must apologize, it would seem, for deceiving you," she said. "*Will* you dismiss me?"

His dressing gown draped in supple folds as he sat opposite her. "Perhaps. What's your real name and history?"

"Sylvia Georgiana White. My friends call me Sylvie."

Sweet tea scalded down her throat. She had planned a tale for just this eventuality—governess, traveling companion—the second false trail she had planted across France. It all sounded splendidly convincing. Even if he sent agents to check, they'd find witnesses who would swear to it, because part of it was true. He listened in unquestioning silence, and unwittingly made it easy for her.

"Your antiquities business," he asked at last. "Why did it fail? You have all the skills necessary to run such a venture."

"My warehouse burned down."

"You lost everything?"

"Not such a great loss," she replied. "It was anyway too difficult to get customers to take me seriously."

"Because you were young, blond, beautiful, and female?"

"Just the 'female' was reason enough. How long have you known?"

"Since that first day, when I discovered you tied up to my bedposts like a trussed hen."

Her teacup rattled hard as she set it down by the grate, but her ironic sense of absurdity outpaced the shock. She stared at him with incredulity for a moment, then dropped her face to her hands in liquid hilarity and laughed till her sides ached.

"You really have known all along?" she gasped at last. "How the devil did you find out?"

"Faith, ma'am! Credit me with eyes."

Dying gurgles caught in her throat. "So you knew throughout our first dinner, over the roast beef and the bread and the fruit and coffee ices, when you said all those outrageous things?"

He nodded, his face alight with mirth.

"At Number Eighteen and Mr. Finch's bakery? During our sleigh race? When you made me ride double with you on Abdiel? Our adventure with skates in St. James's Park? You have *always* known?"

"Yes."

She pointed to the rug lying between the bed and the fire. "Even when you bathed right there in front of me that first evening?"

"You did not, as I recall, ask to leave."

Sylvie stretched out her legs, glad of the freedom of her breeches, and retrieved her teacup. Thank God that Dove was making it so easy for her!

"So my modesty is *not* something that concerns you, after all. What a very gallant soul you are, sir!"

"I offer gallantry only where it is earned, ma'am."

Her long twist of hair had begun to unravel across her shoulders. "And you think that the vast majority of women neither earn nor deserve it? Perhaps you're right. I *had* invaded your house without warrant, with all the resulting smoke and destruction. Why didn't you unmask me immediately?"

He abandoned his teacup and walked away. "I had no idea of your motives or identity, but if I'd admitted that I knew your sex, I couldn't have hired you as my secretary."

She watched the long strides, the gray flow of his robe. What she had learned about him didn't stop her wild awareness, her body's visceral reaction to all that male power. Her scalp tingled at the thought of his combing her hair across his pillows while she slept. What the devil had he been thinking while he had done that?

"But if you knew I was lying then, why hire me at all?"

He reached the far side of the bed and fingered the blue hangings. "I was intrigued. I did need a secretary—and perhaps I thought that in time I might win a new mistress, as well. You're obviously experienced. It didn't seem like an unreasonable hope."

"Ah," she said, staring at her toes in the thick boy's stockings. "So we're going to be honest. I wondered if it might come to that. But you really couldn't be sure about the mistress part. I am not, like Berthe, very partial to lace."

"Oh, I have other blandishments," he said lightly, as if he were still merely teasing. "We'll see, shall we, in the fullness of time?"

She glanced up. "Then I *do* have more time?"

"I see no reason to dismiss you, just because you're a woman. I never did."

The breath came back to her lungs in a rush. She hadn't realized she'd being holding it. "I was afraid to tell you. I thought you'd be angry."

He folded onto the bed and flung himself back against the pillows. "Angry? Why? I had the choice all along to reveal what I knew. I just decided to wait."

"Because you weren't certain how much lace I would want—though now you are?"

Elegant fingers thrust back over his scalp. "Lud, Sylvie! What the hell do you think? Though if you stay now, that's simply a risk you must take."

"Risk? What risk?" She stood and pushed her straying hair off her shoulder. "To decide that I am enamored of your lace cuffs, after all?"

He gazed up at her, wry amusement still lurking in his eyes. "If you could be so easily seduced, ma'am, you would not have tried to live out this mad masquerade. You'd have tried to forge a quite different bargain. I have done my best to respect that."

It was generous. Stunningly generous. She had deceived him. She was spying on him. She intended to betray him to his enemy. Yet he would neither turn her out on the streets, nor insist that she pay with her body for his forbearance? Though it had been there—hadn't it?—all along. Looking back, she saw all the small signs, carefully restrained, of a man who desired her—who even, perhaps, had already begun to seduce her. She just hadn't consciously noticed, because she had so enjoyed being male and a friend?

"I don't know what to say," she said, horrified that it was true.

"I've never coerced any woman into my bed, though I am not above offering temptation. I would prefer you to be openly female. I would prefer you to live here with me as my lover. I would like us to plunge together into that shared enchantment. I would like to see you flushed with passion as we drown in our mutual surrender. If I cast sufficient lures, might you yet stoop to take them?"

Rivulets of desire and trepidation coursed through her blood, yet fear ran deeper. She turned her face away to hide the betraying color. "I don't know! I would rather— You cannot hire a woman as your secretary."

"And you would still rather be secretary than mistress? Damnation," he said mildly. "Like any male I am staggeringly impatient. However, I can still use your services and you still owe me a debt. So you may continue here solely as George, if you like, and I'll take the risks—on one condition."

In spite of her pounding heart, she tried to match his light tone. "Which is?"

"Left to your own devices, your disguise wouldn't fool a blind beggar on Michaelmas Day. If you're to keep up this deception in public, I really must teach you how to be a better man."

It was a new shock, though a less serious one. "What, sir? After all that gallivanting about in the snow? Lud, Lady Charlotte wanted to bed me!"

He exploded with mirth. "Only because she was as foxed as a peahen." Lean muscles flexed as he rubbed his fingers over his eyes. "Fortunately, I was there to rescue you, before we were all faced with an impossible dilemma."

Her shadow danced over the walls as she began to pace. Once again she had achieved everything that she wanted. No, not wanted, but what she needed. Her pulse beat hard and fast, racing like a drumbeat. After learning so much from Yveshire, what she *wanted* terrified her.

"I think I make a perfectly satisfactory boy as I am," she said. "In spite of my recent hysterical collapse, I'm not usually very partial to excesses of female emotion. I shan't let you down."

He opened one hazel eye to look her up and down. "So you won't weep in public, or blush at a crude jest?"

"Weeping and wailing and gnashing of teeth isn't my style. Is that what you believe you need to teach me?"

"Alas, I need to teach you everything."

"And I thought I'd been doing so well! Do you want to start now?"

His eyes were alight—with mystery, with humor. "Tomorrow! Tomorrow! We'll start your lessons tomorrow, when you are safely disguised in your ugly wig and cravat."

He pulled a pillow over his face, as if choked by sorrow, or by laughter.

"Why should that make any difference?"

"Faith, ma'am! If you march back and forth by my bed like that much longer, the sight of your hair will unman me."

She stopped, riveted to the carpet, pushing the blond strands from her forehead with both palms as her blood surged and pounded.

"Is this the first lure?" she demanded. "Compliments? A declaration of desire?"

Dove flung the pillow aside and stretched, arms flung out to each side, dark hair in disarray on the pillow. The pure line of his hip and thigh took her breath away.

"Lud, no! Our awareness is already mutual. Declarations of appreciation would be superfluous. Surely you've recognized that my lures will be far more devious than that?"

The breath caught, choked, in her throat. Her hands fell uselessly to her sides.

"This is a warning?" she managed to ask. "There are subtle snares simply in being taught how to be a better man?"

"No, I shall teach you that entirely for my own purposes. The deadly snare lies in the sheer beauty of your being a woman."

"I don't deny my gender, but the mere fact of being female does not make me vulnerable."

"It makes you vulnerable."

Lost for an answer, she turned to walk away. At the door she stopped to glance back at him, lying long and lean on his bed.

"You're so sure," she said. "I really fail to see why."

"Sure? I am absolutely certain of only one thing—"

"Which is?"

"That whatever mad arrangement we may agree on tonight, you and I are destined for ecstasy."

The latch snapped open. Sylvie stepped into the hallway, her skin alight, her blood running in molten channels. She tipped her head back against the cold wall and wished that she knew how to wail and gnash teeth.

She was soul-wrenchingly afraid. Her determination threatened to collapse before such desire—piercing, even when she had been shown that he was corrupt, deceptive, a man of many masks. She had undertaken to destroy him. Now she stood for the first time on the brink of a terrifying unknown: the dread she had been unable to admit to Yveshire and could barely confess, even now, to herself.

I don't fear his lovemaking because it might prove to be depraved, Your Grace, but because it might prove to be beautiful beyond bearing.

SYLVIE PACED ABOUT HIS STUDY THE NEXT DAY. THE BLEACHED light of the dying winter afternoon shone dully through frost-flowered windowpanes. She had lain awake through what had been left of the previous night, then slept late. Dove was out. He had not sought her out, nor offered to teach her how to be a better man. Was he avoiding her?

God forbid that he had seen the agony his declaration of interest had produced in her heart!

He didn't need to cast lures. She was already enchanted, caught in the devil's spell. Though Yveshire had shown her the truth about Dove, she was still stunned by the force of this one man's attraction. It was a terrible flaw, a weakness that she was determined to root out: to long so fervently for his touch, to want so desperately to believe that he wasn't dishonorable and duplicitous, that he would not have been capable of planning with such brilliance another man's destruction.

It was as if Desdemona had indeed fallen in love with Iago. There was only one escape: to find and give Yveshire everything he needed to send his enemy to the scaffold, even if the thought sent shudders of horror down her spine. Yet what if—instead of confirmation of his venality—she somehow found proof of Dove's innocence? Something to reconcile what she had experienced in his company with the evidence Yveshire had shown her? A disturbingly cowardly thought! She had seen the proof in his own handwriting. When had she ever before shirked from the truth?

Restlessly she walked out into the corridor, listening distractedly for his step, painfully aware that her fingers drifted over surfaces he had touched, her shoes trod over carpets marked by his passing. It was absurd, wretched. She was behaving like a lovesick milkmaid.

She marched to the window at the end of the hallway, then back again, trying to formulate a plan, trying to understand, devastated that her instincts could still be so wrong. Nothing made sense. Her shoes ticked out the rhythm. *No sense. No sense. No sense.* There must be something she had missed. She had examined cabinets and drawers. Nothing was locked against her, but something must be hidden here. What?

She gave up at last and walked back into his study, striding the eight paces to the fireplace.

Eight paces?

Her pulse fired. Just to make certain, she strode back into the corridor and counted again. The discrepancy leaped out at her. The hallway was longer than the room next to it. Almost faint with excitement she tore back into Dove's study. Both end walls were part of the same outside wall, so the difference must lie with the fireplace.

She ran her hands over the paneling beside the chimney, pushed and prodded at every embossed carving. How could she not have noticed before? A hidden cupboard must be built into the wall. Yet no latches clicked, nothing gave way. Nothing. The two paintings on each side of the grate were solidly attached to the paneling. In a fury of thought she walked back to his desk and stared at the ledgers she'd slaved over that morning.

"You've finished work?" Dove asked behind her. "Don't tell me you're bored?"

Sylvie spun about to face him, but he was smiling.

"Not at all, sir." She hitched her hip onto the edge of the desk and folded her arms. "I've been searching for a secret compartment."

She waited for surprise, anger, indignation, denial, but he laughed.

"A dangerous quest! You forget the story of Bluebeard?" He tossed his gloves onto a chair and walked up to her. Her pulse reared wildly, like a horse out of control. "What will you give me if I show you how it opens?"

"That depends on what you have hidden inside."

"How about terrible hooks holding the remains of all my past wives?"

She grinned to cover up the pain in her heart, all her senses aware: of his scent, his height, his magnetism. "Or past mistresses? You blame me for being curious?"

"Not at all. I'm impressed that you're so astute. You noticed that this room is too short, I gather. What were you doing? Pacing the corridor?"

"Yes. Exactly that."

"Then I'm happy to show you. I'll exact payment later." He reached into a pocket and brought out a small key. "Here," he said. "This unlocks it."

Sylvie took the key, amazed that her hand remained steady, though her heart seemed to swoop and leap. "Unlocks what?"

"The door."

She stared at the fireplace wall. The linen fold paneling gleamed softly. The plasterwork was flawless. The carved frames of the two paintings had revealed no secrets to her searching fingers.

"Which door?"

He walked across the room to pick up the poker. Coals rattled in the grate. "The one with the lock, of course."

Blood rushed uncomfortably to her face, but she laughed.

The paintings were both cracked with time, but each showed a horse peering out of a rustic stable. On the left a dappled-gray gazed forever into the painted distance. Behind his bold head and silver mane, yellowed trees and fields stretched to the horizon. A chestnut with a dark, liquid eye stared from the other painting. A padlock fastened its stall door. The tiny keyhole had been impossible to see among the shadowed shapes.

Sylvie marched up to it and inserted the key. The lock clicked open. With a tug at the frame, she swung the painting aside. A large cavity yawned.

"A priest's hole," Dove said. "I learned of it when I acquired the house." He took a candle from the mantelpiece and lit it at the fire. "Here. You'll need a light."

"I may cast out shadows?" she asked. "I may examine murky spaces and hidden corners?"

"It is anyway already getting dark," he replied. "I have no objection to clarity of vision, though I must admit I wonder what you expect to find."

Dove propped himself against the desk, booted feet crossed at the ankles. Sylvie stepped over the low threshold. She stood in a narrow closet lined with shelves. The candle flame flickered over an assortment of everyday objects—the ordinary contents of any seldom-used cupboard. She picked up a broken dish and set it back down. A stack of ugly cups. A bundle of spare candles. An extra poker, a little bent. A carpet brush. A pile of old books.

"What a dreadful disappointment," she said. "No bodies? No gory hooks? No murdered women?"

"What, no proof that I'm Bluebeard, after all?"

"I would seem to be the fool once again," she said, frustration breaking in her voice.

He strode up to peer over her shoulder. His scent enveloped her, ice fog and leather, fired with that wild undertone of maleness. "On the contrary. However, I would like to know why you're still so suspicious of me."

Intensely aware of him, Sylvie took a deep breath. "Suspicious? Am I? Not because of Bluebeard—"

"Careful, don't break that!"

"What?" She glanced down. Her distressed hands had closed on a small box. "Why not? Is this where you keep evidence of all your dead wives, after all?"

Dove walked back to the desk. "Look for yourself, if you like."

Sylvie stepped out of the little cupboard, the box still in her hands. "Why? What is this?"

Her shoes rapped as she marched up to the desk and set down the box. She felt uncomfortable, like a child caught prying. Dove strode away to light a taper, then moved about the room lighting candles. The window at the end plunged into sudden darkness.

"Probably not what you expect," he said.

It had once been a lady's sewing casket, perhaps. Beautifully made and divided into many small compartments. Tiny drawers pulled out. Miniature partitions sprang open. Small trinkets lay in each one. Bits of ribbon. Lockets. Buttons. A tiny doll. A pack of cards. Little shapes made from twigs, twisted straw, entwined lavender stems: mostly crosses, a few rings, and one woven with human hair into the shape of a heart.

"Not wives, then," she said. "Mistresses? These are lovers' tokens?"

"Of a kind. The truth is both more touching and more disturbing than that."

"You hesitate to tell me?" She tried to make it teasing, but her voice died in her throat.

He glanced around, his gaze fathomless, but he smiled as if to answer her with equally ironic mockery.

"Faith! I'm only reluctant because the truth tends to induce female histrionics, which—in spite of what you claimed last night—might seem coercive under the circumstances."

"Coercive?"

"A lady's tender feelings are often enough just one step from a man's passionate bed."

She set down the box and closed the lid, hiding the mysterious trinkets. "Curiosity is a besetting female sin, of course, but you're wrong, sir, if you think that I share many of the emotional vulnerabilities of the weaker sex—certainly none that will carry me wailing into a man's arms. Perhaps I should offer you a wager? If you think you can make me weep, I will win it hands down."

"I cannot accept any such wager with honor, when there's no chance of your winning."

"Try me," she said.

"What do you offer, if I accept?"

"The pleasure of knowing that you successfully manipulated my sentiments."

He laughed. "False coin. If you weep, you will owe me a kiss on any part of your body of my choosing. If you sob aloud or faint, of course, you'll wake in my bed."

"And when I win?"

"If you win, you may have Abdiel."

Dove strode back to the desk and rang the bell. A footman came in and bowed.

"Hire a horse," Dove said. "Mr. White and I are going out."

"We are?" Sylvie asked. "Where?"

His smiled as if she were infinitely precious, as if they were already lovers. "I'm going to take you to St. John's."

Her heart hammered painfully. "St. John's?"

"Where Tanner Brink's recalcitrant pony deposited you at my feet the other night. Another merry venture in the dark, but perhaps this one will shed a little more light at the end. Shall we don boots, hats, and coats, and go?"

THE CARVED FIGURE OVER THE GATEWAY CARRIED THE SAINT'S lamb and staff, as she had guessed, but the Latin motto was too weathered to read.

"It was a nunnery once," Dove said.

He looped Abdiel's reins through a ring set in the wall.

Sylvie slipped from her hired mount, tied it, and climbed the steps after him. The door opened onto a shabby hall, where a motherly woman instantly appeared to greet them. She and Dove exchanged a few sentences, then she led them off down a corridor. The tour did not take long. The woman walked them through dining rooms, workrooms, laundry, pantries, kitchens. The ancient walls were cleanly whitewashed. Rag rugs covered the stone floors. Cared for, even if dilapidated.

The woman beckoned them up a flight of stairs, quietly opening door after door on dark, breathing silences. Her candle flame flickered over round, sleeping faces, anxieties lost in dreams, lips open like petals. Where nuns had once spent their celibate nights, children now slept in long rows of cots, two or three to a bed, only a little overcrowded.

"We do our best here at St. John's," the woman said to Sylvie. "We do our best for the poor homeless mites, for if they're not orphans when they arrive, they soon will be."

A baby wailed, waking suddenly from sleep. The matron excused herself and left to attend to it.

Dove strode off in the opposite direction, back down to the front hall. Sylvie clattered after him, her man's shoes harsh on the wooden stairs, her breath acrid with sorrow.

A foundling home. Where he comes on Wednesdays.

And an endless sink for funds.

"Those things in your priest's hole?" she asked. "They are connected with all this?"

He indicated a wooden bench at the side of the hall. "Wait there. I'll fetch Martin Davis."

The man who came in a few seconds later behind Dove wore a clerical neck cloth. Candlelight gleamed on pink cheeks and round spectacles. He came up to Sylvie and shook her warmly by the hand.

"Mr. White? I hear you made good use of the prayer book I left in your room, sir? Of course it wasn't your room then—"

"My secretary would like to know about the children's tokens, sir."

Dove stood staring from the window into the inky courtyard. The priest glanced at him and cleared his throat, then smiled back at Sylvie.

"The trinkets, young sir? You asked about the children's trinkets?"

She nodded.

"The mothers leave them," Martin Davis said. "We cannot feed all the children in London, but it doesn't stop them coming. Almost every day a woman will arrive with a baby in a basket, or bring a small child by the hand and send him to knock at the door by himself. They bring the things then, the crosses and the hearts and the toys. The mothers make them. They set them in the baby's basket, or leave them clutched in the hands of a toddler, as a remembrance. That's all that they have, you see. Nothing else."

"But you take the tokens away?"

The pink cheeks swelled as he pursed his lips. "Regretfully. We cannot let the children keep them. They have no value other than sentiment. Just bits of ribbon and straw. They're too fragile, too easily broken. It leads to rivalry, trouble. When we can, we return them to the children when they leave here, but not all of our babies survive. So Mr. Dovenby takes those things home with him."

"They are," Dove said quietly, "as you surmised, George, a token of love. My own mother left one with me."

"A straw heart?" she whispered.

"No, a baby's rattle, tied up with ribbons like a prize at the fair."

Martin Davis looked from one to the other, then cleared his throat again. "If there's nothing else, good sirs? Then I'll get back to my work."

Sylvie watched the cleric leave. His footsteps echoed away down a corridor. A large clock ticked into the invading silence. Dove still stood quietly at the window, but the room had filled with distress.

"So it was his *Book of Common Prayer*?"

" 'I stretch forth my hands unto thee; my soul gaspeth unto thee as a thirsty land.' He came to see me the evening before you arrived, desperate for more funds. It became too late for him to return home, so he spent the night." Dove turned to gaze at her, his eyes dark. "I, of course, own nothing as holy as a prayer book."

"So Martin Davis runs this place?"

"I have too many other demands on my time. He's a practical man, as well as a compassionate one. St. John's is in good hands."

"What future is offered to the children?"

"We find them work. They're schooled, apprenticed, trained for useful employment. A little business in those workshops we walked through helps to defray expenses. The boys color prints. The girls learn to sew and mend."

Tension made her voice harsh, though her heart felt like breaking. *"Samplers?"*

"You would have us remake society in your image? The girls learn the skills they will need."

"That's why their mothers have to bring them here to start with," she said desperately. "Because women cannot earn their own living, except on their backs."

His boots echoed on the stone floor. "I cannot reform England single-handedly. I cannot clear the streets of gin and vice and squalor. Neither can you. The girls learn to read and write, but they must also learn trades appropriate to their sex. Don't preach to me, Sylvie!"

She blushed scarlet, anguish beating frantically in her heart. "But if this place cannot feed them all, how does Martin Davis choose which children to take?"

Dove laid his palm on a large brass bowl that sat on a table in the center of the hallway.

"Here," he said. "Put your hand in here and show me what you find."

She stared at him for a moment—at the clean lines of his jaw, at the wild, angry tilt to his mouth—then she did as he asked. Little wooden balls rattled under her fingertips. She grabbed one and pulled it out.

"What color is it?"

"Black," she said. "It's a black ball."

He strode away, then turned at the front door to face her, his eyes dark.

"I'm sorry, ma'am, we cannot take your child." His tone was bitter. "You must pick a white ball, if you wish us to take him in today.

A red one and we'll add his name to our waiting list and hope he won't die in the meantime. But a black ball means you must go back without hope into the hideous streets and the gin alleys and the brothels. Yet abandon your baby here without undergoing our lottery, and the child will be handed without compunction to the parish. Because even though I have packed London's lost infants into every nook and cranny of this building, I can stretch my funds to cover only one child out of ten."

"Oh, God!" Sylvie said, closing her eyes. "You pay for *all* of this? This is where your money goes?"

"You ought to know, sir," he replied. "You've been keeping the ledgers."

The wooden ball slipped from her hand. It clunked onto the stone floor to roll away and be lost. One more baby's soul to disappear into darkness. She turned her head to hide her face, supporting herself with both hands braced on the table, while salt droplets splashed on the backs of her fingers.

"I don't see how you can stand to turn any of them away," she said at last, her voice choked. "How you can bear not to sell every last item that you own, every silk shirt, every painting, every beautiful thing that you have."

"Apart from what's left of my clothes and a few books, I own nothing. I rent the house with all of its contents."

"I thought the house, at least, was yours?"

"Like these lost children, I, too, was a foundling—remember? My foster father's estate was entailed. Everything was inherited by his nephew. I'm obliged to earn my living, as you are. I own nothing that isn't vital to my survival."

She couldn't stop the tears. Desperate to hide them, she marched away into the shadows, yet her vision swam and her cheeks flooded with moisture.

"But this place must have taken huge amounts of capital to begin with," she said. "Where did that come from?"

He didn't reply. Sylvie pulled out a handkerchief, dried her face, and turned to look at him.

Dove was standing beside the brass bowl. A handful of balls—red, white, and black—rippled down into its mouth from his lean fingers. The metal rang like a peal of bells.

"Many places," he said at last. "Though most of her estate belongs to her son, Meg helped—she still does."

Sylvie walked up to him, knowing that her eyes and nose were red.

"So I wept," she said. "You may collect your winnings. Where do you wish to kiss me?"

His expression darkened for a moment. He brushed his thumb over the corner of her mouth. His fingers touched her cheek, fleetingly, tenderly, as if she were infinitely fragile, infinitely precious, though there was nothing in his eyes but regret.

"What I wish is for you to offer your favors freely, ma'am. In the fullness of time, that might happen. Meanwhile, the wager was, as I told you, inherently dishonorable. Did you really think I would collect on it?"

ERTHE SAT IN THE EMPTY STABLE AND WAITED FOR TANNER Brink.

"Ah," the Gypsy said in her ear. "Here you are. Pretty as a daisy on a cow turd."

The French girl blushed, not sure if it was really a compliment.

"I'm taking her messages to the duke," she said. "I'm good at spying. I learned a lot about her when she lay sick in St. Omer. She's worked for Yveshire for years. On her back much of the time. But you already know that, don't you?"

Tanner sat down on the truss of straw next to Berthe. "Yes, I know all about what she did in Austria and France. It was all a sight more honest than what you do with men."

She turned wide eyes on him, indignant. "I don't know what you mean!"

"You tease a man. Tease his cock. Pretend to offer everything, but you don't mean it. You don't even like it. That's much worse than an honest seduction, whatever your reasons."

She looked down at her hands and bit her lip. Tears pricked at her eyelids. "Well, *he* didn't want me, anyway."

"Then you're a foolish girl," Tanner said. "Why did you offer it?"

"I thought I might learn something."

"From a quick tumble in a gentleman's bed? That won't heal what ails you. Any girl deserves better than that."

Berthe swallowed hard. Mr. Dovenby had said something similar, hadn't he? Perhaps she did deserve better, but the rejection still hurt.

"You do already know about the duke, don't you?" she insisted. "And how she's been involved with him?"

"Everything from Vienna to London," he replied. "Which is why the Dove hires me. There's no secret in the world safe from Tanner Brink."

"Has she gone to visit Yveshire? Is that where she goes?"

"The Countess of Montevrain has gone to the duke through alleys and over rooftops, creeping like a mouse. But the real question is: Are they still lovers?"

Berthe shrugged. "I don't know. How can I tell that? But you know everything *and* you've followed her, and still you're not telling any of it to him, are you? Even though he's paying you, you're keeping all of her secrets for her?"

"No more than you are." Tanner winked and tapped his finger to the side of his nose. "A duke offers a better future for any ambitious soul than a mere gentleman—and him a simple foundling, no less."

"Why should the duke offer *me* anything?"

"Ask yourself: Can Yveshire trust her this time? Can the duke trust her to be objective about a man like the Dove? He's very charming. He's courting her. He's going to teach her how to surrender like a lamb. How will His Grace feel about that, when he learns what's going on?"

Berthe bit at a fingernail. "I meet one of the duke's footmen in Shepherd's Market and give him her notes. They're in code, but it's all under my control, isn't it?"

"Maybe it is. But first, tell me something. She pays you well. She saved your life by taking you out of France. Why aren't you more grateful?"

"Grateful?" Berthe wrinkled her nose. "I am grateful. But that doesn't mean that I owe her anything—and as for him, I owe *him* nothing at all!"

Tanner Brink picked up her limp fingers and turned her hand over. He began to weave little circles in her palm, as if tickling a child.

"Your fortune, Berthe?" he said. "Wealth, long life, or true love—which would you like?"

The French girl giggled and pulled her hand away. "All of them," she said.

CHAPTER NINE

*F*AITH, DID YOU REALLY THINK I WOULD COLLECT ON IT?
They rode back, fast, in the dark.

The defiant line of her shoulders and back made him feel desperate. He had longed to kiss away the sorrow from the corners of her brave mouth. He had no idea whether or not she was really an enemy. In a deliberate move to up the stakes, he had taken her to St. John's, knowing that she would sooner or later—thanks to a bloody interfering Gypsy named Tanner Brink—find out anyway.

A woman will arrive with a baby in a basket, or bring a small child by the hand and send him to knock at the door by himself.

It was enough to break anyone's heart—man or woman. She had wept openly as they rode home through the night. So why must she pretend now that none of it moved her? Could she never risk genuine emotion, never risk vulnerability, or did she guard herself so ferociously only with him?

The empty stable yard waited. The groom came out with a lantern to take care of Abdiel and return the hired horse to its stall. Dove led the way into the house and walked straight to his study. Her heels clicked behind him. Tension—of grief, of suspicion, of desire—lay starkly, like an unexploded bomb, between them. He knew only one way, other than sex, to dispel it.

"So you still want to become a convincing male?" he asked.

"Yes, of course." Her courage as she made herself smile snatched the breath from his lungs. "Even though I shed tears over those damnable black balls and failed your test so miserably. Do you want to talk about it?"

"Women talk," he said. "Men act. Lesson one: *Catch!*"

He picked up an inkwell and threw it. She stumbled, surprised, and lunged after it, but the silver globe missed her fingers and crashed into the grate. Ink spilled. A black slick sizzled beneath the firedogs. The smell was dreadful.

"Men know how to throw and how to catch," he said. "Ladies flinch and close their eyes. They're afraid of anything that moves too fast."

"I did *not* flinch."

"You missed the inkwell."

She swooped down, picked up the silver pot and tossed it back. Dove snatched it from the air with one hand.

"Not bad. Try again. Like this."

He tore off his coat and wig, grasped her wrist, and showed her how to swing her arm. How to put her back and shoulder into it. She still threw like a girl.

He tried to show her how to catch. She still missed.

Dove threw everything he could lay his hands on: lumps of sealing wax, a brass paperweight, a spill holder, books. It felt like a kind of madness. She careened from chair to desk, fireplace to door, catching some, missing most. She threw things back wildly, uncontrolled.

"It's all in the gaze. Never take your eye from what's coming at you, or from what you're aiming at! Concentrate!"

He wrenched open the priest's hole and fired a barrage of cracked cups. Sylvie dived and scrambled. Crockery crashed to the floor, smashed into paneling and bookcases.

"Forget your hands!" he said. "Use your eyes!"

Her teeth snarled at him, neat and even and white between

bloodred lips, as a plate careened past her outstretched fingers to shatter in the fireplace.

"Stop!" She bent double to catch her breath. "We're littering the floor with broken china. I can't catch it all!"

"No boy would have missed a single deuced thing that I've thrown at you. Not one!"

She straightened up, still panting, to pull off her jacket and wig. She yanked out pins. Her hair shone gilt as she braided it and swung the long plait behind her back. She was magnificent, glorious, beautiful. Her skin and eyes glowed. Images swarmed forcefully in his mind: of that feminine blaze surrendered into passion in his bed.

"Now," she said. "Throw any damn thing that you like."

"I've only tossed you the discards so far." He strode back across the room, kicking aside potsherds like pebbles on the beach. "Every bit of that junk deserved breaking, but now come the valuable things. Catch them, or pay my landlord their value."

"Miss them and I'll be working for you beyond the grave?"

Dove shrugged, mad with desire. "It's your choice."

He seized a small jug and tossed it. The porcelain turned in a lazy arc, handle over spout. Sylvie captured it with both hands, then stood grinning for a second before setting it down.

"I did it!" she said, as if amazed at herself. "Though I think you made it very easy for me."

He laughed as flame roared through his blood. "Did I? Then this time I'll make it harder!"

The empty inkwell whirled, accurate and fast. She caught it.

A pen holder spun, wickedly shedding quills. Grinning like a merry fool, she grabbed it from the air and tossed it up once to catch it again, beaming.

"Hah!" she said. "It's just a knack, like opening a fan."

"If you had any sense," he said, "a fan is exactly what you'd be wielding right now, instead of flitting about like a moth playing boy's games. With a fan you'd win instantly."

She stopped to gaze at him for a second, slender in shirtsleeves and waistcoat. Loose-limbed, abandoned, piercing in her allure.

"Perhaps I don't care to win," she said. "Isn't playing games the whole point of this exercise?"

He grabbed a decanter. "As far as I'm concerned, it's just an excuse to see you so charmingly aroused." The cut glass whirled through the candlelight, sparking diamonds from every facet. "It'd be a deuced sight more rewarding—to both of us—to achieve that heady exhilaration in my bed."

With a quick lunge she grabbed the decanter with one hand. Without missing a beat, she threw it back, hard and fast, with all the force of her shoulder and back, straight at his head. His hands full of silver candlesticks, Dove ducked. The decanter sailed into the window. Glass shattered, raining frost flakes and ice shards. Brandy fumes filled the room.

He dropped the candlesticks, threw back his head, and roared with laughter.

Sylvie leaned one hand on the desk and clapped the other palm to her side. Her blond plait had already begun to unravel, framing her face in a halo of gold.

"Devil take it!" she said, grinning wildly. "I've got a stitch. And I'm damned if that brandy isn't mingling sickeningly with the smell of burning ink."

His legs folded until Dove collapsed onto the Turkish rug, to sit among the ruins of broken china. He wanted her. He wanted her there on the floor with him, disheveled and passionate—

"Lud!" he said. "I can't stand it, ma'am! Let's go to bed."

"No," she said.

He pushed both hands back through his hair. His blood pulsed, hot and urgent. She delighted him. She enthralled him. She was driving him crazy.

"What will it take? I've just sacrificed silver, brandy, china, and ink at the altar of your virginity."

"I'm not a virgin."

"That's debatable."

Shards crushed as she walked toward him. Her calves curved, limber and maddeningly feminine beneath the boy's stockings. Her instep arched like a bow. His palm ached to touch it. His soul ached to know her laughter forever. She stopped just out of reach, but she trembled as if battered by an invisible wind.

"*Debatable?* I was widowed several years ago, but it was a real enough marriage. You already know that."

Helpless with mirth, his blood alight with his craving, Dove subsided until he lay full length among the debris.

"But you're still a virgin where it counts—in your soul."

"You're mad."

He gazed up at her face, framed in its halo of gold. Her eyes betrayed her longing. Her skin was moist and flushed. Passion flamed so damned sweetly!

"You are lovely in the candlelight," he said. "You are beautiful beneath the ceiling. You have learned how to catch and how to throw. Yet your psyche lies untouched. Whether you've known a hundred lovers or just one, you're still a virgin and I love you."

"Though he swore undying love—and though she was most definitely not untouched—Psyche was abandoned by Cupid."

"Only because she tried to uncover his secrets. Yet a handful of arduous tasks for Venus, and all was reconciled. Either come here, Sylvie Georgiana, bend down like a wood nymph and kiss me, or go to bed. Some poor fool's going to have to clean up all this mess. It might as well be me."

"Let the footmen do it in the morning," she said.

"And have my staff think me mad?"

"You *are* mad."

"Of course. But it's meant to be a secret."

"You can't stop there," she said. "You'll have to tell me why."

"Certainly not! I'd rather leave you with the Bluebeard impression. Wickedness is more mysterious, more seductive, and more compelling than goodness any day. Go to bed! Tomorrow you will learn how to bow like a gentleman. So far you've been scraping out an obeisance reminiscent of a duck trying to clean its feet. Go to bed! Go to bed! Before I forget that I'm a gentleman and carry you with me to mine—"

The door slammed. Dove stared up at the maze of leaves and flowers in the plaster on the ceiling, contemplating the progress of his seduction. To launch into something so spontaneous—where such intense sensual desire and an oddly innocent joy mingled so maddeningly together—was entirely new territory, but to his immense surprise he thought he might like it.

*H*E FUNDS A FOUNDLING HOME AT ST. JOHN'S, YOUR GRACE, she wrote in code. *It's certainly in an area that most gentlemen would be unlikely to frequent. That, perhaps, is where part of your brother's wealth disappeared. I will find out. He is starting to trust me. With a little more time, he will tell me everything.*

Sylvie read over her note, sealed it, and gave it to Berthe to deliver to Yveshire's man during her daily round of shopping.

He trusts me. A shiver of discomfort ran over her skin. That was the essence of her work. To win trust—and then betray it. Did Dove assuage his guilt at St. John's? Was that how he made amends with his conscience? Or did he in truth have no conscience, and was the foundling home just a cover for something quite different?

Whatever the truth, she cared far too much.

She glanced at the clock. Dove was late. He had said he'd be back by dark, to teach her how to bow like a gentleman.

"Other than the slight scent of brandy and burned ink," his voice whispered in her ear, "no trace would seem to remain of our battle last night. I'm so glad that the glaziers managed to repair the window this morning. Deuced cold in here otherwise."

Sylvie jumped, crashed her head into his chin, and banged her elbow on the desk, before she dropped back to her chair. His soft-gray velvet jacket beckoned touch like the sleek coat of a cat, his cuffs and cravat crisply white in contrast. In defiance of convention, his own dark hair, shining and clean, tumbled about his forehead, the longer strands gathered carelessly in a ribbon at the back.

"What the devil?" she said. "The door is still closed!"

Rubbing his jaw he pointed behind her. The painting of the chestnut horse sat at an angle, darkness yawning behind it.

"A secret passage behind the chimney from my bedroom to the priest's hole. It would lend itself to splendid intrigue, if one were so inclined. Do you want to see?"

She pulled off her wig and rubbed at her bruised skull with both hands. "Not really!"

Dove laughed and walked back to close the painting over the priest's hole.

"Lud, ma'am! The unveiling of the secret stair was designed to lure you through its dark passageways into my bedchamber. But, alas, I'm a hopeless Bluebeard."

"I've given up on Bluebeard," she said. "I cannot think you have anything very dastardly hidden in there, or you wouldn't invite me to see it. Besides, I have already spent time in your bedchamber. What other secrets do you have?"

"Enough." He propped his shoulders against the chestnut horse and folded his arms. "But let's see about that disgusting bow you've perfected. Pray, go across the room and do your damnedest. I promise to be just as impressed as it warrants."

Sylvie stood and marched to the center of the room, where she turned and swept him a bow. She tried to make it precise, faultless. "How's that?"

"Monstrous," he said. "Neither elegant nor commanding."

Though he said it with a grin, the words stung—absurdly.

"Commanding? I thought a bow was a gesture of subservience."

"Lud, ma'am! If you think that, you won't survive a moment among the *ton*. A good bow commands a room. It makes ladies swoon and other men furious."

She tipped her chin and propped her hip on the desk. *I can't afford to care! His approval mustn't matter!* Yet it did; to her shame nothing much else seemed to matter very much. "Show me."

Lithe as a cat, he walked toward her. A snuffbox appeared in one hand. He stopped to take one elegant pinch. As if the candles had suddenly dimmed, a chill permeated the room. His hazel eyes narrowed.

"Good evening, sir," he said. "Terrible weather!"

The box disappeared, as if by magic. He bent at the hips, one foot in front of the other, and bowed. A wave of lethal force swept from the gesture, as if he might straighten with a dagger aimed for her heart. Her pulse hammered. *Ladies swoon!*

"Faith!" she said. "How the devil did you do that?"

The candles warmed, their light friendly and innocent again. He winked. "I thought about the children. Now it's your turn."

She was glad of the support of the desk. "I expected a lesson in how to arrange my limbs, not an attempt to become Richard the Third."

"Your limbs could not be more prettily arranged, but you still have the mind of a woman who thinks a bow is just a gesture, like a curtsy."

"A curtsy is never just a gesture."

"Then you already understand. Imagine the men who father those foundlings, only to abandon them and their mothers. Imagine the babies left in their baskets who aren't discovered until it's too late, or who must go—against every humane instinct and inclination—into the hands of the parish. Imagine anything that fills your mind with distress—"

"So imagination is what it takes?"

"Effrontery mixed with contempt is what it takes."

Her heart thumped heavily. "You always feel contempt for other men?"

"Not at all, but unless they're real friends, no two men ever met yet without baring their teeth, like dogs waiting to see which will tuck tail and slink away first. Our modern age hides those fangs behind a gloss of lace and elegance, but we're all curs at heart."

She studied the long line of his coat. The set of gray velvet over male shoulders and trim waist. The white linen at cuffs and cravat. In spite of his careless hair, a picture of wickedly civilized elegance and devastating male attractiveness. Yet he had destroyed Yveshire's brother, arranged an innocent man's death. She must not forget it.

"I only know how men behave with women," she said.

He smiled, apparently carefree in the candlelight. His skin glowed, and his eyes—bright with irony, intelligence and passion for life—impaled her through the heart like a moth spiked with a pin.

"With flirtation and seduction?"

"The knowledge lies much deeper than that," she replied. "It's in the blood. I haven't been male long enough, obviously."

"No, but whether man or woman, you feel contempt enough for my sex."

Coals crumbled and fell in the grate. Sylvie spun away and walked to the fireplace. "You think that I don't like men?"

"Not much. But that's your problem, not mine. I, too, prefer women."

She bent to poke at the flames. "You may prefer women, but do you respect them?"

"Oh, I think so. Far more than you respect men. Pray, stand up, ma'am, and think about that. Then bow to me as if you mean to bring about my destruction."

The poker clattered. She almost dropped it. She spun about, fixed her eyes on Dove's face, and swept him a bow.

"Careful. Limit it. Too much only makes you vulnerable to a man with more control."

"Yet be ruthless, or the dogs will come in for the kill?" Sylvie choked back her distress and bowed again. "That's how you impress your enemies?"

"Not consciously." He grinned. "I've been impressing my enemies for so long, it's almost second nature."

"Do you resent your natural father that much for abandoning you?"

Her barb failed. His fingertips lay lightly on the desk top, relaxed, his palm open. They didn't change, nor did his easy, carefree expression. "My mother abandoned me. My natural father probably never knew of my existence. Keep your back straight and try scorn instead."

Her lip curled. "Scorn? Is that what makes ladies swoon?"

"No, scorn is what makes men want to kill. Desire is what makes ladies swoon."

She was arrested mid-bow. "How the devil do you think about desire and scorn in one breath?"

"I don't know," he said. "I was hoping you'd tell me, since that would seem to be something you've perfected. An understanding of the fickleness of men runs far too deeply in your bones."

Blood rushed to her face, hateful, feminine, vulnerable. With her gaze locked on his eyes, she stepped a little more with one foot, kept her back straight, and bent her hips.

"Faith, I was never abandoned by a man, except when my husband used death to desert me. After that, the abandoning was all mine. I intend it to remain so."

"Perfect," he said. "You've learned how to bow. Do it again."

She bowed again, letting her mind flood with a savage mix of lost emotions, projecting power and disdain and a carefully banked anger. It was disturbingly easy.

"Excellent! I'm impressed."

She glanced at the fire, as if the flames could explain the sudden rush of warmth in her blood. "I made you want to stab me to the heart?"

"Yes. Very physically. With all the abandon you like." Mirth colored his voice. "Which is of course exactly the result a man wants when he bows to a lady he admires—depending on how soon he wishes to get her into bed."

"Ah," she said, looking back at him beneath her lashes. "Then let me see the bow that tells her that tonight isn't soon enough."

"Since that skill is also all in how one thinks about it, that might prove to be a dangerous game, ma'am."

She laughed. "I'm not afraid of a little danger. Are you?"

"Not at all, but since it could prove awkward for me to entice as many ladies as you've been doing recently, I must leave that up to you."

"Oh." Sylvie grabbed a china figurine from the mantel. "I've also learned how to throw like a man—remember?"

The painted shepherdess sailed hard and fast for the window.

Dove vaulted over the corner of the desk. Graceful, infuriatingly precise, he caught the little figurine and set it down.

"Well," he said, smiling. "You've just proved my point. You thought only of the target and forgot your own body. Nothing else, except practice, is relevant."

"So in everything a man does—shooting, riding, fencing, pursuing a seduction—his skill depends entirely on the state of his mind?" She dropped into the safety of a chair by the fire. "I'll remember that."

Dove stared at the little china figure, the pretty painted clothes, the gilt crook, as if he didn't quite trust himself to meet her gaze. "And in everything a woman does, her skill depends on the state of her heart?"

"I wouldn't rely on that for a maxim," she replied.

"It depends," he said, glancing back at her and grinning, "on the woman."

Ah, what a man! However hard she tried to stay hostile, he undermined her, made her laugh. She had never enjoyed any man's company so much, which felt almost more dangerous than his physical attractions—though they were real enough and perilous enough.

Sylvie pushed her feet up onto the fender to lean back like a boy, her hands crossed behind her head. Pins stabbed her palms. She pulled them out. Blond coils slid over her neck and cheeks. She combed them with her fingers and rubbed her fingertips over her scalp. She had accepted a mission. When had she ever retreated from danger?

"So there's no skill that cannot be perfected by mastering the mind, rather than the body?" she asked. "Even those skills that are primarily those of the hand and the mouth and the skin—like sex?"

He froze for a moment, before meeting her gaze once again, but he was smiling. "Now you're not fighting fair. Pray, don't insist that we puddle about in base metals, then offer me a glimpse of the forbidden philosopher's stone."

"You're afraid to answer my question?"

"Making love is a skill for the heart."

"Ah, you liar!" She laughed. "When did any skill you ever practiced involve your heart?"

He grinned back. "What a shame that you think we must wait before we discover quite how far Psyche and Cupid may go, once they've repaired their dumb quarrel! But when it happens, it will without question involve hearts."

"I'll remember that, too," she replied with mock gravity. "Thank you for the lesson, though you are wrong. What else do you wish to teach me?"

Dove picked up the shepherdess, strode across to the fireplace, and set the figurine back on the mantel. He turned to gaze down at her. Something new glimmered in his eyes, as if perhaps she really had wounded him.

"It's my turn to learn something from you."

She raised both brows, though her pulse thundered. "You think I have anything to teach *you* about being a man?"

"Not at all. Yet you bowed to me earlier with such easy ferocity. Before I go much further in my campaign of seduction, I would like to know whether or not it is really your intention to betray me."

The breath stopped in her throat as heat flooded her face. "Betray you? How? To whom?"

"That's exactly what I'm asking. Shall we have chocolate and chat about it at the fireside like two civilized young men?" Shadows traced over his sleeve as he rang the bell on the mantel, the bones of his hand clean and hard. "Pray, replace your wig, ma'am," he said, "before the footman arrives."

She hastily bundled and pinned up her hair. Before she could prevent him, Dove slipped her wig over her head. His fingers brushed her temples, touched deliciously at the back of her neck, as if he deliberately wanted to feed the frantic beat of her heart, intensify her shock at his accusation with this mad awareness of his magnetism.

A footman appeared. Dove requested the hot drinks with the easy courtesy of any man giving orders to a subordinate. She gathered her wits.

"How can I betray you?" she asked as soon as the servant left. "You think that if we became lovers, I would sleep with other men, also? Would that wound?"

He sat down and leaned back, watching her. "Perhaps. I don't know. What's more relevant is that I've never bedded an enemy in my life."

"An *enemy*? How can I possibly harm you? You control everything in our relationship."

"Then take this chance to even the scales. I put myself at your disposal. I have one question for you, then I will answer anything, within reason, that you like."

"Anything?" Her heart beat too fast. *In spite of what he is saying, he trusts me—or he would never bring this out into the open.* She tried to calm her rapid pulse. "You have just said that you think I might be your enemy—though I'm damned if I see how—so why would you reveal any truth to me?"

The door opened and the footman entered carrying a silver tray. Bitter chocolate had been ground with sugar and hot water in two cups. The aroma was heavenly. The man bowed and left.

"Let's begin with my question," he said. "Then we can decide about yours."

She hid her tremor of nerves by testing her hot drink with the tip of her tongue, but her heart thumped hard, as if she were running a race. "What do you want to know?"

"When you first went to Lady Charlotte's to collect on your wager, I followed you."

"I know that. I don't blame you. When you found me in your bedroom, you must have thought I had all kinds of nefarious personal designs on you. It was only reasonable to be suspicious."

He stirred his chocolate with a long silver spoon. "But you crept out of Number Eighteen and returned later like a thief. I watched you climb back in through the window. A most inventive method of exit and entry. Where had you been?"

Her heart dived, like a hawk swooping fast onto prey. Hiding her face, Sylvie sipped at the chocolate foam, then licked her upper lip, before she replied. She must just bluff it out.

"To the necessary. At least, that's why I climbed out of the window to begin with. There wasn't a chamber pot in the room. I was afraid that if I ventured back into the corridor to hunt for one, I might be waylaid again by Lady Charlotte."

"Rather a long time to be gone just for a call of nature," he said.

If Dove had followed her to Yveshire's, he would know she was lying. But if he *had* followed her to Yveshire's, it was all over anyway. She tried to breathe deeply, let her distress add credence to her story.

"Once I was done, I went for a walk. I had to think. I had no future. No idea how I would make a living in London, nor even how I might survive. To be honest, I felt desperate."

To be honest. Her desperation had been true, at least. He had seen it that next morning when he offered her the post as his secretary—he was bound to remember that.

"Why should I believe you?" he said. "Can you prove any of this?"

She bent to set down her cup, so he wouldn't see her face. This deception was vital. She must discover what drove him, and then—if he really was guilty—she must indeed betray him. Yet her cup rattled clumsily against the grate. Annoyed at herself, she took another deep breath. Lud! Why the sudden shakes? She was a professional at this!

"No, of course not. I don't usually take witnesses with me to the privy, nor do I plan alibis when I do something as stupid as to stroll off into the unknown streets of a city I don't know in the dark. But I had to walk. Don't you see? If I'd just lain in that study doing nothing but thinking, I'd have gone mad." She glanced up, in control again, and gazed straight into his eyes. "Anyway, where could I have gone? I don't know anyone in London."

"It's all right," he said gently. "I believe you. I just had to make sure."

The kindness in his voice almost unnerved her. After this assignment was over, she would never do this again! In all those other missions for Yveshire, she had learned how to cajole and beguile. She had learned how to seduce. She had learned how little most men could be trusted, how deceptive appearances could be. Yet she had never before been offered this gentle compassion.

"I'm guilty of only one thing," she said. "I arranged that Lady Grenham would find me here. I thought she would distract you, if you returned, so that I might escape with your cravat. You must have guessed that by now. I'm very sorry for it. I misjudged—and of course I had no idea that she would tie me to your bedposts."

It was a risky admission, but it was partly true and might allay more suspicions. He lifted the spoon from his chocolate to catch a droplet on his tongue. "Yes, I know that. I've seen your note. Now you've satisfied my interest, it's your turn."

"So you don't think I'm an enemy now, after all?"

"No. And I know you must be curious about me."

She gathered her wits. "Curious? Of course. It's a besetting sin of mine. It will no doubt one day bring about my demise, like a cat."

Dove laughed. "I'd noticed." He glanced at the clock on the mantel and stood up. "But it's time to go."

"Go? Where?"

"My dear George, now that you've learned how to bow like a gentleman, it's time for us to venture into the fair streets of this devilish city."

"Wait," she said. "What about my questions?"

He stopped in the doorway and grinned. "What's the matter, ma'am? Are your questions too intimate to ask me outside?"

THE STREETS WERE FILLED WITH MEN, JOSTLING, TALKING, passing witticisms like sweetmeats. Sylvie and Dove walked rapidly past the jumble of houses and shop fronts. Londoners swept by them in a wave. Dove walked next to her casually, exactly as if she were another man, without offering his protection against the throng of carriages and pedestrians. It was rather refreshing to stride out, swinging her arms, elbowing through the crush with the best of them.

"Where are we going?" she asked.

"The river."

"The Thames?"

"There is only one river: the driving heart and unfathomable soul of this wicked place, both lifeblood and sewer of our fair capital." The crowds began to thin. The smell of fish and decayed weeds filled the air. "Be glad that it's winter. The Thames is not a place to enjoy much in summer. *It stinketh*."

"No worse than the streets, no doubt."

He laughed. "In truth, in summer almost anything is better than the streets."

They strode on together until darkness leaped into a great void beyond the last of the buildings. Young girls hovered in the shadows and eyed them as they passed. Directly ahead lay a bridge.

"You were never before out in a city at night on foot?" Dove asked as they walked up onto the bridge and stopped to gaze out.

It was almost entirely dark now. Warehouses loomed on the south bank like great blocks tossed there by giant children. Farther down the river a forest of masts cast a spider's web of rigging.

"No. Never. I have lived most of my days inside, or at least within garden walls."

"I thought so," he said. "That's really the only reason we came here."

"We came to see the Thames?"

"I thought you might also like to see our new Westminster Bridge. It's barely a dozen years old. The pride and joy of King George's new London, the result of incalculable amounts of gold and a modestly limited sacrifice of lives."

One of the bridge lamps shone on his hat, shadowing his clear profile. The tail of his dark hair lay like spilled ink down his spine. Both lean hands rested on the parapet, the fingers clever and precise. Distress beat hard somewhere beneath her rib cage. His voice sounded so caring and relaxed. *I believe you. I just had to make sure.*

"A city always under construction," she said. "All to make a playground for men."

"And for women—especially those of a certain vocation. Whether dressed as a lady or a lad, don't try to walk alone anywhere in London at night." His gaze scanned the far skyline, rooftops gaping like ragged teeth. The dome of St. Paul's. The jutting church spires. "There's a dangerous city out there."

Her heart began to beat even faster. Yveshire's words during her first visit, after she had crept from the window at Number Eighteen: *He visits parts of London that no normal gentleman would dare go.*

"You must be familiar with all of it, I suppose, because of St. John's: not only the haunts of the quality, but those of the tradesman and the artisan and the apprentice?"

If he hesitated, it was for only a moment. "Yes, most of it. Few places in London hold any fears for me."

The lamps of a few small boats scattered over the water like glowworms. Sylvie closed her eyes, remembering the glitter of ballrooms, the sparkle of diamonds, a world of artifice within walls that had never held any safety for her. Of course, she had already been out alone in London at night—though only through the deserted streets of the more fashionable new squares.

"I want to see it all," she said. "I want to see this whole wicked city."

"I was planning to show you the clubs and coffeehouses," he replied.

"But the rest of it—all that teeming life! You could take me to places I would never have the chance to see otherwise. Not again in a lifetime. You could do so without risk. Why not?"

"It couldn't be entirely without danger."

"Lud, sir! Nothing in life is entirely without danger. I learned that on a smuggler's boat in the Channel, and I am reminded of it whenever you and I spend time together. Yet here I am, still in one piece."

He glanced down at her, smiling. "You would really like this?"

"Yes!"

"But perhaps I don't wish it."

"I'm not supposed to learn something new? Take away some lesson?"

"Perhaps not that, not yet."

Sylvie looked down. She couldn't risk pushing the issue. "Then you owe me a question," she said. "You said I could ask anything I liked."

"So I did. Deuced foolish of me—must have been a weak moment. What do you want to know?"

"I may truly ask anything?"

"Within reason." He glanced away as a wagon began to trundle toward them.

"Then I'd like to know why you fund St. John's. You're not a wealthy man. I assume it's because you were a foundling yourself?"

She held her breath, but when he glanced back, his smile was open, with no trace of bitterness or self-pity.

"Of course. I, too, was left in a basket, clutching that token of my own."

"Where were you found? Here in London?"

"About as far away as you can get and still be in England. Near a tiny place called Dovenby—thus my surname—in the Lakes."

"So you have no real name?"

"Dovenby's as good as any," he said. "Imagine if I had been left nearer Cockermouth! Then I doubt if I'd have survived my boyhood. Instead I was discovered mewling pertly like a kitten beneath a bush, and raised by a childless couple who lived near Derwent Water."

The wagon rumbled past, its iron-shod wheels creating an ungodly racket on the stones. The driver sat bundled in a woolen blanket. The horses' breath cast little clouds of ice mist about their warm nostrils. The man touched his hat once, in acknowledgment of the two gentlemen.

"You grew up there? In the Lakes?"

He grinned, as if the memories were precious, filled with joy. He couldn't—surely?—be faking this! Yet Yveshire had shown her all that evidence—

"The wilds of Borrowdale, Rosthwaite, High Seat—from Maiden Moor to Armboth Fell, the Lakes were my playground. Whenever I could escape my tutor, I rampaged over the hills with the lads from Keswick and ran into wild adventures every once in a while with a certain group of Gypsies. I had no idea that the world was filled with less fortunate foundlings."

She closed her eyes for a moment. She could imagine it so vividly: a boy reveling in the freedom of the wild peaks. It didn't sound like a childhood designed to produce envy or bitterness, but perhaps the knowledge that he'd been abandoned by his natural mother ate like a canker at his soul—too deeply to be apparent on the surface.

"Your foster parents still live there, by Derwent Water?"

Discord chased over his mouth and eyes, like a shadow. "Sir Thomas Farlow and his wife raised me as if I were their own son. My mother is still there. My father is dead."

Perhaps his foster parents had not been very kind to their foundling, after all. They must have wanted children of their own. Who knew what damage they might have done to this false son, found beneath a bush?

"I'm sorry," she said.

"Thank you. But you have lost both parents. Your loss is greater. You have my condolences, Sylvie."

Sylvie bit her lip, regaining control before she looked back at him.

"Is this why you've chosen to come here in the dark, with the river hissing its icy slurry beneath our feet? Did you guess what I would ask and fear that I would disgrace myself once again with sentimental tears?"

"Perhaps. You were happy as a girl?"

"Yes—but I was my parents' only child and the light of their lives. How did you cope with not knowing who you really were? Your true parents could have been anybody."

That new hint of guardedness betrayed him—no wonder he had wanted to escape the clarity of candlelight! "Yet I was lucky. The rattle left in my basket was made from amber and gold. I was raised as a gentleman. I was even sent to Oxford, a place for young gentlemen to learn debauchery along with their classics."

It was a small avoidance, not one that anyone would notice unless they were already suspicious. But perhaps this was it: *What if your true parents might have been vagabonds or criminals? Had the open friendship of a duke's son, supremely confident in his identity and position, been too much to bear?*

"Oxford made your fortune?"

"Oxford came close to helping me lose any fortune I might ever have hoped to gain. Fortunately, I came to London before I was completely ruined."

"Where you met Lady Grenham?"

Sylvie watched his lean fingers. The beautiful hands stayed relaxed, easy, as if nothing about any of this bothered him at all. Yet she knew he was restless, that their talk about his childhood had disturbed him in some way he wouldn't quite admit.

"Yes. Which brings us back to your original question about St. John's. Meg also tends other charities, just as pressing, but she arranged that I meet Martin Davis. I was, temporarily, in need of a place to funnel a great deal of money. A foundling home was the obvious solution."

Her heart thumped hard. Had she already stumbled to the core of the issue?

"Where did the money come from?"

He didn't answer. A party of young men, bold with drink, had surged up onto the bridge. They gathered around the wagon, forcing the driver to halt. The dark echoed with their merriment. Dove watched them, lithe tension in his stance. His right hand had drifted toward the hilt of his sword.

Sylvie swallowed.

The wagon moved on. The young men came caroling toward them, then surged past without a backward glance.

"Any other questions?" Dove asked.

The chance for an answer or for any more intimacy was gone. Yet a shadow still lay at the corners of his mouth, in the tiny tension in his nostrils. He had offered her something of his past. She thought everything he'd told her had been true, as far as it went. But something lay at the heart that disturbed him too deeply to name, something dark and dangerous. Something she must uncover.

"Oh, I think that's plenty for one night, sir!"

"Then since you will not let me take you back to my bed, where we could be languorous and warm, let us go somewhere harsh and noisy," he said.

CHAPTER TEN

E BEGAN TO STRIDE BACK OFF THE BRIDGE. SYLVIE HURRIED
to keep up with him.

"We are to visit the artisan and the apprentice, after all?" she asked.

Dove turned to look at her, raising one brow. "You would *like* somewhere harsh and noisy?"

"Faith! Why not?"

"Then how about the Bull and Thimble? The ale is execrable, but the company might amuse you."

He started down a set of steps that led to the river. The stone was slimy, green, as if the steps were seldom used. Black water and ice floes jostled beneath Westminster Bridge, leaving a slick, soapy film of frost on the arches.

"What kind of company?"

Dove stopped to grin up at her. "The best kind. Thieves and pickpockets and vagabonds and whores. You said you wanted to see the other side of London life. Shall we see now whether you really mean it?"

A small boat rocked at the base of the stairs. Dove leaned in to shake the shoulder of a man draped across the seats. The boat listed precariously to one side.

"Blackfriars Stairs, my good man!"

"Wait!" Sylvie grabbed Dove's sleeve. "This man's foxed! Lud, his boat's a leaky tub."

"Is it?" His tone was suspiciously innocent.

The boatman sat up. Inky water sloshed lazily beneath him. Shrugging from Sylvie's grip, Dove stepped in to stand, feet apart, on one of the seats. The small craft dipped like a leaf.

"Lud, sir! Be careful!"

"Concerned, George?"

As relaxed as a street gymnast, Dove pulled off his hat and held it out in one hand to aid his balance. The boat wallowed. Rotten boards creaked ominously. The waterman gaped up in a half-drunken stupor, but light from the bridge lamps high above flooded over Dove's face. His eyes and mouth shone with audacity and humor.

"You scurvy wretch!" Sylvie hissed, though she felt an answering mirth bubbling up to match his. "Surely the new bridge created new water stairs, too? This man is no professional waterman!"

Teetering precariously, hat waving as the boat tipped, Dove peered down. "Couldn't say who he is. No acquaintance of mine. Appears to be struggling to stay upright, but he can surely take us to Blackfriars?"

"We'd sink before this boat went two hundred yards."

He grinned up at her. "You can't swim?"

She stepped back, skidding on the slimy stone. "Of course I can't swim! Where the devil would I ever have learned how to swim?"

"Then I must teach you that, too."

Sylvie backed up several more steps. "Oh, no!" she said. "Not in the frigid Thames!"

She turned and raced back up to the street to lean over the wall at the top of the stairs. Dove had stepped back onto the stone steps, then thrown aside his hat to peel off his jacket, as if stripping for a swim.

"Where's all your vaunted courage, George?" he called up to her.

"Enough to defy you in this!" she shouted. "I've heard all about the dangers of shooting the bridges on the Thames, especially in the dark dodging ice floes. I shan't do it now for the first time in a keel-sprung barge with a waterman who's had more to drink than any fish in the river."

His shirtsleeves shone white as Dove flung wide both arms. "You don't trust me to rescue you?"

The waterman was trying to climb out of the boat to reach Dove's discarded hat.

"I don't intend to find out."

Dove snatched his hat from the boatman's unsteady fingers. "My apologies, sir," he said to the man. "I can't afford another hat right now." He spun a small coin into the upturned palm, shrugged back into his coat, and ran fast up the steps.

"Truce!" he said, laughing openly. "I won't throw you in the river tonight. Tomorrow will do just as well."

"Alas, sir, I believe you have no intention of taking me anywhere at all."

"Do you? And now it's getting ready to snow—or sleet, which is worse."

Sylvie glanced up at the sky. The stars and moon had disappeared. Chimneys and rooftops had dissolved away into blackness. Cold drops stung her face. Within minutes the air filled with icy wetness, and she and Dove were soaked.

They strode back to his townhouse through deserted streets. She didn't believe for a moment that he had really intended to take her anywhere. The waterman must just have been some vagrant sleeping in an abandoned boat. But she had learned vital information, more than she could possibly have hoped for when the evening began: a small knowledge of his past, where something had happened that must be the key to understanding what drove him—perhaps whatever had made him destroy Yveshire's brother. And the name of a low tavern somewhere beyond the Blackfriars Stairs: the Bull and Thimble, haunt of whores and vagabonds.

It would all go in her next report to Yveshire. Against all odds, she was succeeding in her mission. Why the devil did that make her feel so deuced miserable?

WATER DRIBBLED FROM THE CORNERS OF HIS HAT. SYLVIE sloshed beside him, her shoulders bravely hunched against the falling sleet. How could anyone mistake her for a man? Yet perhaps men only ever saw what they expected to see.

"You don't really think me a coward?" she asked, as if aware of his glance.

"A coward? Absolutely!"

She ducked beneath an overhanging doorway for a moment, squeezing out of the sleet, though it left him standing in the full force of the spitting ice, driven now by a fitful wind.

"Because I didn't want to be drowned in the river?"

"No, because we're going to arrive home drowned anyway—or at least, I am. Yet even if I cajole or plead or insist, you won't abandon all this folly and let me take you to my bed."

"We've discussed this before," she said, grinning up at him.

"There will be a roaring fire in my bedchamber. Clean sheets heated with a warming pan. Hot mulled wine or hot chocolate with brandy—"

"I'd never come to your bed for hot wine," she interrupted. Cold had stung her cheeks, making her eyes brilliant. Otherwise she was dark: wet hat; soaked shoulders; the tail of her wig a pulpy mass on her collar. "Though, who knows, I might yet do it for chocolate."

He laughed. There was no tavern that he knew of called the Bull and Thimble. He had watched his wagon make it safely out of

London. He had given the man in the boat his coded signal to let the others know his plans for tomorrow. The entire evening a success— until he ended up in his lonely bed with his mind filled with longing for this one infuriating woman.

"Your choice," he said. "But what if I tell the maids you're not to have a warming pan until you change your mind?"

Her lips stretched, ripe and inviting, as her grin widened.

"If I change my mind, I won't need one," she said.

SYLVIE WAITED FOR DOVE THE NEXT MORNING WITH STUDIED nonchalance. He had not followed through on his threat to remove her warming pan. Her bed had offered cozy, welcoming sheets. Yet she had lain awake, her arms about her pillow, staring up into the lavender-scented darkness—the innocent, sweet aroma of childhood—because to fall asleep would be to dream.

Her dreams would not be innocent, nor childlike. She would dream, with a desperate, passionate longing, about this one man. She had never longed before for a man's bed, though she had known many men's beds. The longing was incoherent, disturbing. *I am afraid of it,* dream voices would whisper insistently. *I am afraid of it.* So she fought sleep. Then she would wake, not sure why she ought to be afraid.

She copied more receipts into ledgers, wrote a handful of innocuous letters to tradesmen, then wrung one hand over her dry eyes almost as if to wipe away tears.

He came in quietly and walked up to the desk. "You're sleeping no better than I?" he asked.

Sylvie turned to look at him, at his buckled shoes and silk stockings, the wide flare of coat skirts, the embroidered waistcoat, such a stunning contrast to the male power hidden beneath. At last, she raised her eyes to his face. His skin shone like bronze against the silver strands of his wig. He was smiling, deep creases bracketing his mouth.

A hot wave of disturbance ran through her blood to pool, like a spring tide, deep in her belly.

"I slept like a kitten replete with milk," she replied.

"Liar!" His smile deepened. "You slept as badly as I did: haunted, restless. Yet the cure is so simple—"

"You're about to suggest I take brandy in my milk?"

His scent enveloped her, soap and witch hazel, the smell of clean male skin, as he leaned over the desk to inspect her work. "Just breathe on your milk, ma'am. That should be intoxication enough. It is for me."

"Ah, how very restrained you are, sir, when I thought you were about to suggest something far more satisfying to take to my bed than a warming pan."

He raised both brows and gave her an innocent grin. "But what could be more satisfying in bed than hot coals in a brass pan?"

"—which you did not take away," she finished. "Thank you for that. Other than pretty compliments, dusted with subtlety like plums with sugar coating, what more could I possibly need?"

"Scents other than lavender? Sensations more gratifying than your arms around a pillow?"

She covered her face with both hands. Ah, but he knew exactly how to do this!

"You practice necromancy? Unless you crept in to spy on me, how can you possibly know how I arranged my pillows?"

"I don't need to spy." His voice was light, reassuringly noncommittal. "I already know. As I said, you sleep just as I do—lonely, desperate, and dreading your dreams."

Her palms dropped as if numbed, but she instantly gathered her wits. "What dreams do you have that you must dread?"

He leafed through the letters she had written, then grasped a quill to add his signature to each one. The firm bones of finger and wrist betrayed once again, without question, that he was the author of those papers that Yveshire had shown her: papers that had led the duke's younger brother to ignominious ruin and death. Sylvie forced her mind back to her mission.

Dove walked away to stare at the thin winter daylight beyond the window. "I dreamed last night that you were drowning in the Thames. I wanted, with absolute desperation, to save you, but my boots were stuck in ice, my arms bound with tentacles of hallucination. I struggled and shouted, but you were sinking, sinking, with your lapis lazuli eyes pinned silently to my face."

"What happened then?"

He turned back to her, his face shadowed. "You disappeared, as I fought and watched, without uttering a sound. Then I was suddenly able to leap into the water, only to be bound once again by dream weeds. I struggled as if fighting hands holding knives, but I was still unable to reach you."

"Lud!" she said. "We were doomed to drown together? I trust that isn't prophetic?"

"Prophetic? It might be, unless you let me teach you how to swim."

"You assume," she said, "that I intend to enter the water with you in the first place."

"I must at least assume that you have very good reasons for not doing so."

"It's nothing personal," she said. "I just prefer the dry land."

He walked back to the desk and began to fold, seal, and stack the letters. "Oh, no, ma'am," he said. "Whatever your reasons, they are very personal indeed."

It was a terrifyingly astute observation. The thought flashed into her mind that Dove knew all about Yveshire, knew her real purpose in being here, understood her reasons for insisting on still dressing like a man. Why had he told her that dream? *I wanted, with absolute desperation, to save you—* No man had ever before wondered whether she needed saving. No man would ever have cared so much that he would tear himself apart in the trying. *Why tell her?* Didn't he realize that she could never allow herself to believe for a moment that he truly cared?

"So you have something else to teach me today?" she asked. "Besides swimming?"

Dove set the letters on a silver tray, where a footman would later come to fetch them. He glanced down at her, his expression surprisingly tinged with laughter.

"If you're really to accompany me into my world, you had better learn to take snuff."

She leaned back in her chair. "Ah, the deadly inhalation, the flare of disdain in the nostrils, the flick of fingers that dismisses every other man in room?"

"—and makes ladies die away on the spot."

"I seem to recall that I've already survived witnessing your taking of snuff."

His grin widened. A gold snuffbox with elaborate enameling appeared in one hand. He opened the lid with a practiced flick. "But perhaps you're not truly a lady?"

"I'm doing my very best, sir, to keep my position as your secretary." The truth, though not one that made her any more comfortable.

"Yet you're damned if you care to inhale snuff? I don't blame you. A filthy habit, fit only for sailors."

"I didn't say that."

"But I did. Never mind, you don't need to take much. It's all a bluff, a chimera, like everything else in the fashionable world. Gesture is everything. Substance nothing."

She stood up. "Allow me in return to teach you how to wield a fan," she said. "Then gesture and substance are all one."

"I can't wait. But until then?" He held out the snuffbox.

Sylvie took it.

"Close the lid. Now open it as I just did."

She practiced for a few moments, beginning with both hands, before progressing to one. He stood beside the desk and watched her. Inevitably, her heart began to spin into a breathtaking new rhythm. His steady gaze wasn't intrusive. His eyes didn't speak openly of kisses or seduction. Yet small flames of delight danced in their hazel depths, as if she and Dove shared some intimate, lovely, hilarious joke—as if she were already seduced, long ago, and was replete and satisfied in a way she'd never known.

She swallowed. "Show me again," she said.

"You recognize, of course," he said as he retrieved the box, "that the opportunity is here—waiting like a flying carpet to carry us both to a magical world—for us to touch hands."

"Accidentally, I assume," she said.

His gaze locked with hers. "Little fleeting, apparently careless brushes over your wrist, or of my fingers against yours—like this." Exquisite sensation throbbed between her legs as his fingertips brushed over hers, as direct, as lovely, as if he had kissed her. Hot blood rushed to her cheeks. "With the snuffbox as our excuse, I could so easily enfold your hand in mine, caress the sweet center of your palm while I shaped your fingers with my own—"

His fingers followed his words, feeding tinder to that furnace of sensation, making her knees weak, her breath unsteady. Her palm gripped his convulsively. She stared into his eyes, her heart hammering, as he opened his hand and dropped the enameled gold box into hers.

"But I cannot afford it," he said, his breathing as disordered as hers. "It is far too hard to stop there."

She turned away, her hectic pulse pounding. "Then we'd better concentrate on taking snuff." She held out the box, though her hand trembled, and flicked open the lid. "How was that?"

"The tender grace of it sears my heart," he said. "Now, with just a little more flourish?"

"Like this?"

With lean, lovely fingers, he plucked the snuffbox from her hand, yet with exquisite care, he didn't again touch her bare skin. Maddeningly, she knew that she craved it.

He flicked open the lid, his eyes never leaving hers. "Like this. Try again."

She took back the box and tried to copy his gesture exactly. "Since you won't risk more naked contact, I'm trying to imagine what it would really be like to become a man like you, to be inside your skin."

"What an exhilarating, if unsettling, thought—it certainly is whenever I imagine being inside yours!"

The snuffbox tipped and spilled half its contents onto the carpet as she laughed. "Faith! I suppose I asked for that!"

"You begged for it, ma'am. But if you would really *like* more naked contact, I put myself at your disposal."

Sylvie gazed into his eyes, though his fire might burn her yet. "Alas, nothing must be allowed to interfere with the taking of snuff."

"What a pity!" he replied. "I must be teaching you too well."

She proffered the gold box and snapped open the lid with an elegant flick. "You're teaching me the perfect combination of wariness and hauteur," she said. "There, is that it?"

"Faultless! Now set a few grains on the curve below your thumb and inhale them, one nostril at a time."

Sylvie pinched up a little powder to set it in the depression on the side of her hand. She sniffed. Sensation exploded. Eyes streaming, she sneezed violently.

"Faith, sir!" She sneezed again, then burst out laughing. "It's like lifting off the top of one's head. What toxic, foul poison!"

"Exactly." He spun away, as if to hide mirth, or desire, or concern. "Why else would the taking of snuff with absolute indifference so impress other men?" On the other side of the desk he turned back to face her. "Try again, not so much."

"Only if I may let most of it drift unmolested to the carpet." She took another pinch, making faces at him, though this time she barely inhaled any powder.

"I am humbly, though most pleasantly, impressed, ma'am," Dove said. "What a perfect blend of superiority and distaste! Combine that with your deadliest bow and you'll be London's darling by nightfall. Shall we go out in shining formal attire later this afternoon to invade the coffeehouses?"

$\mathcal{D}$OVE AND SYLVIE STEPPED OVER THE THRESHOLD TO BE instantly engulfed in smoke, the reek of lamps and candles, and a wall of talk and laughter. Groups of men sat at tables, drinking coffee, playing cards, making bargains, passing witticisms, reading newspapers and scandal sheets.

"Welcome," Dove whispered in her ear, "to the malevolent world of the London gentleman."

Faces glanced up beneath powdered wigs. Faces with tiny patches, the skin powdered and rouged above lace cravats and satin coats. Men's faces. In his elegant gray coat and silver wig Dove led the way into the room as if he owned it.

"Not exactly malevolent," she replied softly when he paused to nod to an acquaintance. "Though certainly distrustful, as if the dog pack isn't sure how much to grovel and how much to snarl."

"More malevolent than you know. Think of Richard the Third, murderer of little princes, then make a nice bow to Lord Bracefort. Behind you. He's an ass."

She turned toward a man who had just risen to greet them. Lord Bracefort wore puce with a great deal of lace. His smile was forced, uncomfortable, a little swaggering.

Bracefort bowed—a dog that groveled.

Yet Sylvie stood dumb and entirely forgot to return it. Another man sat at Bracefort's table. Tall, powerful, a man of obvious status, his face inflexible beneath his neat wig. His eyes locked onto Dove's face, while he pointedly ignored her.

Dove swept both men a deep obeisance.

Bracefort blushed scarlet.

The other man became livid, as if he'd just been slapped.

"Your Grace," Dove said. "How charming that you should be here! Perhaps you haven't met my new secretary, Mr. George White?"

Sylvie bowed, doing her best to project unconcern, though her heart hammered so painfully she thought she might faint.

Bracefort slumped back into his chair. "Very pleased, I'm sure."

"I'm simply devastated to see you unable to rise, Your Grace," Dove said, taking a pinch of snuff. "Age fatigues, no doubt?"

Obviously fit and not more than thirty-nine, His Grace remained sitting, absolutely still, his dark gaze boring into Dove, before he turned his head and snapped for a serving man.

"My hat and cane," he said. "The company palls. I am leaving."

"Allow me." Dove took the tricorn and cane from the hapless servant's hands. He spun the hat on the table in front of the duke, then twirled the cane once before offering it, like a benediction. "May I offer my assistance in honor of your aged limbs, Your Grace?" he asked. "Or we could instead meet at dawn with seconds, if you like."

"My distinct preference, sir, is that we not meet anywhere," the Duke of Yveshire said, standing with icy dignity. "You will not find me in this coffeehouse again."

Abandoning both hat and cane, the duke stalked from the room.

*   *   *

SYLVIE STOOD RIGID AT HIS SIDE, AS IF STRUCK TO THE HEART. Forced to trust that she would follow him, Dove walked farther into the room, greeting friends, nodding to acquaintances.

A small titter had already chased about the coffeehouse. *Lud, sir, the Dove baits Yveshire, of all people! Is he mad?*

He overheard one reply. "Lunatic, sir! But one must admire the man's nerve—and that deadly charm, of course. You heard all about the sleigh race at Meg Grenham's? Saved Hartsham's life. Hero of the hour."

The man's companion—the Earl of Fenborough—shrugged. "I've known Dovenby longer than you have, sir. Brilliant, beyond a doubt. But without the interest of the glorious Grenham, Yveshire would have crushed him long ago, like a bug—"

Dove led Sylvie into a corner, commandeered a private table, and ordered coffee. She sat down awkwardly, stiff with bravado.

"A dangerous moment," he said dryly.

"Is that true?" she asked, her head bent, her voice almost a whisper.

"About Meg's benevolent parasol protecting my shameless head? Yes, of course. You already know that."

She stared at her hands, lying flat on the table, as if willing them not to shake. "Powerful connections are everything, of course."

"Then perhaps next time you won't try to destroy them quite so enthusiastically?"

Her cravat lifted as she took a deep breath. "You refer to her bonfire of clothes in the street? Lud, no wonder you were angry! In truth, sir, you have been very forbearing with me."

Coffee appeared, welcome and steaming. Dove sipped at the hot liquid, strangely bitter on his tongue.

"So why didn't you tell me that you were already acquainted with Yveshire?" he asked.

Her head jerked up, her face blanched like paper. "I didn't—Faith! A *duke*!"

"One of the more powerful of England's peers, though not more so than Meg's father and brother. Where did you meet him?"

She wrapped her hands about her cup, as if she were reaching for an answer. A tremor ran through her fingers. Her knuckles shone like ivory. If she denied that she already knew the duke, he'd know for certain she was lying.

"It didn't seem that important at the time. He waylaid me at Lady Grenham's after the sleigh race." She tried to smile. The courage of it touched him to the heart, in spite of the seriousness of this. "He dislikes you."

Nerves were understandable, devil take it, whether she was telling him the truth or not.

"I assume His Grace tried to warn you against me?"

Light flickered over her face as someone pushed past the table, making the candles flutter. "I suppose so. I had no idea who he was, though I guessed he was a man of considerable authority. Now I learn that he's a duke and your enemy?"

"*Enemy* is a powerful word."

Color flared suddenly across her cheeks. "Lud, sir! For a powerful hatred! That became pretty obvious just now. I thought he might murder you!"

"And you cared? I am touched. Why didn't you mention this interesting encounter before?"

She was still upset. She obviously chose her words carefully. "As I said, I didn't think it was important. He didn't introduce himself. He only said that I shouldn't work for you. He thought you were foxed and dangerous to consort with, especially in a lightweight sleigh."

It might be true. Though if she was being dishonest now, she was covering it well. But how could Yveshire have met her before that?

His Grace had traveled, but he would never have strayed far from the most privileged of settings, places that Sylvie would never have been. Unless everything Dove thought he had learned about her was an elaborate concoction of fantasies—which would mean that Tanner Brink was lying to him, as well.

"He was right," Dove said. "I am dangerous in a lightweight sleigh, or out of it."

"But what the devil would a duke know about any of it?" she asked. "I don't imagine he has ever worked a day in his life!"

"This duke works," he replied. "He just doesn't work for money. What else did he say?"

She sipped coffee, her mouth lovely. Now that she had overcome her initial shock, she seemed almost too casual.

"He was impressed, I think, by my dewy innocence and concerned about the resulting perils of your companionship. He believes you have nefarious ways of making a living."

"I do," Dove replied.

Her cup joggled, spilling a little coffee. "So I *am* working for Bluebeard?"

The light was tricky, the air thick. She was still flushed, nervous, but it was hard to read her true feelings.

"Nothing quite so dramatic," he replied dryly. "There's considerable profit in a bakery."

"Oh?" She wrinkled her brow. "Don't tell me—Matthew Finch? He works for you?"

"He works for himself. I'm simply an investor in his enterprise."

Curiosity flared in her eyes, but she leaned back in her chair like a man, then tipped her head to gaze at the smoky ceiling. Her pulse beat too fast in the silky skin just beneath her jaw.

"I can't imagine Yveshire thought me too innocent to know that!"

"Gentlemen—even those of such unsteady antecedents as

myself—do not usually fund bakeries. I can't imagine that Yveshire has any idea of it."

"Then what did he mean? What else do you do? I've been trying without success to fathom it from your interminable ledgers."

He waited just long enough for her to drop back to meet his eyes. "The ledger headings are in code," he said.

"In *code?*"

"To hide the nature of my business enterprises from prying eyes—"

"Like mine?"

"You're my secretary. Why should I hide anything from you?"

"Then what do you really do?"

"Allow me to show you tomorrow."

She froze as if turned to stone. Yet she was able to recover quickly enough to sip coffee, gazing provocatively at him beneath her sinfully feminine lashes.

"Lud!" she said with exquisite indifference. "I wager you fund a butcher's and a candlestick maker's, as well!"

Mirth bubbled in his throat, treacherous, then tension evaporated into laughter. Every muscle caroled its awareness. He had never met a woman like her. She was brave, beautiful, and without question the greatest challenge he had ever faced.

Dove wasn't sure if he would ever truly unmask her, but he knew with burning certainty that he must lure her as soon as possible into his bed. If she was not really his adversary, it would be glorious to love her. If she was—if she intended to betray him—she didn't stand a chance. So he had never made love to an enemy before! What of it? In his bed he would uncover her secrets. Either way, she didn't stand a chance.

"No," he said. "I fund something far more disreputable than that."

To his amazement she laughed, as if the champagne in his blood had intoxicated her, too. "Then I assume that your other work is very wicked indeed?"

"That all depends on your definition of wickedness," he replied.

T HE CHANCE FOR FURTHER PRIVATE CONVERSATION WAS GONE. Three young men walked over to join them. An invitation ensued. Sylvie followed Dove back into the streets and up into some private apartments in a large house not far from Piccadilly. An uproarious company had gathered around the fire—artists, musicians, writers, peers and sons of peers, and a few select ladies. Drink flowed freely, but conversation ran like a river: brilliant, clever, about literature, politics, art, war.

She plunged into an argument in Italian with a singer from Naples, then found herself agreeing in French with a writer from Paris. She disputed with an earl and bandied witticisms with a marquis. Before long she was beckoned to the fireplace, where she bowed over the hand of an elderly lady in diamonds and silver net, a lady who proved to be a duchess.

"Any companion of Dove's is welcome here, sir," the duchess said, peering at her through a pair of jeweled spectacles. "Though it would seem that you are making quite an impression of your own."

After a quick exchange of pleasantries, the movement of the milling guests swirled her away. Another glass of wine was thrust into her hand. On the other side of the room the singer was now arguing with Dove. Floods of voluble Italian swirled back and forth. At last the singer threw up his hands, took a breath, and broke into song.

Conversation died. Power soared to the ceiling in the language that had colored her childhood. By the time the singing was replaced with applause, her eyes swam with betraying tears that she had to blink back.

"Aristocrats and artists," a voice said in her ear in ponderous English. "Which are you, young sir?"

"Neither," she said, swallowing and looking around. The newcomer was fat and rather slovenly, though his eyes sparkled with penetrating intellect beneath a great bushy wig. "Are those the criteria for membership in this company?"

"Being a friend of Robert Dovenby's is criterion enough, young sir. You have my congratulations and my condolences."

"Condolences?"

The man eased himself into a chair. "The companionship of genius is overrated. He will always outwit you and he will never trust you. I should know, sir. I am in the habit of outwitting everyone I meet."

Sylvie laughed, but had to give way before the press of people swarming about the newcomer. Dove winked at her. The Italian baritone beamed at him. The duchess was laughing at something he'd just said. Sylvie walked over to join them. Moments later she found herself bowing her good-byes and Dove was guiding her from the room.

"I hope you were suitably entertained," he said as they walked down the stairs. "You were a success!"

Fine wine and scintillating conversation buzzed in her head like a swarm of summer bees. Italian song had opened floodgates of happy memory.

"*Entertained?* I'm enchanted! But you're a favorite of a duchess, as well?"

"Our hostess?" he asked. "Her Grace finds me amusing. Alas, I'm the only one of her guests that can persuade our Italian friend to sing in her drawing room without pay."

"You did that deliberately?"

"To my shame. I just had to take the risk that you would not break down publicly into puddles of sentiment."

"Oh, but I did. However, mine weren't the only damp eyes in the room. And you're evading the real issue."

He spun about on the bottom step. An echo of that Italian power and beauty still sang in his eyes. "Which is?"

"That you're invited to the private gatherings of dowager duchesses, where you're a great favorite among the flower of the peerage, yet you made me feel guilty over Lady Grenham. You led me to believe that her patronage alone was critical to your position in society."

"It is," he said. "Her father is another duke. Yet the more the merrier. I certainly do everything in my power to shield myself from Yveshire's antipathy."

"And such powerful ladies form the best possible shield?"

"The only one." Mirth sheened over his expression like moonlight on water. "I have no desire to be squashed like a bug."

"*Crushed,*" she said, giggles rising in her throat. "*Crushed* like a bug."

THEY STEPPED OUT INTO THE STREET. A DESULTORY, HALF-frozen fog parted before them as Dove's long strides consumed the cobbles. Mist dampened his hat and broad shoulders, shone like silver on the tail of his wig, ghosted over the tails of his coat. Moisture splashed up onto his stockings from the slush on the pavement. A picture of carefree masculine strength and resourcefulness.

Dovenby is a man from nowhere. My brother was a light in society. Edward once told me that Dovenby was the most charming man he'd ever met—

A man from nowhere, whose light burned like a flame. To open doors. To win influence. To be feted and petted by the most powerful ladies and gentlemen in England. To surround himself with beauty.

Had he ruined and killed Yveshire's younger brother just to gain this?

As he walked, he sang, in a clear tenor. Italian arias besieged the smoky oil lamps, and Dove gleamed as if burnished. Sylvie joined in, though she had a voice like a frog.

She had survived meeting Yveshire face-to-face in public! Dove hadn't guessed. How could he? No one knew that this duke employed ladies like the penniless Comtesse de Montevrain to gather information for the British government. She had survived a social gathering at the home of a duchess—dressed as a young man! She had done it all gloriously, splendidly, without putting a foot wrong. Her heart hammered and soared. She felt as if she had swallowed some kind of mad hilarity, mixed into brandy and sparkling wine.

Tomorrow! Tomorrow Dove would show her—what? Something that would give Yveshire everything he needed to destroy his enemy? Something that would send Dove to the scaffold?

But what if she uncovered proof of his innocence, instead—what then?

"Well, sir," she said. "I believe I acquitted myself quite well in my first venture into your world. You agree?"

"It helps to be a polyglot. As with a performing monkey, society appreciates a nice selection of tricks."

"Thank you! I appreciate the compliment."

Smiling, he glanced down at her. "I was referring to myself, not to you. The duchess entertains me only because I entertain her. If I ceased to do so—or if I offended her, or anyone in her circle—I would be shunned instantly."

The fog enveloped, hiding house fronts and railings.

"So only Lady Grenham smiles at you with true benevolence?"

"Exactly."

"Then it's not really the more the merrier, is it? I'm glad I was able to keep my wits among that collection of literary aristocrats—in spite of your little spat earlier with Yveshire."

"No encounter with the duke can be called 'a little spat.'" His voice held nothing but amusement.

"I was just trying to be polite."

He only grinned—but of course her indignation wasn't genuine and he knew it. A shared understanding sparkled between them, like the ice crystals caught in the frail glow of the streetlamps.

"I'll allow your perfect manners with the duchess," he said. "But you didn't exactly pass this test."

She tipped her head back and caught a droplet of ice-cold fog on her tongue. "What test?"

"In your fragile distress at meeting Yveshire in the coffeehouse, you forgot just about everything I'd taught you. Instead of bowing like a gentleman to pour scorn on our enemies, you gaped like a schoolboy."

She shrugged. "Then they'll just think that's exactly what I am."

He gave her a mock frown guaranteed to freeze any dowager duchess. "I would not hire a schoolboy as my secretary."

Flinging out her arms, she danced a few steps in front of him. "Then set me snarling like a bulldog at the singers from Naples—that I can do."

Enveloped in the dull flicker of a lamp, she bowed with a flourish, projecting as much deadly certainty into the gesture as she could muster.

Dove stopped and folded his arms. His wide grin sent deep creases into both cheeks. "So you haven't forgotten!"

"If you refrain from further encounters with murderous dukes, I'll do just fine," she replied.

The cocoon of sheltering fog enclosed them together in the

intimate glow of the oil streetlamp. His gaze drifted slowly over her body, from her heeled shoes to her man's hat, lingering at wet calves and waist and throat, hesitating like a caress as he studied her jaw and mouth and eyelashes. The awareness between them shifted and changed, as if the sparkle of ice in the air crystallized into diamonds.

He paused for exactly half a heartbeat, gazing straight into her eyes. "Faith, ma'am, in spite of your excruciating disguise, you are already very fine."

Sylvie spun away. Wild glee soared like hawks in her heart. Ah, but he was splendid! Even if he proved to be wicked, he was splendid! She ran up the steps to his front door to lean nonchalantly against the jamb, letting her hat tip forward a little over her eyes.

"Then you have nothing left to teach me, sir?"

Dove walked up until she was pinned with her back against the door. He lifted away her hat. His breath, tasting sweetly of laughter and wine, feathered warmly over her mouth. He seemed to be studying every nuance of her eyelids, cheeks, the corner of her left eyebrow, the little dip beneath her nose. His mirth had dissolved like salt stirred into water, home of dark mysteries.

"I still have plenty to teach George," he said. "But I would much prefer to tutor Sylvie."

Expectation resounded like a drumbeat. Her bones flooded with memories—of another dark night and a maze and a stone Aphrodite. Pleasure pooled relentlessly, drawing heat from her fingers and toes into a flare of awareness deep in the belly.

"Perhaps there is nothing you can teach Sylvie," she said.

"I don't care." His words spiraled softly into her ear. "I am willing to take that risk. I will even take the risk that Sylvie might have something to teach me."

Her hands gripped the door jamb behind her back, denying the longing to search the warmth beneath his coat, to settle intimately on his lean waist. Her head turned, denying the longing to lift her face to welcome his mouth pressed once again onto hers.

Yet temptation seared: a bright, bittersweet temptation—to make passionate love to a man that she had promised to betray to his worst enemy.

CHAPTER ELEVEN

❧

THE FLUSH OF DESIRE FIRED HER CHEEKS, THE NATURAL effect of wine and song and conversation, of what he had worked for tonight with such devotion and knew he had achieved—in spite of the encounter with Yveshire. Her female vulnerability and softening, the yearning clear at the corners of her mouth and in her lovely, clever eyes.

Yet she turned her head away.

"I was widowed," she said. "Afterward I worked as a governess. You're the darling of London society, lover of the beautiful Lady Grenham. How could I teach anything to you?"

Scents of damp wool and clean linen filled his nostrils. Beneath them, like an undertow dragging him to irresistible depths, the compelling perfume of her skin, icy and moist, while her warm, wine-laden breath assailed his senses like a drug.

"Perhaps we could learn infinite delights from each other?"

She glanced up at him with wry self-derision. "My mother warned me long ago against rakes."

"Rakes? I've never been a Lothario."

"What does that guarantee?"

"Not much. Yet it's been my habit to be faithful. If we became lovers, I wouldn't abandon you without cause."

She clung hard to the painted wood, as if afraid that her knees would buckle. "What of Lady Grenham? You loved her."

He replied with the simple truth. "I thought that I did. But perhaps our passion had already died away into friendship. Why else did Meg end our affair so publicly, so absolutely, and with no chance of going back, as soon as she had the excuse? Women are wiser than men in such matters."

She sighed, her lips wine-dark in the dim light. Her shoulders beneath the male jacket were soft, female. Hidden by the cravat and high collar, her neck curved sweetly, waiting for kisses. He was erect, burning for her.

"And now you think you desire me?" she asked.

"We desire each other and more deeply than I, at least, can quite fathom. Why deny it? This masquerade of yours is a kind of madness."

"But it's my *own* madness," she insisted.

"Sharing my bed would be your own madness, too."

She shook her head.

"Yet it would be so very easy." He let his voice tease, offering boundless pleasure, gently, insistently. "Just follow me up the stairs, throw aside your wig and coat, and don't walk on past my bedroom door."

It was as if desperation beat at her. He was certain she couldn't resist much longer. She would surely lift her head to press her mouth onto his? Then she would come with him into the warmth of his bed. She would willingly, openly, share the ecstasy of the body. Anticipation raced sweetly through muscles and bones, filling his empty palms, throbbing in the groin.

"I cannot take the risk," she whispered.

"What risk? A secretary is never an equal partner. A lover always is."

He touched his lips once, softly, to the side of her mouth, letting her feel his absolute control, though honey saturated his tongue.

Her mouth trembled, but she did not kiss back. Though the blood's longing still illuminated her skin, though the fine tremor of desire still fired her lips, her eyes filled with scorn. *How the devil do you think about desire and scorn in one breath?*

"Lud, sir, next you'll tell me that no lover has ever tired of you yet."

"Why is that important?"

"At Grenham Hall, when I so clumsily interrupted, it was obvious that Lady Grenham had just invited you back into her bed. You would no doubt have accepted, except that you were already confident of Lady Charlotte's favors that night—until my presence disrupted that, too. Now you simply look for the nearest female to fill your empty bed."

"That's nonsense and you know it!"

"Nevertheless, I don't feel like obliging you."

"Because you think that I couldn't love you as you deserve?"

"As I *deserve*? And how is that? Perhaps you loved Lady Grenham. I don't know. But if you did, your affection was set aside easily enough. How proud you are of breaking hearts, instead! Even Lady Charlotte's!"

I stretch forth my hands unto thee; my soul gaspeth unto thee as a thirsty land.

His key rattled as Dove unlocked the door.

"Believe what you like, ma'am. But for God's sake believe this: I have *never* shared Lady Charlotte Rampole's bed, nor wished to. I have most certainly not broken her heart. The extent of the intimacy between myself and that lady is what you witnessed yourself on an icy terrace in the moonlight. Faith, Sylvie, since the minute I laid eyes on you, you're the only woman I have wanted."

With a small shock he realized that every word of that was true. *The only woman I have wanted!*

She looked desperate—as if fighting to hide a vulnerability that she thought might destroy her.

"Then how very unfortunate," she said.

The door gaped open onto the shadowed spaces of the hallway. He could not, in honor, press her any further. Leaving her standing in the doorway, Dove strode away. His steps resounded harshly on the treads.

It would be so very easy. Just follow me up the stairs, throw aside your wig and coat, and don't walk on past my bedroom door.

Yet he knew she wouldn't come. In spite of her burning desire, she wouldn't come.

DOVE TOSSED ASIDE HIS WIG AND PACED THE DARK CONFINES of his bedchamber. The great bed lay ready. *There will be a roaring fire in my bedchamber. Clean sheets heated with a warming pan. Hot mulled wine or hot chocolate with brandy—*

Damnation! *So very easy?* To make love to a woman who might only be here in his house in order to destroy him?

I have never bedded an enemy in my life.

Ruthlessly he repressed his desire and made himself think.

She had known Yveshire before. Perhaps it had been exactly as she'd said—they had met for the first time after the sleigh ride. Yet why would the duke seek out a boy he didn't know, just to warn him not to become familiar with a rogue? Worse: Yveshire's town residence—that splendid ducal mansion standing in its own grounds—was close enough to Number Eighteen. That might be a coincidence, but then again, it might not.

It seemed fantastic, impossible, but if it was true, she was part of a plot that had been in the making for a very long time. Her arrival in England, her encounter with Lady Charlotte to make a wager over a stranger's cravat, her note to Meg, nothing had been random. Everything had been planned from the very beginning.

He was burning with desperate desire for a woman who might prove to be his downfall.

And Yveshire might be behind it.

He waited until he was sure that she had gone to bed, then he slipped back down the stairs and walked out into the stable yard. Ice lay dissolved into puddles on the cobbles. He strode through the slush and stepped into the stable. Abdiel lifted his head and nickered softly. Dove pushed aside the black mane to rub his palm down the stallion's warm neck.

He waited for the best part of an hour, while the bay dozed, breathing softly into the hay-scented darkness, but there was no Tanner Brink.

"I TRUST YOU SPENT THE NIGHT IN AN AGONY OF IMPATIENCE, ma'am," Dove said without further preamble as he strode into his study the next afternoon.

Sylvie looked up, swallowing nervousness, forcing herself to act as if nothing had changed. Dove was wearing the simplest of his clothes: charcoal coat, plain ivory satin waistcoat, and white linen shirt. His own dark hair tumbled over his forehead, the gleaming tail pulled back over his collar at the back with silk ribbon.

Her heart skipped as a smile creased his cheeks.

"Impatience? Why?" she asked.

"After our little contretemps in the doorway last night, you're not afraid that I will simply dismiss you?"

"A little—but I'm hardly impatient for it."

He bowed, with no hint of threat or scorn. "You should be impatient, ma'am, for my apology. I was at fault. I was importunate, when I said I would not be. I offer no excuses."

"No apology is necessary," she said. "I'm not a prudish female, given to megrims and fainting."

Dove glanced up at her beneath his lashes, his smile rich with that brilliant awareness of the absurdities of life. "Only once. In my bedchamber."

She grinned back. "Which was very feeble of me! It won't happen again."

"Faith," he said. "I've been wondering ever since why I didn't press my advantage then, while I had you at my mercy in my bed."

She laughed. "I thought so! Your apology is entirely empty."

"Oh, no. The apology is real. I'll just have to make you another one, when I finally *do* take advantage."

"You could have pressed your advantage long before that," she said. "I wasn't in your bed when we first met, but I was very help-lessly tied to it."

"Then you are fortunate that I am so much the gentleman."

Pushing back her chair, she stood and walked to the window. Winter daylight straggled through fog and drifting coal smoke. Frost flowers bloomed haphazardly in the corner of each pane. She laid her palm flat against the glass and watched the ice petals blur and melt into dew.

A *gentleman*. What did that mean? Simply education and good manners? Or did it always imply honor and kindness and gallantry? Discomfort burned, sliding down her throat. When had Dove ever shown her anything less? Yet she had a mission. She had seen proof. And she thought he was still hiding a great deal.

"While whoever I really am, I must be an adventuress," she said, "or I'd never have invaded your life dressed in breeches?"

"Adventuress? That's rather harsh. Shall we just say that you're a resourceful—if brave and foolhardy—young woman?"

"Faith! More compliments? I was ungracious last night. I accused you of callousness, of being heartless. That isn't what I truly believe."

She heard him walk to the desk, where he began to leaf through papers. "I would love to hear what you do truly believe, ma'am."

"I don't think that you're a rake, or that you discard lovers carelessly. That's not why I won't become your mistress."

"It's not?" His voice was light. "Then why not?"

"Because I think you may in fact be the opposite. I think you may be a man who perhaps gives his heart far too easily."

"Whereas you have learned to guard yours like the darkest pirate treasure. You have known so many lovers?"

Her pulse hammered at the risk. She hadn't meant to talk about any of this, yet she heard her voice plunge on, as if desperate—or as if suddenly free? "I thought I had fallen in love once. After my husband died, there was a man I could have loved, or did love, perhaps—"

"What happened?"

The outline of her hand, palm print and fingers, spread moisture over the window, a small transparent space on the rippled glass. *I see a long life. I see riches. I see little sorrows and great joys. I see one great love, almost lost, then regained—*

"There was no possible future for us. He was an aristocrat. He had to make a splendid marriage, not wed a penniless widow. We think that men aren't romantic, that men don't have hearts, yet I believe this man almost broke his heart over me, but only because he'd already lost it to another woman who wouldn't have him."

"If he had loved you, he'd have married you anyway and defied the world to comment."

"Even if he *had* thought that, I couldn't have married him. I didn't love him enough. Don't you see? I don't know how to love with all my heart. I don't know if I ever could."

She dropped her forehead against the icy window, appalled that she had strayed so close to the truth, that she seemed to have forgotten that she was here to manipulate and deceive. How very close to madness, when to enthrall her quarry—and coldly take him to her bed, when and if it became necessary—was her sole assignment here!

"You're telling me that it isn't *your* vulnerability that you wish to protect," he asked, "but mine?"

"Yes—perhaps! I'm not sure. You, not I, said that making love is a skill for the heart."

His footsteps were soft on the carpet as he walked up behind her. "Allow me to take that risk for myself, ma'am."

Sylvie rubbed the cold dampness from her skin and turned to face him. *Honor and kindness and gallantry.* Was it real? *For what if you fall in love with me, Dove, then discover that I've betrayed you to Yveshire: the one man who truly hates you—and the one man I once almost loved?*

"May I—in spite of what now lies between us—remain in your employ?" she asked.

He smiled down at her. "Of course. If I dismiss you, I lose all chance of your redeeming your debt—"

"You can always just have me thrown in the Fleet, instead."

"—and I would also lose every hope of winning your favors."

"A vain hope," she said honestly. "I am afraid of it."

"Then we are doomed to our cat-and-mouse game, ma'am. I shall continue to teach you how to be a man, until you decide of your own free will that—at least as far as I'm concerned—you would much rather become a woman again."

"It won't happen." She tilted up her chin, called on all of her courage, and grinned. "Being male is far too much fun."

"Excellent," he said. "Pray, go and change into your shabby blue jacket. Because I could never take a lady where we're going now."

THEY LEFT THE HOUSE BUNDLED IN PLAIN CLOAKS AND traveled into the oldest part of London. When Sylvie climbed from her sedan chair, Dove was already waiting. It was the first time she had seen him go out without his wig. Beneath his three-cornered hat, his dark hair framed his face with deceptive casualness. He looked dangerous, though the gold-mounted smallsword, Meg's pretty gift to her lover, had been left in his townhouse. Instead he carried a heavy stick with a brass knob. There was probably a blade hidden inside. She knew that pistols, primed and charged, already nestled heavily in his pockets.

He turned and strode away, trusting her to follow. Carriages, wagons, and pedestrians flooded past. Overhanging signs filled the space above their heads: cordwainers, coopers, chandlers. The maze of narrow alleys and thoroughfares was thronged with artisans and apprentices, vagabonds and vagrants.

Each street held a particular odor: of leather or burning metal or wax. Goldsmiths clustered together. Shoemakers vied with each other from adjacent shopfronts or stalls. Every main street was littered with small stands—sometimes no more than a stool and a basket—blocking foot traffic. Their proprietors yelled themselves hoarse, hawking ribbons, buttons, hot pies. All of London seemed to be selling or being sold—unless it was begging, filthy, and covered in rags.

Sylvie kept close at Dove's heels, glad of their inconspicuous clothes. Anyone giving the appearance of too much wealth in these streets would have his pocket picked soon enough. Though the atmosphere might seem to be filled with a hearty good-fellowship, the threat of violence swaggered just beneath it.

A gang of youths burst out of a side alley. A lethal concentration flickered over Dove's face for a moment. He spun Sylvie into a doorway, that lithe tension echoed in the line of shoulder and back, as the boys rudely shoved them aside, shouting insults. One of them slashed at a puddle with a stick as he passed, spraying their stockings with muck, yet Dove let them run on by unmolested.

"You don't leap to defend our honor?" Sylvie asked.

"What the devil does honor have to do with rampaging apprentices?"

His question sounded merely amused, though the side of his cloak was soaked.

"You'll let them get away with that? I thought gentlemen were very prickly about such things."

Someone yelled. She glanced over her shoulder. The boys had overturned a brazier full of baked apples. While gorging on sugar-spiced hot apple, they also snatched uncooked fruit to stuff into their pockets. The apple seller flailed about with a cudgel, without much effect. Fruit began to fly, smashing into passing carriages, knocking the hats from two clergymen, breaking a window in a splendid shattering of glass. Hot coals tumbled over the slushy cobbles, smoking in mounds of horse dung, hissing and fizzling as they succumbed to the damp.

Ragged children instantly swarmed like wasps to scavenge apple pulp from doorways and cobbles. Sylvie choked back heartbreak and anger. This was a world entirely out of her power to influence—except that war was worse, and perhaps her work had helped to delay or limit that scourge, at least.

The boys ran off, swearing like sailors and covering their retreat with another fusillade of produce.

"You suggest that I bring order to London's streets single-handedly?" Dove asked.

"No, but someone should teach those boys a lesson—that's anyone's natural impulse, male or female, I should think. Perhaps if you'd distracted their attention onto us, that apple cart would still be standing upright."

He caught her arm and pulled her to his side as another group of apprentices ran past, snatching the occasional hat or wig from a furious citizen. Dove hauled Sylvie into a narrow alley, filled with stalls selling used clothing. The shouts and yells were instantly left behind, muffled by the maze of fabric.

"So I should have leaped to defend both the innocent apple seller and my own male pride?" Dove asked, pushing past a display of soiled frock coats.

"Not necessarily, but don't tell me that the thought didn't cross your mind!"

He glanced down at her and smiled. "My mind is, apparently, entirely too transparent to your sharp observation. Here were my choices: allow the idiocy of youth to pass by unchallenged, or object to their unseemly manners and demand that they apologize—even though nothing much was damaged except our dignity—which would have led to a fight."

Sylvie pressed past several shirts hanging from a rack. "I do hope it wasn't my shabby presence that hindered you. If it had come to fisticuffs, I assure you I'd have been very proficient at scampering out of the way and throwing things."

"I tremble at the thought."

"Yet you were tempted?"

"Temptation and action are two different things, as you and I have been proving to each other on a daily basis for some time. However, we are—in both areas—now beating a decorous retreat, instead."

She was forced to laugh. "And discretion was without question the better part of valor this time? Faith, I don't blame you. If it *had* come to a fight, in spite of my long-range assistance, you'd have been beaten to a pulp far more soundly than the apples. With one against more than a dozen, you couldn't possibly have won."

"On the contrary, had I chosen to fight, I would most certainly have won."

"Against so many?" She gave him an innocent grin. "I only press the point, you understand, so that I may learn more about the mysteries of the male mind. Your claim of such prowess is obviously just bravado."

"My claim is simply the fortunate truth." He ducked to avoid an entanglement of petticoats slung from a pole. "I am perfectly capable of protecting you."

"So if we were attacked in earnest, I wouldn't need to dance like a dervish and fling cobblestones? After all, you taught me how to throw."

He stopped and turned to her, framed by lengths of silk tossed over a tall rack. The fabric moved, stirred by a cold wind, creating a momentary illusion of chivalry and exotic settings—as if he really would be equally at home in a medieval battle, fighting to the death.

"Fling anything you like, but don't expect me to escalate any confrontation, especially with brainless boys. I am armed and trained in the art of self-defense. Those apprentices are not. If it were necessary, I would use my unpleasant superiority of skill and weaponry without hesitation, but against such odds—and in a street brawl—someone would undoubtedly be killed, though the fatalities would not have been yours or mine."

"Then I'm forced to shelter behind your stout sword arm," she said. "If I were faced with ravishment and fisticuffs, I'd be very glad to see Sir Lancelot thundering to my rescue—unless I had a blade of my own, of course. Can you teach me that, too?"

He turned and walked on. Scarlet and beige, verdigris and crimson were all left behind as they emerged onto another street. A stream ran between the buildings, the clack and slither of a waterwheel resounding somewhere out of sight. The overhead signs creaking on their chains blocked out almost all of the light now. The winter day was drawing in, darkness descending through the misty air like ink mixed with water. A lamplighter was coming their way, dragging the scent of burning oil and damp smoke in his wake.

"The answer is no," he said.

"Why not? Ladies do learn to fence and shoot. Then I could defend myself."

Dove stopped. He touched the corner of her jaw, just below her ear. His fingertips lay lightly on her skin, yet long, deep waves of disturbance eddied out through her blood.

"There are very real differences between the sexes and this is one of them, Sylvie. Your game is amusing, but it is just a game. The one thing I won't—and can't—teach you is how to fight like a man. You do not want to learn how to kill."

He dropped his hand. His linen cuffs immediately covered the long bones and tendons, the network of veins, the lean strength of his fingers. Her own, in contrast, seemed puny, terrifyingly delicate. She hid her hands behind her back.

"It's all right," she said. "If it ever comes to a pitched battle, I'll very happily leave all the killing and maiming to you."

Dove flashed her a quick smile. "No maiming. If it's ever required, I promise to lay all of your enemies stone dead at your feet."

It was a joke, of course. Yet she believed that if he had decided to fight off London's mob, he would have taken on any odds and laughed at the challenge. He would have done it with brilliance and ruthless efficiency and—very probably—a strange and terrible beauty.

Art, he had said. The *art* of self-defense.

The deadly male arts that women pretended to abhor, pretended not to want to know about. Yet—if they were lucky enough to have it—all women kept that knowledge deep at the heart, like a precious treasure: *This man will protect me, even if it means taking the life of another man. No harm can possibly come to me, as long as I am with him. And his fatal skills are* arts, *lovely and awe-inspiring, as his mind and body are lovely and awe-inspiring—and so very, very different from mine.*

It was a powerful aphrodisiac.

"While you and I emerge without a scratch," she said. "Meanwhile, any apples that were lost are now warming the stomachs of children who otherwise never taste fruit."

"Including those apprentices."

"Why aren't they working?" she asked. "It's not a holiday."

"Holiday? They get three one-day holidays a year: Christmas, Easter, and Whitsun. So they make recreations of their own, a momentary escape from exploitation and brutality. When they are forced back to work, as they will be, they'll be beaten for it. But any boy will happily trade a beating for a hot apple and a momentary taste of freedom."

Sylvie looked back up at him, at all that treacherous certainty and confidence. "A satisfactory conclusion for everyone—except the apple seller, of course, who gave more to charity than he could probably afford."

"It won't bankrupt him," Dove replied, "because he stole most of his apples to begin with and will easily steal more. Shall we go in?"

The stream carried a swirl of rubbish and ice beneath the pavement. The noise of the wheel rose and fell. They were standing beside a low doorway. Dove opened the door, ducked his head, and disappeared inside. Sylvie stepped in behind him, then stopped, blinking, trying to adjust to the sudden change in light and the rackety assault on her ears.

"Mr. Dovenby's here!" someone yelled above the din. "Look sharp, lads!"

THE PLACE WAS LITTERED WITH PAPER. PAPER IN STACKS, ON shelves, on countertops. Paper hanging like rows of cotton handkerchiefs from cords strung across the ceiling. Paper bound and unbound, cluttering dingy shelves, bursting from boxes and packets, drifting underfoot like dirty snow.

Over and on and around the paper, ink formed phalanxes of words, marching across page after page. Or ink flowed and danced, forming capricious curves, shaping pictures of people and ships and horses.

The racket was inescapably merry. Men laughed, talked, argued. Presses clacked and turned. The inked pads of the breyers thumped. Metal clattered as nimble fingers sorted through boxes of type, while their owners cursed and mumbled and formed silent syllables, both with earnest lips and on the plates. The entire place stank of tallow and ink. In spite of that first cry, no one seemed to be paying them much attention.

"Welcome to another of my business ventures," Dove said.

"A printer's?" she replied. "You own a *printer's?*"

"I do what I can to further civilization."

Sylvie propped herself against a huge stack of paper and laughed. "*This* is what's so wicked?"

"Oh, it's very wicked," he replied. "You haven't yet seen what we print."

An older man had stepped out of a back room. He came hurrying over, his face beaming beneath the tonsured remains of red hair.

"Mr. Fennimore," Dove said. "Meet Mr. George White, my new secretary. We need to make Mr. White conversant with everything we do here. We shall retreat to your office. Bring us some samples, if you please."

"*Everything?*"

Dove winked as he unclasped his cloak, took Sylvie's, and handed them to the man. Oil lights shone mercilessly on his bald spot as Mr. Fennimore hurried away.

Sylvie picked up a printed sheet from a pile on the table beside her and laughed. "But this would seem to be an exhortation to virtue!"

Dove plucked it from her fingers. "To my shame, among other less wholesome things, we produce improving tracts. This one seems to be encouraging the use of soap." He picked up another sheet from the pile. "Here's one that suggests that infants should be fed more than once a day." He set it into her hands. "You'll probably approve of that."

"But nothing *serious?*" she teased, studying it. "No sermons on *impractical* virtue and morality?"

"Ah, you think we should address less tangible virtues than soap, or milk for babies?"

"Why not?" she said. "Bible verses? Why not expound on the most righteous path to heaven?"

"Why the devil would I want to preach to either the rabble or the quality about righteousness?"

"Obviously, you do not." She seized a bound pamphlet and rapidly perused the cover. The front was imaginatively decorated with a woodcut of a hanging. "The quality read this?"

Dove leaned back against a set of high shelves, arms folded, framed by a snowfall of paper.

"Penny dreadfuls are our bread and butter—the more sensational the better—and everyone reads them from the king to the dung carrier, if he can read. That particular one is an account of the latest murder trial and execution, with the moral painted in shockingly loud colors. That next stack is composed mostly of posters, I believe, proclaiming a mill to be held later next week—another excuse for apprentices to brawl through the streets."

"They'll play truant to attend a boxing match?" she asked.

"They play truant whenever they can. The cause of today's little riot was a bearbaiting involving a rather toothless old bear and a couple of mangy hounds."

"So what else do you print?"

"Come with me and I'll show you."

Sylvie followed Dove deeper into the building. Doors opened and closed. Noise flooded and receded like the tide. In a quiet room near the back of the building, several men sat in rows at high benches, working with metal tools on sheets of copper.

"The engraving is done here," Dove said.

He showed her some of the plates and the original artwork, before they walked on. None of the engravers had risen from their stools. Though smiling and exchanging greetings with Dove, they still sat. Sylvie looked back at their heads, bent in a solemn row, steadily working.

"The maimed," she said quietly.

"Old soldiers," Dove replied. "A carter, a bricklayer, and a drunk who fell asleep outside in the winter. My captive workforce, you could say. So they are missing a limb. They still have human dignity, remarkable talent, and nimble fingers—and they don't play truant. Peter has never touched liquor again."

They climbed a few stairs, shoes rapping over the wooden floor.

A sallow-faced man looked up and winked as Dove walked up to him. His glance seemed sly, filled with secret humor. At a desk in a private corner of his own, he was carefully copying something in longhand. Dove's dark head bent close to the man's wig as they exchanged a few words in private.

"Who was that?" Sylvie asked as they walked into the next room, a tidy workshop where apprentices from St. John's were using the coloring skills they had learned at the foundling home.

"Tom Henley? He was a forger once, until the law breathed a little too warmly down his neck. Very clever fingers and an unbeatable eye for making copies."

"A forger?"

"Don't worry, his skills are no longer used to defraud. Tom Henley openly complains that his unique talent is wasted here, but a decent salary and the fear of the gallows is cure enough."

"Seriously? This man could fake anything?" Wings beat in her blood, fluttering shock and joy and whipping up a mad deluge of thoughts.

"Anything. I caught him once practicing my signature. Rather well, as it happens."

Her heart turned like a bird freed from a cage. "Your *signature*? He can counterfeit your handwriting?"

"Most definitely! Any documents faked by Tom Henley would fool anyone—even me!"

A forger! It was such an obvious solution. Someone like this— even this very man, Tom Henley—might have written all of the documents she had seen in Yveshire's study!

"You're not concerned that he'll use such a skill to defraud you?"

"It's more than his life is worth and he knows it."

"But once a thief, always a thief, they say. How can you really trust him?"

Dove grinned at her. "I pay him enough."

A forger! Her rush of mad exuberance at the idea made her almost dizzy. Someone other than Dove must have destroyed the duke's brother. Someone who wouldn't hesitate to hire Tom Henley—or another villain like him—to fake his master's handwriting for page after page. *I caught him once practicing my signature.* Such a simple answer to all of her distress. Otherwise, it was too great a coincidence that a forger was working here for Dove.

Dove led her through workroom after workroom, then back down the steps into a small office, where a welcome fire crackled in the grate. He closed the door. Their cloaks hung from a hook on the back. The noise subsided to a dull hum, only to burst in again when Mr. Fennimore stepped in a few moments later with arms overflowing. An avalanche of books and paper slid onto the desk.

"Thank you, sir," Dove said. "That will be all."

The redheaded man bowed and retreated, closing the door once again against the racket of a printer's shop in full swing.

Sylvie sat down and propped her feet on the edge of the fender, letting the fire dry her shoes and mud-splashed stockings. Dove set a small stack of booklets into her hands. She leafed through them, barely able to focus for the wild joy surging in her veins. *A forger!*

In spite of the beat of emotion, her hands remained steady. However intoxicating the thought, she must keep it to herself. Yet tomorrow she could tell Yveshire and end her mission: *Examine this man Tom Henley, Your Grace. He has the dishonest skills. He has the access and opportunity. He vents aloud his resentment that Dovenby gives him insufficient outlet for his talent.* Then Dove need never know her real motives for invading his life.

The birds in her veins burst into song.

"We print fiction by the ream," he said. "The very best I can do for London's poor is give them a good reason to learn their letters. I cannot feed all of their bodies, but I do what I can to feed their souls."

Sylvie held up a cover showing a grotesque woodcut of a man stabbing another in the ribs. "This feeds the soul?"

He took it from her fingers. "Absolutely," he said. "Most people's lives in our great capital are risky, dangerous, and cruel. The real world offers plenty of chaos. But within the confines of these covers, the murderer is caught and hanged, the poor widow and her children are succored by a kindly stranger—a childhood sweetheart, who will marry her before the end of the tale—and stability and justice are restored to the universe. The story confirms the moral order and keeps hope alive."

"I am suitably chastised," she said. "I'll never look down my nose at such novels again."

"Lurid tales of murder are especially popular, but they're followed very closely by pretty stories in verse about rogues and ladies who ought to know better—and everyone reads those, as well."

Sylvie leaned back in her chair to gaze up at him. "Romances?"

His eyes seemed luminous with gaiety. "Of course. One of the few really valid forms of literature."

She laughed. "I'm not entirely sure that you don't mean that."

Dove raised both brows. "Faith, I mean every word of it. I offer entertainment, which is just art in a different disguise. You don't think that's important?"

"No doubt, though humans can survive without art."

Candlelight glimmered over his cheeks as he smiled. "Which is where you are wrong. Art is really all that makes us human. Without it, we're little better than beasts."

He laid down the murderous tale and tossed her another small booklet. On the cover, a woman with unbound hair straggling over her white collar wrung her hands at a window, while a man in a wide hat with a dashing feather galloped his horse away into the dark.

"A Cavalier and a Puritan's daughter?" she said. "An impossible conflict!"

"And a tale that confirms ideals of love and commitment, sacrifice and selflessness."

She grinned, opening the leaflet. "Which you know for a fact, because you've read it."

He flung aside his hat and ran both hands through his hair. Shadows and dusk flared beneath his fingers.

"No, but I'm sure I've read far more romances than you have," he said.

" 'Poor lovelorn maid, with heart aflare, her lover's loins still hopes to share—' " She looked up, grinning. "But these verses are execrable!"

Dove laughed. "Yet the message is so vital that it enthralls readers anyway—"

"The Cavalier comes back for her, I suppose? Does it end happily?"

"Ah, so you want to find out what happens—in spite of the hideous poetry?"

She threw the booklet at him. "Of course!"

He caught it with one hand to toss the merry Cavalier back onto the table. "Since I haven't read this particular romance, I have no idea. But the story will affirm the triumph of love over suffering, or readers wouldn't buy it."

A coal fell in the grate. Sparks ran like fireworks across the soot at the back of the chimney as if to echo the surge of joy in her heart. "If only it were so simple in real life," she said.

"It is," Dove replied. "I can't think of anything much simpler than love."

Sylvie leaned forward. Small tendrils of steam rose from her dirt-splashed stockings. *He was innocent. And she was not. She had intended to betray him.*

"There we disagree," she said. "I can't think of anything much more complicated than love."

His heels rapped as he strode the length of the small room, leaving her sitting by herself at the fireplace. Loneliness swirled like a damp fog. Sylvie turned to look after him, as if the sight of his broad back might provide more warmth than the coals. He was standing, apparently examining some prints. Views of London, plans for streets and markets covered the wall.

"Lud, ma'am. Almost everything is more complicated than love," he said. "Especially the absurdity of trying to maintain a platonic friendship with a lady dressed in breeches."

"Why?" she said. "Why can't a man just be friends with a woman, in the same way that he is friends with other men?"

He turned around, leaned his shoulders back against the wall, and crossed his arms over his chest. "Part of your answer is there on the table. Help yourself—if you dare. Though you're under no obligation to do so, of course."

Sylvie picked up another booklet and opened the cover, then dropped it as if the paper had leaped into flames in her fingers. Hot blood rushed to her face, streaming up her cheeks and down her neck. From sheer surprise, she burst out laughing, knowing that she was blushing down to her toes.

"Faith, sir!" Her heart hammered, but merriment raced through her bones. "I don't know what to say!"

"Ah," he said, smiling. "So your courage deserts you, after all? I thought you were made of sterner stuff. By all means, avert your virtuous eyes, if you wish, and we'll go home."

She made a face at him, then retrieved the book from the floor.

"If you laugh at me, I'll never forgive you," she said. "But I never before saw anything like this in my life!"

"And you've tried to tell me that you have *not* led an innocent life?"

Sylvie dropped back into her chair. "Innocence has nothing to say to the matter."

"But you're still afraid to look?"

She bit her lip and shook her head. "Not afraid, just a little taken aback."

Mirth suffused his face, but he had the courtesy to look away. "I told you that what I did was very wicked. Now you know."

Sylvie deliberately turned her back on him and opened the covers. Though her blood still raced hot and fast through her veins, giggles surged to the surface, like bubbles in champagne, as she leafed through the pages.

"I suspect simply being male is the key to all this," she said. "But how could you?"

CHAPTER TWELVE

"I DON'T DRAW THEM," HE SAID. "I JUST PRINT THEM. FORTU-nately, the demand is insatiable—and for far more wicked ones than that."

Sylvie looked up. Unholy mirth still permeated his gaze, danced about the curl of his nostrils and tightly compressed lips.

"They *can* be more wicked than this?" she asked.

He nodded, yet as their eyes met, glee exploded between them. Glee at all the absurdity, mischief, and sheer exuberance of human inventiveness. Instantly they were both roaring with laughter. Cleansing, glorious, uproarious laughter.

"*Far* more wicked than that," he said between gasps. "What do you have there? *The Apprentice and the Duchess's Lady's Maid, Or the Further Adventures of Buxom Bettie?*"

"*Buxom Bettie!*" She clutched at her sides. "Spare me! I'm going to get hiccups."

"Lud, ma'am! If *Buxom Bettie* so undoes you, what hope when a gentleman offers Mr. George White a pinch from his naughtiest snuffbox?"

"A *snuffbox*? Gentlemen carry erotic *snuffboxes*? How could anything be naughtier than this?"

"Allow me to show you—if you promise not to die from an apoplexy of mirth."

"I promise," she said, trying to choke back her hilarity. "Oh, I promise."

Wringing one hand over his mouth, he strode up to the table and began to sort through the booklets still lying there. His lips quivered with barely controlled mirth.

"This one's translated from the French, but illustrated here in London. Far more sophisticated and very wicked indeed. And here's another, pure Parisian, both language and etchings. Hmm, you are fluent in French. I'm not sure you should look at this one."

Sylvie tossed aside the tale of the duchess's maid and leaned over the table to snatch the Parisian book from his grasp. Dove flung both hands wide as, triumphant and careless with laughter, she spun aside out of his reach and opened the covers. Heat, merriment, and scorching embarrassment flooded her bones.

"Lud!" She folded back into her chair, weak with hilarity. "Is this *really* what men like?"

"Alas, to our shame, that's exactly what men like. Unless you understand this, you will never—I guarantee—learn to act convincingly as male."

"Then men are very strange creatures," she said, flipping through the pages. "Absolutely nothing is left to the imagination."

He plucked the book from her fingers as if to peruse the etchings all the better.

"Yet the illustrations are very fine, don't you think? Most lovingly crafted."

"They certainly demonstrate the act of procreation with a great deal of enthusiasm—"

"—and considerable artistry and charm."

She had a killing stitch and tears were running down her face, but she grabbed another booklet, lavishly illustrated with hand-colored prints.

"Oh, I don't deny the charm," she said between rushes of mirth and wry mortification. "But I feel as if a fire had been lit in my neck."

"What's your objection?" he said, looking over her shoulder. "Both ladies are most affectionately drawn. The brunette in particular is very fetching. And the gentleman is showing them both a most appropriate attention in the circumstances, considering that he has forgotten all of his clothing except for his stockings and wig."

Sylvie dropped the book to her lap and buried her mouth in one hand, rocking back and forth as she tried desperately to stifle her laughter. She felt alight. All stress had fled, as if the birds in her veins had flown up to the ceiling in great liberated flocks.

"Though I'm not sure of that one," he said. "If you look at that, you'll never forgive me."

She glanced up at him, at the loveliness of his clever mouth, his clear skin—and her womb melted. Her blood coursed, giddy and hot. Her groin burned for him. Her breasts ached, full and heavy.

"Which one?" she asked in exquisite desperation.

"The illustration now fallen open beneath your fingers. A young man dressed in nothing but his shirt appears to have climbed in at a lady's bedroom window. The lady boasts a rather luxuriant profusion of blond curls, and is smiling with obvious relish at the young man."

Sylvie wiped away tears to look at the drawing. Her blood sang with sensual responsiveness to the clear, erotic invitation of the print. "At least she is dressed in a shift—"

"An entirely transparent shift that has managed to slip from one shoulder to reveal one stunningly round breast and a delectable glimpse of the other—" His hand touched the page, riveting her attention to his lean fingers, the sensitive pad of his thumb. "At the same time," Dove added, "in distinct defiance of gravity—just like the gentleman's shirt—the shift has slid up her legs to display two beribboned garters—"

Desire almost robbed her of breath. She had to swallow before she could speak, yet she interrupted him. "Two garters?" she said gaily. "She is also revealing an expanse of white thigh, along with—"

"Unless you wish to slay me on the spot, pray don't name what else is revealed, ma'am!"

Her soul alight, her bones scorched with flames of desire, Sylvie subsided to the floor. "But it's painted with such allure and imagination!"

Dove rescued the book, which had slipped to the grate. She stared at him, knowing he was no more immune to the erotica than she, that his hands craved her naked skin, that his cock throbbed for her, that his mouth and tongue were as on fire with passion as hers.

"And a most inventive palette," he said gravely.

"—while the young man's anatomy has undergone such a remarkable change—certainly one of a magnitude impossible in nature!"

"It has?" Dove asked innocently. "I didn't notice. I was only looking at the lady's endowments—a further difference between us, ma'am."

She closed her eyes, weak with longing for him, as hilarity surged in a cleansing tide through her blood—then she began, rather painfully, to hiccup.

$\mathcal{D}$OVE PRESSED A GLASS OF BRANDY INTO HER HAND. SHE HAD no idea where or when he'd obtained it. She only knew that they were sitting companionably opposite each other at the fireplace, and that she felt as open and clear-eyed as a child at Christmas. The hum of the printing works had died away to silence some time ago. Everyone except themselves had gone home. The small room felt warm and dark and intimate.

Illuminated by firelight, Dove sprawled in his chair, cravat and coat tossed aside, dark hair caressing his forehead. He seemed more relaxed than she'd ever seen him. Reflected flames teased up and down his shirtsleeves, cast dancing shadows over his lean fingers. A man in a man's world.

The brandy burned its sweet path down her throat. The hiccups were gone.

"Very well," she said. "Now I know. You print blatantly wicked erotica, fully illustrated with every detail."

"Are you offended?"

Avoiding his gaze, she sipped at her glass and glanced absently into the fire. Offended? No, she was charmed and happy and relieved. So this was his secret! The flames flickered, forming and destroying tiny castles and faces and forests. More explicit images also seemed to dance in the fire, tiny men and women coupling and loving and breaking apart. Like those wayward figures, she was still molten, aroused, and alight with feminine awareness.

"No. Not at all! I suppose I should be, yet they're conceived with such simplicity and humor and love of life and real affection—and such a vivid imagination! But who writes all those stories? Are the drawings done here?"

"I hire several independent writers and translators and artists. One of my writers is a gentleman who's using this means to work himself out of debtor's prison. Most of the rest work at home."

"I thought such things would be sordid. They aren't, not at all."

"Perhaps because so many of my artists are female."

She looked back at him, meeting his smile with one of her own. A strange, almost magical bond held them together now at this fireplace, enclosed in the glow of the coal and the one lamp, burning steadily on the mantel. The desk with its sweet feast of erotica slept quietly behind them in the darkness.

"Women?"

"It's one of the few ways a widow—or any woman with children but no husband—can earn a decent living in her home. They're a wonderful pool of talent that might otherwise be used less innocently on the streets."

Her brandy glass gleamed, mirroring tiny flames as she set it down by the grate. "Do women write the stories, too?"

"Yes. You think females are strangers to honest lust?"

Sylvie leaned back and stretched, almost as if wearing breeches and a man's wig had transformed her into a new person: a younger, simpler person, still eager for all the rich experience of the world. Though that person, of course, was feeling very female at the moment and she was rather intensely aware of honest lust.

"It's obvious that these ladies, at least, understand that very well. I imagine this trade is very lucrative?"

"It finances everything else that I do: all those improving tracts that we sell below cost; the romances and the penny dreadfuls that barely break even; the prints and pictures of London that the apprentices learn to color—though the coloring of the erotic illustrations is all done by grown men, I hasten to add. But if it were not for this trade, I couldn't pay decent wages. I'd be forced to exploit the labor of the men and women who work for me, as their labor is exploited in every other workshop in London."

"This is also what pays for St. John's?"

"Gentlemen will pay a fortune for almost any explicit erotic fantasy, and then they'll pay another fortune for a different one."

Sylvie smiled up at him, feeling lazy and safe, and—in spite of the subject of their conversation and the warmth still eddying through her bones—oddly innocent. She hadn't laughed like that in years. Nor had she ever felt quite this wild firing of the senses at being alone with a man. *This* man.

"Those grown men who do the etching and coloring," she said, "like to indulge in a fantasy of overblown wishes."

"Are you sure they're overblown?" he said. "Ours is an age of excess, after all."

She laughed. "Not *that* much excess! At least when it comes to human anatomy. But you're not in danger of prosecution for this?"

"Not as long as we're circumspect. And we are very circumspect. Word of mouth, private subscription, availability limited only to gentlemen of sufficient means and absolute discretion."

"And you keep your accounts in code."

He smiled and reached his long legs to a stool, where he propped up his feet. His eyes closed as his head dropped back to rest against the high wing of his chair. "Am I forgiven for that, too?"

"I do see that you could hardly explain any of this to me before now."

"Then we're friends?" he asked.

The question struck her dumb for a moment, as if he had opened a door to reveal a shining new horizon. She studied his face, the closed lids, the firm mouth—and her womb quaked. She wanted him, she craved him, but yes, they were allies, comrades, *friends*. And now—thanks to Tom Henley—she was certain Dove was innocent.

Coal crumpled, sending up a tiny flame. Light flared over the supple curl of his upper lip, before dying to darkness in his sinfully thick lashes.

Heat pooled in her belly and thighs. She was about to do something she had never done, risk what she had never risked with any man. It wasn't necessary. It wouldn't further her work. Instead, for the first time in her life, she would surrender absolutely, trust absolutely. This would not be in trade for a secret, for survival, for power. This would be simply for joy. Yet perhaps, if she tried to give Dove her soul as well as her body, it might form a mute apology for her more nefarious intentions, because she had so misjudged him.

She stood, doused the lamp, and walked silently to the door to retrieve their dry cloaks. Returning to the fireplace, she spread them on the floor. Dove still lay relaxed, eyes closed, hands folded on his lap. Firelight danced over the planes of his face, the maddeningly desirable curve of male nostril and jaw.

Sylvie slipped off her wig and pulled the pins from her hair, though her fingers shook with nerves.

He didn't move.

She tugged her arms from her coat sleeves, letting the jacket drop to her feet. Fumbling like a child, she stepped out of her shoes and buried her toes in the blue wool, then unfastened her waistcoat.

The flush of desire raced over her skin. A wicked throb pulsed between her legs, heavy and hot. Some of the more sinful erotic books lay open on the table, every man splendidly hard. Honest lust.

Silently she undid the buttons on her breeches. The garment slid down to join the pile on the floor. Her cravat fell open in her hand and she tossed it aside. Dressed in nothing but stockings and long shirt, she stepped up to him and leaned down.

Her heart hammered, pounding strange, exotic rhythms. Her breath feathered over his mouth.

"More than friends," she said.

*M*ORE THAN FRIENDS. APHRODITE SMILED, LAYING OPEN her erotic embrace.

He had lain quietly, eyes shut, the better to hear her subtle movements, the shush of fabric, the slight click of buttons, the tiny resonance like tearing tissue as she combed her fingers through her loosened hair. Aroused, alight, pulse already thundering, he lay still and listened.

Her feet sounded softly on the floor—bare feet. He was fully erect. Using every ounce of self-control he forced himself not to move. Her scent enveloped him.

More than friends. Her lips touched his softly, vivid with brandy.

Her tongue traced his upper lip, following the shape of it, a slick of moisture and heat setting fire to his flesh. He swallowed a groan, concentrating on the sweetness, and opened his mouth. Soft, warm, female, her tongue did the same to his lower lip, her caress firing volleys of madness, pounding away through his blood.

Blind, eyes closed, his fingers clenched on the arms of the chair, he resisted the longing to touch her and allowed her the moment.

She slid her tongue tip inside his mouth, meeting his, then pressed both lips onto his. A man stricken with thirst suddenly offered an oasis, he drank in her kiss and kissed back. Moving only mouth and tongue, eyes closed, hands clamped, he kissed back—a surrender to the long plunge into that profoundly desired dark well. Sensation surged. Intensity fired into white-hot desire.

Sylvie!

Her mouth explored, ravished, seduced. Open, feral. He returned the kiss, thrust for thrust, matching, dancing, heat racing from tongue to groin, throbbing into his erection, cascading into an intensity of aching pleasure.

They came up gasping for breath. Dove thrust both hands into her hair and opened his eyes.

Lapis lazuli had dilated to black, merged into the darkness. Her mouth bloomed, smiling.

She stepped back, flames chasing warmth, as long streamers of blond silk ran through his fingers, capturing her, framing her in gold.

"Sylvie," he said aloud. Her name caught in his stricken throat, as if raked over gravel.

"What did you expect?" she asked. "Showing me all those wicked pictures?"

He released her hair, freeing her. Yet she only moved back one more step to cross her arms, grasp her shirt, and tug it up over her head. A strip of linen had been wound around her breasts. Below the waist, apart from her stockings, she was naked. Curved, female, naked.

"You're the most devastatingly erotic sight I've ever seen," he said.

She stood quietly, looking at him. Her hair streamed in a waterfall over her arms and shoulders. He was on fire. A keen, all-consuming conflagration.

"It's only fair," she said. "I've already seen you."

Mouth suddenly dry, he said nothing.

"I have desired you since that first night. I desire you now. You know that, of course. You have always known it. I thought I had a reason to deny our desire. I don't think that any longer. Make love to me, Dove."

He could barely hear her words over the hammering of his pulse. She was lovely, vulnerable, all the boy's cockiness and bravado fallen away to be replace with exquisite femininity. Her shoulders were rounded, her thighs long and slender. Flaxen dust glimmered, chasing down over her forearms and flank in a pretty fuzz, like the skin of a peach. Firelight stroked lovingly over the curve of her belly, the hourglass of her flank, sparked gold in the delectable down hiding her sex.

Sylvie!

His palms ached with longing as potency throbbed from the groin, scalding his blood and flooding him with concentrated pleasure.

"I'm not a virgin," she said. "You will not be the first."

He stood up and caught a strand of her long hair in his fingers.

"No," he said. "That's where you are wrong. I will be the first."

HIS LONG FINGERS BRUSHED GENTLY OVER HER SHOULDER, moving in her hair as he circled behind her. Warmth cascaded shimmering from his touch, mingled in her blood with the heat from the fireplace, dissolved into the sweet burn consuming her thighs. Sylvie swallowed her gasp, denied the desperate intake of breath as she stood stock still, biting her lip.

He bent his dark head to kiss her once on the shoulder, before he stepped out of his shoes and thrust them away. He pressed tiny kisses across her nape, blowing aside her hair to reach her bare skin, then shrugged out of his waistcoat. Ivory satin slithered to join the pile of clothing on the floor. He moved directly behind her, running tiny bites over the side of her turned jaw, sweetly, sweetly running the tip of his tongue into the curve of her ear. His breeches slid away.

She closed her eyes, recalling that glorious male body striding to his bath, the muscled turn of biceps, carved with beauty and the faint tracery of male veins. Now she felt his arm, smooth as silk, warm as summer, brushing against her own as he deposited his shirt at her feet. His long thighs had been only a sculpture, filling her with yearning. Now they encompassed her nakedness. Now she knew the stark contrast of his hard male flesh and the nudge of his penis, standing erect against her.

She dropped her head back to inhale his scent: dark hair, distinctive maleness, burning brightly beneath the heady tones of brandy and witch hazel and clean linen.

He began to unravel the binding she had used to flatten her breasts, his hands passing nimbly around and around, fingertips feathering over her flesh, as if opening her heart. The strip of linen dropped away. He laid both hands on her waist, moving his fingers reverently, unhurriedly over her flank and hips. Then slowly, slowly, his hands smoothed up over her ribs, over the flurry of her sharp breathing, to cup both breasts in his palms.

"You are so lovely," he murmured.

Sylvie rolled her head against his shoulder and swallowed the delicious, helpless little whimper that shivered up from her belly.

"I promise," he said, "that you will moan aloud. I promise that you will be defenseless in the face of your passion and that I will be the same."

His fingers spread, gently lifting the weight of her breasts, the thumbs circling casually. Exquisite. Ah! Exquisite. A sensitivity so acute at the tips that her knees began to buckle. Soft moans merged into the sensations, sound and touch blending as if a hot sun burned away the distinctions between sky and surf.

"I am already moaning aloud." His erection brushed over her spine and hip and belly as she turned in his arms. "I am already helpless, dear sir. I don't know if I can bear it."

He smiled down at her, his eyes filled with darkness and mystery. "You can bear it," he said.

I HAVE NEVER BEDDED AN ENEMY IN MY LIFE. He smoothed gently over the slender curves of her waist, limber beneath the silk of her hair. Enveloped in firelight, Dove worshipped her slowly, painstakingly, fired with tenderness and lightheaded with ardor.

They kissed until lips and tongue wept with the beauty of kissing. His hands strayed and explored, palms filled with wonder, fingertips trawling through ecstasy. Her breasts swelled hot beneath his palms. Her spine slipped beneath his fingers as he trailed down to the delectable curves of her bottom. Resilient, soft, female. His stones throbbed, pulled tightly against his body, heavy with the sweet ache of waiting.

She touched back, she kissed back. Her hands explored his shoulders and spine and buttocks, massaging muscle and tendon until his blood seared his veins. He bent to suckle at the base of her throat. Her pulse beat beneath his lips like a trapped bird.

"Ah, Dove!" she murmured, whispering, sighing. *"Dove!"*

He lifted her easily to set her down on their nest of discarded clothes and captured her bruised mouth with his own once again. Their naked bodies melded, legs entwined with legs, arms with arms.

If there's one thing I never hurry, it's making love to a woman.

Beneath his seeking mouth her skin was moist, burning, flushed with desire. Her nipples rose hard and hot to meet his encircling tongue. His fingertips slipped along the crevice between her buttocks, strayed into curls and moisture. Tiny moans feathered in his ears as her breathing slid into chaos.

Yet he waited. Even when she folded her fingers over his rigid erection and stroked up and down. Just right! Ah, God! Just right! His blood roared its response. His head dropped back as her palm caressed, firing rapture, until his cock became a scorching focus of pleasure.

Yet he still waited. She pulled her legs up, resting her calves on his back. He rubbed the exquisitely sensitive head of his penis against her wet heat. Burning. Silken. Smooth. Moist with passion. Intensity concentrated into one burning, blind male desire.

Imperious. Demanding. Intoxicating.

"Yes," she moaned. "Please. Now."

Passion roared as he pushed slowly inside her—deep, deep into that velvet-hot, female embrace—and heard himself groan aloud like a man in a trance.

TEARS STOOD IN HER EYES, OR PERHAPS SHE WEPT OPENLY. Sylvie no longer knew. One long, easy thrust, until she was filled, satiated, then the slow withdrawal to make the plunge once again. She clung to him, vulnerable to her soul, her ears full of moans, her heart filled with rapture.

"Dove!"

Perhaps she said it aloud, perhaps the fire sang his name, perhaps the flames in her blood chorused like blackbird and song thrush, warbler and wren, as the sun rose in the eastern sky.

Dove!

He smiled down at her, his eyes brilliant, his face flushed with passion and caring and joy. Then he dropped his dark lashes and closed her lips once again with his own. He pulsed inside her, spiraling waves of intensity. She matched his rhythm, gasping her passionate delight into his open mouth.

Don't stop! Don't stop! Don't stop!

Her heels pressed into his strong thighs. His muscled chest rubbed her swollen nipples. Her spine bent, limber as a willow, as he rolled her and lifted her. She followed willingly, pliant and supple in his hands, lying over or beneath him, caught in his wake or cresting the wave he created for her.

Dove!

The word faded to a sigh, folded to a whimper. Her hands slid on his moist skin, clutched his sweat-slick arms and the hard muscling of his back as if drowning. Abandoned to rapture, her mouth tasted him, hot, salt, delectable, and her nostrils inhaled him like a heady perfume.

Dove! A whisper, a cry. The secret, hidden name of her soul.

Her inner muscles clamped around him, milking, caressing. The rim of his penis swelled, stroking up and down, as he plunged again and again.

Yes! Yes! Don't stop! Don't stop! Don't stop!

Until, while he held her suspended, straddling him, his stones drew hard up against her. He shuddered, groaning, his head thrown back. Fire spread over his chest, flaming red in the firelight. Pulsations suffused. Strong. Deep. She closed her eyes as the heat rushed, spreading, spreading—his fire blazing into her womb, racing over her aching breasts and the hard nubs of her nipples.

And for the first time in her life she was convulsing and convulsing, a shouted ecstasy that opened at last into the intense, silent, delicate bliss of absolute surrender.

Sylvie collapsed, her face moist with tears, her arms and belly and neck damp with sweat, her womb flooded with honey, words lost on her exhausted, kiss-benumbed tongue. Slowly his erection slipped away. She sighed as if her heart would break at the loss.

Dove smiled and pulled her down into the cradling circle of his arms. He wiped away their mingled moisture, kissed her once on the forehead, then let his head fall back, still holding her.

His heart beat steadily, fast and strong, beneath her cheek.

He is charming. Attractive. Handsome. Witty. Brave. Intelligent. His manner is impeccable. Of course. But you know very well that charisma is one of the Devil's most useful attributes.... Yet perhaps angels possessed all of that as well.

"A promise kept," he murmured. "Oh, God! A promise kept."

She was replete. Languorous. Satisfied to the bone.

But you're still a virgin, he had said, *where it counts—in your soul.*

She had discovered, at last, what he meant.

DOVE LET HER SLEEP, SECURE IN HIS EMBRACE, PULLING HIS cloak over her shoulders as the fire died down.

He felt as if she had just laid a priceless treasure in his hands. He lay bemused, wondering whether the treasure might—like a Faerie gift of gold—turn to dust and dry leaves by morning. Yet morning lay in the far distant future, while *now* shone brightly around his heart.

I have never bedded an enemy in my life.

He had deliberately, even heartlessly, seduced her with other men's words, with other women's artistry: the elegant, sweet, witty erotica of their libertine age. She had said she was experienced. She had known a husband, lovers, perhaps several. Yet she had never before learned of the spontaneous bliss of the body's true passions. The keenness to be found in the inspired firing of ardor, or in the uninhibited revelation of lovemaking's most natural and innocent joys.

He felt oddly honored and just a little humble—which seemed like a kind of madness, when she might yet be intending to destroy him.

She had been a little shocked at the French pictures and tales, though not shattered. But then, with exquisite bravery, she had opened herself to the whimsical seduction of those etchings and engravings—and the wicked written word. Whatever else she might be, she was brave. And more vulnerable than she knew.

Ah, Sylvie!

He kissed her slumbering eyebrow, the soft skin of her temple.

If she was indeed working for his enemies, everything she had seen here tonight was easily discovered by anyone who asked the right questions of the right people. Yveshire had been having him followed. If she was working for the duke, unlikely as that seemed, he had perhaps shown her just enough of the truth to confuse the trail. Who would imagine that he would take a spy straight into the heart of his most dangerous activities? It was—like his entire life—a calculated risk.

Yet—what if she was guiltless? He tightened his arm protectively around her shoulders. What if she was guiltless? What if her decision to make love had not been as cynical, as deliberate, as his? What if she was not using him? What if all of her vulnerability and passion were real?

Aching with tenderness, he smoothed a strand of blond hair back over her ear.

Either way, God help him, he was in love.

* * *

SYLVIE WOKE WITH THE FIRE BURNED ALMOST TO ASH, WARMTH burning only where naked flesh touched naked flesh. Dove still cradled her, his arms around her, keeping their makeshift covers over her back and shoulders, sharing the protective flame of his body. Yet the floor beneath its thin covering of coats and shirts stung like iron.

"Alas," he said, pressing kisses on her drugged eyelids. "It won't do for Mr. Fennimore to find us here when he comes in to work." He hunted for his watch, lost in their nest of clothing, and read the hands by the dull light of the embers. "In about two hours. Alas, alas, we must go."

Ten minutes later Sylvie ducked her head as wind-driven snow flurried up from the cobbles. Dove grinned down at her. The street was deserted. While they had made love, while they slept, while they'd made love again, it had snowed, a fine dusting, like sugar on a cake. The fresh powder whipped up in a cold, dry wind. Icy showers surged against her face.

Dove brushed snow from her cheek. Oil lamps smoked up into the darkness.

"Now," he said. "We must make it home without freezing to death. Are you hungry?"

As he asked it, her stomach growled. "Starving! I could eat an ox, horse and mountain, all at once."

"Faith, ma'am," he said. "Your appetite wasn't satisfied last night?"

She grinned up at him. "Satisfied? How can you ask that? Yet we missed dinner and I could still use a solid breakfast."

He laughed. "I wasn't solid enough for you?"

A hot wave flushed over her cheeks, melting the ice nipping her skin. "You know perfectly well what I mean. I am satiated to the marrow. But would Matthew Finch have more pies?"

"A vain hope. Tomorrow—today—is Sunday, when he takes the day off. Never mind. I know a tavern that serves food all night, whether Sabbath, saint's day, or spring tides. Stay close. Act like a man. And maybe we'll survive it."

She laughed back at him. Her heart felt as buoyant as cork.

*I*F SHE STRETCHED OUT BOTH ARMS, SYLVIE COULD TOUCH doors and windows on each side of the alley. The Dog and Duck was marked by a painted sign in the shape of a malevolent, red-eyed retriever clutching a green mallard in its grinning jaws. The inn's facade was ice-sheened pitch, but a single lamp illuminated the dog, making its eye shine.

"A low dive," Dove whispered in her ear. "Haunt of sailors, thieves, and unsavory women. Keep your head down and leave everything to me."

He broke off a piece of icicle hanging from the sign, pushed open the door, and ducked inside. A wall of heat, noise, grease, and tobacco smoke hit Sylvie in the face. She kept close at his heels as Dove elbowed his way into the taproom and ordered them breakfast.

"Honest ale, the best, five tankards. No gin or grog. Bread and beef for two."

Dove installed her in a dark corner, placing his body between hers and the bawdy, drunken room. He had laid aside their hats and cloaks. Snow crystals winked like diamonds on the dark fabric, then disappeared.

No one, obviously, slept at the Dog and Duck. Fiddle music fought with talk, song, and laughter, rising to the rafters in raucous disharmony. Smoke wreathed: from tobacco, the temperamental fireplace, myriad oil lamps and candles. The air felt as thick as flannel.

A young brunette, slender in red silk—though her breasts perched above her corset like pears on a plate—set down three tankards and grinned at Dove.

"Well, love," she said. "Come to pay sweet Nance a shilling?"

A second girl at Nance's elbow gurgled with merriment. Also dark-haired and dark-eyed, she carried a tray laden with sliced beef and fresh bread, which she set down in front of Sylvie.

"Get off, Nance! Dove never paid for it in his life, and he ain't going to start with an old scrag like you!"

Dove laughed as he stood and spun a shilling on the table. "Yours, Nance, and you don't need to lift your skirts for it."

Nance grinned and reached up to kiss Dove on the mouth, before she seized one of the tankards and took a long swallow.

Another coin spun. "And one for you, Bess, if you'll sit here and guard my young friend from your overeager sisters. Mr. White isn't used to girls like you. He's a virgin."

"Never you worry," Bess said, sitting down opposite Sylvie. "I'll take care of the lad and a Romany curse to any that question it. But if you're gone more than an hour, he won't be a virgin when you get back."

Dove tore a chunk from the loaf, wrapped the bread about a slice of roast beef, and grasped two of the tankards in his other fist. Then he winked at Sylvie and disappeared, Nance at his elbow.

"Well," Bess said, her dark eyes filled with mirth. "Nance won't get what she's wanting, but Dove will."

The bread was fragrant and hot. Beef dripped savory juices onto her chin. Sylvie had never been this hungry in her life. "What does Nance want?"

"Why, she's a whore, cully, though she'd do Dove for free, if he'd have her."

Sylvie leaned back carelessly, like a boy, though her heart thundered. "And what does Dove want?"

"Not the favors of a girl who's in it for the gold or her own advantage. God didn't make too many like him, but he made a few and Dove is the best of them. Yet there's not a girl in here will win him, not even for a night. Even the street whores know that."

"Though he likes women," Sylvie said, gulping ale.

"Ah, yes, but he's that rare bird: a one-woman man. One of these days he'll give his heart for good, but it won't be to a harlot like Nance. Any day now he'll meet the woman he's destined for. Then Dove will fall, like spray in a waterfall, and be lost."

"What do you mean, he'll be lost?"

Bess set her hands on the table. "It's written in his palm, cully. Love and death sit there together. His bride'll be a virgin, a huntress, but when he finds true love, he dies."

The bread stuck in her throat. Sylvie washed it down with more ale, hoping the honest glow of alcohol could melt the sudden ice around her heart. "How can you possibly know that?"

"Took a peek at his hand once when Dove wasn't paying attention. The mark of Diana is inscribed like a bracelet around his thumb. His heart's reserved for the spotless, white-limbed lady of the moon, but when he gives his heart, he embraces his doom." Bess shrugged, her eyes dark. "His fate was determined long ago, just like yours, just like mine."

It was superstitious nonsense, yet the chill spread. "Then what will he get from Nance?"

"Just talk," Bess replied. "And a word with my cousin."

"Your cousin?"

A pretty girl in powdered wig and blue ribbons sidled over to them, smiling, and refilled their tankards.

"Forget it, Sue," Bess said. "The boy's taken."

The girl pouted, but left.

"Your cousin?" Sylvie asked again, before downing another swallow. There were perhaps advantages sometimes to drinking like a man.

"Tanner Brink," Bess replied. "We're all family here. Even Dove."

* * *

THE GYPSY WAS SITTING IN A BACK ROOM, SLOWLY DRINKING himself into a stupor. Dove kicked away the footstool supporting the man's boots, lifted him by the collar, and dropped a little ice—carried in from the street for the purpose—down his neck.

Tanner Brink jerked upright on his bench, opened both eyes, closed them again, and laughed, though he took Dove's proffered tankard and gulped a long draft.

"You took her to the printing works?" the Gypsy said. "Heigh-ho! You're a bold lad, Mr. Dovenby!"

Dove hooked a chair with one foot, then sat down. "I thought I'd better do it myself, before you took it upon yourself to show her the wrong things."

Teeth grinned like white mushrooms popping up from brown sod. "You think I'd betray you, just because I took her to St. John's?"

"I have no idea, but you're a damned interfering and useless informant, sir. You *were* planning to take her to the printer's, of course."

The Gypsy shrugged. "Why not? There's nothing to hide— unless you know where to look—from her or from Yveshire. The man's your enemy, but he's not a prig. What do you want to know today?"

"Whom you are really working for."

Tanner Brink opened one eye, while that brief hesitation told Dove everything he needed to know. "Nobody but myself, and you when I feel like it."

Dove drank a long swallow of ale, then ate another chunk of bread and beef. "It's the part about your working for yourself that worries me, sir, and always has, whenever you've chosen to burst in or out of my life."

The Gypsy grinned. "Your problem, my lad, is that you believe that what we do matters. It doesn't matter. Our fate was determined long before either of us was born."

"Yours may have been, not mine."

"Let me see your palm, then I'll tell you. Sixpence for your fortune, Mr. Dovenby."

"My fortune is worth more than sixpence, Mr. Brink. It's worth at least as much to me as the Duke of Yveshire's is to him."

"Then you can't be sure, can you, whom I'm working for?"

With a laugh Dove drained his tankard, then ordered another for the Gypsy. "I'm sure enough. I should have known better than to trust the Romany."

"Why? We share the same beliefs," Tanner said.

"About freedom, perhaps." Dove stood up. He had other men to find here tonight. "But I don't believe that our lives are preordained by the stars, or our palms, or tea leaves, or a crystal ball."

"Fate can never be avoided," Tanner Brink said. "Ask Bess, who can tell you yours." He winked. "A fortune can be stolen as well as paid for."

"Much as I love Bess, I don't give a fig for her fortune-telling. Our destiny is ours to wrench from fate and shape to our liking."

"No true Romany would say that."

"Then tell me your own future, Mr. Brink," Dove said. "It ends on the gallows?"

The Gypsy kicked his feet onto the stool and grinned at Dove, a grin apparently sweetened with real affection.

"There's nothing but trouble written in the stars for me—and a nice, troublesome long life to enjoy it in."

DOVE LED SYLVIE BACK TO HIS TOWNHOUSE. ALE AND SMOKE buzzed in her head. An indolent, sweet peace had invaded her bones. It was easy enough to dismiss what Bess had said when she was in Dove's company. His step was lovely. His height, his grace, took away her breath. His smile, his hazel eyes, his fluid hands—edged in ice, in gold—were entrancing.

Just follow me up the stairs, throw aside your wig and coat, and don't walk on past my bedroom door.

He'd been right. It was easy. Indeed, it was impossible to do anything else.

Dove knelt at the grate and built up the fire. Sylvie stood with his closed chamber door at her back and kicked off her shoes. The bed lay ready, warm, inviting.

He glanced up, radiant, smiling. "I do believe, Mr. White, that you're just a little foxed."

She shrugged out of her waistcoat and untied her cravat, while her hot pulse thundered.

His bride'll be a virgin, a huntress . . . a spotless, white-limbed lady devoted to the moon. Ah, well! Ah, well! Not me, then! Not Sylvie Georgiana, who had sold herself long ago and was—at the heart— no different than Nance, or Sue, or Bess, or any other woman who had been forced to earn her living, in one way or another, through deception.

When he gives his heart, he embraces his doom. And that's not me, either—so his fate doesn't lie in my hands, after all.

Yet this was no longer just another task. This was no longer a deception, even if it had begun that way.

Blushing like a sunrise, peeled like a withy, Sylvie stripped away cotton and linen and wool.

He sat back on his heels to watch her.

"Very foxed," she said. "Or I wouldn't stand before you now in nothing but my hair."

"As I," he said, standing, "am drunk as a lord at the sight of you."

He strode toward her, tossing aside garments. Ivory satin fell with a sigh. Linen pulled up over his dark head to fold behind him

like a reefed sail. Breeches and stockings, rolled down and abandoned, revealed him naked, magnificent, and as aroused as she.

We shall bend, his eyes said. *We shall dance. We shall drown together
in a delirium of passion. Will you dance, ma'am? Will you drown
with me?*

He held out one hand. Sylvie walked straight into his embrace.

*Even if it is only for this one more time, I will dance, beloved. I will
drown.*

A WATERY SUN WASHED IN THROUGH THE WINDOWS. THE
false promise of spring fired her hair to gilt: the labor of
Rumpelstiltskin spilled over the pillows. Outside, echoing about
London's rooftops and steeples, the call of church bells. Sunday.

Her eyelids lay heavy with bliss. Her lips curved, warm and
lovely. Longing bloomed in the palms of his hands. Beneath the
covers her long legs and slim hips flowed in hills and valleys, firing
the impetuous ardor of arousal, once again, in his groin.

But it was time to face what was left of the day. Dove had already
slipped from the bed and dressed in a long gown. Now he stood
gazing down at her, his heart aching, his body on fire, and held out
a steaming cup.

Her nose twitched. Sylvie opened sleepy eyes and smiled.

"Ah," she said. "Coffee."

"And a second breakfast." He set down a covered plate, then
flipped the cloth back to reveal warm sticky buns.

Her shoulders curved, female and lovely, as she propped herself
against the head of the bed, the covers pulled up over her breasts.
"I'll get crumbs in the bed."

"My bed is already filled with sweetness. Honey spills from the
hangings. How could it matter?"

She bit into a bun and glanced up at him, cornflower innocent, pansy bruised. "But what do we do now?"

"This minute? We eat. We drink. We make love again."

"And later?" Her blue eyes gazed up as if to search his heart. "What do we do about what lies between us now? If we live openly as lovers, your household will discover that you've been employing a very odd secretary. What do we do about that?"

"Become Sylvie. George can disappear back to France. Or if you like, become both of them. I don't mind if George keeps my ledgers, as long as Sylvie joins my life."

"In your bed, at least?"

"That isn't your desire, also?"

She licked her fingertips. "I can hardly deny it. That is my desire, also."

He strode away. Before he swept aside coffee cups and breakfast, before he lost himself once again in her honeyed embrace and forgot everything that he knew or thought that he knew.

A false promise of spring. "First," he said, staring from the window. "There's something I must ask, though I had hoped you would tell me on your own without my asking."

"What's that?"

He turned back to her. She lay as lovely as liquid gold and as treacherous, no doubt, as Rumpelstiltskin. His body derided the concern. His mind focused his attention on her eyes, as blue and wide now as the ocean, watching closely for her reaction and hating the necessity.

"How long have you been working for Yveshire?"

I T HIT SO HARD, SHE THOUGHT SHE MIGHT FAINT. THE SOUND of the church bells echoed and re-echoed, as if ringing in her head. Coffee spilled, soaking into the pillow.

"Yveshire? What do you mean?"

"Sylvie, I'm not a fool. I could lose myself right now in your gaze. I have lost myself in your body. But do you still expect me to believe that you came here accidentally? That you make love to me only from desire?"

The temptation to confess everything was so overwhelming that it kept her pinned for a moment like a moth to the pillows. He was so lovely! Brilliant and terrible, a lean silhouette against the morning light, gold edging his hair and shoulders, his face lost in darkness. How could she have thought she could ever deceive him?

Yet if he learned the truth now? When her mission for Yveshire had just become irrelevant, though the reality of that assignment and her past still lay like a terrible trap, waiting to destroy her? *His bride'll be a virgin, a huntress.* There could never be a future with him, but to have it end now? She couldn't bear to have it end now!

"I made love to you last night from desire," she said. "How can you doubt it?"

"I don't. My heart and my loins both know that truth. But I need to know why you really came here to begin with, Sylvie. I need you to tell me for whom you are working."

"What if I'm working for no one?"

"I would like to believe that. I cannot believe it. I have shown you many of my secrets. What are yours?"

"I have no secrets," she lied.

"And Yveshire? How much comfort do you offer to my enemies?"

"I told you," she said, frantic with grief, compounding her sin. "We met for the first time at Lady Grenham's, after the sleigh race. He warned me against you. It seemed too fantastic at the time, though his misconceptions might explain why he considers you an adversary."

"What misconceptions?"

It was the one part of the truth that was surely harmless now that she had discovered Tom Henley? She would tell the duke that all of his evidence about his brother's death was undoubtedly counterfeit. She would make him swear to abandon his persecution of Dove. Then it might be as if her mission had never existed. Sylvie wanted that so badly, she felt faint.

"It was to do with his younger brother, Lord Edward Vane," she said. "Something about ships and timber and investments. I couldn't follow it all. Did you know Lord Edward? Were you friends?"

"I met him when I came to London," Dove said. "He went to some lengths to befriend me."

"And everyone knew that, which made it easy for someone to thrust blame onto you when Lord Edward was killed. I know it's absurd, but Yveshire believes that you deliberately pursued an elaborate campaign against his brother, defrauded him, ruined him, then sent him to his death. He claims to have evidence, documents in your handwriting, that prove all of it."

He stood in silence for a moment. When he spoke again, the words were edged in ice.

"Does he? How very unfortunate that Yveshire should share that with you."

Panic began to throb beneath her ribs. "Is it? Why? Surely those documents are forgeries?"

Dove walked to the bed and peeled off his robe. Gilt highlighted his shoulders, the dusting of dark hair on his arms. The dressing gown draped from his outstretched hand.

"Put this on and go back to your own room," he said. "Leave today, if you wish. All your debts are forgiven."

The panic bloomed, thudding loudly enough to threaten to beat her to her knees and defeat her. "Why?"

He stalked away, the pure line of back and buttocks and thighs lovely enough to weep over.

"Because everything His Grace told you about my persecution and destruction of Lord Edward Vane happens to be true."

CHAPTER THIRTEEN

RESSED ONCE AGAIN AS GEORGE, IN HER WIG AND MAN'S coat and boy's buckled shoes, Sylvie left the house. The morning sunlight had shattered among the chimneys to be lost in a miasma of coal smoke and ice. Shapes loomed and disappeared in a glittering yellow fog.

It was totally irrelevant now whether Dove was having her followed. He had made love to her, stripped her to her soul, then casually agreed that he was guilty of destroying Lord Edward Vane. He would hardly be surprised if she went to the duke, though ironically nothing in that spoke of complicity now. Even if she were innocent, it would be natural enough that she would want answers, after what he had admitted.

Pain numbed her heart as she strode through the streets. Yveshire had mentioned where he attended divine service. Would it be the house of a just and merciful God? Or just a mockery offered by Satan to lead sinners further astray? Either way, it meant nothing to her. She had lost the faith of her parents a long time ago. She had never before, of course, been foolish enough to put her faith in a man.

The hurt stabbed. If she didn't hold on hard to anger, she thought she might even stumble and gasp.

The church soared into the fog, elegant columns fading softly into yellow-gray fleece. The cream of London society streamed out into the cold, clutching fur muffs, then ducking powdered heads as it climbed into carriages. Stamping hoofs and turning wheels created a moment of confusion as coachmen tried to jockey into position. The carriage lamps did little to ward off the murk of a winter noon in front of the most fashionable church in London.

Sylvie lounged in the shelter of a pillar and watched. There was little enough holiness evident in this crowd. She had made love to their darling, the toast of their drawing rooms, and thought for a moment that she had stumbled into the arms of an angel. Instead he had admitted that he was Lucifer, an angel fallen, the evil genius who had written all of those letters, planned all of that devastation for an innocent man, then sped him to his death.

When Yveshire stepped into his carriage, Sylvie swung in through the opposite door and sat down beside him.

"Lud, ma'am," the duke said. "You've seen a ghost?"

"Just a goose walking over my grave. I'm sorry to accost you like this, though I doubt that anyone noticed me in the fog and confusion. I had to see you immediately."

In a clatter of hooves and jangling harness, the coach started forward. Yveshire caught her by the chin and turned her face toward his.

"For God's sake, what has happened?"

"What you hoped for, I should think. Dove confessed to me. *Confessed!*"

The duke rapped with his cane. A small trapdoor opened.

"Keep driving," he said to his coachman. "Around the Park. Anywhere. Just keep driving."

The horses broke into a trot.

"But you knew he was guilty," the duke said. "I've shown you the proof. What the devil made you question it?"

"A forger named Tom Henley. I thought all that evidence must be counterfeit. I convinced myself Dove wasn't guilty. I can't believe I was such a fool!"

"Faith, Sylvie! Pray, don't weep!"

"Weep? I shall have his guts for garters!"

Yveshire pulled her into his arms. Seconds later she was bawling noisily onto his lace-edged cravat.

"Hush, hush," he murmured, while she wept as if her heart would break. "No man is worth this!"

She pulled back, trying to laugh, though tears flooded her cheeks. "Two beans for my professional objectivity!"

"Hush, now!" He handed her a handkerchief, beautifully monogrammed with the Yveshire crest. "This is my fault. I should be horsewhipped."

Feeling wretched, Sylvie blew her nose.

"It's not your fault," she said. "You warned me. I went into this mission with my eyes open. But we overreached. The plan was lunatic. He saw through me from the beginning."

"If it was lunatic, it was my blunder, not yours." The duke's voice seemed tight, filled with pain. "I will do what I can to make it up to you. Can you tell me exactly what happened?"

Leaning back companionably beside him, she dragged the story from her heart, piece by painful piece. The laughter and flirtation. The mad game of trust that was not—and could never be—real trust. Every gesture of friendship she had made betrayed by those small notes in code to his enemy. Every move of his contaminated by his knowledge—or guess—that she was doing it.

My men are waylaid, misled, sometimes even set upon—though in ways that seem random.

"You said he was clever," she said. "You said I should be careful. I wasn't careful enough. You recall, of course, how you told me that every time you set a tail on him, he loses it? When did your men last follow us?"

"Last night when you went with him into the City. I received a report that you suddenly disappeared, lost when a brawl broke out over an apple cart."

She hated it, more evidence of his manipulation, of his deviousness.

"Dove probably paid those apprentices and the apple seller to create a diversion. While your men dodged flying fruit, we slipped away down an alley. I had no idea what he was doing. I was having too much fun. I should have guessed that all that gallivanting past shirts and petticoats was simply to throw off your spies."

"And your final destination?"

"A printer's. With a waterwheel and dozens of workers." She described its location as accurately as she could. "He owns it, runs it, decides what should be printed."

"He took you there? Even though he already suspected that you're working for me? Then this is all a bloody red herring!"

"Yet he had a purpose. Among more mundane things, he prints some rather fanciful erotica. Amusing, shameless, charming, exceedingly naughty, but not in the least offensive. In fact, the illustrations were beautiful."

"Devil take it!" The duke's laugh was dry, empty of real humor. "I've probably purchased some of it myself."

"He likes beauty." She didn't mean it to sound so bitter. "He would do nothing in bad taste. Could he be prosecuted for it?"

"I doubt it—not unless it's blasphemous or truly seditious."

"No, not at all. It was sophisticated, lovely—filled with delight and joy."

"Then it wouldn't even harm his reputation very much, if all that came to light. It might even enhance it. We live in liberal times."

She took a deep breath. She didn't want to have to share this! Yet the duke must know everything, if she was to continue with her mission. And perhaps she was angry enough, or hurt enough, to want to make him face it.

"Then you won't be surprised when I admit that he used a selection of such prints to seduce me? That was why he took me there."

Yveshire wrung one fist over his mouth. "You were seduced?"

"Oh, yes. I still am. He did it without compunction, yet I'm in love with the bastard. I can't help it."

To her surprise, the duke pressed a kiss, soft with regret and compassion, on her forehead. Framed by the wig, his lean face and dark gaze spoke of real caring, yet the barrier was still there, as it had always been there. *If he had loved you, he'd have married you anyway and defied the world to comment.* Had she never truly loved—or been loved?

"Why did you stay, Sylvie? Why not walk out on this mission weeks ago?"

"Because I rather liked it that the Comtesse de Montevrain had been left behind in Vienna and Paris."

He looked puzzled. "Living as a boy is hardly a new future."

"Yet for a few precious moments, it seemed like it. I was wrong. It seems that I shall never escape who I am."

"Would you like me to kill him now, quickly, and have this over and done with? I can create any excuse to challenge him. No one would be surprised."

"You would abandon all of your plans?"

Yveshire pressed back into his own corner of the carriage, as if he didn't quite trust himself to sit so close.

"It's what I should have done to start with. Instead I have been obsessed with revenge. That was wrong. God, it was deuced wrong of me to involve you. I must have been mad."

"If you fought a duel with Dove, who would win?"

He glanced back at her, as if her question was absurd. "With swords, I would, without question."

"Lud! Are all men so boastful? How can you be certain?"

He stretched out his right hand and spread the fingers. Fine, strong fingers, tastefully decorated with rings. She had known them once, with a certain tenderness, with a certain passion—though that was long before she had discovered what passion really meant.

"My brother and I were taught by experts, professionals from France and from Italy, the best. We had the resources of the dukedom at our command. Dovenby is good, but he learned only what a ragtag collection of provincial English fencing masters could teach him. If we fight a duel, he dies."

"So a duel has always seemed too unequal to be honorable?" She glanced down at the ruins of his damp handkerchief in her lap. "Because you would simply cut him in ribbons?"

"Not only because of that. I wanted a revenge as long and drawn-out as his torment of my brother. I hardly care about that now—none of it is worth such a cost to you! Say the word, Sylvie, and I will slay him and weave you a basket from his remains."

She fought for control. If she once gave in to hysteria, she might disappear forever into this terrible void in her heart.

"But I'm assured that Dove's fate is to fall in love with a lady of virtue before he dies."

"His *fate*? What the devil do you mean?"

"A Gypsy girl named Bess read his palm. There was no mention of his imminent death, unless he has first found true love. So for God's sake, don't fight a duel with him."

"Unless I, too, have my palm crossed with silver to discover whether my fate, like my brother's, is to die at his hands? Do you expect me to give credence to such nonsense?"

"Your Grace," she said with careful composure. "Pray bring him to justice, if you can, and keep your hands clean. Though unfortunately the scaffold does not seem to be part of his destiny either, unless he first gives his heart to a lady as spotless as the goddess Diana."

"Superstitious rubbish!"

"Either way," Sylvie continued, "he'll pursue nothing more than a temporary fling with a fallen woman like myself, so your concern for me is entirely misplaced. I intend to finish this mission. It's too late now to make any other choice."

The duke sat in silence for a moment. His profile seemed set in plaster.

"All of this is my fault," he said at last.

"All of this, if you listen to the Gypsies, was written long ago in the stars."

Yveshire glanced back at her. "So his fate depends on Diana the Huntress? Perhaps the Gypsies forgot that the gallows belong to Hecate, associated with the infernal regions, who is just another aspect of the same goddess?"

She swallowed mirth and tears, like two phases of the moon, both aspects of one single agony.

"I should ask them to cast his horoscope. Though since he's a foundling, I suppose nobody knows exactly when he was born."

"Devil take his horoscope! Rest assured that Robert Sinclair Dovenby is destined for destruction and death at my hands. I cannot help that, Sylvie. I bitterly regret now that I involved you. Do not return to him."

"It's too late!"

"If you go back to him after this, I cannot spare you or save you."

"I most certainly don't want to be saved." She looked up and made herself smile. "Any temporary infatuation of mine is totally irrelevant. What I didn't tell you is that he also thinks that he loves me. This is my profession: to bind a man's trust with my body."

"I cannot bear the thought of it."

"Then don't think of it. For, mad as it may seem, I believe what Bess said. I'm not in any danger, Your Grace, though if you fight him, you may be."

The duke rapped again on the roof. The horses dropped back to a walk.

"Not if Diana is the new name of my rapier," Yveshire said.

OVE WAS WAITING FOR HER IN THE STUDY, IDLY ARRANGING quills on the desk. His dark hair tossed in wild disarray, as if he had just galloped a horse twenty miles. Sylvie walked in and threw aside her hat.

"You've been out," he said.

"To church."

He glanced up to meet her gaze. He seemed dangerous, self-contained. "I trust that you prayed over my wicked soul and for our mutual salvation?"

"Not at all. I spoke with the Duke of Yveshire."

"The puissant duke, filled with chivalry and honor. Would you believe me if I told you that I rather like him, in spite of his implacable hatred of me?"

A tremor ran down her spine, forcing her to take a chair by the fire. She held her hands out to the flames. Like damsels in distress, her fingers quivered. "Then it's only fair to warn you that His Grace has dedicated his rapier to Hecate, so that he may run you through with it."

"I was afraid it would come to that. Such an honorable method to rid the world of one's enemies. If I were to tell you that I killed Lord Edward Vane in a duel, would that help?"

Shock sank like a stone. "You fought a *duel*?"

"No. Unfortunately for the sake of everyone's finer sensibilities, I did not. Though what lay between us was certainly an affair of honor."

"How can I believe that?"

"Unless I explain everything, you can't, of course." Tension vibrated in his voice. "Unhappily, I cannot explain anything."

"Why not?"

"Firstly because the truth is not mine to reveal. Secondly because that revelation—if it can ever be made—must be reserved to the duke first and he would not be able to hear it."

"After what you did to his brother, he cannot bear the sight of you."

Dove turned and stalked to the window. The new pane, where she had thrown the decanter, was slightly greener than the rest.

"It's a quandary, isn't it? Especially for you, now you work for both of us."

"Not really. His Grace intends the world—and my burden in it—to be lighter quite soon. He's certain that if you and he fought with rapiers, he would kill you. Is that true?"

He glanced back at her. "Very likely. Though I can guarantee my prowess against the rabble, the duke's education with a blade was far better than mine."

Desperate to avoid his gaze, she studied the painted horses on each side of the fireplace. "The duke and his brother both learned from French and Italian masters."

"Then I would be slaughtered without question."

"Which is why you didn't settle your quarrel with Lord Edward, whatever it was, with swords? He would have killed you too easily?"

"Lord Edward was a renowned swordsman, but there were more things at stake than his death."

She closed her eyes, feeling painfully tired, as if anguish had drained her of blood. "It's monstrous."

"I did what seemed essential at the time," Dove said. "The man needed to be ruined first and it was worth it, even at the cost of this conversation."

The pain coalesced, making her suddenly frantic. She stood up. "What cost?"

Light from the window cast him in bronze. *Only last night!* her blood sang. *Only last night!*

Dove smiled as he might smile at the angel of death. "It is usual for a man to wish his lover to think well of him. Instead, you are standing there before me like the avenging seraph, filled with scorn and accusations."

"Why should that matter?"

"I am rather desperately in love with you. You think me a worm. Forgive me, ma'am, if I seem a little frazzled."

Sylvie caught the back of the chair to steady herself. "You cannot be in love with me!"

"I am in love with you. I mean that. In Mr. Fennimore's office and in my bed upstairs this morning I meant it. Every last piece of it. Meanwhile, desire and doubt, dread and disappointment, all fight a ferocious battle in your heart. There's not much I can do about it. It would be bloody absurd to ask you to trust me. So leave, if you wish, but know that if you do, you take most of my soul with you."

The wooden chair rail gouged into her palm. "I cannot believe you."

"Then you're going to leave?"

"How can I? I promised the duke I would search for evidence he can use to see you hanged."

His lip curled. "You mean you will *continue* searching. You've been reporting to him ever since you came here, of course. Just as you have lied to me all along about your past."

She felt tired. Tired enough to curl up in the chair and sleep. Tired enough to weep away her dreams in an agony of loneliness and regret. Instead, she strode up to the desk and began to sharpen a quill.

"Yes," she said. "Berthe takes my reports. One of Yveshire's footmen meets her in Shepherd's Market."

"But it's all such a waste of time and effort. I do many things that I don't particularly wish to be broadcast to the world. I don't do anything for which I'm likely to be hanged."

"Perhaps that's a matter of opinion," she said. "But as your secretary, it shouldn't be too hard for me to find out."

To her immense surprise, he laughed. "Then, George, you had better take care of these damned receipts. I have to go out."

Half an hour later she caught a glimpse of him through the open door of the study. Immaculate in white wig, silk stockings, buckled shoes, dove-gray coat—and with Meg's elegant smallsword shining at his hip—he stepped out into London to break hearts and create havoc wherever he went.

A CLOUD OF SCENTED POWDER FELL OVER NAKED SHOULDERS. Dove waited in the doorway and watched, aware of nothing but calm affection where once he'd have expected the more straightforward fire of lust. Meg seemed too frail to him now, a lovely icequeen sparkling in her pretty boudoir like a diamond. The maid looked up, blushed as she saw him, and curtsied.

Meg opened her eyes to meet his gaze in her mirror. She pulled her wrapper up over her shoulders.

"Go," she said quietly to the girl. "Send wine."

As the maid left, Meg turned and held out a hand to Dove. "My dear! What is it?"

He walked in and bowed over her fingers, then kissed her briefly on the mouth. Her lips were soft and aromatic, like a rose after rain. Cool, lovely, and passionless. The lips of a friend.

"I need your permission, ma'am, to tell Yveshire the truth about his brother."

Color rose slowly beneath her powder. "That truth is not yours to tell."

"Sylvie suffers for it. The duke suffers for it."

Meg's rings shone like tears on her fingers. "And you suffer for it, I know."

"I would never ask only for myself."

"I cannot, Dove. That decision doesn't belong to either of us. There is still one true innocent in all this. We swore a solemn vow to protect her at all costs."

The maid entered with a silver tray, set it down, then closed the door behind her as she left the room.

Dove poured wine into two goblets. He set one in her hand. "Then what solution is there, Meg?"

Powder shimmered around her in a fine haze as she stared at their reflections in the mirror. "So your secretary has become your lover?"

"Yes—and then this morning she asked me about Lord Edward."

Meg spun about on her stool to stare up at him.

Dove leaned back against the wall beside the dressing table to give her a wry grin. "I am, as you will have noticed, very helplessly in love. Pray don't gloat, Meg! I know you predicted it. Sylvie has been working for the duke all along, of course. I feel like a bloody fool."

"Love has a way of making fools of all of us at least once in a lifetime, Dove. How long has she has been working for Yveshire?"

"Since she left France. Probably before that. My own spies are lying to me very merrily, I believe, including Tanner Brink. It seems that everyone would like to protect her from me."

"Except Yveshire! The duke didn't hesitate to throw this lamb to the lion, in spite of what he believes about you. Damn the man! He's obsessed."

"With good reason. I would really like that to be over, Meg. It's deuced tiresome."

"Tiresome? Devastating, more like! Yet we can manage. Sylvie can manage. There is another who cannot."

"To sacrifice myself is just a jolly little exercise in self-abasement, of course," Dove said. "But I'm not prepared to sacrifice Sylvie. She's looking for evidence to see me hanged. If she doesn't find it, I think the duke might create it. What do you suggest?"

Meg hugged the wrapper to her chin. "Make love to her. Your lovemaking will bind her loyalty, whatever she thinks about you."

"Being a man of due humility, but little modesty, that was what I believed, too. She still intends to betray me."

"Then seduce her again, until her doubt shatters in the face of her passion. If you hold nothing back, you will enslave her. Her mind may tell her not to trust you. Her heart will tremble at the edge of the abyss. Her body won't be able to deny you." Meg stood in a shimmer of ivory satin and lace. She gave him a genuine smile. "Mine never could."

"You don't expect me to answer that, surely? You were a flame to a moth, Meg."

"And so we consumed each other? I love you very dearly, Dove. I am no longer in love with you. Though—to my shame—I was for a while." Meg swallowed wine. Her lips were stained red, like blood. Her smiled opened into a wry grin. "I pray you will keep that shocking revelation to yourself. It would be far too damaging to my reputation, were society to hear of it."

"Find a man worthy of your love, Meg, someone who is truly your equal."

"Now I've sent Hartsham away, perhaps I should set my cap at Yveshire, instead?" She looked away as if to hide her real feelings. "The duke must be persuaded to abandon this madness."

"I doubt if his mind is on dalliance. His Grace is polishing rapiers."

"Because there's nothing like a nice, sweaty brawl to soothe the troubled masculine soul? A duel might cleanse the bad blood between you, at least."

Dove trailed his fingers through the powder on her dressing table, the fine dusting over the mirror, then rubbed his fingertips against his thumb to allow a tiny rain of scent to fall to the carpet.

"Alas, we're talking real blood, Meg, and real hatred. Neither of us deserves death over this, least of all Yveshire."

Fine wrinkles marred her lovely forehead, spread in tiny bird tracks at the corners of her eyes. "You're not clever enough with a blade to fight him to a standstill, then talk some sense into him?"

"Perhaps. But the experiment might prove fatal first."

"Then—other than throwing my lamb to the lions—what can I do, Dove?"

He leaned down to kiss her. "I would like to see my secretary emerge as a lady. You can send dresses to my townhouse."

Meg was surprised into laughter. "She would wear them?"

At the door he bowed, allowing the witty extra flourish that would make any lesser woman swoon.

"She will wear them," he said. "To my cost!"

DOVE RETURNED TO HIS TOWNHOUSE DEEP IN THOUGHT. IT was late. A cold drizzle soaked the pavements and hissed around the streetlamps. He stepped aside to allow two drunken revelers to pass, then watched them disappear. God, he was sick of winter!

"I would like warmth," he said aloud to the oil lamp that smoked before his front door. "I would like sunshine. I would like a beneficent life with a clear conscience and without intrigue."

The lamp said nothing, so he ran up the front steps and unlocked the door. The house lay quiet. Everyone, by his orders, had long gone to bed.

I don't do anything for which I'm likely to be hanged.

That was true, as far as it went. Yet he did several things that could certainly cost him the smiles of society, and therefore his livelihood and the charitable funding for St. John's. Though it might shock the ladies, a little erotica was the least of his disreputable activities.

He shrugged out of his damp hat and coat and took the stairs two at a time. The hallway slept, hushed with cold and beeswax polish.

A thin stream of light beamed beneath his bedroom door to shine across the wooden floor.

Berthe? Not after the last time! In which case—

He opened the door.

She turned to face him. Defiance resounded like a thunderclap.

"Ah," he said. "So we're still playing?"

In the light of the candles, silver tissue shimmered and streamed, falling straight down her back from her shoulders, the fabric shaped at the front into a long bodice set with a row of tiny, pearl-encrusted bows. Enclosed by the deep neckline, her white skin swelled into the delicate curve of round breasts. Shining like gold, her hair swept away from her white face and lapis lazuli eyes, dark with rebellion.

Though he had planned it and expected it, a sweet shudder pulsed directly to his groin.

"I am the happy recipient of dresses," Sylvie said. "Did you think I would not try them on?"

*T*HE BOXES HAD ARRIVED EARLIER THAT EVENING.

My dear Mr. White, the note had read. *Mr. Dovenby, assailed by distress, has shared your secret with the one friend who most certainly won't tell another soul. That friend is both charmed and intrigued at your motives, but if you really wish to enslave him and uncover his mysteries, you might find this gift more effective than breeches*—Meg Grenham.

With Berthe's help, Sylvie had unpacked cobalt satin, ivory brocade, buttercup silk, silver tissue. A shimmering cascade of rich fabric spilled over her lap, while the French girl exclaimed and held up gown after gown. Another box contained petticoats, corsets, fans, stockings, and shoes—

She had learned enough, perhaps, to know when destiny could no longer be avoided.

Vienna and Paris had finally caught up to reclaim her.

A scented bath. Aromatic powder. A touch of rouge on her pale cheeks and on her lips, trembling now at the enormity of what she was doing. A touch of scent on her neck and between her breasts, touched gently in the bend of her elbows and between her legs. The chemise with its lace-trimmed sleeves. The stays, laced tightly by Berthe to maximize her cleavage. The underdress, overdress, the precise shaping of the folds. The maid's bony fingers tweaking at the bows on the bodice. Garters of blue ribbon with tiny bouquets of silk violets tied above her knees. The dressing of her hair, swept up from her face to support a toy lace cap with long streamers of ribbon.

And at last the silver slippers with their blushing rosettes and red heels. The delicate shoes of the siren.

Comtesse Sylvia Georgiana de Montevrain stared back at her from the mirror. She had used this shell before to entrap men into betraying their secrets. Because Yveshire needed information, because she had needed to make a living, she had taken virtual strangers to her bed. Like Bess, like Nance, like Sue, she had practiced until she had learned how to have sex without love.

Dove might forgive her for spying. He might even forgive her for betraying him to Yveshire. Would he ever forgive her for this?

*H*E CLOSED THE DOOR. POWER, MASCULINITY, AND THE COLD winter streets had stepped into the room with him. His wig framed his face, creating that stunning contrast of smooth male skin to the formal gloss of fashion. Without taking his gaze from hers, Dove flicked open a box and took one elegant pinch of snuff.

"I had no idea that such gowns would distress you," he said. "Though the result is magnificent."

The corset fenced in her ribs, making it difficult to breathe. She had forgotten that, forgotten the great weight of the train burdening her shoulders, forgotten that her arms, pinned in their tight sleeves, could no longer reach above her shoulders. Yet perhaps only the armor of dress and corset and petticoat made this possible.

"You asked Lady Grenham to do this?" she asked.

"Since we are to duel, ma'am, it seemed only fair to allow you this choice of weapon. You didn't have to accept it."

She fluttered her fan. Ribbons stirred at her neck and breast. "I'm working for your enemy. I intend to use every weapon at my disposal."

"I'm very glad of it," he said. "Since every other lady that ever graced this room before has also shared my bed before morning."

With a click of red heels, she walked, still fanning, toward him. Candle flames bent and danced as she passed. Light and shadows streamed over his face.

"There is always a first time for that not to happen."

"Oh, no, Sylvie," he said. "There is not."

Hot color rose up her neck. "You think that I cannot deny you?"

"Of course you can deny me. But you cannot deny the fire that is consuming this room. You cannot deny the flames that run across this carpet, that lick over your skin and mine, that run molten in our blood, that threaten to turn all of that silver tissue into ash. Especially when you intend to use your body as a sword to flay open my heart."

"How do you intend to use yours?"

"To convince you to trust me."

She stopped in front of him and closed her fan, turning her head in deliberate presentation of the soft skin of her neck and shoulder, the framed swell of her breasts.

"Were our positions reversed, would you trust me?"

His breathing did not waver, though the heat of his desire scorched her bare flesh. "Probably not. Yet I might risk it, if I decided I had nothing to lose by so doing."

In one practiced movement the fan cascaded open in her hand. She gazed up at him over the delicate tracery of silk and carved ivory. "And if I betray you tomorrow?"

He stepped forward to catch her around the waist. "By tomorrow, ma'am, you won't want to betray me," he said. "Shall we begin our sweet battle?"

Her fan fell like a leaf to the floor.

He kissed her until he felt drunk with kissing. His tongue thrust, his mouth explored. Like an explosion of honeyed, hot wine, she kissed back, firing ardor deep into his heart, blinding him. She tasted of spiced oranges and woman, sweet on his lips. Her heady scent enveloped him, offering oblivion and madness. Desire consumed, like a furnace.

Her teeth bit. Her throat sighed. When he broke away at last, her neck bent, offering her hot pulse to his hungry exploration. He held her, bent back over his arm like a willow in a gale, then rained small kisses down her long throat, over her firm bones, her soft flesh, down, down to the swell of her breasts. Though he ached, though his pulse thundered, he kept his touch controlled, subtle.

The secret to every woman's ardor was patient worship. Waiting to touch until, with small sighs and shudders, she begged to be touched.

Yet this time was different. This time was a fight, as if to the death.

"My hands are filled with silver tissue," he said against her ear. "Your ribs are encased in whalebone and thousands upon thousands of tiny stitches, like a shell. Do you think you can hide beneath the recklessness of this dress, with all its layers of petticoats and corset?"

She gazed up at him, the beauty of her blue eyes and dark lashes like a drug to his senses. "Why not? You are using all the power of your own silk and powder. Your dangerous male throat is wrapped safely in your cravat. Your lean animal body can pretend to be

civilized only because of an ivory silk waistcoat and a white linen
shirt. Allow me to peel away the layers, sir, and we shall see who is
hiding from whom."

"But now we know that we're enemies, don't you think the vulnerability of nakedness too risky?"

"I'm not vulnerable to this," she said. "You are. Even knowing
that I shall betray you to Yveshire, you will tell me all your secrets
and be happy to do so. Passion won't win me to your side, but your
desire will destroy you."

He spun her against the wall. "I beg to differ," he said. "But let's
find out. One layer at a time."

B ERTHE STOOD DEFIANTLY IN THE DOORWAY OF THE STABLE,
tapping one hand against her skirts and occasionally biting
at the thumbnail on the other. Snow had been falling on and off for
three days. The yard was softened by white drifts, folded like a cov-
erlet around pump and dung pile.

"Now then, stop that," Tanner Brink said quietly in her own language. "You'll spoil your pretty hands."

The French girl jerked. "You make me jump out of my skin!"

"Do I? Well then, we're even, since you just about make me
jump out of mine."

"What do you mean?"

He took her elbow and led her back into the shadows. Warmth
steamed gently from Abdiel's stall. The bay raised his head and
nickered softly.

"Oh, quiet now," the Gypsy said to the horse. "Your master is
proving himself every bit as fine of a stallion as you are."

Hot color washed into Berthe's face. She hated it, but at least
Tanner Brink couldn't tell in the dark.

"So how long has it been now?" he asked.

"Since they've been locked in his bedroom? Three days. Lud, but you think they'd have had enough by now!"

He pushed her down onto a truss of hay, then squatted opposite her, his back against the stable wall.

"Tell me."

"Like I told you before, it began Sunday night. Someone sent clothes. Was that the duke?"

"No, not the duke. So you helped her to dress as a lady."

"That's what I'm paid for, though she's no better than me."

"Wrong again," the Gypsy said.

Berthe thought her skin might catch fire with rage. "She's not a lady. She's a whore. Yet she's the one he lusts after."

"Hush, hush," Tanner said. "So he's a man. Now, Sunday night? Tell me again."

"They were locked in there for hours, missed their supper."

"I imagine they were more aware of another kind of appetite," the Gypsy said.

Berthe almost choked, but this odd brown man wasn't going to see her lose control. "Long after midnight, he rang for wine and food and hot water for washing. The footman wasn't allowed in. Mr. Dovenby took the tray at the door, but his man caught a glimpse of the room."

"And?"

"She was still dressed. So was he. The bed hadn't been slept in, but the hangings were torn down and strewn across the floor. He could tell from the master's face what had happened."

The Gypsy grinned. "And Monday morning?"

"When the footman brought coal and coffee, Mr. Dovenby still wouldn't let him in. But he was no longer wearing his jacket. And her silver tissue overdress was flung over a chair."

"What did he say?"

"Nothing. He ordered more hot water and food. Monday night,

when the man brought supper, Dove opened the door in his shirt-sleeves. She was standing by the fireplace, wearing nothing but her petticoats, like a painting of sin."

"But Mr. Dovenby still wore his wig?"

"Yes. And she still had her hair dressed like I'd done it. Why?"

Tanner Brink hugged himself. "Nothing. Go on."

"Tuesday morning, he'd tossed his shirt and her petticoats out into the hallway with the dirty dishes. They were all stained with wine and with butter."

"*Butter?*"

"Well, butter or cream—how should I know? When he opened the door last night, the master wore just his robe. Though he still had his stockings on. And his wig. The candles had been doused, so the footman couldn't see her, but he thought she might be in the bed."

Tanner Brink buried his face in both hands. His shoulders shook in silent merriment.

"And this morning?"

"He rang for a bathtub and his shaving gear and hot water and fresh sheets. Normally he has clean sheets every day."

"Well, then. They didn't use the sheets till last night, did they?"

"You think he didn't have her on Sunday and Monday? The foot-man swore to it."

"I think a man and a woman can make love without using the bed." The Gypsy thrust his fist against his mouth for a moment, stifling more laughter. "So now it's Wednesday. What did the footman say about how Dove looked this morning?"

"He looked like a pirate. I saw him. His wig and stockings were gone. With the closed door at his back, he made the men leave everything in the hall—a ranking of buckets like you never saw in your life. He carried it all into his bedroom later by himself. His hair looked like a crow's nest, and he had bruises on his throat and chest."

"Bruises?"

"Love bruises. You know."

"Ah, bruises! And then?"

"I don't know. He hasn't opened his door since. The staff keep taking away the ashes and dirty dishes and slops without ever seeing into the room. And now it's Wednesday night, when he always goes out."

"But Dove's not going out tonight, is he?"

"No," she said with a toss of her head. "And meanwhile it's been up to me to report to the duke by myself."

"Well, well," the Gypsy said. "You are a merry little trouble-maker, aren't you?"

CHAPTER FOURTEEN

L ET'S FIND OUT. ONE LAYER AT A TIME.

Sylvie slept. Her hair streamed out across his pillows in a pale fan of gold.

It was Wednesday, but he would not be going to St. John's.

Dove built up the fire, then once again left the ashes with the used dishes in the hall. Wrapped in his long robe, he walked to the window. Though the streetlamps were lit, no one was about. A few tracks, from servants or tradesmen, crisscrossed through the fresh snow like threads in a net. It had snowed intermittently for three days. Most of social London had prudently slid to a halt.

Sylvie sighed and turned over, but she didn't wake.

Dove pressed his forehead against the cold glass. Memories jostled.

Had either of them expected a repeat of that sweet ardor in front of the fireplace in Mr. Fennimore's office, or the gentle lovemaking that had followed the next morning? That was forever gone, burned away in their desperate, soul-wrenching plunge into passion.

We can find our pleasure, ma'am, without removing a stitch, he had said. And so they had. On that first night, as wild urgency and mutual defiance had trapped them there at the door, they had made love fully clothed, standing up, knowing they were both about to be carried into uncharted lands.

Uncharted lands: new, all new, for both of them, as if they were inspired by folly, while the pagan gods laughed at their presumption. *Uncharted lands:* where intensity waited to enthrall, madden, possess two foolish mortals—and potency seemed inexhaustible.

Ardor carried them next from the door to the bed, but they had made love again before reaching it. To his eager flesh she was hot and wanton, naked below the waist, encased in whalebone above it. Her legs clung about his hips, while her hands gripped the blue velvet hangings at her back and he supported her in both arms. The gods of Olympus tossed back their wine and cheered.

Dove smiled wryly to himself. Ah, Sylvie!

Had she meant only to goad him? Drive him into a frenzy? No doubt. In the end she and the ripped hangings and his own self-control all slid together, conquered by passion, to the floor. In the afterglow, as he stroked her hair and kissed the sides of her mouth, she had gazed back at him from heavy-lidded eyes, smiling with lazy content, her mouth lovely.

"I feel a little like a maiden carried away by Zeus—"

"In the guise of a bull, or a swan, or a shower of coin?" he asked.

"All of them! But the maiden isn't sure if she has woken to find that the monster is truly a god, or—"

"Or if it's just that the gods are all monsters?"

She curled deeper into his embrace and laughed. "Everyone knows that the gods aren't required to tell the truth to mere mortals, so perhaps she no longer cares."

A strand of her hair curled about his forefinger, gilt as a buttercup. How very imprudent to feel such a helpless love for a woman who still, for all he knew, planned to destroy him!

"But what if Zeus has discovered that he hasn't carried away a mere mortal, but the triple goddess of love and wisdom and passion, who is more powerful than he is?"

"Then we shall have war in heaven." She glanced up at the torn canopy. "I think, perhaps, we already have. Have we broken your bed?"

Her sheer loveliness unnerved him and her courage took away his breath. "Nothing is broken, ma'am—just the heart."

"Whose heart?"

"That remains to be discovered."

She propped herself on one elbow to run a fingertip along his roughened jaw. As her eyes searched his, her breathing became ragged and her pupils dilated into darkness.

"This is not something," she said, "that I have ever done before."

"What exactly have you never done before?"

She grinned. "Destroyed the bed hangings."

"I promise we'll discover far more interesting new things than that, ma'am," he said.

She leaned closer. Her scent enveloped him in a kind of lunatic bliss. His pulse leaped, uncontrolled.

"Yet to repeat what we've already done may be enough." Her lips robbed him of vision as she feathered tiny kisses across his lids. "Neither have I ever done it before with all my clothes on," she added. "It's oddly vulnerable *not* to be undressed."

"That's the idea. Our only purpose is to uncover vulnerability."

"Yours or mine?"

"You intend to prove that you're the better armored," he said. "I already know that you are, but I still intend to disarm you."

"Though your risk is greater than mine?"

He slid his hand beneath her skirts. Her thigh curved, a woman's thigh. Lovely. Soft. Smooth. Heat streamed up his arm, firing longing. He was instantly erect once again.

"Perhaps it's not. You've just admitted that to allow a lover free access beneath your clothes feels even more intimate, more hazardous, than simple nakedness."

"A lover?" she asked. "Or an enemy?"

His fingertips lingered at the smooth indent where her leg joined the sweep of female hip, the slight swell of her belly and the gilt fuzz below it. His blood pounded with importunate promise.

"You think you're my enemy," he replied. "Yet I am not yours."

"You will be," she said as her head fell back. "Don't think that I won't take from you everything that I can!"

"Everything I give is freely given. You will give back in equal measure."

"No," she whispered. "I shall not."

Dove closed his palm over moisture. Her eyes closed. Her breathing scattered into fragments.

"Then you're a coward, after all," he said.

"Perhaps."

He rubbed gently in small circles until her breath exploded and she cried out: inarticulate cries, moaning into his ear as her fingers clutched at his sleeve. His own ardor raced in his blood, throbbing its demands. Calling on all of his self-control, he ignored it.

"And now, no doubt, you're a starving coward?"

"After that? Hardly!" She swallowed and opened her eyes. "I am honest enough to admit that."

He smoothed her skirts back over her legs. "I meant for food and wine. No woman, however much she may otherwise be satisfied, ever fell in love on an empty stomach."

Her pupils were still dilated as if she were drugged. He kissed the lids closed, as she had done earlier to his. Somewhere in the house a clock chimed.

"It's three in the morning, ma'am." He stripped off his jacket to make a pillow for her head. "My coat. Now you owe me a layer. Meanwhile, allow me to order our supper."

Did it seem like a truce? Behind the screen in the corner, replete for the moment and without removing more clothing, they washed each other in turn using a basin of hot water. Though touching her with the washcloth launched him into a kind of lunacy, though his cock stirred and hardened again as she sponged him, though she kissed the head briefly, charging him with helpless pleasure, he only smiled at her and invited her to eat cold meat and sip wine.

But for the rest of that night, wild urgency drove them all over the room once again. Amidst the ruins of their meal, they made love on the carpet before the fire. Then on the window seat. Once using one of the chairs by the grate. She aroused him, fired him, drove him into a frenzy of potency and aching tenderness, as if he were being flayed alive by desire.

One more layer?

They slept at last, exhausted, wrapped once again in blue velvet and the embrace of her skirts, while her silver overdress glimmered like a ghost from the dresser where he'd thrown it.

In the morning his sheets and pillows lay as untracked as the fresh snow that had fallen during the night.

*L*ATER THAT DAY—MONDAY—SHE SHED HER SKIRT AND bodice, and he peeled off his waistcoat. Still the bed lay untouched. Still their ardor seemed inexhaustible. As night fell she stood beside the fire—lovely as honeysuckle, dangerous as nightshade—in her lace-trimmed stays and silk petticoats, while he flung open the door and called for their supper.

"We're to have lobster and oysters and wine," he said, turning back to face her, "with the mad luxury of fresh grapes, asparagus, and cucumber, harvested from a hothouse. After which, I believe my chef has prepared syllabub and spiced fruit."

"I'm to be suborned next with ambrosia, food for the gods?"

"Why not? You think I won't enlist all of the senses?"

"How could I think that?" She smiled at him, recklessly. "When I already know to my cost that you will. But perhaps you've forgotten that one taste of ambrosia may confer immortality? Then we may be trapped here in our battle forever."

"Then let us feast," he said, "to make sure of it."

Dove took the tray from his footman and set it down before the fire. He poured wine and knelt to break open the loaf of fresh bread. Steam curled. He lifted covers from hot dishes. His mouth filled with anticipation as scents rose and mingled. He was hungry. Very hungry. Though not only—in spite of twenty-four hours of lovemaking—for food.

"When I was a boy," he said, "this was how I imagined bliss."

Sylvie slipped onto one of the chairs, leaned forward, and inhaled savory scents. "What was?"

He sat back on his haunches. Her naked throat gleamed like silk in the firelight. "To eat lobster and oysters in front of a fire."

She accepted a plate filled with food and bit into succulence. "A simple enough idea of bliss."

"That's because I was a child," he said. "I didn't know about the more adult forms of bliss, which are so much deeper."

Rue stained her laugh, as if she couldn't quite help herself. "And everyone knows that seafood only enhances those adult games?"

He winked, freeing an oyster from its shell as he stretched out to lie, propped on one elbow, at her feet.

"You think that you and I need any aphrodisiac? Lud, ma'am, from that laugh anyone would think that you were filled with contentment already. Has it worked?"

She frowned mockingly at him and took a spear of asparagus. "Has what worked?"

"Are you induced yet to my side? Will you cleave to me forever? Will you tell Yveshire to go whistle in the wind for his evidence?"

"No," she said, licking butter from the corner of her mouth. "Offer me whatever delirium of sensual pleasure you wish, you won't win."

Dove refilled her wineglass. "Then we must try another layer."

She dipped a second stalk of asparagus, set the tip between her lips, and sucked off the melted butter. He thought he might explode.

"I've already lost my dress, sir, and you seem very dangerous in nothing but your shirtsleeves."

"I can be a great deal more dangerous than this. Meanwhile, I will offer you my neckcloth for the sight of your bare arms."

"So to prove you wrong, I must eat my oysters in my stays and chemise?" She gazed down beneath lowered lashes. "How will you reward the removal of my petticoats?"

"With cream. You will not want to stain all that silk."

"Cream? But we're still enjoying the savory course. You *want* to hurry past the oysters?"

"Never! I will linger for as long as it takes over every remove. Yet the sweets still inexorably follow."

He offered her a slice of spiced pear, pinioned on a fork. Lemon-honey sauce dripped into the cupped palm of his other hand. She bit into the pear and swallowed. Then, supporting his hand with her own, she leaned down to lick up the drops of sauce, freely offering the swell of her breasts to his gaze. Transfixed, with every sense aflame, Dove tore away his cravat and tossed it aside as her tongue swirled over his palm.

"A cravat alone is no fair trade for both panniers and petticoat," she said.

She lifted her glass. Burgundy trickled, then broke in cool rivulets across his chest. The stain bloomed like a rose on his white linen shirt. Her tongue touched as she licked wine from his throat.

"Very well." He tipped back his head in a kind of blind ecstasy. "You've just earned my shirt, too, but now the price is most definitely both hoops and petticoat."

"Then take them," she said.

His palms closed on her slim waist, his fingers fumbled in tapes and laces, while his lips found her wine-rich mouth. She trembled like a stricken waif in his arms, madly kissing, as he untied, then accidentally knotted, then ripped at the tapes. Hooks scattered as he cast aside hoops and silk, leaving her clad only in her white, beribboned corset and the sleeveless, knee-length chemise beneath it.

"Time now for cream," he said.

"But you haven't yet fulfilled your part of the trade." Firelight caressed her naked arm—ivory smooth, firmly modeled—as she reached for a cut-glass dish. "Then you may feel the cool slide of this syllabub on your naked belly."

"Certainly, ma'am." He ripped his stained shirt down the front, then cast it aside. "Since I intend to eat the rest of my supper from yours."

She tipped the dish. Sweetened, port-flavored cream chased the burgundy down his chest to follow the indent of muscle all the way to his belly. She dropped to both knees to run her tongue after the stream in a merry torment of pleasure.

"I think," he said, grasping the silver jug that contained the lemon-honey sauce, "that cream and wine and syllabub and desire are all about to mingle into one ferocious, satiating feast."

"If I allow that, will you tell me your secrets?" she asked, glancing up at him, her eyes pools of azure. "Will you betray your soul to me for it?"

"Yes and yes, but not simply for that," he replied. "Only for love."

*U*NCHARTED LANDS: WHERE PASSION MOCKED AND MESMER-ized, reveled and consumed, and potency proved not be inexhaustible, after all.

In the moments between food and sleep and lovemaking, he talked.

After she had sponged warm water on his skin and allowed him to do the same for her, while he held her head pillowed on his shoulder, while his fingers traced the sweet curve of her neck, the delectable corner of her jaw, while he watched the candles flickering on the mantel, he told stories. Long, rambling stories about his childhood in the Lakes. Little anecdotes about the life of a bachelor in London. He didn't expect her to reciprocate.

"It's very lovely where I grew up," he said. "Magical. The stark wildness of Borrowdale wore a furrow in my soul. When the mists flow down from the hills; when the sun suddenly cracks open the clouds to spin diamonds across the water; whether ice frosts the bare trees, or summer stamps them into full leaf, it can be breathtaking. Yet on long winter evenings when wind and rain trapped us inside, I found myself craving other kinds of beauty: that of paintings and sculpture. I thought that I wanted to make a fortune, so that I could collect art."

"And did you?"

"What?"

"Make a fortune?"

"A small one, which I squandered later in less innocent pursuits. The cost to oneself of acquiring a real fortune is far too great."

"Because it can rarely be done without robbing someone else?"

"There are many personal costs to making money. That is one. No collection of paintings and sculpture was worth it."

"So you collected women's hearts, instead," she said. "Without ever really giving yourself to any woman."

Her voice was so drowsy that he didn't reply. He just kissed her and let her sleep, while he wondered whether that was true.

IT WAS TUESDAY MORNING, AFTER THEY HAD SPONGED AWAY the residues of another night, before they touched on the personal again. He had been talking about his youth, that last innocent moment before the simple friendships of his childhood had begun to change in his hands—like the fairy Melusina—into something quite different, long before he'd met Meg.

"You speak of love," Sylvie said. "I believe you did love Lady Grenham, at least a little. Other than those boyhood infatuations, was there ever anyone else?"

He was kneeling at the grate, taking care of the fire. At her question he stopped and looked up.

"There was another lady that I believed I could have loved, though Meg was still my lover at the time, and I was faithful to her, always."

"What do you mean—*could* have?"

Dove washed his hands and set the basin outside the door. Sylvie sat down by the fire and stretched her feet onto the fender to warm her toes. When she'd been dressed as a boy, the pose had seemed merely natural and comfortable. Now, with her bare arms and shoulders—and her long legs encased in nothing but silk stockings and beribboned garters—the effect was mesmerizing.

"I hardly knew her," he said, his mouth dry. "I just witnessed something that happened between her and the man she later married. She thought that she hated him, yet her heart knew that love takes sacrifice and trust and risk. Because she was brave, she didn't shrink from taking the gamble."

The faintest tinge of color washed up Sylvie's neck. "And was the man worthy of her valor?"

"Oh, yes. Though he had no idea of it at the time. Men rarely do."

The color deepened. "And you think I should take that risk with you?"

Dove walked up to stand behind her. He stroked his hand over her hair. Such lustrous hair, the arrangement tangled now, as if skeins of silk had been played with by kittens. He pulled out a few more pins, destroyed a pretty arrangement of silk flowers, and watched the freed strands of gold slide across his fingers.

"I'm already doing so with you," he said.

"And perhaps I'm already in love with you," she said, "and have been all along."

His heart stopped, then skipped back into motion, thudding heavily in his chest. Dove leaned down to kiss the tender curve of her nape. "But you don't yet believe that love is enough?"

She turned to gaze up at him, then stood to slide her arms around his back, while she laid her head into the hollow of his shoulder.

"I don't know," she said. "Perhaps it takes another layer."

*A*NOTHER LAYER. A LAZY, SENSUAL DAY, THAT STRIPPED away his breeches in exchange for her stays. So apart from his stockings and underdrawers, he was naked, while she still wore her short white chemise. Sleek, translucent, it slid over her hips and breasts like light dancing on water. It made her seem almost innocent. It made her so damned alluring, he thought he might die of desire.

Over meals and between lovemaking, they discussed, argued, laughed, over art and philosophy and literature. Later, when he again had breath to talk and was roaming over topics at random, she began to talk back. It began with little tales of her dimly remembered early childhood in England. Small, silly anecdotes. Then her family's flight to Italy, when she had still been too young to quite comprehend what it was all about, followed by a girlhood of long, hot summers and cool winters. She had been taught by Italian nuns and by private tutors, and believed—as all young girls believed—that she would grow up to marry well and have children.

She revealed nothing incriminating—nothing of that other past that Tanner Brink, too, seemed to be hiding from him—but they were precious insights, all the same.

"I never really expected to see England again, though in a way it was the promised land," she said. "My mother never forgot, never quite accepted Italy. She talked about English roses and woodlands, as if nowhere else in the world had such flowers or such trees. When Jack climbed the beanstalk, the magical land above the clouds was this one. Whenever there was a place, once upon a time, far, far away, it was Sussex or Rutland or Wiltshire."

"So now you've come home."

"Home?" she replied, as if truly taken aback. "Lud, what a strange word! I don't have any home."

"You think so only because you've seen nothing of England but London in one of the nastiest winters we've had in years. In the spring I could show you—"

"I won't be with you in the spring," she interrupted. "I will have betrayed you long before that."

Yet that night, washed and fed and replete, they curled up together in his bed. There were no layers of clothing left.

S YLVIE STRUGGLED UP FROM SLEEP AS IF SHE HAD BEEN drowned in dreams. Her bottom fit snugly against his belly, their legs spooned together, his arm about her waist. She lay quietly for a moment, feeling the security and allure of that warm presence. *Home.* Foolish thought!

Without waking him, she extricated herself and sat up.

Slowly her eyes focused on the room. It was already light. Everything was neat, comfortable, even the torn-away bed hangings, which he had folded beneath their discarded clothing. The fire had burned low, but it still warmed the room. For three days Dove had efficiently cleaned and ordered, while stripping her piece by piece to her soul.

He sighed in his sleep and moved his hand as if to reach for her. She slipped from the bed, wrapped herself in his robe, and crossed the room to see to the fire. The flames soon leaped up, burning brightly.

Dove turned over. She glanced back at him. Light caressed his closed lids and olive-smooth skin. His jaw was forbiddingly shadowed with stubble. She had known it during the night, tantalizingly rough against her cheek and belly and thighs. There was nothing left of the elegant rogue of the silver wig and exquisite grooming. He slept like a dark angel, his hair tossed wildly about his ears.

Yet he was a man. He was Dove. He was her first real lover.

"You were wrong," she whispered to herself as treacherous tears burned and threatened. "Nakedness is far more vulnerable."

Now his lovely body and mind and skills were all lost in dreams—his tongue robbed of stories and laughter and philosophy and kisses—while Sylvie choked back her weakness and resisted the impulse to climb back into his bed to be ravished once more.

When she looked up again, his eyes were open and gazing into hers.

"Ah," he said. "My secretary, frowning at me like Aurora."

"Dawn doesn't frown," she said. "Aurora is always all smiles."

Dove pushed back the covers. He looked at her in silence for a few moments, then swung from the bed and walked naked toward the door. Even after so many days, the sight of his body took her breath away.

"Exactly," he replied. "Aurora's frowns are inevitably false, because dawn is always followed by day, even in winter."

He grabbed a towel, covered his hips, leaned his head into the corridor and shouted. There was an instant thumping and scurrying of feet.

"Lud," he said as he closed the door behind him. "The kitchen staff get a raise tomorrow. I've just demanded the bathtub."

Half an hour later he dragged the tub into the room by himself and filled it, bucket by bucket.

"Come, ma'am," he said. "This is for you. Your modesty, what's left of it, may remain undisturbed. I'll see to our bed."

While she bathed, he stripped the bed and made it up again with clean sheets. He came back to help rinse her hair, running strands through his fingers, while pouring clean water over her head from a jug. The sensation was delicious, both innocent and sinfully wicked. Instantly she wanted him to touch her further. Instead he held up a large towel for her.

Wrapped once again in the robe, she sat at the fire to dry her hair and drink hot coffee, while he emptied and refilled the tub—bucket by bucket—before he at last sank into the water himself.

"Ah," he said, leaning back and closing his eyes. "Nothing like hot water to soothe exhausted muscles—pray, ma'am, do not ask which muscle."

She laughed and threw her empty cup at him.

Spraying water he reached up to snatch it from the air. "God forgive me for teaching my secretary how to throw!"

"Be glad that you didn't also teach her how to kill."

"She doesn't need to be taught that, ma'am. I'm already slain." Dove sank beneath the water and blew bubbles like a child.

Sylvie marched up to the tub to retrieve the cup from the floor where he'd set it. He surfaced, his face infused with laughter, his jaw outlined in darkness—another few days and he would have the beginnings of a real beard.

"I don't stand a chance," she said. "You're not slain yet."

"Yes, I am." He rubbed one palm over his wet chin. "But if you would like to murder my flesh along with my heart, then it's time you earned your keep."

She grabbed a jug of cold water. "I've not earned that yet?"

"Your lovemaking earns my heart and soul, ma'am. It does not earn your keep. As my secretary, on the other hand—" She began to tip the jug, but his arm moved, trapping her hand. "One of your duties is to shave me."

"No," she said.

"I made this clear when I first hired you, Mr. White," Dove said. "You refuse my direct orders?"

He opened his fingers and she set down the jug. "We're surely past all that now?"

"We are? Then you capitulate?"

"Never!"

Neat as an otter, he rubbed a towel over his face. "So your choice is clear: if you wish to remain here as my secretary, you must shave me."

"You would allow your enemy at your throat with a razor?"

"That depends on the enemy, ma'am. My shaving supplies are on that washstand."

She walked up to the washstand and opened the brass-bound mahogany case. Everything inside was beautifully fitted: silver-mounted brushes, little bottles, soap—and in its own long case, an ivory-handled razor.

Sylvie stared at the straight blade, already honed to a deadly edge.

"You would trust me with this at your throat?"

"Why not?"

"Because I've never before shaved a man in my life," she said. "What if my hand slips?"

"Then I expire, bloodied and conquered."

Razor in hand, she came back to the tub. "You really want to be the first to allow me that experiment?"

He grinned and sank deeper. "I believe I've already been the first in almost everything that counts."

She leaned close to whisper in his ear. "I think your experience has been just as unique as mine, sir."

"Yet you think male pride will allow me to admit it? Pray shave me, sweet Sylvie, or my chin will frighten ladies and children, and throw horses into fits."

He closed his eyes.

"What do I do?"

"Scrape that pretty thing over my face to remove the stubble." He nodded at the washstand. "But soap comes first."

"You already have soap," she said.

"Shaving soap, ma'am. In the case. A common enough commercial variety."

She returned with the soap, wet her hands, and began to massage suds over his chin. Next would come the prickly lines of his jaw and upper lip, the vulnerable angle below his ear, the column of his throat: the intimate knowledge of every plane of his face, a knowledge sinking deep into her bones that could never be eradicated—as long as she lived, as long as she lived—as the knowledge of his body could never be eradicated. Deep in the bone. As long as she lived.

Yet he caught her hands in both of his. "Alas, delectable as your touch may be, I cannot insist that you take the skin off your palms. This is what the brushes are for."

Sylvie wiped the soap from her hands. Her palms tingled. Her blood surged, hot and urgent. "Why didn't you say so?"

"Because the feel of your fingers on my face was so erotic. However, allow me to explain—"

She followed his instructions, using the shaving cup and brush.

"And now the lethal blade?" she said, picking it up.

"Yes. The lethal blade."

Dove tipped his head back, displaying the devastating lines of his throat and jaw. His eyes remained closed. His breath came deep and even. Sylvie stood over him with the razor in her hand. *The lethal blade.*

As if stricken into ice, she was stone. She was one of the Nine Maidens, turned into granite for dancing on the Sabbath. She was Long Meg, a stone finger pointing at heaven, never to be sensate again. Yet she was also heat and ice and prickles of awareness, in her breasts and belly and legs. She still claimed to be his enemy, and he offered his naked gullet to her dangerous fingers.

"If the soap gets too dry," he said, "it won't be as easy."

"The blade is sharp?" Her voice sounded rough.

"As a shrew's tongue. If it's not, I'll have my man's hide." He held up a washcloth stretched between his two hands. "Try it."

She slashed down. The cloth sliced neatly into two halves. She barely stopped the sweep of her hand in time. The blade hovered a few inches above his heart. Jerking back, she dropped the razor to the floor, where it fell with a clatter. Her heart leaped back to life, pounding in her chest like a drum. Her hands shook.

"Damn you! What if I'd cut you?"

He opened his eyes and grinned at her. "I'd probably have noticed."

"Are you lunatic? You could have bled to death!" Before he should see her mad tears—of fear, of regret?—she spun away and stormed to the fireplace. "Shave yourself," she said. "I cannot do it."

"Lud, ma'am! You're afraid to scratch me? I thought you intended to see me hanged?"

She rubbed away the betraying moisture. "Hanging doesn't shed blood like a broken bottle of burgundy."

"Yet it results in death just as convincingly."

Tears still burned, salt and bitter. She gulped them back. "Logic was never a female strength, they say, and nor is it yours: you *knew* I might cut you."

"Lud, I was sure of it! So I have escaped rather lightly."

She spun back to face him. "What the devil made you risk it?"

"I just wondered, ma'am, if you'd take care or if you'd kill me."

"Oh, I will kill you yet," she said. "And I will torture you first. Just not in that tub."

Water splashed as he slumped back. "Oh, you torture me already, Sylvie. Very nicely. So now I have to grow a beard?"

"I'll bring you the mirror. You may shave yourself." She took the mirror from the washstand and stared at her own face. Her skin was pale, yet hectic color burned in both cheeks. "I'm not afraid of the looking glass," she said. "But I'm very afraid of you."

"It's not fear," he said. "It's love."

Dove ducked to wash away the lather, leaving his incipient beard to remain darkly on his chin. He looked like a vagabond. Sylvie stood and held the mirror, watching him, while her pulse thundered.

It's not fear, her heart repeated and repeated. *It's love.*

AFTER BATH, BREAKFAST, AND A GRAND ARGUMENT ABOUT some unimportant topic that he could no longer remember, he took her back to his bed for another afternoon of lovemaking. When he woke, she was gazing at him, her eyes shadowed, but she was smiling.

"Of course, there was no robbery on the journey," she said. "You've probably guessed that by now. The duke took care of all those details. Thus, no smugglers, only some desperately shady characters that Yveshire hired to see Berthe and me safely to England."

"More of Tanner's cousins, no doubt," Dove said.

"You think so?"

"I damned well know so." He grinned at her genuine surprise, though her smile might yet break his heart. "If Tanner's not also busily involved with Yveshire, why the devil didn't he tell me the truth about you? He must have discovered it. Unless, of course, he just decided—for mad reasons of his own—that you're my fate."

"Ah," Sylvie said. "So you paid Mr. Brink to uncover my true past? What did he tell you?"

"Only some cock-and-bull story—the same one, no doubt, that you've been telling me?"

"It's nothing that matters," she said, blushing. "I'll tell you the truth now, if you like."

"I don't care," Dove said, and meant it.

He pulled her into his arms and kissed her. The kiss led to more kisses and yet more, in every imaginable crevice of her delectable body. She returned them, licking, suckling, holding nothing back, fulfilling every wildest male fantasy, until they were both satiated and sliding inexorably back into sleep.

IT WAS DARK: WEDNESDAY EVENING. SYLVIE SLEPT, HER HAIR spread like Faerie gold over the pillows. For the first time in months he would not be going to St. John's. Dove lit candles and rebuilt the fire, then walked to the window.

A carriage trundled through the snow in the street. One brave soul who had decided to venture out in spite of the weather. Dove touched his jaw, where the new growth of beard still prickled. Her suckled marks on his throat ached sweetly. His back and shoulders, he knew, were a little scratched—when in her tumult she had scored him faintly with teeth or nails, and not even known she had done it.

At calmer moments he had given her one or two gentle little bite marks of her own, but only in spots where no one would ever see them and where the bruises would fade in a day.

Whatever her previous experience, no one had taught her that before, such a simple, innocent game for lovers.

He was glad that no one had taught her. It was precious to him—though he had no illusions about wanting chastity or virginity—to feel that he alone had revealed this new world to her, that together they had created something unique and theirs alone. She was experienced, yet she had come to him with a strangely innocent joy.

Yet he was also sorry that no one had taught her. It meant that she had gone to other men's beds with indifference, or unconscious resistance, or even fear. It meant that she had been used. It meant that other men had exploited her loveliness and not even known that they abused a work of art.

That thought kindled a bright flame of possessive anger—something he had never experienced before and wasn't even sure he should allow. Alas, it also explained why she might still be able to resist him, even after everything they had shared. In which case, he had lost and the game was Yveshire's. Because he had nothing else left to give her, except a lifetime.

He pressed his face against cold glass and felt a shiver like a sword thrust run through his heart.

"What is it?" she asked behind him.

Startled, he looked around. Sylvie was standing like a Valkyrie beside the bed. Like sunlight on water, her gilt hair streamed down over the robe he'd had his servants bring for her.

"Dove," she whispered. "What is it?"

"Only that our combat has come to an end. I have no weapons left."

"You don't need them."

For a moment he stood stock-still, listening to the pounding of his heart.

"What do you mean?" he asked at last.

"You have won," she said. "I am ripped apart, like Prometheus, as if I had stolen fire from the gods. I cannot pretend otherwise any longer. You have won."

"No," he said. "No win. No loss. We are equals, Sylvie."

"Perhaps not that," she said. "It's taking every ounce of courage that I have to say this. In spite of everything, I trust you. To my shame, I trust you. I can't help it. You have nothing left to fear from me."

Was she telling him the truth? How could he possibly know if she was telling the truth? "What about the duke?"

"For the first time in my life, I'm trusting to instinct. I don't know what happened with Yveshire's brother, but I cannot believe that you're an evil man, or that you acted entirely without honor. Whatever you tell me, whatever I discover, I won't betray you to the duke. I promise."

Instinct—the only reason he believed her and would now freely gamble their future on that belief?

"If you'd known the truth about Lord Edward Vane, you'd have pursued him as vengefully as I did. I cannot explain why, because others are involved. We must just trust each other. I love you, Sylvie."

She smiled with heartbreaking bravado, as if she were trying to tease. "You will even show me the rest of your secrets? I'm prepared to tell you mine: even about Yveshire."

His heart missed a beat at what he might be risking if his instincts were wrong, if she was lying now—

"I have no *hanging* secrets, though I do have secrets that might ruin me rather thoroughly in society. If you'll dress once again as George in your breeches and wig, I'll take you into the City and show you."

"You can trust me," she said. "Yveshire must pursue his vendettas in his own way—"

A loud knocking thundered, interrupting her.

Dove strode across the room to fling open the door. A man stood in the hallway. Snowflakes traced like lichen over his moleskin cap.

"Trouble," Tanner Brink said.

CHAPTER FIFTEEN

"Mr. Brink," Dove said. "I've been wanting to talk to you."

The Gypsy grimaced. "No time for that. Tom Henley has fled. You'd better come to the print works now. It's not wise to take Abdiel. I've brought ponies."

"How many?"

"Three." Tanner Brink nodded at Sylvie. "One for each of us and one for your secretary."

"Even though you know that she's been working for the duke all along, even though you lied to me about what your cousins really discovered about her in France?"

Tanner shrugged and grinned, rubbing one finger over his nose as he winked at Sylvie. "She won't harm you. Nor will I."

"I believe it," Dove replied. "But while she and I were otherwise engaged, my merry forger has been running his own enterprise? And now an untrustworthy rogue like you thinks that my secretary should come with us to see what it is?"

"Of course I must come," Sylvie said, while his words echoed in her heart: *I believe it*.

"And if I tell you that it might be dangerous? That I would rather you stayed here?"

"Then now that I've committed myself, I should insist on coming."

"Very well." His smile warmed like the sun. "We may assume, whatever happens, that Yveshire will protect you."

Now that I've committed myself! Such a blind, absolute faith, both heady and terrifying!

Her soul had opened to him, unfurled as the heart of a rose unfurls to the sun. Her feet sang, her hair streamed with desire. This was all new. All new. This craving and this ecstatic joy. The brilliance that seemed to shimmer about him. The deep softening in her bones, as if his glance melted her. And he *had* melted her, entering her so deeply, so profoundly, that her womb had risen with soft kisses to meet his arousal every time they'd made love.

She would risk everything and abandon all prudence in the face of these mad new feelings?

Yes, her heart said. *Yes. Yes. I will risk everything. I put my fate in his exquisite hands, and devil take tomorrow! I love him*—

Armed with sword and pistols, Dove rode ahead of her. Tanner Brink followed at their heels. She was dressed once again as George. With his dark growth of stubble and without his wig, Dove seemed indistinguishable from any of England's most disreputable rogues.

Snow muffled and disguised, as if London were wrapped in cotton ready for shipping to the Indies. The ponies trotted through streets like black tunnels, while white flakes piled onto buildings and signs, railings and pavements, and settled coldly on her flushed face. They took a different, perhaps more direct, route. Until she heard the wheel turning sluggishly, dragging at the water, she had no idea where they were, but the stream rumbled as it pushed its way under the bridge, a hollow sound like distant thunder.

Still wrapped in his cloak, Dove swung down and unlocked the door. He ushered Sylvie inside, while Tanner Brink waited with the ponies. The rooms lay silent, cold and dark, only the thud of the water-wheel breaking the silence.

"The wheel always turns?" Sylvie asked. "Even when no one is here?"

"Either that, or it freezes in place," Dove replied. "Though it's disengaged right now, driving nothing."

He struck a spark and lit candles, then led her deeper into the building. Everything they passed—papers, copper plates, stacks of leaflets—received a quick perusal. In the corner where the forger had once sat, a door now stood open. A door, she realized, that had before seemed to be part of the paneling. The flame in his hand flickered as Dove disappeared.

Sylvie followed. At the bottom of a flight of steps lay a basement. Dove lit a lamp. Light flared over a small brick-lined room, jammed with stacks of paper and another printing press. A desk for inkwells and quills, well used, sat in one corner.

"A secret room," she said. "Is this where you print all that erotica?"

Dove was examining piles of paper, cases of bound booklets. "Lud, no! That gets printed abovestairs, along with the rest of my more respectable trade."

"If *that* was respectable, sir, I dread to think what you do down here."

"I indulge in the most scurrilous and ungentlemanly of pastimes: I write."

"*This* is where you go every day?"

"When I'm not out and about collecting material." He tossed a set of pamphlets into her hands. "This is what might get me in trouble."

Sylvie propped herself against a stack of bound boxes and began to read.

"Oh," she said, after a few minutes. "So you're a reformer, Mr. Dovenby? You would abolish the trade in slaves and end indentured servitude? You would reorder children's labor and introduce new rules to govern apprenticeship? You would even improve the status of women?"

"Someone must make the arguments for change," he said, still leafing through papers.

"But you're wise to print such things in secret?"

"None of that is illegal, exactly, but it would certainly get me barred from most drawing rooms."

"Faith, you don't pull any punches," she said, turning a page. "You use your access to those drawing rooms to name names? Lud, you expose every detail! Does this work?"

He was still searching methodically. "Awareness is where all reform starts. I send wagonloads of this stuff all over England."

"Yveshire doesn't know?"

"No one knows. Except some of my workmen, of course, and Tanner Brink, who helps to arrange my transportation networks—and now you."

"Mr. *Brink* is part of all this?"

Dove pulled out a knife to slash open some bound cases. "The Romany are rather strongly wedded to the idea of freedom, and all of Tanner's family love secrecy and intrigue. Remember that wagon on Westminster Bridge? The driver was another of our friend's cousins."

"And the drunken boatman? No, don't tell me! He was working for you, too?"

He glanced up and grinned. "Another member of Tanner Brink's fecund family, alas!"

Laughter gurgled in her throat. "I'm completely mortified! Though I do see that you couldn't share any of that with me at the time. Are you sure you should now?"

"I trust you." He tore into more cases, creating a confusion of paper. "And I thought, after everything we talked about these last few days, that you might even approve."

Heat rushed and burned in her heart. *I trust you!* "I do approve!" she said, reading on. "But how do you unearth all these personal histories?"

"At places like the Dog and Duck, from sailors and workmen and whores. And from Matthew Finch, who learns things from his countrymen that would make your blood run cold. Through these pamphlets and leaflets, I do my damnedest to see that the rest of England learns about it, too."

"You hesitate at nothing! You openly attack members of the peerage and hold them up to common mockery. You even list the great ladies who've employed African children as pages, then abandoned them. Lud, you ridicule them—"

"Without mercy! A woman who buys a child as a disposable accessory deserves the contempt of every civilized person. Pour on enough scorn and we may even change the fashion."

Paper slipped beneath her cold fingers. Her heart thumped uncomfortably. "If it became known that you were behind this, you'd be thrown out of every coffeehouse in London. No one would ever receive you again. It would ruin you. Someone might even prosecute!"

"Yes," he said. "Though I skirt the edge of that with very great care, since my arrest would rather dampen my activities. However, certain members of the *ton,* who would prefer that these truths did not come to light, would merrily see me whipped at the cart's tale for it, if they knew. Considering the influence of such persons, I definitely risk the pillory."

The image chilled. "Dove, you're risking everything!"

His laugh echoed against the muted thud of the turning wheel. "Enough. Though not my neck, as yet."

"So you print nothing truly seditious?"

"Not quite." He pulled more freshly printed paper from a box and read in silence for a few minutes, leafing through pages. At last he looked up and held out a sheet. "Except this!"

"What?" Sylvie slipped from her perch and walked up to him. "What's that?"

"Hanging material," he said.

She felt almost blind with distress as she took the paper. "Explain," she demanded. "Why is this different?"

"It's a direct incitement to rebellion." He picked up another and read rapidly. "Lud, this one is really defamatory. Menaces the king himself! Alas, what we have here is treason."

Paper crushed in her clenched fingers. "Then you were mad to print it!"

"I didn't print it. And—though my signature decorates every sheet—I most certainly didn't write it."

"Then who did?"

"Very likely, Tom Henley himself—an uncertain villain and one who would do whatever it took to save his own neck were it threatened. But not, I think, the impulse behind all this, though he certainly had the opportunity to run the presses secretly these last few nights. I imagine he was paid very well for it, then helped to leave the country."

"By someone with enough wealth and power, who knew what you were doing here?" She collapsed onto a box. "Oh, God! It's my fault! I told Yveshire about Tom Henley. I told him about this place. Yet I can't believe that the duke would try to trap you with a forgery!"

"The upright duke? No, it's not quite his style, is it? Though he might do it, if he were given enough direct provocation. So who, I wonder, was the instrument of that?" Dove slashed open another box. "Lud, there are cases and cases of it, and each worse than the last!"

"Then we must destroy all of them!"

"Too late," Tanner Brink said from the doorway. "Militia, coming this way! Caught like rats in a trap."

Sylvie dropped the ball of crushed paper. Her blood was ice. It was her fault. If Dove was caught and hanged for this, it would be her fault!

"The ponies?" Dove asked.

The Gypsy's grin split his face, though sweat stood visibly on his forehead. "Turned 'em loose. They'll leave a false trail."

"Though that hell-bound pony of yours will run straight to one of your brothers? Save yourself," Dove said. "They're not looking for you. Alert the others. I trust you to get away."

The Gypsy disappeared, not back up the stairs, but toward the dark corner behind the silent press. The muffled tramp of booted feet and the rattle of arms sounded above their heads. Dove leaned over to kiss Sylvie on the mouth.

"Don't waste time worrying about what you did or didn't do," he said. "I love you. None of this happened only because of you. But now the hunt is on and we are the hunted."

"At least we're on the same side," she said with false gaiety.

"Faith, ma'am, so we are!"

He dropped his candle onto a case of paper. Hot wax spilled, then flamed.

Grabbing her hand Dove pulled her with him into the shadow of the printing press. In the flickering light of the growing fire, she saw that a small ladder led up the wall beside it. Dove climbed a few rungs to the open trap door above. He clambered through, then hauled Sylvie after him. Behind them burning paper raised its voice from a crackle to a roar.

Dove wrenched open another small door and crawled through on hands and knees. The clanking of the wheel was deafening. Sylvie scrambled after him. She was instantly knee-deep in frigid water. Great wooden slats dripping slime and ice rose one after another above her head. Dove was busy with something: chains, machinery. The wheel creaked to a halt. The water level began to rise alarmingly around her legs, then suddenly dropped as diverted water began to pour down a shaft he'd just opened.

"That'll create merry hell," Dove said.

He dragged her past the wheel and out of the stream. Snow still swirled from the black sky.

"You're flooding the basement?"

"Thereby making a mess, while providing the soldiers with enough water to douse the fire." In the dim flare of a streetlamp, she saw his fleeting smile, filled with wild mirth. "That should delay some of them, at least."

"Though it may mean that not all of those papers get destroyed!"

"Alas, ma'am, even to save my own neck, I can't quite justify burning down the entire neighborhood."

Light flared as a group of soldiers carrying torches burst over the little bridge and raced around the corner. An officer on horseback led the rest, his mount's hooves skidding.

"There! Those men! Stop them!"

"What was that wise saying about discretion and valor?" Dove asked.

He spun her with him into a narrow alley. Sylvie glanced back, just in time to meet the officer's gaze: he was young, red-faced. In numb horror, she saw his naked blade cleave the night.

She and Dove began to run, with an entire troop of soldiers at their heels.

The next hour was a confused impression of lightning speed and laughing defiance.

Dove leaped and swung, cloak flying. His sword slashed. An entanglement of cloth signs fell about the officer's head. Barrels of fish tipped into the path of the pursuing soldiers, so horses slid and shied. A parked coal wagon mysteriously lost its brake and began to roll downhill to dump its contents across the road. Soldiers swore and danced, torches were dropped and went out, muskets fired blindly or flashed in the pan.

"Bless the snow," Dove said, laughing as he stopped for a moment to let her catch her breath. "It blinds and conceals, and makes their powder damp."

"Yet we can't elude them much longer!" Her words burned. She couldn't catch enough breath. "I'm slowing you down. Leave me here!"

"*Leave* you? Never!"

"Save yourself! No one will recognize you unshaved. Yveshire will protect me."

"Alas, but the duke isn't here. You've already burned your bridges, ma'am." He kissed her once, his mouth warm. "Trust me!"

They raced into another narrow space. The renewed tramp of running feet burst into the mouth of the alley behind them. Shots rattled from the brick walls.

"Dove! It's a dead end!"

But he had seized her around the waist and tossed her above his head. "Reach up!"

She glanced up, then flung up her arms. Strong hands caught her wrists and hauled. Moments later Dove stood beside her, balanced on the scaffolding of a half-built house.

"Well, now," Nance said. "Don't you look a treat with a beard! Was that worth a kiss or not?"

Bess tossed her head back and laughed. "I did half the hauling, you ragged harlot! So if any bussing of bearded fellows is to be done, it's one for me, too!"

Dove kissed both girls on the mouth, while a ragged troop of women poured from the house to begin throwing snowballs. Sylvie wildly joined in, scooping snow from the timbers. The soldiers ducked and swore under their barrage.

"Excellent shot," Dove said as she hit a man with a musket in the center of his forehead.

Leaving the other women behind, he caught her hand to drag

Sylvie through a maze of passageways, dodging the chaos of construction. At last a short ladder spat them out onto the rooftop of the house next door.

"An icy path, but a sure one," Dove said.

Then with Sylvie's hand still in his, he began to lead her across the snow-patched roofs of London.

She was encased in a moving sphere of crystal, the snow-blinded sky, rank with coal smoke, the gloomy rooftops beneath her feet. Without Dove, she'd have been instantly lost—or fallen. Ice hung from eaves, and snow piled in crevices. Yet every ridge and chimney stack proved passable, due to the constant fires burning beneath. From roof to roof, sliding down layer after layer, or up over balconies, or scurrying across the face of more scaffolding—once to send a tumble of loose bricks to the deserted street beneath—or balanced on the stout wooden crossbeams that held the largest street signs: at every step, Dove supported, encouraged, and laughed with her.

When they at last slid back to the ground, she had no idea where they were, but a lone horseman sat blocking their way, holding two ponies by their bridles.

"Well," Tanner Brink said. "We've half London to cross yet. Though not to worry. Bess is still entertaining herself throwing snowballs at what's left of the militia, and Nance is challenging the poor lads to show that they've better ballocks than she has."

Dove laughed and tossed Sylvie into her saddle.

"But they must know where you live," she said. "Won't they be waiting for us at your townhouse?"

"No doubt," Dove replied. "But I've friends left yet."

HALF AN HOUR LATER SHE WAS WARM AND FED AND CRADLED in blankets, curled into a bed in a hidden niche behind the ovens at Matthew Finch's bakery. She had cast in her lot with a man who'd have a traitor's price on his head by morning—thanks to her. Anxiety thrummed like wire fretted by wind, more insistent and more disturbing than mere worry.

With his network of Gypsy traders, Dove could probably smuggle an army out of London, so he could surely save his own life. Yet even if he escaped capture, this meant permanent exile. If only she had not accepted her assignment for the duke, if only she had not helped to bring things to this head—

Dove would be an outcast. Without position. Without money. Without a livelihood.

She had destroyed his world.

Why would he want to begin a new life with the woman who had precipitated that?

Yet Europe had been her playground and the war with France was over. She tried to tell herself that this was the one thing she had to offer Dove. She could be an equal partner there, though they would start with nothing. They had a chance. They could make a new life. But foreboding filled her heart, as if an ax were about to fall.

While she tried to cling to logic, to make plans, to have faith, her bones whispered their anxiety. Not only of fear for the future—she wasn't simply afraid. No, the muttered refrain was more like a drone of absolute negation, the threat of the abyss. If she listened too closely, would panic overwhelm her?

Fighting sleep, she half listened as Dove and Tanner Brink talked. They were sitting just beneath her, close to the fire in the baker's private sitting room.

"You took *Berthe* there?" Dove was saying. "Lud! Why?"

"It's in the stars," the Gypsy said. "My doom is written in her palm."

"*Your* doom?" Dove replied, and laughed.

Sylvie barely woke when Dove later slipped into the bed to join her. She responded sleepily as he kissed her heavy eyelids and slack mouth, so he curled behind her like a shell around a pearl and let her sleep. Yet in some dark hour of the night they were awake and making love with a quiet, intense passion. Sylvie opened to him, welcomed him, in a trance of bliss. So why did she dream later with such deep desperation, as if it might have been the last time?

RHYTHM. A WONDERFUL, BLOOD-STIRRING RHYTHM. CAdenced like a heartbeat. And a human voice, a man's voice, chanting in a language she'd never known existed. Sylvie struggled awake.

Dove was gone. His place next to hers in the little bed was empty. He must be in the bakery. Or perhaps he had gone out to use the necessary—

The song rose and fell with the drumbeat. She looked down into the room. Tanner Brink and Matthew Finch sat, one on each side of the fireplace, making music. The African baker clutched a small cylinder under one elbow. The fingers of his other hand skipped over its stretched skin top, while his voice rose and fell, as if his mouth were just another musical instrument.

Tanner Brink perched on the edge of his chair, leaning forward, staring intently into the other man's eyes as he wove chords on a fiddle, quavering in and out of the baker's theme.

"Ah," the Gypsy said, looking up. "Our young friend is awake."

Instantly the music stopped and the baker laid aside his drum.

"What was that?" Sylvie asked. "I felt as if my soul were being drawn from my body."

"No, no," the African replied. "It's just a song about home."

"About your home? About Africa?"

His dark eyes shone, calm and certain. "About all of us who wander lost in the world, dreaming of paradise: you, me, Mr. Brink."

"That is the melancholy joy of my family," Tanner Brink said. "Everyone is lost, but the Romany know it."

Sylvie felt uncomfortable, almost as if she'd been prying into something sacred. "And now I seem to have lost Mr. Dovenby," she said.

"Ah," the Gypsy replied. "So you think he's yours to lose?"

Matthew Finch had walked to the door. He stopped with his hand on the latch to look back into the room. "Everybody would like to possess Mr. Dovenby."

"But will he be careless enough to lose this young person?" Tanner asked.

The African grinned. "Perhaps she's not his to lose either. I'll have hot water sent in, and breakfast."

The door closed behind him.

"Who *is* Matthew Finch?" Sylvie asked. "How did he get to London?"

The Gypsy glanced back at her, not blinking. "On a ship. As a small child. He became a page boy, but after he became too tall for his little turban and jacket, he was turned out to starve." Tanner Brink's expression didn't change. "Fortunately, he met Mr. Dovenby instead, who would tell you that Matthew Finch has a mind like a whetstone and the soul of an angel."

"He doesn't want to go back to Africa?"

The Gypsy shrugged. "Why would he want to go back? His own people sold him into slavery."

"That's not what his music said," she replied.

"Do you think that music cannot lie? A man can long for something he shouldn't have, or is afraid of—just as a woman can."

She glanced down, not wanting to think about the implications of that. "Is Matthew Finch his real name?"

"He chose it when he became free: Matthew for the Bible and

Finch for the bird. The lady who turned him out called him Crocus. His real name, his African name, he's told no one, not even Dove."

"And is Tanner your real name, Mr. Brink? Surely no one was ever christened Tanner?"

The walnut face split in a grin. "What makes you think I was ever *christened*? My mother called me her little corn bunting: a plain brown bird that can live anywhere on anything, and likes to crow from his song-perch to impress his harem. His song is a discordant enough jangle, as most infant cries are."

She laughed. "And your father?"

"My father called me his kestrel."

"Brown enough and small enough, but a good deal more dangerous than a corn bunting!" She lay back to stare at the ceiling. "I would seem to be lost among the birds. Will we fly to Holland or to France?"

"Fly wherever you like," the Gypsy said. "The Dove has already flown."

Her heart stopped, then lurched painfully. Sylvie sat up so suddenly she banged her head on the low slope of the ceiling. "Flown? Flown where?"

"Why, straight into the eagle's nest. He's gone to see Yveshire."

"*I* HAVE BEEN BROODING LIKE A HEN, CREATING FANTASIES OF revenge," the duke's voice hissed. "That stops here. I was wrong to plot. I was wrong to wait. You die now."

Sylvie crouched down, frozen in place, her heart thundering like the waterwheel. Tanner Brink had eventually allowed her to leave for Yveshire House, but only after she had cajoled, begged, insisted—while Matthew Finch's breakfast had gone uneaten. She had at last ridden out into the London morning huddled inside a long cloak, mounted on a Gypsy pony, feeling too sick to be hungry.

Meanwhile, Dove had placed himself directly into the hands of his adversary. Why? Didn't he understand the depth of Yveshire's hatred? Didn't he know that once the duke had committed himself—even abetted fraud to entrap his enemy—he would allow himself no way out except to bring about Dove's death? There would be no talking, no explaining. There would only be an arrest for treason—or perhaps this: that Dove would first goad the duke into fighting a duel.

Thank God Yveshire's house was old, embellished with ornamentation and balconies. Impossible, while she was still dressed as George, to march up to the front door to confront the duke's servants, so she had been forced to break in. All the ground floor windows were fastened and locked. A secretary worked in the study. Maids were cleaning in the duke's bedroom. Footmen stalked the hallways. But the back of the house was easy to climb.

As the snow turned to rain, she had found an entrance from the roof: reached only by inching her way across ice-slick cornices, which led her inside and onto a narrow gallery. It seemed to be only an accident of construction—used for nothing except cleaning the windows, perhaps—just a space above a carved partition fronting some ornamental clerestories, but she had immediately heard voices.

You die now!

"If you insist," Dove replied. "Though I do feel obliged to try to prevent it."

"Death lies very light and easy in my hand," the duke said. "You will not prevent it."

Sylvie crawled to the edge of the partition and looked down. She was close to the vaulted ceiling of a ball room. Far below, a few candles flickered in the dim daylight. Yveshire stalked across the wooden floor, his back arched, his head thrown back. A white satin waistcoat hugged his lean torso. Stripped of coat and shoes, the duke held a naked rapier in his right hand.

"I shall not play games," Yveshire continued.

"But I shall," Dove replied.

He was immaculate, elegant. His stubble was gone and his dark hair lay hidden beneath a new wig. While she had argued and pleaded with Tanner Brink, Dove had stopped somewhere to shave and bathe, then change into fresh clothes. Yet Dove's coat and shoes also had been cast aside, a layer peeled away to make both men's bodies more deadly and more vulnerable. His embroidered waist-coat was blazoned—as if to mock her anxieties—with scarlet birds of paradise on ivory silk. His muscles flexed beneath a translucently fine white shirt.

He, too, brandished a sword.

"Only if you think death is a game," the duke said.

Dove bowed. "This duel is certainly a game, Your Grace, where the odds are entirely in your favor."

"Your loss, sir! I will see you in abject terror before you die."

As if a snake struck, the duke lunged straight for the throat. Dove parried and fell back as Yveshire drove him across the room. *Thud. Ring. Shiver.* Thudding feet, steel ringing on steel, and always the duke forcing, driving, as Dove gave way before the older man's furious onslaught.

He is certain that if you and he fought with rapiers, he would kill you. Is that true?

. . . I would be slaughtered without question.

Dove was younger. He was fit. He was obviously skilled, grace and scope sparking from his blade. With every thrust of Yveshire's sword, Dove's steel was there to meet it. Yet Yveshire had learned to fence from French and Italian masters. He was lean, powerful, and brilliant. And death glowered in his gaze.

There was nothing she could do. She was just another carved boss in the ceiling, dumb, wooden, staring with horrified eyes at the fight in the room below. Any interference, any distraction might wing death directly to Dove's heart. She had arrived too late. She had nothing to offer him now but her silent witness and her prayers. Though if there was a moment—any moment—when her shout or scream could save him, she would be ready for it.

It was a fast battle, with long runs. Always a hideous clashing of blades, before the men swept apart. In spite of the duke's deadly purpose, their movements were elegant, lovely. Dove remained always on the defensive. Strong, swift, and clever, he only met and parried, and steadily gave ground.

Again and again Yveshire beat Dove to a standstill, before he spun and stalked away, only to turn at his leisure for another attack. Every renewed clash splayed across the floor like strokes from two brushes painting a masterpiece—a dance of death that was terrifyingly beautiful. No undefended moment allowed a strike through Dove's guard, but neither did the duke seem to tire or give ground.

Suddenly Yveshire threw up his sword, leaving his heart undefended. Dove's blade halted, hanging in the air like a hawk. The duke strode away.

"If you are not trying to kill me, Mr. Dovenby, you are making a mistake. Unless I die on your blade, sir, you will most certainly die on mine."

Breathing hard, Dove lowered his rapier. "Unfortunately for me, Your Grace, I have no desire to kill you."

"Yet you slaughtered my brother without mercy." Yveshire, too, was struggling for air, sweat standing in beads on his forehead.

"Though the hand that struck him down wasn't mine, I certainly intended to kill him—and would have done so without compunction."

Yveshire's body contorted, as if in pain. His breath whistled between his teeth. "Though you were too much the coward to meet him face-to-face."

"If Lord Edward hadn't been felled by the husband of a lady he'd just tried to murder, I would have met him on the dueling field. I won't say *honorably,* for your brother had no honor—"

Steel flashed. Dove was driven back, fighting for his life. "You ruined him deliberately!"

Thud. Ring. Shiver. "Yes."

"*You* arranged his humiliation! *You* arranged all the circumstances that led to his murder!"

Parry. Retreat. Spin. "Most of them."

"Then try life for a hour or so with only one arm, Mr. Dovenby."

In a blur of white, the duke struck. Dove reeled backward—and a new bird of paradise unfurled scarlet feathers on his left shoulder.

"First blood to you, Your Grace," he said.

"And second—" The duke thrust again. Another small bloom of blood opened and spread—a long scratch on the back of Dove's wrist. "Perhaps you would like to greet death with only one eye, sir?"

"Alas, I need both of them to keep you engaged until you tire of this."

Dove lunged. The duke sprang back. His arm budded a small calyx of silk petals: white petals with a bleeding heart.

"Hah!" the duke exclaimed, glancing down at his wound. He grinned. "So you *will* fight!"

There was nothing beautiful left now. The contest became grueling, ugly, merely a test of stamina. The men fought, bloodied, blinded by sweat. Even if Dove wished it, he could never prevail against the duke's masterly swordsmanship. Yet he still met and parried, sidestepped and blocked, as the dance slowed, until both men fought on through a haze of exhaustion.

At last the duke lowered his rapier and stood with both hands propped on his knees as he struggled for breath, shaking his head from side to side. Dove walked away, his blade vibrating in his fingers like a harp string. He stopped and looked down, as if unable to summon enough willpower to prevent his hand shaking. The ragged red birds had spread wings, on his shoulder and cuff and another on his thigh.

Yveshire wiped sweat and a trace of blood from his face. He, too, had a new scratch—along the side of his cheek. "Damn you!" he said. "Damn you! I cannot best you, sir!"

"I'm quite thoroughly bloodied, Your Grace. You are barely touched. You have won. I concede."

"You're not dead."

"I refuse to lie down and simply expire, but honor is surely satisfied? Had I the energy left, I would present my sword hilt and bow like a gentleman."

The duke threw back his head and laughed. "One of those deadly little bows that slays the ladies?"

Dove flung aside his sword. The blade clattered on the floor. "One of those deadly little bows that your brother taught me, Your Grace. No one could deliver an insult with quite his aplomb. I'm willing to talk about it, if you will listen."

Yveshire pulled out a handkerchief to mop at the graze on his face. "It makes no difference now, Mr. Dovenby. If you had not fought so well, I'd have spared you the hangman, nothing more."

"Ah," Dove said. "So we come to that?"

"We come to that." The duke walked to a side table to pour himself a glass of brandy, which he downed in one swallow. "You have been running a printing press."

Dove dropped down to sit on his haunches. He leaned his head back against the wall. "True. London cannot get enough of all the naughty little stories that I print there."

"You refer to your erotica? I hear it is very fine."

"I do my best."

The duke turned to stare at him. "I shall be sorry to deprive England of your talents in that regard, sir. But I have evidence that you have indulged in something far less innocuous."

Dove stretched out his legs. He sat entirely relaxed on the floor. "So my merry little experiment with fire and water didn't succeed?"

"Sufficient remains to prove you guilty of treason, sir."

"Which I didn't print, but of course you know that."

"Yes, I know that. However, you cannot prove it."

"Even if I could, the evidence remains and it's very nasty. Someone will have to hang for it."

Still holding his brandy glass, Yveshire dropped into a chair by the fireplace. "The militia captain has already given those papers to his superior officers. They cannot be suppressed now. Someone, as you say, must hang for it."

"Unfortunate," Dove said. "I should have let you slaughter me with your rapier. Far cleaner and less public. I can't say I'm looking forward to a traitor's death."

"I only wished to execute you myself," the duke said, "for Sylvie's sake."

"Though it was your idea to involve her—"

"I have come to regret that very bitterly, sir, which is why the responsibility for your dispatch is mine also. Alas, I have just failed, so she will have to watch you hang, after all. Who the devil taught you to fence?"

Dove glanced up to meet Yveshire's gaze. There was no amusement left now in his eyes.

"Lord Edward Vane, Your Grace. Your brother taught me everything I ever needed to know."

Sylvie folded back into a corner. She put both hands over her mouth, only to find that her cheeks were damp. Had she wept and not known it?

"Under the circumstances," Yveshire said, "can you give me one good reason why you should not be found guilty of treason and hanged?"

"No," Dove said. "I can't."

"*But I can,*" a woman's voice said.

Sylvie lurched forward to peer over the partition.

Meg, Lady Grenham, wearing white satin and diamonds, stood like a winter goddess in the doorway of the room. Her hair was powdered, her skin white as chalk, though her cheeks and lips were delicately rouged.

"*I can,*" Meg repeated. "But first, my dear Yveshire, I would like some refreshment." She began to peel off her gloves. Her fingers trembled. "Men are always so determined to begin with the physical, when a few moments' sensible conversation over wine could clear everything up with a great deal more delicacy."

Yveshire stared at her for a moment, his face frosted with ice, then he bowed.

Meg curtsied, the personification of elegance. "You will also be pleased to find Mr. Dovenby a fresh shirt, Duke? And remove all this evidence of your mutual animal natures? In his present state, he is just as offensive as you are." Her fan cascaded open in her hand. "In the blue drawing room? In ten minutes? Mr. Dovenby?"

Dove had risen to his feet. He bowed.

Her skirts shimmered as Meg led both men from the room.

A T THE END OF THE GALLERY A SMALL DOOR OPENED ONTO the top of a steep stair. Sylvie ran down, her heart soaring like a skylark. Lady Grenham would prevail upon Yveshire to let Dove escape. If Meg failed, she would add her own voice to the argument. The duke had loved her once. She would call in every favor, every debt that Yveshire owed her, to save Dove's life and allow him to flee to Europe.

At the bottom of the stair she stepped out into a hallway. A couple of maids scurried past carrying linen. Sylvie dodged behind a lacquered cabinet. She was still dressed as George, in wig and breeches.

These were the same clothes she had worn yesterday, when she had raced across London, splashing through icy puddles, climbing over rooftops. If she was caught lurking here, she would simply be dragged away to Newgate to be hanged as a thief. No servant would ever allow such a disreputable intruder a personal interview with the duke.

The maids disappeared. Sylvie crept along the corridor in the opposite direction. Though she had visited Yveshire's study and bedroom, the whereabouts of the blue drawing room were a mystery. It was, presumably, on the ground floor somewhere near the large room where the men had fenced. She hurried down through the house, passing through several reception rooms, their mirrored walls reflecting her image as she passed—a filthy young man in a bedraggled wig, with a face that seemed strangely bereft.

Corridors replicated. Rooms multiplied. The house lay silent, much of it unheated. Some hallways lay empty. In others footmen stood or sat dozing, causing her to make detours back through the rooms she had already passed. Her heart began to beat hard. Townhouses like Dove's were usually laid out very simply. Historic palaces like this—remodeled innumerable times to suit the whim, power, and wealth of the Yveshire's—could be impenetrable warrens. She had nothing to rely on but blind faith and luck.

She had doubled back through another set of rooms when she heard voices at last—still somewhere beneath her. Following the sound, she discovered a musician's gallery built into a high corner like a small turret, designed so that two or three men with violins could serenade the company below without being seen.

"Yes," Dove said. "I am very deeply sorry, Your Grace."

Three slender arches opened onto the room—an elegant blue-and-white fantasy of plaster. Her heart hammering, Sylvie looked through the tracery.

Dove stood at the window, his hands folded behind his back,

looking out. He wore an elegant slate-blue jacket that she had never seen before. His wounds were presumably bandaged beneath the fresh shirt. His face was invisible. Yveshire sat beside the fireplace. He looked ill, his skin plaster white. The scratch marked his cheek with a narrow track of bright red.

"Lud, sir!" The duke's voice sounded thin, as if stretched to dry on a rack, as if about to break. "So am I."

Lady Grenham walked slowly up and down between the two men, nervously opening and closing her fan. Small tracks ran down through her rouge, as if she had been crying.

"I have proof," she said. "You don't need to doubt that."

"I don't doubt it." Yveshire stared at his clenched hands. "Perhaps I am not even entirely surprised."

Silence stretched for a few moments. Meg turned to look at him. Though still lovely, she seemed frail. *I can almost see the face of the old lady I will one day become. It lies like a shadow—*

"Everything that has happened is my fault," she said. "But you do understand, Duke?"

"Faith, ma'am," Dove interrupted. "If His Grace hadn't hired Sylvie to entrap me, none of this need ever have come to light. Our present predicament is not your fault!"

"But now it *has* come to light," the duke said. "And I am the man forced to swallow this bitter pill. My little brother. I thought that I loved him. For the sake of that love, I hounded you, sir. I even tried to entrap you with false evidence."

"It doesn't matter," Dove said. "You had reason enough. Whatever Meg says, your brother met his fate because of me. I, too, took the law into my own hands."

The duke steepled his fingers over his eyes. "So if—for Meg's sake and for the sake of what she has now told me—I no longer intend to destroy you, Mr. Dovenby, what do you propose to do about the discoveries at your print shop? I cannot undo what has been done."

"We can easily make a case that I didn't direct Tom Henley's activities," Dove replied. "That is, after all, the truth. It's unlikely that any of the soldiers recognized me there last night."

Yveshire dropped his hands. "I imagine that until Lady Grenham loaned you a razor and fresh clothes this morning, you cut a sadly disreputable figure, sir."

"Yet blame must be placed somewhere," Meg said. "No one will believe that the forger acted alone. The *king* will have been told by now. Lud, Yveshire! Why did you have to force us all to this pass?"

"If you could have brought yourself to trust me with this story before, ma'am—"

Meg looked away, her cheeks flushed. "And cause you so much pain?"

"The truth, however painful, is better than to continue my unwarranted persecution of Robert Dovenby."

"It doesn't matter," Dove said again. "And none of those facts need ever leave this room. As for the business at the printer's, all we need is a plausible tale of a dastardly plot foiled just in time. For that, I won't have Lady Grenham involved—"

Yveshire's laugh was sharp. "Or you will slaughter me yet, sir?"

Dove turned from the window. His eyes seemed cold, as if his soul had absorbed the bleakness of winter, and his face was white. "No, Your Grace. Even if I wished it, I don't have the skill."

The duke stood up, as brittle as glass. "Perhaps we can never quite be friends, sir, but to undo what I can of what Tom Henley created at my bidding, I will back any tale you care to tell."

Dove walked up to shake the duke's proffered hand. "Thank you, Your Grace."

"But thanks to all those false documents," Meg said, "the law will be crying out for blood. Unless Dove is removed entirely from suspicion, they'll hang him yet."

"Indeed, ma'am!" Dove replied. "And since I now have far too much to live for, I believe we should name someone else for our traitor. Someone reckless and heedless enough—"

"You would pin a charge of treason on an innocent man?" the duke interrupted.

"Why not?" Dove smiled as if a wild spirit of humor had suddenly winked at him. "I thought that was the fashion of the day? Fortunately, we already have a perfect scapegoat."

"Who?" Meg asked.

Dove took her hand, bowed over her knuckles, and kissed them. The gesture spoke of love and respect, with something of a heartfelt gratitude. Sylvie watched him, her heart open, vulnerable—

"The one person who is completely expendable in this entire situation," Dove said, "and always has been—Mr. George White."

CHAPTER SIXTEEN

DOVE WHISTLED SOFTLY AS HE RODE BACK TO MATTHEW Finch's bakery on the horse he had borrowed earlier from Meg. Fatigue drenched every muscle. His wounds had been neatly stitched and bandaged by Yveshire's valet, but he ached like the very devil. He had barely escaped with his life: one mistake, one slip, and Yveshire would have run him through.

Water ran and dripped everywhere. Little rivulets wove along the streets. The thaw had begun.

The words of his tune echoed beneath his breath: *Alas, my love, you do me wrong . . . for I have loved you so long, delighting in your company . . .*

He had lost enough blood to be a little lightheaded, but he had crafted a solution to almost everything that had plagued him.

His merry mood dissolved instantly when he found that Sylvie was not at the bakery.

"She left with the Gypsy and without her breakfast," the African said. "Neither of them have come back here."

"Where the hell did he take her?"

Matthew Finch smiled. "We are all savages, we men, when it comes to the right woman. I don't know."

Thinking hard, Dove rode back to his townhouse, abandoning Meg's horse into the hands of his groom. Abdiel leaned his head from his stall and nickered. The stallion was saddled and bridled.

"What the devil's the meaning of this?" Dove demanded. "Abdiel is ready to go out? You should have exercised him at dawn."

The groom tugged at his forelock. "I did, sir. Sorry, sir, but Mr. White insisted that he needed to take the horse out now and had your permission."

Dove raced into the house and flung open the door of his study. She wasn't there. He took the stairs two at a time. Her room lay empty. A small noise made him spin about. She had just opened his bedroom door, his saddlebags flung over one shoulder.

Her eyes opened wide, lapis lazuli on ivory, as the color drained from her face.

"Lud," she said. "I'm sorry to foil your plans for me, but I'm just leaving."

Dove strode up to her, his heart hammering. "What plans?"

She stepped back. A boy again, she was neatly and plainly dressed in the blue jacket she'd worn when they'd first met. She looked frantic, desperate with rage and heartbreak.

"I don't suppose you've alerted the authorities as yet? In truth, I'm gambling that Yveshire insisted that I would make just as good a scapegoat fled as captured? Or did he refuse your plan and suggest something else? You would betray me very happily. The duke, I think, would not."

"*What plans?*"

She tipped up her chin. "With Tanner Brink's admittedly reluctant cooperation, I followed you to Yveshire House. I'm flattered that you think I'd make such a plausible traitor, though I do see that it's a perfect solution to everything. My parents were known Jacobites. Now we're near the end of this troublesome quarrel with France, I must have come to England to foment revolution. You've won, Dove, and I'm leaving."

"If you leave, I have lost."

"So have I!"

"I won't let you leave!"

"You won't *let* me?"

He slammed the door closed behind him. "Not like this!"

She backed a few more steps. "I've already determined I must borrow Abdiel to get me as far as the coast, though I am not a thief. I will send him back. Now, sir, if you'll kindly stand aside?"

"No."

The saddlebags hit the carpet as she grabbed his dress sword from the desk. The corner of her mouth quirked, as if with a poignant regret. "Meg's gift. I regret that I must borrow it, also. Pray, sir, let me leave!"

"Sylvie, we must talk!"

The blade hissed from the scabbard. "You think I have neither the heart nor the skill to kill you? Perhaps not. But I have a blade. You do not. I believe that gives me the advantage? Stand aside, Mr. Dovenby, and let me pass."

She lifted the rapier to point directly at his heart.

"This is insanity," he said. "I haven't betrayed you."

" 'Fortunately, one person is completely expendable in this entire situation—and always has been—Mr. George White.' "

"And you immediately believed the worst?"

Light glimmered from the sword, lethal even in untrained hands.

"What the devil was I supposed to believe? I hid like Polonius, though not behind the arras, and was similarly struck to the heart. Alas, I also neglected to eat breakfast. Perhaps my distress at hearing your plans for me undermined what was left of my fortitude. Like any feeble woman, I fainted. I hit my head on the wall. When I recovered my senses, you'd all gone. It seemed only politic to flee the country before I was arrested."

Where to even begin? His wounds throbbed. His fatigue was absolute.

"What you overheard was said to *Yveshire*! The duke would never agree to anything that would harm you. You know that!"

She stepped closer. The rapier tip hovered at his throat. "Yes, I know that. But did you? Were you *certain* of it?"

If he moved too fast he would impale himself. "Yes, absolutely."

"Because you guessed that Yveshire was my lover?" Her hand shook. Reflections glittered treacherously from the blade. "Would it matter if he still was? Would it matter to you if I were to visit his bed now, or if I'd been doing so all along?"

He hauled up the words, one by one. "But you did not, Sylvie."

"No. I was foolish enough to give myself so absolutely to no one but you—even to fall in love with you—when the only man who ever deserved my trust is the duke."

"Yes," Dove said. "I know."

"Yet without consulting me you forced him to agree to sacrifice George White." She blinked back moisture. "And you lied to me long after I began telling you the truth."

"Yes," he said. "I had to." He didn't know how to reach her, how to make her understand. "But our bed spoke its own truth, Sylvie—"

"Faith, sir!" Tears spilled, ice-cold runnels of grief. "All that glorious enchantment? Yes, but the body can deceive the soul so very easily. Passion by itself is nothing but a prison of gold."

He wanted to kiss her, take her jaw in his hand and force his lips over hers, compel her to acknowledge what lay between them. Instead he stepped back until his shoulders hit the door.

"Our passion was never a prison—"

"Don't tell me any more lies! Whether you meant to betray me or not, your splendid imitation of it forced me to face a reality I'd been denying far too long. Let me go!"

"What reality?"

"There's no future for us."

"I don't believe it."

"Then believe this!"

She stiffened her arm and lunged straight for his heart.

In spite of his exhaustion, his body reacted like a coiled spring. Dove sidestepped, kicked, and disarmed her—and tasted desolation on his tongue.

She dived for the fallen blade, but he seized her and dragged her bodily back across the room. Biting and kneeing, she fought him. A blow caught him across the cheek. Another struck hard over the cut on his thigh. Her teeth closed on his wrist. When her shoulders struck one of the posts at the foot of the bed, he released her and spun away.

Panting, she flung out both arms to grasp the blue velvet hangings in each hand, her jacket crumpled at the shoulders, her face white above the defiant tilt of her jaw—and the lapis lazuli of her eyes blurred by anguish and pain.

"So this is how we first met," she said with exquisite bravado, "and how it all ends between us."

The temptation to press his mouth over hers roared in his brain. He had lost all claim to cool judgment. Stunned, he staggered to the window, reeling like a drunkard.

"That choice is yours," he said. "But first I beg that you'll hear me out."

"*Choice?* When have I ever had choices with you? I'm once again to be your prisoner? Yet I'm no longer struggling, sir. I'm not screaming for help. Heaven knows, there's no one in this house to help me now. Will you bind me to your bed?"

Clenching his fists he pressed his forehead to the glass. As if to mock him, the sun had broken through the clouds. Melting snow raced and tumbled. "We tried that," he said. "It didn't work."

"But you are wrong, because it did work and that is our tragedy." She dropped her arms and walked to the fireplace. "Where is Berthe? She was gone when I returned here, another innocent victim of our madness. Even though she's penniless, she's taken her things and fled. Or has she deceived me, as well?" She spun about to search his face. "You know? Tell me!"

"You crave the truth? Berthe was taking messages to the duke."

"Yes, of course. I sent her."

"Messages of her own, Sylvie."

Her chin jerked up. "What the devil do you mean?"

Lovely, beloved, betrayed Sylvie—and now he could neither save her, nor spare her.

"Berthe has been busy plotting on her own. She took false tales about me, about us, to the duke's man in Shepherd's Market and then directly to Yveshire. She was well paid for it."

"*Berthe?* Why?"

"I don't know why! You talk about choices. You long for your own power. Perhaps Berthe did, too. Perhaps she felt ignored, unimportant, jealous. Perhaps she hated me for rejecting her that night. Perhaps she simply couldn't bear to see your growing involvement with me. I don't know."

"No." Her voice sounded broken. "Yveshire told me nothing of this—"

"His Grace didn't want you to know that your maid was acting behind your back. He wanted to spare you. Like fools, we have all wanted to spare you. So we have all lied to you: the duke has, Berthe has, and I have."

As if fighting for dignity she sat down and kicked her feet out in front of her. "What did she tell him?"

"Anything that would confirm his hatred of me. Her tales were welcome enough to his ears, and he rewarded her well for them. In the end, Berthe told Yveshire that I'd forced her. That's when—sick with worry and guilt over you—he broke with his own code of honor and paid Tom Henley to create those pretty little pieces of treason. For your sake. To save you from the embraces of a rapist."

Her back was lovely, soft, female, but for the first time she looked fragile, while he was pinned at the window, turned away from the sunlight.

"How very flattering that he loves me enough to do something so very out of character!" she said. "And no, I won't pretend that I believe you raped Berthe. She has her own reasons to fear and distrust men."

"As you do?"

"Yes, if you like. But you still didn't consult me or consider me—"

"I've done nothing but consider you. I couldn't consult you, because when I left the bakery I couldn't know what would transpire at Yveshire House. I only knew that whatever happened, the duke would protect you."

She glanced up and from some deep reservoir of courage seemed to find a little humor.

"But this is what's happened, sir: I have tried to kill you. However, I'm perfectly calm now, so will you please let me leave?"

"No," he said.

Dove sat down on the window seat and leaned his head back against the glass. He felt as if he had spent days without sleep, as if he had led armies through cannon fire. His stamina had been consumed. His brain dragged through a fog even to find speech.

"I am trapped," he said at last. "I cannot find any way out of this."

"Because if you claim to trust me, I'll want to know why you went to Yveshire House without first sharing your plans with me, why I wasn't included? Yet if you admit that we cannot trust each other, what the hell do we have left? I thought I had fallen—Lud, not *fallen,* but plummeted headlong, head over heels—into love. I trusted blindly for the first time in my life. I let down my defenses, became truly vulnerable. Then you used me as a cog in your machine and excluded me from your machinations, while you told me and yourself that you loved me."

He closed his eyes. "What can I do, Sylvie? How can we ever re-create what I thought we had found together?"

"It doesn't matter." Using her boy's handkerchief, she rubbed her moist cheekbones. "You and I cannot, do not, and never did, trust each other. I'm the duke's creature and was all along. Whether you're still his enemy or not, I have nothing to offer you. Let me go, Dove. I have very little courage left."

"No." He stood, then retrieved his sword and placed it on the windowseat. "When did you last eat?"

She looked incredulous, though her eyelids were still stained red. *"Eat?"*

"You didn't eat at Matthew Finch's this morning. I don't imagine you've stopped since then for a meal. I will escort you gallantly to the dining room. We'll have breakfast. You'll hear me out. Then you may do whatever you damn well please."

She stared at him in silence for a moment. "Very well," she said at last. "If the alternative is to spend the rest of my days imprisoned up here like a goat."

"A *scapegoat,*" he said. "But first, I pray you will change out of those absurdly charming clothes and put on one of the dresses that Meg sent you."

"Why?"

"Because Mr. George White—a person who doesn't exist and never existed, but who can conveniently be said to have fled to France—is indeed to be sacrificed. Not to save my neck, but to save yours. George White was recognized last night at the printer's. Whatever Yveshire does, whatever I do, that officer can identify you."

"If you hadn't taken me with you, that wouldn't be the case. Though, of course, I wanted to come. But you manipulated that, too, didn't you? As you had Lady Grenham send dresses for just this eventuality? Lud, I was your fool!"

"I'm not laughing."

"Oh, neither am I," she said. "So what's to become of me?"

"George disappears. Sylvia Georgiana, Countess of Montevrain—with her new private income as promised by the duke—emerges unscathed and unsuspected to take whatever place she chooses in London society."

"Faith!" she said. "I'm blinded by the brilliance of all this merry plotting. It's regrettable no one thought to consult me, though I'm not foolish enough to disagree." She stood up. "So, George White will vanish and only I will regret his passing."

"Not only you," he said.

"No? What does that matter? I cannot bear what we have done and undone. I cannot go on from here as if nothing has happened. So I assure you that whatever place in London society Lady Montevrain may choose, Mr. Robert Sinclair Dovenby will have no part in it."

He looked at her across the expanse of carpet where they had shared such a delirium of passion. "And you think that won't be an almost unbearable loss to me?"

"The loss is mine, also," she said, her eyes brilliant with courage. "You will find another lover and I will be your court jester."

"When I left for Yveshire House this morning, it was my intention—if I survived—to ask you to marry me. That makes me the fool, ma'am. So for God's sake, let us have breakfast."

*D*OVE WAS WAITING FOR HER, STANDING BESIDE THE FIRE-place in the dining room.

Sylvie ran her fingers over the lustrous skirts of one of Meg's dresses: a blue day gown with a wide underskirt and lace-trimmed petticoats in blond silk. Panic beat hard beneath her ribs, that deep, desperate panic that was indistinguishable from desire.

Dove had also bathed and changed. His dark hair framed his face. His broad shoulders filled his own plain charcoal-gray coat. As she met his gaze, yearning flowed like a waterfall from her heart, so she gathered defiance. Otherwise she would be entirely lost and carry him to destruction with her.

"To see you dressed like this," he said, "leaves me breathless."

"I could say the same. Between my stays and the state of my emotions, an easy breath is difficult to come by."

He pulled out a chair for her. Savory steam rose gently from the dishes on the table. Her eyes burned like flatirons. She couldn't think about the French maid. Or about Yveshire hiding Berthe's betrayal from her. Or even about Dove. It was hard to think very clearly about anything. She only knew that she was tired.

"Breakfast," he said. "Violent feelings are easier dealt with on a full stomach."

"We may sit," she replied. "I don't think I can eat."

"I assure you, ma'am, that this food will taste like unpaid bills to me, also. Yet I will eat and so will you. If our combat is to continue, we shall both need our strength."

Silk rustled as she sat down. "It takes two to fight, sir. I have no intention of taking part."

He filled a plate with eggs and meat and slices of fresh bread, poured hot chocolate from a jug, and set it all down in front of her.

"But you will eat," he said.

Sylvie picked up her knife and fork. The eggs were delicately seasoned. They tasted like dust. She ate them anyway, gulped at the chocolate, and began to feel a little warmth creep back into her bones.

"Your skills at persuasion are unmatchable," she said. "But then everyone in your life is just something for you to manipulate."

He sipped chocolate and gazed at her. "Perhaps. However, here are some facts. When I left Matthew Finch this morning, I went straight to Meg's townhouse. The truth that Yveshire needed to hear could come only from her. Meg let me shave and gave me fresh clothes and a horse, so that the duke's servants wouldn't turn me away at the door. I begged her for more than that, but I left without knowing whether she would come to Yveshire House or not."

"Yet she came."

"Meg has her own motivations and her own autonomy. Just as you do. Just as Tanner Brink and Berthe and Yveshire do. I was bound by an oath. I still am. I had no way of knowing what Meg would decide. How could I involve you then, when I had no way of predicting the outcome?"

A bread roll crumbled in her fingers. "Very well, I accept that. Yet it would have cost you nothing to have confided your plans to me, consulted me. Instead you went to Yveshire's knowing he would try to kill you. If I'd come with you, I could have prevented that."

"You think so? Do you really think I should have tried to use you as a shield?"

She pushed her plate away. "Lud, sir! Am I supposed to admire your courage? That you risked your life to face the duke's wrath? I already know that you're brave. I already know—to my cost—that you're brilliant. I know to the depths of my soul that you're a magnificent lover. I can never treat you with indifference. But can you deny that you've used me, outwitted me, ever since I first came here?"

He ate ham and eggs and drank more chocolate. "I had to. It was your intention to destroy me."

"Even when we made love in Mr. Fennimore's office? Even during those three days upstairs in this house?"

His fork paused halfway to his mouth. "What was *your* intention, ma'am?"

"Exactly," she said. "There is nothing more to be said. You can offer me explanations. You can tell me about Lord Edward Vane. I can tell you about Berthe and my real life in Europe. I can admit that I haven't slept with Yveshire in many years. All our lies can be uncovered and it won't make any difference."

"If we don't try, we can't know that."

She stood up, terror beating hard beneath her stiff bodice. "I know it, because you've made me think that I love you. You've stolen my heart without my permission. You've made me feel that I would be nothing but an empty shell without you. You've torn me apart and left me with nothing but my own vulnerability. Passion alone isn't enough to heal that. Even love isn't enough, when its foundations were all built on quicksand."

Fatigue glimmered in the bones of his face. "Did I give you permission to steal *my* heart? You did it anyway. If you walk out of here now, you will indeed take my soul with you. I love you, Sylvie."

She clung to the back of her chair. The blue skirts shimmered away to the floor. She felt like a stranger in her own body.

"Love? Yes, perhaps. Yet Tanner Brink once told me my fortune: 'I see one great love, almost lost, then regained—' He didn't say that it would be lost again quite this bitterly. If we reaped love, we also sowed the seeds of its destruction from the very beginning."

What did she hope for? That Dove would rant at her? Shout out his love? Insist that no other man should ever have her? Seize her to tie her to his bed once again? Ravish her, heart and soul, with the sheer beauty of his passion? Perhaps she could never really make him understand, but she knew him better than that. Yet she bit her tongue to stop herself pleading, while agitation filled her mind.

"This is madness," he said.

"We've both known madness." Her knuckles turned white as she fought the impulse to abandon honor and principle, to obey the shattering desire to try to solve everything in his bed. "But if I give in to you now, I'd be nothing more than your slave for the rest of my life, which terrifies me to my soul. If you give in to me now, you will one day only hate me for it, and I fear nothing more than I fear that. There's no answer, no future for us. Let me go, Dove."

"Then allow me to call you a sedan chair." Elegant, deadly, he stood up. His eyes echoed only a wasteland. "I'll have your new dresses delivered to Yveshire House immediately."

"Yveshire House?"

He walked away to stare from the window, leaving her nothing but the heartbreaking line of his back and long legs. "You'd better go to him, Sylvie. He's in dire need of a friend. This morning His Grace learned something of what his brother really was and what that has cost him, and his world fell about his ears."

DOVE STRODE OUT TO THE STABLE, WHERE ABDIEL STILL waited, saddled and bridled. He led the horse from the stall and straight to the mounting block. The stallion needed no urging. Water sprayed as the bay cleaved a path down the thawing streets, diamond droplets catching the sun, drenching the horse's bloodred coat. Iron shoes clattered and splashed as they spun around corners, until the paved streets became the muddy ruts of the highway.

He galloped straight west. Market gardens and refuse tips and brick kilns soon gave way to open country. A tracery of bare branches whipped past overhead. Blue skies soared, one of those rare, clear February afternoons, with the fogs of London left behind. In less than an hour he swung the horse through a pair of wrought-iron gates. Cattle scattered, starting away from the fences, as he rode up the long driveway. A groom ran out as Abdiel skidded to a halt before the grand entrance to Grenham Hall, Meg's country house. The front door was flung open.

Dove tossed the reins to the groom and raced up the steps. The butler stepped aside. Leaving a trail of mud-spattered boot prints, Dove strode down the familiar hallways.

Meg opened the door of her sitting room herself. She was still wearing a long cloak and clutching her muff. Her carriage could only just have arrived from town, for her face was still stained with tears.

"It is spring," she said. "I am told there are snowdrops in the woods. Since you are already as wet and bemired as any hunting dog, my dear Dove, would you like to see them?"

"*Y*OU ATTEMPTED TO FLEE THE COUNTRY?" YVESHIRE ASKED. "Without coming to me first? Lud, Sylvie! Even though you didn't overhear most of our conversation, surely you realized that none of us meant to see you hang as a traitor?"

A fire burned brightly, warming her cold face and hands. The duke's servants had not questioned her arrival: a lady in silk and satin, with her feathered hat and fur muff—all the finery that Lady Grenham had sent at the behest of her lover.

Yveshire had come to join her in the blue salon. The little musicians' turret where she had fainted that morning—where she had overheard Dove plotting her future without consulting her—was now simply part of the ornamental fretwork.

"I wasn't thinking very clearly, Your Grace," Sylvie said. "I was experiencing a little unbalance. I still am."

"You have come to berate me about Berthe? I deserve it. I used her without telling you."

"She had her own needs. Perhaps she used you as part of her own drama. It doesn't matter. She's gone. Meanwhile, it feels very odd to be sitting here pretending to be a lady in all this borrowed finery."

The duke leaned back in his chair and steepled his fingers together. His skin held the gray tinge of old paper, the thin red line of the cut on his cheek still vivid in contrast.

"You *are* a lady! Now that your mission for me is over, George White can vanish. In fact, it's a brilliant solution."

She held her hands out to the flames. Her fingers seemed different. Foreign. Female hands. She could no longer prop her feet on the fender, or sprawl in a chair, or put her hands behind her head. She was a lady.

"But I'm not sure that I really wanted to let go of George White."

"It's been a trying morning for all of us," the duke said. "It wasn't easy to admit that I was wrong to persecute Dovenby over Edward's death."

Sylvie tried to smile at him. She had never seen him so drained. "Dove deliberately allowed you to do so. It wasn't your fault."

"He had his reasons." Yveshire wrung one hand over his mouth. "There were things about my brother that I didn't know. Didn't want to know, though somewhere deep inside perhaps I suspected it. Dovenby became an easy focus for all that anxiety. I hated him, because if I didn't, I might have to face what Edward really was. The more rumors I heard, the more evidence I discovered, the more I loathed the wrong man, because the alternative was to know that my brother was evil, someone my father should have been ashamed to defend."

"He was your brother. Whatever Lord Edward had done, you weren't wrong to love him."

"If I had known what he'd done, I'd have destroyed him myself." His mouth twisted in wry self-mockery. "Instead, this morning I tried heart and soul to slaughter Robert Dovenby."

"So did I," Sylvie said. "He's so damned irritating, it's amazing more people haven't tried."

The duke's head snapped up. "You tried to slay *Dovenby?*"

A fold of blue satin pleated under her fingers. "I tried to kill him with his own sword. It was grotesquely dishonorable of me. He was unarmed and—thanks to your noble efforts this morning—already wounded. Of course, I didn't really think I'd succeed."

The ghost of a smile crept over his features. "What happened?"

"He disarmed me instantly. He's invulnerable."

"Did you *want* him to allow you to run him through?"

"No! But if he'd been anything other than invincible, I would have stopped my lunge in time."

Yveshire stared at her. "You're still in love with him?"

"Is this love? He overwhelms me, defeats me. I feel enslaved by my cravings. If I were to allow him to touch me again, I would be enthralled, captivated." The blue satin creased as she fought for courage—to admit the truth, to let her one friend know that she was a coward at heart. "I feel as if I might destroy myself over loving him. I don't think I can bear it."

"What can't you bear?"

"He's everything that you told me, everything that your brother saw there, and more. All that intoxicating glamour! Should I live as just another sycophant, another desperate victim of his skills?"

"Is that what you believe would happen?"

"Dove can't enter a room without everyone in there, man or woman, wanting him. Everyone falls in love with that kind of charisma: duchesses, poets, musicians, Lady Charlotte Rampole, Lord Hartsham, Lady Grenham. Even my maid, Berthe, though she hated herself and him for it. Even Tanner Brink. Even you, now you've allowed yourself to really see him. Even your brother."

The duke's eyes burned in his pale face. "You think you would be just one more face in an adoring throng, infatuated with this man's allure?"

She shivered. "I hope that it isn't just pride, but I don't know. I only know that I'm petrified."

"Why? Why are you afraid? After all, you're that kind of woman."

Silk swished as she stood up. "What do you mean?"

"How the devil do you think you've made your living all these years?" He surged to his feet and took her by the elbows. "Lud, Sylvie! Don't you know your own power? Even as George—even as a young man without social standing or wealth—you made a stunning impression on London society. When I first met you, you were barely more than a girl, yet you shone among the others like a diamond."

"Any shine you noticed when you and I first met, it was only reflected from you," she said.

His grip tightened. "I was a duke's eldest son and now I am Duke of Yveshire myself. A certain glamour comes with the position. Whereas, even if you were a scullery maid, you'd fascinate every man that met you. Faith, you and Dovenby are made for each other!"

"No," she said. "You don't understand. He's stronger than I am. I cannot cope with his glamour. I don't know if what I feel is really love, or if it's just infatuation. If I were to try to live with him, I would fail, and marriage—"

"He asked you to marry him?"

"I tried to prevent his asking. I had to. Why else do you think I attacked him with a sword?"

Yveshire opened his fingers to release her and walked away to the window. He stood framed in sunlight. Tall, lean, edged with gold.

"Then the position here is still open, if you want it."

"What position?"

"Must I enumerate my desirable qualities? I am a duke. I have immeasurable wealth. Six country properties with all their vast estates, this palace in London, a great network of investments and businesses. I promise to be an understanding husband—"

Sylvie sat down, her heart hammering. "You're proposing *marriage*? To *me*?"

"Why not? It's what I should have done years ago. Sylvia Georgiana, Duchess of Yveshire—it has a certain ring to it!" The duke held out one hand, palm up. "I am offering you my hand, ma'am. No woman in her right mind would turn that down. Say yes, Sylvie, and the power of a dukedom is yours."

* * *

"WHY WOULD I WISH TO SEE SNOWDROPS?" DOVE ASKED.

"To remind you of innocence," Meg said. "To remind you that some things can be simple."

He peeled off his riding gloves and threw them aside. "What the devil is simple about this mess?"

"You don't believe that she loves you?"

Dove ran both hands back over his hair. "I know that she does. As much—perhaps—as I love her. She believes it's impossible."

"Where is she now?"

"She's gone back to Yveshire."

"But perhaps the duke is a man without passion?" She said it lightly, as if to obscure deeper undercurrents.

Dove met her eyes. "Lud, no! He's a man of very deep passions, Meg. I like him. He may have believed the worst of me, but he has absolute faith in Sylvie."

"And you don't?"

"I love her. I love her. But she's a lone tigress, which is particularly damnable for me. She's right. The distrust that we've shared makes all of it intolerable."

In a rustle of silk skirts, Meg sat down. "Oh, my dear! What fools we all are!" she said.

"I AM OFFERING YOU MY HAND, MA'AM. NO WOMAN IN HER *right mind would turn that down. Say yes, Sylvie, and the power of a dukedom is yours.*"

The room began to spin. In two strides the duke was at her side.

"Breathe," he said. "Drop your head."

Sylvie lowered her head to her knees. Yveshire crossed to a side table, poured brandy, and pressed the glass into her hand. "Drink this."

The brandy burned, scalding away what was left of her breath.

"I did not expect my proposal would cause any lady to faint," the duke said dryly. "Especially you!"

Sylvie set down the glass. "My dear friend, I am honored, but you cannot really mean it?"

He began to pace. "We are not in love, but we're old friends. You know I would never force you to my bed, but we were decent enough lovers once, which is more than most couples can claim." He stopped to stare up at a painting on the wall, a lady in Venetian dress of perhaps two centuries before. "As my duchess, your future would be absolutely secure."

Her hands clenched on the blue fabric. "But what can I offer you, when I'm obsessed with someone else? You really don't want to marry me!"

The duke spun about to face her. "So you're refusing me? You will not trade your favors simply for money and you never have. You really do want love, after all?"

"Love?" Sylvie looked up at him. "Isn't that what *you* truly want, Your Grace?"

His cheeks creased in a smile of infinite self-mockery. "Like all of us, I want something I can't have. Haven't you realized yet that Dovenby has always taken everything I ever really wanted?"

She gazed into his dark eyes as understanding slowly bloomed. "Oh, God! How could I not have guessed? You're in love with Lady Grenham?"

"There was a time, when we were young, that I hoped to marry her, but we quarreled—Lud, I believe it was about Edward!—and she married Lord Grenham instead. Then later, after she was widowed, it seemed that we might have another chance. Yet—like you, like all women—Meg prefers her wicked lover. By persecuting Dovenby over my brother's sins, I only drove a deeper wedge between us."

"What else could you have done?" Sylvie asked. "Dove had sent your brother to his ruin and death."

Yveshire wrung one hand over his mouth and dropped to a chair. "I told you once about rumors, about foulness. The rumors were true. The foulness was real. A secret society where the members practiced unholy revels, using women and children and young boys, using drugs." He shivered. "Country girls picked up off the stage-coaches when they arrived in London looking for work, then abandoned later without even knowing who'd abused them. If they died, no one missed them—and sometimes they died."

Sylvie swallowed. "I surmised something of the sort."

"My brother told me that Dovenby was the mastermind behind it." The scratch on his cheek shone vividly against his white skin. "Meg never contradicted that. But the perpetrator of those crimes and many others was not Robert Dovenby. *It was Lord Edward Vane himself!*"

Numb with grief for him, Sylvie buried her face in her hands. "And Lady Grenham knew that all along?"

He nodded. "But why the devil didn't she tell me? Why didn't they expose Edward publicly at the time? Why did Dovenby instead pursue such a wretched crusade, so entirely devoid of honor?"

"He swore Lady Grenham an oath," she said. "He will never explain."

"Yet are you not afraid—as I am—that all that deviousness only personifies what most troubles you in yourself? That we are all monsters? Doesn't that question still eat at your soul, Sylvie? It does mine!"

She lifted her head, dread sinking into her heart. "If I accuse Dove of dishonor, the pot will indeed be calling the kettle black. No, that isn't what has come between us. He is invulnerable, but he is honorable to the core. He must have thought he had good reason."

"Then there has to be even more." Yveshire stood and paced to the window. "A secret so terrible it will bind him and Meg together forever. Dovenby has nothing. His printing business is ruined. Any other wealth he ever accumulated is tied up in a trust for St. John's. Yet if poverty were the only issue, you would live with him in a gutter—and so would she."

"No," Sylvie said. "She would not."

His shoulders were rigid. "I have been forced to forgive Dovenby over the death of my brother, but you think that it doesn't twist like a rapier in my gut to know that he's with Meg now? I have spies other than you, Sylvie. She went straight to Grenham Hall when she left here this morning. Dovenby has gone after her, galloping like a fiend."

"Because he owes her everything," Sylvie said.

The duke spun about to face her, his eyes bleak. "I warn you, Sylvie—if I were to discover there what I fear, I should yet run him through!"

"Then you would take his life only because I wouldn't have him when he asked me."

He stalked back to stand over her. "Faith, ma'am! I offered you a dukedom and you turned that down, too."

"All I ever wanted was autonomy." She felt cold to the bone. "The prerequisite that all you men take for granted!"

"A dukedom doesn't confer independence; it creates nothing but responsibilities."

Bravado lay over the pain in his voice like ice over a frozen ocean. Suppressing her own anguish, Sylvie reached out to clasp his hand.

"Then thank God I'm no longer one of them. You're mad with grief about your brother, Your Grace, and about a lady you've never been able to court and now think you never can. What the devil would you have done, if I'd said yes to your mad proposal?"

"I'd have married you," Yveshire said.

CHAPTER SEVENTEEN

❧

SYLVIE HAD RIDDEN HERE THE LAST TIME IN MEG'S CARRIAGE with Dove. Now she sat alone, dressed as a lady, a fur cloak wrapped over the blue dress and blond petticoat, her hair dressed in ringlets. As the duke's coach horses trotted up the long drive toward Grenham Hall, anxiety exploded into panic.

Was this madness, grief, or courage? Sylvie no longer knew. She only knew that she had just turned down marriage to a duke, because she was so passionately in love with someone else. The servants received her without comment and showed her into a large drawing room, flooded with late afternoon light. Meg rose from a writing desk near the fireplace. She walked up to Sylvie with both hands outstretched.

"You're a woman of remarkable bravery, Lady Montevrain," she said with a smile. "Dove is here. You didn't think you might find us in bed together?"

Hot color washed up Sylvie's face. "No. Though I wouldn't have blamed either of you, if I had. But I don't believe that he is so fickle, or that you would truly wish it. Yet I don't know if he'll want to see me. I only came here because of the duke."

"Yveshire?"

"He's suffering a great deal. No one has thought of what all this is doing to him."

Meg waved Sylvie to a chair. Her hand seemed quite steady, yet she had lost color. "I have thought of it, but I cannot undo history."

"Why not?" Sylvie sat down in a rustle of skirts. "I've believed the same thing, but I wish to God I were wrong!"

"Yet history is what this is all about." Her silver skirts sparking sunlight, Meg began to pace. "I think you must hear the whole story."

"You believe you can trust me?"

Meg stopped to smile at her, though there was something of heartbreak in her eyes. "Yes, of course. Absolutely. Or Dove wouldn't be so in love with you."

Sylvie sat in silence, her heart pounding.

"Lord Edward Vane was dazzled, fascinated, when he first met Dove," Meg began. "Yet Dove was openly cool to him. Yveshire's brother was furious to be rebuffed by a nobody, but he was also determined to win Dove's favor. Lord Edward could never tolerate failure. He also liked to uncover secrets, collect information on people. He wanted to learn something that might give him power over Dove, so he traveled to the Lake District to meet Dove's foster father, Sir Thomas."

"I don't understand what he could possibly have hoped to gain by that," Sylvie said.

Meg turned at the window. Her skirts shimmered as she walked back. "I believe he had some vague notion of discovering Dove's true parents."

"But I don't imagine that Dove really cared. He had foster parents whom he loved."

"Exactly. And Sir Thomas had never discovered anything about Dove's natural mother, even though she'd left a rattle worth a small fortune in his basket. Nevertheless, he must have been impressed to receive a visit from a duke's brother. Sir Thomas agreed to let Lord Edward help him with his investments."

"Did Dove know that?"

Meg shook her head. "Not then. Neither did he know then that Lord Edward was already employing Tom Henley, so that with the help of the forger he was cleaning out other men's fortunes in ways that could never be traced."

"But surely Lord Edward had excellent prospects of his own?"

"Oh, yes, but not enough." A fine wrinkle appeared between Meg's brows. "Being a younger son was simply too hard for him. He was filled with resentments. His goal was to become the richest man in England, richer than his own father, create an empire of power and capital—but it was all being built on fraud and deceit. Like innumerable others, Sir Thomas Farlow was ruined."

Sylvie sat in silence, listening to the rap of Meg's shoes and the hammer of her own pulse.

"Dove only found out," Meg continued, "when his foster father drowned himself in Derwent Water."

Sir Thomas Farlow and his wife raised me as if I were their own son. My mother is still there. My father is dead. Her new understanding engraved a furrow in her heart. She rubbed away tears.

Meg spun about. Her eyes glittered. "Yes, it was terrible for Dove and for his mother, but—thanks to Tom Henley's skills—he couldn't prove anything. That's when Dove decided to accept Lord Edward's friendship, or pretend it enough to enter his confidence. Little by little, he learned all about the scheme with the forger. Then he uncovered something much worse."

"Yveshire told me: Lord Edward's club, the young girls?"

"Yes. Dove was sickened, incensed. He planned to expose that and all of Lord's Edward's fraudulent schemes. Something else happened to change his plans. Lord Edward acted first." Meg took a deep breath. "He truly believed he'd finally won Dove's friendship, but what he wanted was his love. Jealousy was eating him alive."

"Jealousy? Why?"

"London society had welcomed Dove as if he were a prince. Like everyone else, I fell madly in love. My marriage had been miserable. I took lovers both before and after I was widowed, but I was—I am—quite a prize on the marriage market. Lord Edward Vane wanted that prize. He tried to court me, though I could never tolerate his company and I made no secret of it. It was a blow to his pride that he could never forgive. While Dove . . . I was wild for him and couldn't hide it—"

"I know the feeling," Sylvie said.

"Yes. Well." Meg smiled, though her skin glistened like ash. "Lord Edward had tried to make Dove his pet and instead become a sycophant himself. He thought that was my fault. Then Yveshire, his older brother, began to pay me his attentions—" She took a deep breath. "Ironically it was the one moment when my infatuation with Dove might have wavered, but for Lord Edward it was the last straw. Before Dove could publicly expose him, Lord Edward took his revenge."

"On Dove?"

"No," Meg said. "Yveshire's brother had no idea that Dove even suspected him of fraud, let alone knew about his secret society. *He took his revenge on me.*"

Dread avalanched in Sylvie's heart. "If this is too painful—"

"No. You must hear it. If this hadn't happened, Dove and I would no doubt have drifted apart long ago, but I was desperate. I used his kindness shamelessly. I made him swear to help me destroy Lord Edward completely. Yveshire and I are very alike in that!"

"Yet Dove had his own reasons for revenge. What had happened to his father—"

"Yes, and his revulsion over the secret club. Dove's first impulse was to issue an open challenge to a duel. I bound him to an oath of secrecy instead. For my sake Dove agreed to destroy the club without Lord Edward's knowing that he'd done it. Dove had acquired the printer's by then. He began to print leaflets. Lord Edward's cronies became afraid. The game wasn't worth the scandal. The secret society collapsed."

"But no one could trace any of that back to Dove?"

Meg shook her head. "Then we turned our talents toward Lord Edward's financial ruin, since money was the only thing that he really cared about."

"Beginning with Tom Henley?"

"I paid enough to suborn the forger away from Lord Edward. Tom Henley had no loyalty, other than to money, but the man was absolutely discreet. If he'd talked, his own neck would have been at risk. By this time, Dove had become Lord Edward's most trusted business partner."

"He thought that they were building up a great shipping empire," Sylvie said. "Yveshire showed me the papers."

"Yes, Dove wrote them, but he was also using the forger's talents to secretly repair the fortunes of the men that Yveshire's brother had destroyed. We funneled any extra money to St. John's. Once Lord Edward was ruined, I intended to reveal what we'd done. Then Dove would kill him in a duel. But other circumstances got in the way and Lord Edward was slain by someone else. A lot of people wanted him dead by then, and more than one gentleman was prepared to die trying to rid the world of him."

"Yet Lord Edward had already told the duke his version of events?"

"He did so all along, planting poison. Yveshire tried to warn me against my own lover. We quarreled very bitterly. Yet not even to save Dove's good name, not even to annul Yveshire's hatred—" Meg stopped, framed in sunlight, silver sparkling in her skirts. Two red spots burned on her cheekbones. "I could never have told Yveshire the truth."

"Why not, ma'am?"

In white wig and brocade coat the Duke of Yveshire stood watching them from the doorway, the cut on his cheek a slash of scarlet against his white skin.

"*Why not?*" The duke walked into the room. "What is it that you still cannot tell me? You may have hated my brother, but your rejection of me was equally ferocious. Why?"

As pale as the plaster ceiling, Meg shook her head.

"I have no right to ask," the duke said. "I know that. You may send me away now and I shall never seek you out again. But why did you not come to me with the truth about Edward? Why did you abandon all claim to honor and swear Dovenby to secrecy? Your lover even practiced his skills as my brother's fencing partner, while plotting to kill him. It's diabolical!"

"Dove had to be good enough to kill him," Meg said. "And your brother had to taste enough humiliation before he died."

"And for this you have sacrificed everyone, including Dovenby, including Sylvie." Yveshire strode to the fireplace to stare up at the mirror over the mantel. "Even this morning you told me only enough to save your lover from the gallows."

"I wanted to spare you," Meg said. "I have never hated you. Yet to keep my secret, I was prepared to sacrifice even you."

The duke's hands clenched on the marble ledge. "You have been protecting far more than my tender emotions, ma'am. *What was the exact nature of my brother's revenge?*"

Meg sank to a chair and closed her eyes. "You overheard that?"

"I overheard it," the duke said. "And I cannot bear it. The pain of not knowing is far worse than anything more you could tell me now."

"I didn't want you to know," she whispered. "I wanted no one to know."

Yveshire's back was rigid. "If you claim not to hate me, Meg, please tell me! Did he dishonor you?"

"Me? No!" Moisture stained Meg's lashes. "His revenge was far more cruel than that. Lord Edward took out his hatred on my little girl."

"On *Sophie?*" He sounded incredulous.

"Yes." Tears ran openly down Meg's cheeks as she looked up. "Sophie and her maid were kidnapped and taken to the club. Edward arranged it, bribed the maid. Dove rescued the girls, but my daughter had already been used, just like all the others. She was only thirteen."

The duke pressed his forehead onto the backs of his hands. His shoulders sagged, then shook as, with terrible noises, he began to weep.

Meg sat as if pinned to her chair. "Don't, Duke! Pray, don't! He only did it to punish me."

Sick with grief, her face wet, Sylvie walked up to him. She put one hand on his sleeve and laid her cheek on his shoulder. "I must go," she whispered. "This no longer involves me."

The duke turned, his face haggard, his eyes bloodshot. "No! Stay! It concerns you." He looked back at Meg. "And Sophie?"

"She was drugged. She doesn't remember it. Now she's perfecting her French with her cousins in Brussels, she thinks it was all just a bad dream. She'll come back to England next year to be presented at court with no reason to believe that she's not a virgin." Meg stood up, her gaze like winter. "Do you blame me?"

"No!" Dashing one hand over his eyes, Yveshire stepped forward. "The only person who is to blame for all this is already dead."

Meg looked down. "But now I have broken your heart—"

"*My* heart?" The duke reached out as if to touch her bent shoulder. "*My* heart? I should think you would hate the sight of me forever!"

Yveshire dropped his hand, spun on his heel, and stalked out. The door banged shut behind him.

Blindly Sylvie walked up to Meg and put her arms about the older woman. "There are no adequate words," she said. "But I'm so very sorry."

They remained wrapped together in silence for a moment, before Meg kissed her, then pulled away and sat down. "Yet Lord Edward has cursed us all. And now I have put my daughter's fate into his brother's hands—"

"And into my hands," Sylvie said. "I am honored, Lady Grenham. You have my oath that her secret is safe with me. You must know it is safe with the duke. He loves you. He has always loved you. He didn't know why you rejected him, because he had no idea of what his brother had done."

"I wanted to protect him and I wanted to protect my little girl. Yet everyone has suffered because of what I decided that night. Dove was magnificent, Sylvie, so careful and tender when he brought Sophie home! I didn't realize how unfair it was to bind him to me in such a way. Yet I couldn't bear to let him go. Not until I found you in his bedroom."

"*Me?* Why?"

Meg rose to her feet and paced to the fireplace, resting her hands where the duke's fingers had been. "You looked so young and so fierce dressed in your mad wig and breeches! The kind of woman he was meant for. It was as if the scales fell from my eyes. I knew I must free him to pursue his own destiny and that I must do it right away, without hesitation, without any possibility of going back. Of course, Dove was too clever for me, even then. It wasn't quite that easy to set him free."

"The Gypsies would say that none of us control our fate," Sylvie said. "Yet either way I cannot offer him enough. I cannot give him the surrender that he needs."

"I must go after the duke." Meg turned, tear-stained, lovely, and smiled at Sylvie. "But don't you think Dove should be the judge of that? He's in the woods, admiring snowdrops."

* * *

THE SUN HAD BEGUN TO SET, CASTING LONG, CHILL SHADOWS across the grounds. The herb garden was a mess of soggy brown plants and wet walkways. The sundial counted out the hours and minutes with a lengthening wedge of shade. Sylvie hurried down a long path through the woods. Her heart leaped and pounded like a startled rabbit. *I have no real courage,* she thought. *Only this blind bravado.*

She saw Dove before he noticed her. Cold rays of sunlight slanted through the bare branches of a birch spinney, throwing his hair and coat into dark relief against the white trunks and the shimmering backdrop of an ornamental lake. Leaning his shoulder casually against a tree, he stared down at the brave defiance of snowdrops rioting beneath the birches and down to the water's edge.

Her pulse quavered. Intense yearning ran liquid and painful through her bones. She folded her hands across the embroidered stomacher of her dress and forced herself to walk forward.

He looked around. "Ah," he said. "Diana, the Huntress!"

Sylvie stopped dead. "How did you——? Do not make fun of me!"

Dove smiled. "I don't make fun of you. I love you."

"Yveshire is here. Lady Grenham has told him everything."

His eyes searched her face. "They are together?"

"I hope so. He walked out, but she went after him. He couldn't bear to let her see him weep."

"Then now you know that I was—indirectly—the cause of everything that happened."

"Because even Lord Edward Vane wanted your heart?" Sylvie asked. "You could have done nothing else. How could you abandon Meg after what happened?"

"I couldn't. Yet our campaign of retribution was deeply dishonorable."

She glanced down at her hands. Her heart pounded heavily. "No, it was not! Sophie could never have been publicly avenged. The innocent men Lord Edward had ruined deserved to be repaid. You shirked neither compassion, nor justice. You were right."

"Then are you indeed my fate, Sylvie?"

"Your fate?" She reached for courage and gazed up into his eyes, dark, lovely, filled with tenderness. "Then you should know what else Bess said: 'His heart's reserved for the spotless, white-limbed lady of the moon, but when he gives his heart, he embraces his doom.'"

"Lud! Did she really say that? Remind me never to allow any of those damned Gypsies to look into my palm again."

Sylvie swallowed, twisting her hands together. Her heart yearned to touch him, to lay her head on his shoulder, feel the comfort of his arms, but if she was to risk offering him her soul as well as her body—

"She also said that you would marry a virgin, a huntress." She tried to smile. *Then Dove will fall, like spray in a waterfall, and be lost.* It was only an excuse, a delay, but maybe she only had this much courage, after all. "That rather eliminates me, doesn't it?"

"Don't you know that your soul is dedicated to Diana and that I wouldn't have it any other way?"

He stepped forward, firing hot waves of longing in her blood. Sylvie closed her eyes and plunged blindly, taking the ultimate risk before she lost her nerve, before she let passion once again obscure the truth.

"But you still don't know what I really am, Dove. After I lost my parents, I married for money, not for love. I sold my body to an old man, because he promised me security. When he died, I discovered that he'd lied. There wasn't any money. I did try to revive the antiquities business and it did burn down. That was true. Otherwise, all that stuff that Tanner Brink told you, and that I told you, was a tissue of lies, a fabrication. I was never a respectable governess or companion. I traded my favors for my survival. I lived as a kept woman."

She looked up. He had turned away to gaze out over the water.

"Then I met Yveshire," she continued, sick with nerves. "We, too, became lovers, but he gave me another option: to spy for him, send him information from Europe about anything that might help British interests. Within the clear limitations of our relationship, I trusted him and he never let me down. For the first time in my life, I had a secure source of income. Yet even then, when occasion warranted, I took men to my bed that I didn't love."

"Because you fought for autonomy." His profile was clear, beautiful. His voice calm. "What other options does our world offer a woman left alone? I would have done the same. Why does this matter?"

"I lied to you, Dove. I allowed you to think that you might be able to love me. It was all based on lies. Yveshire could never really understand. A duke is too removed from what the world offers to any female left penniless. Yet I thought perhaps that you would. How can an empty shell love the storm?"

He turned back to face her. "I won't walk away. I will beg your forgiveness."

"*My* forgiveness?"

"Of course. You were correct to accuse me. You were wise to doubt me. I was, bound by oath, unable to share certain secrets, but I was wrong not to accept your right to self-determination. I should have consulted you before arranging anything with Yveshire. I should have risked more—" He glanced down at his empty hands and she knew that he, too, ruthlessly repressed the impulse to solve everything with one searing touch. "It was my sin, not yours, that came between us."

"But it was only armor, a shield we had each learned to erect. The sin was equally mine."

The warmth in his smile threatened to break her heart. "No," he said. "It was not, but I care only whether you love me now. I'm ready to risk unarmed, undefended encounters forever, if you are. Can we embark without subterfuge, as equal partners, without fears, without prejudice?"

"Hand in hand?" She tried to smile, though she felt like crying. "I don't know. I will try because I love you, though I'm still afraid that at heart you might be invulnerable—"

Something detonated, shattering among the white trees. Birds scattered, their wings sharp on the air.

He jerked, then crumpled—as a dropped cloak might crumple—fold upon fold.

As her ears rang, as her heart stopped, Dove slumped at Sylvie's feet. His head fell back into the ice crystals and wet, brown leaf litter. Snowdrops bent, green stalks snapped. All color drained from his face. And the front of his shirt wept blood.

"Devil take it!" he said. "I am, hideously, all too vulnerable."

Skirts crushed as Sylvie collapsed to her knees. Delicate white-and-green flowers nodded against his dark hair. The red stain spread, seeping through his fingers. His eyes closed. His lean hand slid away to spread its bloody devastation among the flowers.

Frantically she tore at his cravat. The knot jammed. Forcing herself to breathe, she tried again, but her fingers fumbled and shook. *Dear God! Please, God!* He would bleed to death while she fought for control! She abandoned the cravat and felt in his pockets. A handkerchief! She pressed the folded linen over the hideous scarlet and pressed hard. *When he gives his heart, he embraces his doom.*

"You cannot die!" she whispered. "Don't die! Please don't die!"

The handkerchief came away soaked in red. She folded it again to press it back over the wound. Helpless. Hopeless. Green-and-white petals—as flawless as porcelain, as lifeless as lilies—lay broken against his ear. His face was carved marble, that perfection of bone and flesh made suddenly meaningless in death.

Was he breathing? Dear God, was he even breathing? Sylvie pressed her lips over his cold mouth and tried to force her own breath into his lungs, a kiss as heartfelt as any given the living.

A twig snapped.

"I don't care," she said without looking up. "Shoot me as well, if you like, but if you have any mercy left in your heart, I insist that you go for help."

A muffled sob echoed among the damp trees. From the corner of her eye, Sylvie saw skirts. Skirts and a pair of stout country boots. With the smoking pistol still clutched in her fingers, a girl stood with her back pressed against the paper bark of a birch. Her face was red and swollen, blotchy with tears beneath its dusting of freckles.

Berthe!

Sylvie sat back to stroke trembling fingers over Dove's lips. "I don't think he's dead yet," she said. "I cannot leave him. You must go for help."

The French girl licked tears from the corner of her mouth and shook her head.

In a white rage Sylvie shouted at her. "Berthe! Go for help! Now! Tell someone, anyone! A gardener, a footman: tell someone! Then you can run away, if you wish."

"I want him to die," Berthe mumbled. "I don't care. I want him to die. I thought you despised him as I do. I thought you would never surrender to any man. I thought you were free, a free woman, who could do as she liked. But you've let him corrupt you with all his pretty ways. You think you're in love with him. I hate him. I want him to die!"

Sylvie moved her fingers beneath his jaw, searching for a pulse, but the frantic throb of her own heart was too hard. She couldn't move him by herself, nor could she leave him alone with Berthe. The French-woman had begun to sob openly, wringing her hands over her face.

"If he dies, you'll be hanged. Please, go for help!"

"I'll be hanged either way," Berthe said. "I don't care."

"Heigh-ho!" a man's voice said. "That's not true, sweetheart. Your fate is to die of old age with your children and grandchildren at your knee. There's no hanging at stake, just the life of the lad who's been causing us all so much grief: Mr. Dovenby."

Tanner Brink was just swinging from his pony. Footsteps came pounding after him through the woods.

"Heard the shot," the Gypsy said, his brown eyes dark with compassion. "Help's on its way."

IN A DRAMATIC DISCONTINUITY OF STYLE, TANNER BRINK WAS sitting on a gilt stool: his leather leggings and muddy boots and moleskin cap incongruous against Meg's priceless carpets and silk wallpaper. He did not seem in the least uncomfortable. The Duke of Yveshire stood beside the fireplace, his face set, his eyes rimmed in red. In her cloud of satin, Meg sat opposite him, fine lines marring her forehead.

Dove had been carried in from the woods. A surgeon had been called from London. While the others waited and Sylvie clung to Dove's hand, the man had dug into his flesh to extract the bullet. Now Dove lay bandaged and bloodied in one of the guest beds in Grenham Hall. He had not regained consciousness, but he was alive.

In white-faced defiance, Berthe sat in the corner.

Sylvie stepped into the room. She had washed her hands and face, but the front of her dress was still stained with Dove's blood. Her heart thudded beneath the stiff brocade. *He is alive.*

"He's sleeping," she said. "He's lost a great deal of blood, but the surgeon thinks no vital organs are damaged. There's nothing more we can do."

"Ah," Tanner Brink said. "Mr. George White! You make a better lady, lad. If Dove dies, will you marry this mad duke?"

Yveshire spun about, but he smiled.

"No," Sylvie said. "I shall not. You do not fear that His Grace will run you through on the spot for your insolence, Mr. Brink?"

The Gypsy grinned. "We Romany recognize neither rank nor worldly position. All men are equals to us."

"Then I will have you hanged for your republican sympathies, sir," the duke said.

"How can you be merry?" Berthe glanced about at them, as if they all had two heads. "Even if he lives, he cannot run the print shop now. He has nothing left. He is ruined. I did that. What's the matter with you English?"

Tanner Brink turned to look at her. For Berthe's sake they had all being speaking French.

"Hush, now. It's just the English way of dealing with tragedy, their way of being brave. But he won't die and he won't be ruined. I've had a look in his palm myself. Bess had it wrong. His fate is to defeat death and find love. As yours is, sweetheart."

Tears began to roll slowly down Berthe's face. "I don't know why I did it. I don't know! I didn't really mean to shoot. The duke's footman told me that Dove was an evil man. He said he'd run a club where terrible things happened to innocent girls. But even then I just wanted to frighten him, make him recognize me."

"My *footman*?" Yveshire asked.

"Yes! He told me when we met in Shepherd's Market. You think your servants don't listen at doors? Draw their own conclusions? Have their own thoughts? Look at all of you! You take it for granted that people like me will simply revere you and be happy to serve you. It's not fair!"

"Fair?" Tanner Brink said. "No, it's not fair for the lad upstairs to have a mind like a razor, when other men must make do with being stupid. It's not fair that one lady is beautiful, and another as plain as a cart tail. It's not fair, but it makes for a jollier world. Just think!

What if every man were as clever and easy on the eyes as our Dove, and every woman as foolish and as plain as you are."

Berthe blushed scarlet.

"It's my fault," Sylvie said. "I brought you to England. I didn't think how lost and lonely you must feel. It never occurred to me to explain, but all those stories about Dove were false, Berthe."

"Everything's been false," Berthe said. "How was I to know?"

"You couldn't know," Meg said. "But what do you want now?"

The French girl dropped her head. "I wanted to get out of France. I didn't want to be a whore any longer. I don't want to be hanged for a murderess."

The Gypsy stood up. "No one is going to punish you, Berthe Dubois, because what you want is what we all want. You're just too foolish to know how to find it."

He winked at the others, then walked over to the Frenchwoman and leaned down to whisper in her ear. Berthe glared at him. Tanner Brink laughed.

"She wants love and she wants freedom," he said. "Now then, lass, you're just a little girl, but what do you say, sweetheart?"

"You're sure that Mr. Dovenby will live?"

"I'm as sure of it as I am sure that you're my fate," Tanner Brink said.

Berthe made a wry face. "Well, if it's all in the stars anyway, why are you asking me?"

"So you can say yes. Our fate may be predestined, but it still matters whether we say yes or no to it."

"Then, yes," Berthe said.

"What the devil are you arranging with her, Mr. Brink?" Yveshire asked.

Tanner Brink pulled off his moleskin cap and scratched at his head like a mouse with a flea. "If Dove dies, I'll deliver her to the gallows myself. But he won't die, because his secretary won't allow it. In the meantime, Berthe Dubois has just agreed to become my wife."

Sylvie sat down. Meg reached for her hand and met her eyes. Suddenly the two women were giggling together.

"I don't see how you can laugh," Berthe said, "when the man you both love is lying upstairs with a hole in his chest."

Meg released Sylvie's fingers and wiped her eyes on a lace-edged handkerchief. "Because that's what he'd do, Berthe, if he were awake to hear this. For God's sake, take her away, Mr. Brink. I wish both of you every happiness."

Tanner seized Berthe's hand. He led the French girl to the door, but stopped for a moment to set his cap back on his head. "She's my fate," he said with a wink, "not my happiness. Come, sweetheart! You're going to have to learn all about horses."

The door closed behind them.

"Faith," the duke said. "What a deuced odd couple!"

Meg turned to Sylvie. "You must eat and sleep. Let me find you something fresh to wear. You will stay here, of course."

"As long as Dove is in danger, I shall stay," Sylvie replied.

"Excellent," Meg said. "You're exhausted with stress and heartbreak. You must rest. When Dove opens his eyes, I want your face to be the first thing that he sees."

"You are generous, ma'am," the duke said.

Meg glanced up at Yveshire and smiled. "Do you think I still want him for myself, Duke?"

He stood very still. "I think you were very desperately in love with him."

"Lud, just an indisposition that was traveling around, like influenza! Dove was only ever a distraction for me."

She stood up and put her hand on the duke's brocade sleeve.

He stared at it for a moment, then set his long fingers over hers. "Yet you loved him?"

"I threw myself into loving Dove so that I could avoid the impossibility of loving the brother of the man who'd tried to destroy my little girl. Yet if you will come here every day to inquire after his health, Duke, perhaps we can discover whether there might yet be an advantage for the two of us to contract a brilliant society marriage?"

"I don't want a brilliant society marriage," Yveshire said. "But I have wanted Meg Grenham for a very long time."

*H*IS EYES OPENED ON SUNSHINE. IT HURT, SO HE CLOSED them again. Pain seared his right side. A gunshot. His breath caught. It hurt like the very devil to breathe. Bandages. So he lived.

Thank God for small mercies—and large ones!

The scent of snowdrops and woodland drifted like snowflakes. Something rustled.

"Sylvie," he said, the word as insubstantial as the wind.

"I'm here." He heard her rapid footsteps and felt the blessed cool of her shadow. "I've been rather prettily arranging flowers for your sickroom. You were shot."

Dove opened his eyes to focus on that fierce lapis lazuli glare. Sylvie stood over him, mercifully blocking the sunlight. Her hair was caught back in a simple knot, a shimmering crown of gold around her face. She was frowning.

"I'm nursing you," she said. She twisted her fingers together, as awkward as a child. "In a modest white gown and spotless apron. A vision of angelic meekness and rectitude."

He laughed. A knife stabbed into his ribs. "Pray, don't make me laugh! Don't even make me smile. Who the devil shot me?"

"Berthe."

The absurdity of that almost demolished his self-control. "Faith!

And you thought me so competent? I failed rather thoroughly, it would seem, to charm your French maid."

"Oh, no," Sylvie said. "She was thoroughly charmed. That was part of the problem."

"And is it still yours?" Lud, but he loved her, every fine golden hair, every frown.

She backed away, flooding his face with sunlight. "Now I have you so absolutely at my mercy?"

"You may have me at your mercy, but you're a terrible nurse. I would like the curtains closed. I would like sips of water placed on my lips from your dewy fingers. I would like a cool hand on my fevered brow—"

Her heels tapped as she walked away to tug at the curtains, casting him into the shade. "Is a nurse what you want?"

"You are what I want. Your love. Your forgiveness. Your hand in marriage. Can you love me yet, Sylvie?"

"Yes," she said. "Yes, I love you. I will always love you." She gave a small laugh. "Yet I am still quaking with fear. You almost died. I was so terrified that I would lose you, that the world would lose you. I bargained with God that I would happily forgo your love, just so long as you didn't die." He tried to sit up. Her footsteps hurried back to the bedside. "No! You must rest. Here's some water."

Damp fingers brushed over his lips, carrying the ambrosia of simple moisture. He kissed the soft, wet pads, then tasted salt.

Skirts crackled as she spun away. "Lud, sir! It wasn't my intention to weep over you. You must sleep. But I love you. I promise on my honor to be here when you wake up again."

Her heels beat a rapid staccato across the wooden floor and the door closed behind her.

* * *

WHEN SHE CREPT IN THE NEXT TIME, HE WAS SLEEPING. Sylvie sat for a long time beside the bed, gazing at his face. Quiet suffused the room. Nothing moved but the clock ticking, his labored breathing, and her own thoughts.

He had slept and woken, tossed in and out of dreams. Sylvie had quietly nursed him, or quietly settled herself beside the bed to watch and to wait. They had talked and not talked. There were no more falsehoods between them now. Piece by piece as the days passed, she told him everything. Her easy, loving childhood. Her wedding with the Comte de Montevrain.

"Though our marriage was entirely empty, though I was frightened of him—even repulsed by him—I learned how to be a lady," she said. "In other words, I learned how to be a good actress, how to keep up appearances, even when my world seemed to be a very dark place—all of which stood me in good stead later."

"It must have been a very bitter introduction to life as a woman," he said. "No wonder you carved such a brave, brittle existence for yourself after that."

"Not so brave! But yes, I'll admit it was bloody brittle at times."

"I know the feeling," he said. "There were times I thought I might expire with self-disgust in my deathly struggle against Lord Edward Vane. It was the loss of weeks and months of my life."

There was no self-pity in it for either of them, she realized. It was simply a recounting of the facts and a recognition that all that past had now become strangely irrelevant.

"It must have been vile," she said. "What sustained you?"

"Thoughts of my mother and father. I don't mean the blood parents whom I never knew. I mean Sir Thomas and Elizabeth, the parents who raised me and loved me. That's what counts, what's always counted. Not the single grand gesture, but the day-to-day sacrifices and caring and concern, which is what love really is, after all."

"Yes," she said. "That's what enabled you to sustain Meg when she needed you. I, too, learned that as a child."

"Is that what gave you your courage, Sylvie?"

"You think I am brave?" she asked, genuinely surprised.

"I have never known anyone braver—when you lived with me as George, when we discovered all that nonsensical, innocent joy together as friends, when you fought for your independence, when you fought me. I love you for that. Did you think I loved you only for your body?" He grinned. "Delectable though it is—"

She blushed, pleased because she knew that he meant it. "You're raving," she teased. "Now sleep. I'll be here."

Love for him streamed in her veins. Not only infatuation, but something as deep as the tides being tugged by the moon. She let the force of it wash uncontested through her heart and wondered if she was simply becoming sand, or whether they were both just part of one great unseen ocean.

Within days he was running a desperate new fever. Servants came and went. Meg dragged Sylvie away to force her to rest and eat and sleep. Yveshire brought the best doctors from London. *The loss of weeks and months of my life.*

You won't lose them again, she promised herself. *When you are well, beloved, you won't lose them again.*

HE WAS AWARE OF HUNGER. RAVENOUS, ALL-CONSUMING hunger. A footman gave him beef broth, then left. Dove stared at the bed canopy, then glanced about the empty room. She wasn't there. He yearned for her as a dying soldier yearns for death.

Drizzle trickled down the windowpanes. Here, at Grenham Hall, he and Meg had kept their proof concerning Lord Edward. The proof that Meg had, at last, agreed to show Yveshire. Sylvie could have searched forever at Dove's townhouse and found nothing.

Sylvia Georgiana. Lady Montevrain. Taken as a child by an old man. No wonder she'd been afraid!

The door thudded open.

"You're awake?" she asked. "Look! Daffodils! They grow wild down by the lake, acres of them!"

In her hand golden-green buds and yellow petals nodded on their stiff stems.

"Daffodils? It's already March?"

She nodded.

"They're as lovely as day," he said. "As lovely, though no tidier, than you are."

Sylvie glanced down. Her hair hung in bedraggled little tendrils, like damp flax, around her flushed cheeks.

"It began raining while I was out." She thrust the daffodils into a large jug beside the bed, then stood back to admire the effect. "They're my offering," she said. "I don't need anything back."

Dove stretched. His wound was tender, but no longer agony. "Lud, ma'am! What the devil can I can give back? I'm very nicely ruined. The print shop—"

"Is still operating," she interrupted. "Basement cleaned up. Waterwheel turning. Surely you haven't worried about that? The authorities now know for certain that any trouble there was due to that treacherous fellow, George White, with his French ideas and Italian sympathies. The rumor has flown around town that he shot you. London is agog with sympathy. After all, you saved the king from a traitor." She grinned. "Your work is very fashionable and you're making a nice profit."

"Devil take it!" he said, and laughed. "You're running the damn place for me?"

He struggled to sit up. Sylvie rushed to push pillows behind his shoulders. "I'm just keeping things going while you're ill. I'm your secretary, after all."

Dove reached up and took her hand. "And what else, Sylvie?"

She glanced away, her cheeks brushed with color, like a sunrise. "Is happening in the world? The duke suggests that you pursue your reformist interests where you can really make a difference. He offers you a seat in the House of Commons. Apparently several small boroughs fall within his control. He also feels obliged to offer recompense for what his brother cost you and Sir Thomas, which would seem to amount to a small manor or two, with a little fortune in rents—"

He pulled her down so that she sat on the bed beside him and stroked one finger over her palm. "I shan't pretend to be upset about any of that. In fact, it's a great relief. Unless you decide to use it as an excuse not to marry me."

"Ah," she said, looking back at him. Her eyes were the blue of a summer sky. "So now we come to the affairs of the heart?"

"I will ask you again to marry me and this time you'll say yes."

"When you are well." She lifted his hand to run her tongue over his fingertips. "When you are strong again."

He traced her mouth with his thumb, her upper lip soft and warm. "As strong as when I was able to kiss secretaries in mazes?"

Her color deepened to scarlet, vulnerable, infinitely appealing, but she laughed. "So you did know it was me. I was such a fool!"

"And that's also what you have been afraid of?" he asked. " 'A man becomes a fool over his desires in a way that a woman never does.' "

Her grin widened. "Lud! I have certainly made a fool of myself over you. My passion for you has been my undoing, sir. But am I still so desperately in love? Yes and no. I have sat here many days watching you sleep, letting myself understand who you really are."

His forefinger stroked down her long throat. "Do I really want to know?"

"Lady Grenham told me once that love demands surrender, but I know now that no one else makes you love them. Love is your own to give. Perhaps I thought that I was so desperate for love that I'd destroy myself over it. Perhaps that's why any admission of love seemed like defeat."

"Because it was safer that way?"

"Yes," she said. "But true love isn't safe. It's a risk."

"Love is a gift," he said. "Like life."

"Freely given and received." She trapped his palm over the sweet curves of her breast. Her heart beat steadily. "You are indeed my fate, Dove. Yet I know now that you're as human as I am—riddled with imperfection, forever hidden within your own individuality. What I feel now isn't simply the infatuation of being in love. Even when we cannot share our physical passion, my love for you is as real and as deep as the ocean."

"As is my love for you, Sylvie. So you won't let Yveshire's gift of wealth stand in our way?"

"Out of pride? Out of fear that you'll think that's all that attracts me?"

"I'm not such a fool as that, Sylvie."

"Thank you," she said. "Anyway, you don't need to be. Yveshire has showered me with plenty of gifts of my own, as well as the money he owed me for my work. I'm a wealthy enough woman in my own right."

"Excellent," he said. "I always wanted a rich bride." He trailed his fingers back up her bare neck. "As for physical passion . . . there are many wicked ways that even a man pinned to his sickbed can share that exquisite pleasure with his beloved—"

Passion for him flared in her eyes. They were both instantly aroused, awareness firing between them. Sylvie pushed back the covers.

"Then perhaps I should marry you with the sweet buds of May? With the blooming of all those English flowers my mother told me about?"

He tipped his head back and closed his eyes. "And will you?"

She leaned down to press her mouth onto his and let her lips inspire him with the truth.

MARSH MARIGOLD, BUTTERCUP, CUCKOO FLOWER, CAMPION, ragged robin, speedwell, herb robert, and charlock bloomed in all their multicolored glory over Meg's estates. The dog violets and wood anemones were over, snowdrops and daffodils long dwindled to nothing but leaves. All the delicate, shy flowers had retreated before the springing onslaught of the strong green growth of May.

With Sylvie at his side, Dove rode up to Grenham Hall over the stream where Lord Hartsham had been forced to abandon his sleigh. Ahead lay Meg's formal gardens: the hedged enclosure at the center of the maze where he and Sylvie had made love three days ago under the benevolent gaze of Aphrodite; the orangery where they had collected sprays the following day, the day before their wedding, then made love among the blossoms.

He was healed, Berthe's wound no more than a fading scar. Tomorrow he and Sylvie would leave for the Lake District, where Dove's mother, Elizabeth, waited to meet his new bride. On the way they would visit the properties that Yveshire had deeded to them, in compensation for what his brother had done and as a wedding gift.

Yet Dove glanced at Sylvie, her face lovely and serene beneath her feathered hat, and knew that—as long as they were together—they were both forever *home,* wherever they might happen to be living.

Water gurgled like a flock of baby birds beneath the arches. The sky arched blue and clear above their heads. The two horses, Abdiel and Sylvie's new gray gelding—a present from Meg—walked step for step together, their shoes ringing on the stone bridge.

Where the track turned, where Lord Bone had flashed in and out of the light of a bonfire like a green beetle, Tanner Brink sat waiting on his dun pony. A grin split his face from ear to ear.

"Well, well," he said. "So marriage suits us all, it would seem. Your natural mother never married your father in a church, Mr. Dovenby, but he married her just as I have married my sweet French wife."

"My *natural* mother?"

"The parents who conceived you jumped over a broomstick together," Tanner Brink said. "I should know. I was there."

He felt no real shock. It was something he must surely have known his entire life—bringing with it a further poignant sense of homecoming—though he had never openly recognized it until now.

"My dear sir," Dove said. "I think I may have always suspected it."

"So you guessed? Yes, yes, yes." The Gypsy winked. "Your father was a cousin of my mother's. Why else would I have bothered with such a troublesome lad as yourself for all these years?"

"For my virtues and sins? The feeling is mutual. What happened to them, sir?"

"Your father stole a golden rattle for you and—though he made a gallant enough figure on the gallows—your mother perished of grief."

Dove sat quietly for a moment, as if to offer a wordless prayer for their souls—a prayer without any particularly coherent thoughts. Sylvie reached out and took his hand, her understanding as profound as a heartbeat. Then he shook his head and smiled as he silently asked her to articulate their shared curiosity.

"The priceless rattle that Dove's mother left in his basket?" she said. "Where did his father find such a thing?"

"Why, he stole it from the Yveshires, of course. He went to deliver a horse and found it lost in the gravel. They had so much, how could they miss a little thing like that?"

"But they did miss it," Dove said.

"No, no," Tanner replied. "They never knew it was gone. They hanged him for stealing ribbons at the fair the next day. Well, well! So you were orphaned and left in a basket. I'd have raised you myself, till I saw how well you'd landed in the world with Sir Thomas and his wife. Folks who could make a gentleman out of you, instead of a rogue. No regrets, sir?"

Tanner Brink offered his hand and Dove shook it. "No regrets, Mr. Brink."

"Though you still turned out to be a rogue," Sylvie said.

Dove winked at her and she laughed. "And the world is full of my bloody cousins! You and Berthe are happy, Mr. Brink?"

"Who wants happiness?" Tanner grinned. "We're not bored, which is far more important. And you?"

"We're as happy as clams in seaweed, Mr. Brink," Sylvie said. "Dove's mother's basket is to become a cradle for our first child, who will play with the Yveshire rattle without fear."

"But why the devil would you think that happiness is boring?" Dove asked.

"Oh, I don't," the Gypsy said. "Ask the duke. He sent me to fetch you. He and his lady would like your opinion: Is marriage the beginning of passion, or the end?"

Dove's eyes met Sylvie's in a glance of absolute shared harmony, excluding the entire world. Suddenly they both began to laugh. Abdiel snorted and tossed his head. Sylvie's gelding joined in. Bits jingled like wedding bells. They laughed harder. A hare started up in alarm and bounded away across the meadows, running straight into summer.

"What the devil do you think, Mr. Brink?" they said together.